THE HIGH ROAD
Spellkeeper Flight – Book One

Ken Hughes

Windward Road Press

Los Angeles, CA

Windward Road Press
11923 NE Sumner St Ste 879426
Portland, OR 97250-9601

Publisher's Note: This is a work of fiction. Names, characters, places, and incidents are a product of the author's imagination. Locales and public names are sometimes used for atmospheric purposes. Any resemblance to actual people, living or dead, or to businesses, companies, events, institutions, or locales is completely coincidental.

Book Layout © 2017 BookDesignTemplates.com

The High Road/ Ken Hughes. – 2nd ed.
ISBN paperback: 979-8-2-014782-3-0
ISBN ebook: 978-0-9850484-3-3

For my father – soldier, scholar, traveler, wit, caregiver,
and the first one to read to me.

CONTENTS

FIRST 1

THE MESSENGER 7

A TEXT 29

THE TRAP 31

DESCENDANTS 45

RUINS 63

FROM THE EDGE 85

A TEXT 105

GONE 107

FASTER 125

FALL 143

THE LOST 159

PREY AND HUNTER 173

A TEXT 189

SOMEBODY 191

TRANSIT 211

STILL NIGHT 231

WHO'S WHO 249

BIRDWATCHING 269

THE DIVE 285

FLY 309

GATEKEEPER 327

from FREEFALL 333

ABOUT THE AUTHOR 349

FIRST

This time it couldn't be hide-and-seek.

Nine-year-old Mark Petrie trotted across the grass when he saw Angie break from the trees and run toward the park's edge. The way her father had dragged her out of the park that afternoon, he'd thought he'd never see her there again.

So he went straight after her. He barely gave a glance back to the picnic table where his uncle was arguing about that "politics" stuff with his grumbling friends, their dinner still not unpacked.

When the grass changed to hard street-side sidewalk under their feet, Angie glanced back at him, her face just level with his. "I'm not stopping. I'm not waiting for him to catch me."

"Your dad? But we were only—"

She rushed on up the street, dodging between the scattered people in her path. Mark followed her red hair in the deepening twilight, still trying to work out why Mr. Dennard—a cop, as much a hero as any of Angie's other relatives she talked about—would have turned so angry at their playing with some of the family's old coats and belts.

Mark twisted around an old couple and their yapping dog, trying to keep Angie in sight. He passed sizzling burgers at the food stand, and his stomach clenched, reminding him the day was late and his uncle had been putting off their dinner. He tried to hold the emptiness down by thinking of the fun they'd had that afternoon—

Playing *Defend Sha Ta Ruath*—wherever that was—and letting their make-believe tell him *anything* could be about to happen—

But he was just hungry, and confused.

They reached the street corner at the edge of Rosewood Park's huge block, before Angie slowed and looked around.

"Where're you going? What happened?" he asked as he reached her side.

"I have something to ask my mom." She started across the street.

The word froze Mark a moment and he had to scramble to catch up again. Angie was going to her mother, after… how had she said it once, that mothers could run out on you? He still remembered the pain in her voice then, like Angie was better off with her gone.

She glanced over at him and added, "This is the way? If we keep going it's easy to hit Heat Street?"

"You mean Heath Avenue? The rich place? I think so."

She only moved faster now, with the sidewalk clear of park-goers and only the thinner evening crowds to weave through. Streetlights glowed along their way, just starting to stand out as night deepened, drawing the line between them and the stream of cars on their left.

By the second block, the sidewalk was even clearer. Now and then Mark passed people wrapped in scattered conversations, wreathed in cigarette smoke that added to the stench of car exhausts. Even some of the summer laughter he'd been hearing around the park seemed to thin away, while the air cooled and his feet hurt. Again and again, he saw the people Angie raced past turning to look at her flight.

Mark had lost count of the blocks they'd traveled before he managed to catch her arm. "It's getting dark. You can't just—"

"He said," and she spat the words at him like a weapon, "Dad said Grandpa died in a crazy-house! But he was my *mom's* father, Dad must be wrong, he has to be lying about him—"

She stopped, looked around the street. She must have seen something behind Mark, because she slipped from his slack grip and twisted away, heading up a side street, out of sight of the main road.

Mark scrambled after her, his thoughts pounding harder than his feet. The way Angie always talked, all her games about her family and its exploration of Sha Ta Ruath, and its soldiers and leaders and all the rest, and now her father said the things she *lived* for only ended in something awful?

At least he's not in jail like my *dad,* came an even darker thought. *And her mother's alive.*

The air felt colder now. They trotted past a construction barrier in the street and on through the shadow of a tall brick shape, and their feet sounded louder as the noise of cars fell away behind them.

The buildings pressed closer here, but a block ahead Mark could see the skeleton of a half-finished building silhouetted against the night. His nose itched at the construction dust in the air.

"Mark—" Suddenly Angie was turning back, toward him, past him.

He couldn't see what she had, only lines of darker brick pooling shadows into the slightly-paler street ahead. But that dimness, and the street traffic sounds so faded away behind them, brought a new shiver to his skin as he followed. Her footfalls were slower than they'd been all night. Hushed.

Then—

"You just keep going."

Growling right in front of them, appearing from around a corner, a huge man with some kind of black cap and a snarl of teeth flashing—

Angie, stumbling a step to put herself between Mark and the stranger they were backing away from—

Dim streets, alone, but the cars droning by not so far away, *people*—

The man took a step toward them. His arm reached out.

"HELP!" Mark yelled, with all the power his lungs had.

The next second, the big man had an ugly, blocky tunnel of a *gun* barrel pointed at them.

"Now you done it," he grated. "Wrong night for that. So you keep your holes shut or…"

Don't look at the gun, Mark told himself, feeling his heart stampeding, trying to tear his chest apart. If he looked to the side he could see Angie staring around, and another man—with the same kind of black cap over his scalp—moving up from where they had been headed, with a knife in his hand. Dust, so much dry, dead dust filling the air.

The gun tilted upward, relaxing the threat for a moment, and the man behind it grinned at their helplessness and lumbered toward them.

Then the gun swung higher as something yanked that arm toward the sky and a shape that had closed in behind the gunman's back twisted, spun, and sent the big man slamming to the pavement.

The gun clattered away. The man with the knife swore and broke into a run toward them, only to duck away inside a door as their rescuer reached inside his coat.

Angie gasped "Dad—" and there was awe in her voice.

Detective Dennard roared, "Just *go!*"

His tone, there was something wrong, like it was too fierce to fit inside his throat. And his hand drew back from his gun holster and brushed the belt at his waist…

In the next heartbeat, Angie's hand had locked onto Mark's arm and she pulled him into a run. His feet flung him along the pavement with her, toward the open streets. But he still stole a glance back, for a glimpse at her father chasing after the other thug.

Except Mr. Dennard was gone.

They ran. Ran through the night, forcing already-aching legs to carry them, with nerves on fire from the danger they'd brushed up against. In the rush of his heaving lungs, Mark at first missed the booming sound far, far behind them, until he realized it had spread and cascaded into a wild chorus of gunshots.

Blocks later they met a police car screaming toward the sound, and their shouts brought the cops over and let Mark gasp out a few words of what they'd seen. As he did, he realized Angie's father was closing in on them, as if he'd been only a few steps behind.

Angie flung herself into her father's arms without a word, or a single sob. Mark could only stand back, struggling for breath and watching them.

"*Listen* to that!" one of the uniforms said, raising his voice over the gunfire. "There ain't enough backup in the city to get me in there. That's got to be more than one gang killing each other—and you almost walked in right when something set them off?"

Almost walked in? Right, Mark thought, the three of them must have been blocks away from where the shots had sounded like they'd started. They had to have been.

Then Detective Dennard said "I… don't think I can be a cop anymore."

He kept his face bent over his daughter as he said those words. But Mark heard something in his voice, something that sounded too bitter to be the fury he'd shown before. Was that—shame?

Mark felt the two pieces in his head, refusing to go together. Angie's father had been running with them while the gangs started shooting far behind them… but that voice now… he couldn't make them fit.

No matter how he tried.

THE MESSENGER

Dammit, Angie…

Mark threw his weight on the pedals, legs pumping, fighting for any extra distance he could get from the gang closing in behind him. Through the rasp of his breathing, the Blades' pounding feet sounded like only inches from his heels. All because even on his first day of work he'd *had* to stop for her call.

The alley's end loomed up ahead, and he squeezed the back brake to slow and skid around the poster-covered brick corner. He heard one shrill "So what's in the box?" before he swung out into the Anchor Street crowd, safe.

Easy as that.

Swerving narrowly around two lumbering dockworker types, Mark lurched to a stop to answer their shouts with a breathless, "Sorry, sorry," before walking the bike on. His breathing settled as he worked through the crowd, maneuvering along a sidewalk full of people, probably some afternoon shift letting out—one of the thickest crowds in Lavine city. Darkening clouds thinned the light around them, and his sweat swam in the air, making him shiver in the growing cold.

Tired, but safe. "Beats telling Gene my new phone got me killed," he muttered.

But what was the point of him learning every street in town if he couldn't use the time he saved on a message run to stop in at Angie's—or when she wasn't home, pull over to take her call? That bit of slack in his day was supposed to be the good thing about this job, he'd figured on that benefit ever since his junk Chevy had died and started him thinking of options besides waiting tables.

Didn't matter; the danger was over. Just because it was the Blades again, or they'd been near Angie's, didn't mean the gang had any reason to keep after either of them.

He glanced back again, and his knuckles tightened on the handlebars. The punks were still behind him.

They were just strolling along, some twenty feet back. Two silent figures with their leathers and black do-rags, already drawing uneasy glances from the workers they passed.

Still on me? But only two of them, where'd Rafe *go?* Mark stared up and down the street, trying to think if they'd really bother staying with him much longer. Or, he could put his knowledge of the street routes to use again and lose them, if he could find one gap in the crowd.

At that moment a car pulled out from its parking space, leaving a hole at the edge of traffic, and Mark leaped forward. A woman shouted as he twisted his bike past her, and he barely swerved clear of a wrought-iron lamppost, but he broke through onto the street. Free.

Once his tires dropped off the curb he hopped onto the saddle and began pedaling, finally able to move. *Faster, faster, I'm lightning, I'm a bullet train, I'm the damn Sha Ta Ruath Express if it has one...* He swept down the narrow space between the honking rush of traffic and the parked cars, eyes alert for any door that might pick just that moment to swing open into his path.

The light ahead turned red, but instead of slowing he only banked for the corner and angled onto the cross-street's sidewalk to rush along the new angle. But just as he turned he saw the black-capped rider away to his left, roaring down at the intersection on his Harley.

The crowds wouldn't last... that motorcycle would get closer by the second... so, he could stop while he still had some witnesses and hope he could brazen it out without the Blades remembering his face later. Unless the gang really had been lurking near Angie's because after all these years—

Besides, he *knew* the streets. Another twist of the handlebars brought him up a side street, with a parting glance back that showed he'd have a few moments out of the biker's view. The way ahead was just as empty and riddled with alleys as he remembered, and he arced to the side and ducked into one.

With a van parked squarely in its middle. A battered red barricade.

"Of *course,*" he spat, and jumped down, trotting with the bike toward the narrow gap even as he heard an engine thundering in behind him. He heaved the front wheel up, twisting the handlebars to make as narrow an angle as he could, and pressed in... a tip just catching and scraping on the graffiti... then his heart restarted as it squeezed free. The low box bungeed over his back tire wobbled and almost came loose, but it didn't matter. Now he had only open space ahead.

The Harley's roar rattled off the buildings behind him, dropping to a lower growl as it crept up the alley like a prowling beast. Mark leaned back out of sight, against the van's rear, listening for any pause in that motor... but it only crawled slowly by and finally gathered force and roared away.

He drew in a deep breath and let it seep out. Even in the thick stormy air, he could smell exhaust from the van, still *fresh*—would the alley have been clear just a minute earlier? He reached down to tighten the bungees around his box. At least his old green Raleigh could wriggle past where their motors couldn't, and foot soldiers wouldn't bother chasing him for long. Just as he'd thought, he'd ridden rings around them.

"Mark?"

The voice from around the van was low, worse than a shout: the calmness itself told him who it had to be.

Rafe went on "Still running errands for small bills? I always said you need someone who's got your back."

Mark's fists clenched. *We're a year out of high school, and he still thinks he can make me one of his thugs?*

I can't let him rattle me. Rafe couldn't have seen him duck back here; he had to be bluffing, calling blindly up each corner to see if he'd get an answer.

Then Rafe spoke again. "*This* time, the best place you can be is away from Joe Dennard. This won't stop until it comes out the far side of ugly."

Dennard. The night of the gang war. Suddenly that was all Mark could think of—even after ten years, after most of the Blades who'd lived through it must be dead or in prison. What could Rafe and the rest of them know, or *care,* about what might have happened back then?

But if they did—Mark found he couldn't breathe. If the gang was after Dennard—and they'd spotted Mark for being outside Angie's— were they already closing in on the father and the daughter too?

Then he heard a footstep, then another, the sound receding as Rafe walked away, up the pavement, to be swallowed up by the sounds of the city. He hadn't seen Mark after all.

Mark stayed flattened against the van for five more long, controlled breaths. Then he crouched down to look under it—he hadn't been so well-hidden, after all, not if anyone stopped to look for his feet—but saw nobody lingering out there.

His hands were trembling as he started the bike up the alley. At least his tires were silent as they built up speed, not like running feet would be. But he had to go faster, faster, get some space to stop and call the Dennards.

"Bastard!"

The sudden yell twisted his head back, to see the other two Blades charging up the alley at him. He flung himself forward.

Then the handlebar lurched and tipped, and he wrenched it blindly to keep it clear of the wall, clinging for balance, still looking back at the Blades... seeing the bungeed-down box working loose from the rack...

It's dangling over to foul the wheel—

Somehow, somehow, he kept the bike steady as he leaned forward and kicked back wildly, then felt the box break free. He scrabbled for the pedals again, fighting to build speed and hoping the gang would duck away from the falling box—or even stop to tear it open to discover the sample suit coat some designer had been so damn eager to have delivered.

Push! The street ahead still looked empty, no barriers to him, but also no witnesses if they caught him. Still, the thought of racing blindly into the lane made him twist, sweeping around the corner onto the sidewalk past a flash of red hair that had to be—

He heard the curses first, so fierce he had to steal a glance back. In that one instant he saw two recycling bins falling by the corner in a mess of green and blue and strewn metal. And a door, closing. Angie must have already ducked through it after knocking the bins into the Blades' path.

Mark had to imagine the rest as he powered up the street: how the first Blade might twist around the bins, but maybe the other would slip on some of the scattered cans... his mind kept supplying the sound of bowling pins crashing down together, but of course what mattered were the seconds Angie had bought him to get up to speed at last. And that she had spotted the bins and the open door in the one split instant he'd raced past her. Of course.

He rushed past block after block, keeping to the clearer side streets and zigzagging between them when he could. As he worked on picturing the evening streets' layout he remembered his new cell's GPS tracker app; of course, when he had broken off his call with her to run from the Blades, Angie could have used her own cell to find him. That could have given her some little warning that he was doubling back here, enough to set her trap.

With that guess in mind, it was only a matter of time before he settled onto the bike lane on Garcetti, and looked back to see a motorcyclist wearing a familiar denim jacket and red helmet moving up from behind him.

The old relief at seeing her was colored with an odd stain of envy, now that Angie's nimble Kawasaki had held up while his Chevy's breakdown had sent him back to pedaling. *Not that that matters, if the gang* is *hunting her father.* He pulled over to wait.

As his feet touched the pavement he felt his head spin, tension suddenly squirming up and down his muscles and turning them to water. The Blades had almost... and Rafe had...

A sudden thought made him burst out laughing, sagging against the handlebars.

Angie pulled up beside him, frowning at him as he fought to get a full breath. "Mark? Did I miss something?" Concern softened her voice more than usual.

"Just realized," he gasped out, trying to show her he hadn't lost his mind. "Even without your help, they... they lost that chase years—years!—before they met us..."

Her eyes narrowed suspiciously. "And why is that?"

He hauled in some air, and tried to say it properly. "When the first punks started their 'club.' Motorcycles couldn't squeeze through where I did, and runners couldn't keep up... but e-e-ever since they named themselves the Blades..." The laughs broke through again and he collapsed over the bike.

A moment later he heard her finish "...they wouldn't dare chase you on skates!" and break out laughing herself.

When they both had their breath back, Mark drew himself up, his lanky frame looming over her compact one. The one friend he'd kept by him, the girl who'd gone from severe pneumonia to winning track records. The girl who still held on to even bigger dreams, if she could get away safe from what he'd just learned.

He made himself meet her eyes. "Except… it was Rafe Martinez himself. And when they spotted me, I think it was because they were watching your place, and… he said they're after your father. I mean, if they finally found out he was there, and he really did know something about how the gang war started—"

"He threatened Dad—and you think it's for *this* thing again?" Her simple features tightened in frustration. "For the last time, give it a rest." She spun away, glaring up at the blackening clouds. "And it's been ten years. What could Rafe 'find out' that can have dug all of that up?"

"I don't know. I don't even know why he warned me; I've already turned down enough of his damn *offers*. But what I *think*—"

Mark stopped and bit back the flare of anger; he should have known arguing this with her wouldn't be easy. He met her gaze and settled his voice to its gentlest, steadiest tone.

"I think *something* had them waiting around your place, when I rode by it, and they even knew me, all of them. And that means they'll be back for you again, if you stay around here." He stopped there; no need to say again how he still couldn't forget the fury Dennard's face had held that night—or the shame after, then and when he turned in his badge, after weeks of bloody inter-gang warfare.

But Angie must have guessed where his doubts led, because she sighed "But years back—while he was saving our lives!—he was a block away when the 66s opened up on the Blades, and yet somehow it's *his* fault? No, this has to be about what he is now. If they can control the park's guard, they control the park, control the drugs and God-knows-what else they can do there. And they want me as a way to get at him."

She glanced around the sidewalk traffic, as if the gang might already be creeping through the crowd toward them. In just moments, Angie had it all figured out—without blaming the man they both wanted to trust. And he had to admit, her answer did make more sense.

A car honked on the street beside them.

"Mark?" She was looking back toward him.

"Yeah," he sighed. "Look, maybe it doesn't matter what they want from him. If they were at your place, they want to use you against him, but you're leaving the city anyway—and you still are, right? Staying isn't supporting him, it just gives him more he has to watch out for. And don't think about putting your plans on hold, that's one more way the gang wins."

"I… oh of *course* I'm leaving, I know that. I should like it more when you're right." Her head sank, then straightened a second later. "But you both have to keep yourselves safe, too, or I'll just be right back here." And she grinned.

"Sure, *anything* to keep that from happening." The joke came as a reflex, while his thoughts scrambled to catch up to how she'd be safe again, free, gone. He added, "If they're watching your place, I can round up some reinforcements to help while you pick up a few things—"

"No, I should just call Dad and go, and work the rest out later. Besides, *you* still have to explain to your boss about that package. And aren't you seeing Grace tonight?" she added as she started her engine.

That's over; it's Lucy now. But he didn't say that, only smiled back and dug out his phone as he pulled onto the sidewalk. He only had to keep the smile up a few more seconds, and then she was gone.

She's gone off to learn to fly planes, and when I'm trying to show her I'm the fastest courier on a bike, I get shot down. "Nice going," he muttered as he dialed.

Gene Chung answered on the second ring. "So, the delivery's done?"

With someone else, Mark would have tried softening the blow. Instead: "I'm afraid I lost the coat."

He heard a spluttering sound.

"I was robbed on the street," he went on.

"On a bike?" Gene snapped. "You just had to keep moving and… no, never mind. Mark, you *begged* me for this job, and all your ideas for expanding sounded good, but on your first day—"

"Just let me talk to the client. I *was* risking my—"

"Stay away from them! You pick up what's left of your check, and then leave us alone." He hung up.

Mark glared at the cell, but he wasn't really surprised. *It's what I deserve, and he never really liked me anyway. I must have caught him on a desperate day when he hired me at all.*

But at least he had kept himself ahead of the Blades, and Angie was on her way across the state. Now he just had to find something worth doing next.

He wiped the sweat from his forehead, glad he'd given up his usual long hair before starting the courier job. He poised a thumb over the phone. He could call Henry and tell him he was a bit further from paying him back for the rent, but his cousin deserved better news these days. Or he could go straight to the job boards and look for options. Or work up the nerve to call Roger Winton again—not that buying a few sketches in three years made the "king of food carts" an art patron.

"Or that a 'Mark' should be an artist," he muttered, and put the phone back on his belt. Taking one more look at the stormclouds moving in from the north, he calculated how long it would be until Lucy's shift was over, and turned toward the park.

It was a stupid risk, going near Dennard now, but he hated to let the Blades' threat chase him away. Mark promised himself he'd stay out in public, and meet Dennard just long enough to ask him about an idea that had been growing in his mind. To stop running packages around and try joining the police.

The lowering September sun peeked between the taller buildings now, adding shadows to the thickening air and making him stare harder to watch for any more of Rafe's friends. And here Mark was going to ask a man who'd left the force about joining it… on the day they were both saying goodbye to Angie, too. The same day as Mark's own brush with danger, and him pushing Angie out the door. What a mess.

But, maybe I've been letting myself stay just the jailbird's son, and that can change. Angie never *let herself be just the disgraced cop's daughter.*

When the street ahead softened into the uneven, lower shadows of the sprawling city park, he tried to forget the Blades and force a smile. Angie always claimed it had been named Rosewood for her mother's mother, and in the end it had been the place her father had found work. Mark glided along the bikeways between the evening picnickers, looking out for the old-fashioned navy blue uniform.

It didn't take long. He was only partway to the pond when he saw a chubby figure scrabbling to pick up some dropped wrapper, with Dennard standing behind him. Just standing, with his arms behind his back, probably doing nothing more, but standing closer than anyone else would. Park Officer Joe Dennard had a way of making whatever he was doing seem more menacing than it actually was, and somehow he always made it work.

It must have been something he picked up from his police days. Mark wondered if he might be learning that trick himself soon.

Dennard waited for the repentant litterbug to wobble away, then turned around, a worried frown spreading. "Mark? Are you sure you want to be around me now? Even Angie says she's keeping her distance."

"I'll make it quick; I still have to get out and meet Lucy," Mark grinned back, trying to let the familiar banter keep his mind away from his renewed doubt about what Dennard might have done. "Um, can I talk to you?"

"I'm about finished here for now," was all Dennard said, as if Mark's sober tone had been nothing out of the ordinary. He motioned off toward the park's edge, and his home just beyond it. And he nodded to another man in Rosewood blue, a way up the path—he already had a reinforcement against the Blades, Mark realized.

Mark fell into place beside Dennard, walking his bike silently between the park visitors and wondering how the man could be so calm.

They just missed the light across Summer Street, so they had to stand for a while, watching the evening traffic. Mark tried not to worry, though he could almost feel the storm pressure swelling around them. *It'll reach us soon.*

Then an engine rumbled up and slowed, and Angie walked her motorcycle up beside them. "Looks like I'm late. But I wanted to see you while I could."

Of course she did. Why should any of them stay back from danger? Mark sighed.

"Just come on," Dennard said, as the light changed. He led them across at a quick march.

On the far side of Summer Street waited an apartment complex, a scattering of pleasant orange shapes, and the tiny house almost at the street's edge that Mark and Angie once imagined had started out as an old toolshed. Somehow it still belonged to the park, given over to Joe Dennard and, until last year, his daughter.

And she might never stand here again, came Mark's sudden thought.

It made the little house suddenly feel different. It was still the familiar place, with the trunks squeezed into the corners, but now its stubborn musty smell seemed so much thicker. The wall by the door looked wrong without the picture of Angie's grandparents that she had always kept there.

Mark turned a chair round from the tiny dinner table just as Dennard settled onto one edge of the sofa and looked up at his daughter. "Alright, what are these 'rumors' that the Blades are after me?"

Angie stayed standing, and she dove right in. "I didn't want to tell you the rest on the phone. They aren't rumors; the Blades were looking for me today—"

Dennard was on his feet in an instant.

She finished "—so unless you just tossed one of them in the pond, they must want me as a hold on you and the park."

Her father's face was white, and Mark saw his hands twitch at his sides, as if they wanted to grab at her. "Don't you joke! Not about the gangs. Did they hurt you?"

"No," she came right back.

"Or you?" He glanced over, and Mark shook his head. Dennard turned back to her. "Did you start fighting, did you dig yourself in any deeper with them?"

"Of course not. And they can't hurt me, once—"

"I'll talk to the precinct," and this time he did reach for his daughter's shoulders. "If I can get Peters or Ryerson to—"

She stepped out of his reach. "Don't worry about me."

"Don't talk like that! Of *course* I'm getting you protection, it's the only way to keep them away from you."

"Unless," Mark put in, "she's already out of reach. Didn't she tell you?"

"Right." Angie flashed him a smile, and turned back to her father. "They want to control Rosewood through you, and me? I can do something better than sit here, and Mark's already set it up: I'm moving across the state, for a job that he found out about."

Her father stared at her, then said "So you're… you've got a job? You're leaving town, and this is the first I hear?"

She would have had more time, if the gang had stayed out of it, Mark thought.

"I'm going to be a pilot," Angie said. She turned away and started pacing the short distance she could to the wall and back. "And the first step is that Spitz Airfield needs an assistant, and we worked out pay, and flying lessons, and a place for me to stay."

Dennard sank back onto the sofa, a little quickly, judging by the creak of springs. "You, at a desk?" and he gestured along the path she'd just paced, never still. "And it sounds like it could take years. Can you at least ask your mother for—"

"Not her. I'll make it work, if it gets me in the air someday."

She glanced over at the kitchen counter, nodding to one picture Mark saw was still there: her grandparents, Will and Sarita Rose Fletcher, with one of the mountains they had climbed in the background.

"But Dad, promise me you'll watch your back—until the Blades go on to some other place they can poison instead. Shouldn't take long," she added, and Mark thought he heard a small question in her voice, asking if that was all that was going on.

"It's a big city," Dennard said, and she nodded.

If that was a lie… if she took it and walked out thinking her dad was only in momentary danger… *It's not right.*

"Unless," Mark added, and saw them both start, "they really do have the kind of reason Rafe mentioned."

"Mark?" Angie took a step toward him, a scowl starting to darken on her face.

"I just mean—" and it was easier to turn his gaze to her silent father. "If they were going to keep coming for you, if they even thought that back when the gang war started you had some part in the shots that set it off—if they didn't know you couldn't run that far back—"

"That far?" and Dennard cut off Mark's tumble of words with a laugh. "What matters is we weren't there. You think the Blades got that exactly wrong, and only ten years later too?"

"I don't know." Mark couldn't seem to get a breath, under Dennard's gaze, knowing Angie must be staring at him. But… still, Dennard hadn't been *quite* there with them, he had left them for a few moments… and, impossible or not, there was something *hidden* in that too-confident voice. Mark could only say, "Well, you did quit the cops right after that. Anyway, if there's anything that could give the Blades that kind of vendetta against you, don't we deserve to know?"

Dennard shook his head slowly. "Whatever they want with me, it's nothing like that. The gangs never needed anyone else to make them kill each other. And it's been ten years, and you must be the only one who thinks it… could be my… fault."

And then his head sank toward his chest, as he added:

"No matter what I did."

So few words.

"Dad?" Angie's voice had a tiny shard of pain in it, like cracked glass. "What… are you saying?"

Dennard shrugged, a simple motion, but he didn't meet her eyes. His words seeped out of him, as if squeezed out by too many years of holding up the lie. "I… I stopped thinking. I wanted them to pay, I saw the two gangs lined up there, I didn't think how many other people would get caught in it—"

Angie didn't reply, she only stared at him, slumped in his seat. At least her face hadn't turned to Mark yet.

Only a moment later she shifted her gaze, looking between them, avoiding their eyes. "I need to be alone. I need to say goodbye to the park." She spun away, and three quick steps brought her over to the kitchen, where she snatched up the family picture from the counter. "And my grandparents don't have to look at a murderer."

Then she was across the room again, and gone.

The soft thump of the closing door broke the stillness. Dennard growled "You *had* to keep pushing," but he stayed slumped on the couch.

Mark waited, watching him. *But you did want to tell us*, he could have said. Or maybe, *It must have been hell carrying that around.* Or he could apologize, or say Angie could never have meant what she said. But all he did was let the moments stretch out, accepting what he'd put them all through.

A knock sounded on the door, hard and rapid.

Dennard was up in a moment, halfway to it before they heard a male voice outside. "Joe? I saw your light—"

Then the door was open, and they were looking at the man outside, a short figure whose park blues seemed lost in the twilight.

"They're out there, the Blades! Some kind of gathering, Griggs said not to tell you but I had to, does he really think he can get the rest of us to come in—"

"Lewis. Did you see Angie out there?" Dennard's voice was steady, and the other man seemed to draw calmness from it.

"No. I came right here. I saw at least eight or ten of them, but they're *staying*, storm or no, they even hung some fancy coat above the Nature Station like they were planting a flag!"

In the back of Mark's mind stirred the petty thought *They wouldn't, it* can't *be the same coat I was delivering!* before Dennard said "We have to find her. Mark, where would she go?"

"You think *I* know? Hell, she doesn't want to be found, and she knows the park better than any of us—"

Lewis cut in "But, Griggs wants us at the pond—"

Dennard snapped at Mark "Then you get home, now!" then turned to Lewis and added "So get over there. Don't wait for me, go, just go!"

Mark found himself stepping out into the storm-thickened air. Dennard's voice and the rising fierceness in its last words hung around him a moment, before Lewis trotted out and away down the path, and the door slammed with Dennard inside.

Mark shook his head hard to clear it. He brought out his new cell and tapped Angie's number, but he heard only the usual "Angie Dennard is right in the middle of something, but…" Not that she stopped to answer it half the time normally.

But if he *could* find her and warn her about the Blades in the park… He hopped onto his bike and pushed off, glancing across the street, trying to guess where in the park she'd go. *And I* am *the one who threw his guilt in her face. My fault.*

Then he slammed on the brakes. Angie might be shaken, but the way Dennard had sounded as he chased them out, had sounded *desperate*. Like he'd looked years ago, when he'd attacked that first Blade.

And why was Dennard still in his house?

Mark swung the bike toward it. The light was still on in the window, a crack through the curtains facing off to an angle from him. He moved toward that light from the side, thinking of what the man's rage had triggered once before. *Angie can find a hundred hiding places in the park, but what good is that if her father gets himself killed?*

He drew up beside the window, stepped from the bike to crouch down, and looked in.

Joe Dennard stood in the room's closet, closing an undersized trunk. Some of the family's old belongings, from what Mark could see, as racked clothes fell back to cover it. Then Dennard stepped back and looked down at what he was holding: a leather belt dangling between his hands, ready to strap on—

But it wasn't a gun belt. Just a length of broad, black leather with a brass buckle. So why was Dennard simply standing there, as if he couldn't take his eyes from it? His face was turned away from the window, but Mark almost thought the belt was swaying, as if the hands that held it were trembling.

Reaching the belt around his waist, Dennard took a slow step toward the door.

Then he crumpled the belt in his hands and spun away. His face was twisted in a grimace so tight Mark couldn't look away until Dennard's eyes had already swept past him at the window, unseeing. Just the wake from that look made Mark crouch down and press himself flat against the wall.

The muted *thump* of a fist shook through the stucco.Mark crouched lower, though he knew Dennard hadn't seen him. Why was he worked up enough to pound the wall, but not going after his daughter? Why stop to look at an old belt?

That trunk of clothes looked like some of the things he and Angie used to borrow, family things, for when they were running around the park playing Fletcher Explorers, until Dennard had ripped them from their hands. On the day of the gang war.

A door banged open on the far side of the tiny house. Dennard's footsteps were quick, heading toward the walkway out front. Mark left the bike and peeped around the corner just as the sound stopped.

In the dim light he saw Dennard crouch at one of the apartment complex's brick cooking grills, dropping the belt and some other shape into a small trunk and shoving it under the grill with the scrape of metal on masonry. Then Dennard tore out handfuls of paper—from magazines he'd brought?—and tossed them into the trunk as he crouched down.

A match flared.

Dennard didn't move then, just stayed half-kneeling by the trunk, until a faint breeze ruffled the grass and Mark saw the light wink out. With a hiss that must have been a curse, Dennard fumbled for a few moments and then draw himself back to feed another match into the cracked-open jaws of the trunk.

Orange light kindled inside it, while Dennard struck a third match and added it to the fire. He crouched by it a moment longer, then leaped up and marched off down the path. Mark saw him take out his phone and dial, and heard him say "Lewis, I'll meet you—" before he moved out of earshot. His other arm swung up once, as if to wipe his eyes.

Mark could only stare after him. *What did I just see?* Dennard had looked so desperate, so much like he had years ago, that watching him had made Mark more afraid of what he'd do for his daughter than afraid for Angie herself, out in the Blades' path. So if Dennard was that driven, why had he stopped to burn a piece of Angie's childhood?

The glow grew brighter, filling the inches-wide gap where Dennard had propped the trunk open, like some squat, eyeless Jack-O'Lantern. And…

Whatever it is, nobody will ever have this chance again. Something about that truth sent Mark scrambling forward. The metal trunk was still only warm when he grabbed it from under the grill, spilling the flames out onto the pavement. With a corner of the box, he raked the burning paper away from the belt and what turned out to be a thick canvas satchel, then snuffed the patches of fire out with the bottom of the trunk. Once the embers had faded, he leaned closer, blinking back tears from the smoke. The satchel—it used to store the belt and a few scraps of leather, he remembered—seemed to have resisted the brief fire; the belt felt warm and sooty, but no more battered than it had ever been. The first real scarring his fingers felt was the lettering on its inside.

"Made in Sha Ta Ruath." The writing flashed in his mind, and he realized that after all the games and dares years ago he'd remembered the strange name only as some essence of exotic places he'd never get to see. "But why would he burn it?"

He shook his head, and stuffed the belt into the satchel. He could give them both to Angie later, if he got a chance to warn her about the Blades.

The traffic light back across Summer Street was longer than ever. Angie still wasn't answering her cell, and she'd turned off her GPS app. Mark could only stare at the traffic, fighting the urge to dodge between the cars in the dimming light.

When he could finally start his bike forward, the images began to creep back into his mind: the shapes of Rosewood Park and how Angie might pick a way through them. If the Blades were gathered at the Nature Station, by the northeast corner... her only risk would be if she walked blindly up from the south, or in around the central woods...

Mark chained his bike next to the northwest picnic tables, and his eyes moved to the wilder wood beyond the parking lot. Fenced off, and separating the park from the industrial grounds at its north edge, it might give the best cover to get near the Nature Station. He unfastened the satchel from his bike bag; the fire's heat had already faded from it. Maybe Angie was watching the Blades from in there. Maybe her father wouldn't guess that in time to help her.

"Right," he laughed at his presumption. "It's just me who can save the day, and then we run off to Sha Ta Ruath—"

There!

His eyes flicked to the woods; he was suddenly sure she was there. But he saw only the straight trees and brush leading up the first slope. He felt a twitchiness in himself, an eagerness he hadn't felt since he was a child running around the park. Even with the Blades somewhere out there too.

None of the lingering park visitors paid much attention to him, even when he tossed the satchel over the seven-foot fence in front of the wood and started climbing it. He had to press the blunt tips of his shoes hard into the chain mesh to take some weight off his fingers, and any slip made it rattle, and forced him to dig his other shoe in deeper. All the thrill of a minute ago was gone, leaving only chilling thoughts of what the Blades might do if he let them see him. He could only try to keep hidden, and hope the risk was worth it.

Then he reached the top and dropped, falling into the dimness to land on wood chips. He felt through the brush for the satchel, grasped it, and started up the slope in a careful crouch. The trees themselves weren't so thick—there was always a step or two between the trunks, and their branches were sparse shapes lost in the grayness twenty feet above him—but below, the bracken pressed so close that every step brought a scratching over his jeans. The rich scent of resin filled his nose.

He could still hear the park sounds; just outside the wood some child was arguing with its parents about the coming storm. The voices seemed far-off but he guessed they'd be as loud as the bushes rustling around him. *In this light none of them out there would see me here.* But, Angie could let him go right past *her* if all she heard was someone moving in the brush, if she was even here. Or her father could come searching, keyed-up enough to jump him on sight.

He angled left as he climbed the slope, eyes searching the grays of the brush, ready to sweep up and down all through the wood if it would help them. Soft as he could, he muttered, "Forget Sha Ta Ru-ath."

Again! Something twitched on his nerves, familiar, just as he spoke. He paused in mid-step—

His foot caught on a bush and he stumbled forward, bouncing off a tree trunk, the satchel slipping from his hands.

With a wordless snarl he knelt and felt around again, straining through the shadows. After an endless, helpless moment that left him with scratched fingers, he found the canvas shape again.

And the twitching feeling was back. *Back,* right at the *instant* he gripped the satchel; he pulled his fingers away and it vanished.

Vanished. He felt it close away inside him, clear and real as a window closing on a warm wind, but no wind could blow *inside* his skin, this thing wasn't a touch at all. Not like anything real could be.

Except as a kid, now he remembered, he'd felt it before in this wood—

I'm wasting time. He grabbed the satchel and hugged it closer to press on through the wood. He shifted his search rightward now as he crested the slope, peering through the dim shapes ahead. His clothes still scraped against the bushes, but a steadier breeze had begun to rustle the leaves overhead too, rising and falling all around. Maybe he *could* stay hidden and find her in time to help, if she was here.

Still, that feeling had started by him just saying a word. Just a whisper.

"Sha… Ta… Ruath."

With his words, the twitching grew enough to make him realize it had been starting to fade. He *had* felt this before, as a kid in the park; a kind of stirring outside of him. It wasn't just the storm's approach, and it came from somewhere through the trees ahead. Not inside him, and not something he sensed, but still it was…

He couldn't resist reaching into the satchel to close his hand around the belt he'd worn once, so long ago. With the touch, the twitching, stirring feeling grew, as if he'd opened some door between him and a sound. No, not a sound, but some different knowing, a kind of pressure from the trees ahead and right…

But Joe Dennard had wanted to destroy this belt, and he and Angie were somewhere in the park right now, and so was the gang.

And yet, Mark *felt* that pressure in his head, beyond all doubt, as new and certain as if he'd felt a sixth finger flexing on his hand.

Even as he took a quicker step around a tree, still clutching the belt, he tested it again. This time he rushed the words out, more "Sha-Daruath."

The stirring came in stronger, closer, as the syllables came out closer together. He stared around, half expecting to see Angie or somebody waiting in the brush already, but he saw only the slight dip in the slope to his left, trees a half-pace farther apart, at about where he sensed the strangeness. *What* is *this?*

With another slow step, he tried to recall how the pressure had changed with the words. Like something moving, not so held back from him, now that he'd spoken the sounds more together... like a wave lapping over him, but not one that had fully begun, not quite enough... not at the words' start...

He pushed his voice into the starting word, to buzz *"Zha-Daruath."*

It *surged,* the pressure sweeping through his un-sense with a flood of tingling, making him stagger as though it poured into him from the ground, from the air. How could the leaves be so still, with everything whirling with this lightness, the force of anything possible, straining to start... He took another step, his mouth falling open, lost in sensation.

As he stepped, the wave settled. He felt his feet drifting away from the ground.

A TEXT

—*Message delivered. Ahead of schedule, but D can't miss it. His own people will make sure he makes his move.*

Whatever that move is. And whatever you're really playing for, it had better be worth what I'm risking.

CHAPTER TWO

THE TRAP

Mark rose upward, floating, like a dream. His feet reached down for the ground of their own accord, but found only empty space.

Upward, forward. The dark shapes of branches met him, scratched along him, as he fended them off with a forearm, hugging the satchel closer, his fingers tightening on the belt within—

What the hell is happening? Where will I stop?

With a shock of fear he grabbed for the branches, but his fingers only closed on twigs that rustled and snapped in his grip. The black sky yawned above. He tried to reach down after the trees as they dropped away below, but he could only thrash his arms, couldn't lean back when he hung weightless in the air.

I must be fifteen-some feet up—more each second! In the next instant he tried the only thing he could think of: he let the satchel go and bent his knees to tense for the fall.

Except he didn't fall, he kept rising. He could see the satchel beside him, floating upward on its own. "No no no—" He thrashed in space and stared helplessly around... and his breath caught at the sight.

The branches below were a sea of shadows ruffling in the breeze from behind his back, a breeze that ebbed away into stillness even as he noticed it.

But the wind hadn't faded, he could see that from the trembling wood still passing by below... because he was being carried within the current now, still rising and floating across it. He gazed around in the gloom: beyond the faint trees and rolling hills of the park just below, the crystalline grid of city lights began to spread before him; the streets' night-thinned rumbles and honks filtered up to his ears with clearer tones than they ever had down at street level. Even the smells were different, cleaner, at this distance from the ground. He looked down again, to the scattered lamplight along the park's walkways. Was that a couple walking along?

A rumble of far-off thunder snapped his mind back. The satchel was floating away.

No! He flailed and strained in the air, and managed to snag it again. The damn belt had *broken gravity*—he clutched it and gasped out "Zha-Daruath!" but this time all the words triggered was a faint tingle.

A wave of cold washed that tingle away as he stared at the ground, whole stories below him and still shrinking. What if saying those words really *had* brought him down, all at once?

Or, what if *nothing* brought him down? More and more of the city drew back around him. Moonlight filtered from above, leading upward forever, forever. His heart hammered. Behind him, the endless black storm bore in, ready to swallow him up. He might as well be naked in the sky.

This can't be happening! How can Joe Dennard have something that makes you fly... *and how could I be so stupid as to grab it and get trapped...*

Dennard. Mark remembered seeing him, almost putting the belt on, before he tried to burn it; the thing *had* to be more than just a death-trap. Mark's head pounded, but he locked his eyes on the thin ribbon of darker black below. The park walkway, if he could just reach it. "Think!"

The belt—the words—nothing works, I'm falling upward into space and I need to scream—*It's too late, I was dead as soon as I followed that sensation, what do I do?*

The sense, of the power.

It was still throbbing through him, mixed with the chill in his nerves. Not quite a touch, but some other sensation, in his head. That something buzzed around him… but was the touch in his head more like *feeling* it, or *holding* it… his thought couldn't quite reach…

Something came loose, and the air brushed at again, whistling past him as he dropped straight at the ground. "No, dammit!" He flailed as he fell, clutching the belt and trying to tighten the other grip that wasn't a grip, to *squeeze* or *push* or anything. Time slowed.

No, it was the ground slowing, stopping, and it began to drift away again, still stories below him. Mark let out his breath.

And dropped again.

He clamped his control tighter and felt himself rise, stomach sick as the corners of the belt dug into his fingers. His face twisted, this was stranger than trying to loosen a headache inside his skull, feeling for the twitch in his head that seemed to be all that was holding him up. He shivered as he rose through the cooling air.

Can't think about it. He turned his neck and saw the park's Nature Station drawing near ahead—of course, didn't most storm fronts in town push in that direction, west to east? Straight below him, three people moved down the walkway, hurrying to get inside before the storm.

Or fleeing the Blades. Weren't they at the Nature Station?

Now he was maybe three stories up and rising. As the figures moved on, he stared down at where the soft grass would be, just waiting for him to drop and catch himself and drop again—

Don't think it, just hold on! He couldn't risk breaking his neck, not tonight, not just from grabbing an old belt. "Damn, damn, *damn!*" The outrage that surged through him was a blessed release, a release from looking down at the ground he was hanging over by something thinner than his fingernails. Again and again, Mark told himself that Dennard had thought he could make this thing work.

Hell, Angie's pictures showed her *grandfather* wearing this belt, and with all the stories she told—

Somehow he kept those thoughts from crowding into the center of his mind. He held his grip; the low roof of the visitor Nature Station was just another shape to pass—even if those shadows around it were the Blades, Angie and her father had to be safe, he only had to hold on. Hold on.

Beyond the Station he could see the parking lot, then the sea of dark shapes and cold lights growing beyond it again. All that hard, bone-breaking asphalt ahead to get past; he forced his eyes up beyond it. That long black gap among the buildings would be the river.

Yes! He'd just drop into the water, if he could only ride the wind out to it without falling—

Just by thinking that thought he slipped, lurched down through the air. An instant later he tightened his mental grip, clinging on somehow. *Can't think about it, can't scream...*

Down past his dangling feet, shapes moved among the Nature Station trees. And far off to his right, he saw a knot of figures marching up the walkway toward them—would that be the park crew, was Dennard safe among them? All Mark could do was hang on in the air, at what must be four stories up now.

In one of the pines below, a pale patch was spread out within the branches. The stupid coat he'd dropped; the Blades had hung it up, like a dare. And one leather-dark shape, and another; seen from above their black do-rags made them look almost headless in the shadows. The Blades waited, spread out—were they keeping watch for something?—as the park officers drew near on the walkway.

Hold on, hold on up in the air, don't think of watching them, don't think of drifting on and then falling on the hard street into traffic—

Air rushed in his ears, the roof leaped up at him—

NO! Something surged from him, a force pulling him upward. For an instant he hung in midair, thrashing, and then he let himself tumble to thump down on the Station's roof in a tangle of elbows and pain.

He lay still, barely caring when the satchel with the belt slid away, down the slanting tiles for a moment, before coming to rest a small distance from him. Somewhere nearby voices stirred the air, but for now he could only feel the strangeness of his body's weight against the roof and his bruised breathlessness. The wind brushed at his hair. *I'm alive, alive, I made it down.*

I was flying. I was.

Then a shrill voice filtered through: "…he there? Is that him?"

"You heard the Eel, he's gonna need more bodies than—"

"Just let them walk on up." Rafe, that was Rafe, his voice steadying the other Blades' snarls. "Stay in place."

In place? What's that *mean?* Mark's ragged thoughts couldn't focus, but he pried his head up to look down along the dust-caked tiles, then crawled down the slope to peer over the edge.

Right above two of the Blades. They were speaking in gruff, hungry voices kept low enough that the wind had hidden them: "Gotta be him."

Mark pushed himself backward, out of sight—not as easy as crawling down to the edge, with his restored weight trying to slide him down toward it.

"Hiding in the crowd?" one of the Blades said.

"He better hide, playing us like—heads up."

Mark flattened himself to the roof, but instead of shouts aimed at him he heard only low, half-excited sounds from around the building. They hadn't spotted him. He crept along the side, toward the corner they seemed to be gathering below. Not all of them were there; he heard some of the Blades muttering from other directions. What were they here for?

Then he saw the southern walkway, lined with its mix of different trees and their little identification plaques. The four park officers he'd seen were walking up it to reach the gang.

They stopped when they entered the pool of light at the edge of the Nature Station, revealing the plump man in the lead to be the boss, Griggs. "Alright boys, we've had some complaints about you. I'm afraid we'll have to ask you to move on."

The Blades tensed at the challenge. Mark saw two, three thugs below, at different distances from the light, and knew there must be twice that many lurking in other spots out of his view.

But Rafe, the tall figure in the center, only said, "Complaints about what? Don't we have a right to enjoy this park too?"

He sounded so reasonable, but Mark saw one of his thugs flash a nasty grin. Was all this just some dare for them?

Griggs started to answer, then stopped, glancing back as Joe Dennard began shouldering his way forward from the rear of his team.

And every Blade's head turned to watch Dennard. Dennard stopped in his tracks, glowering past Griggs at the intruders.

The next moment one of the punks shifted, fading a few steps back from the confrontation and toward Mark's wall. He glanced around, like he was searching the trees for something.

What were Rafe's orders before? *They* are *keeping watch,* in case someone snuck up on them. Too bad they never thought of the roof, or the *impossible*...

Or maybe they should have. Mark scowled; the Blades, the belt, Dennard, did it all mean...

Griggs turned back from whispering with one of his men, and said, "Don't you start arguing with me. We have laws against gangs congregating, you know."

"Gangs?" Rafe had the gall to spread his arms innocently. "Are you calling me a criminal?"

Mark's thoughts raced as the two leaders argued.

The Blades were after Dennard, and he'd *admitted* to setting off the old gang war...

And yet Dennard had never been close enough to fire those shots...

But distance meant nothing now; those blocks Dennard would have had to cross impossibly fast must have been left behind just as the ground had dropped away from Mark before. Dennard *had* rushed off to fire a few wild shots and turn two gangs against each other, and then rushed back to catch up to the children. He just hadn't done it on foot.

And now, somehow, Rafe knew enough to target Dennard and be ready for any trick or partner he might have ready. Except, the Blades were watching all directions except the one Mark had used.

A single blare from a siren cut into the noise below. The Blades and the guards turned to watch as a pair of cops marched up from the parking lot.

Mark pressed himself lower to the tiles, grinning. Whatever Rafe had in mind, Dennard was staying safe with the park team. All Mark had to do was sit tight. Not think about Dennard's crime, not think about *flying*.

Below him, Rafe took a few steps back toward one of his thugs, right under the edge of the roof, and muttered something. The little man glanced at his cell and answered, and through a lull in the wind Mark caught what sounded like "...perfect shot..."

Shot?

"We heard you boys were drinking," a stern cop voice said. Rafe came back with some calm counter, but Mark could only stare around at the night.

Shot? A bullet could come from anywhere in the woods, or from the other side of the Station, or the little corner grove at the edge of the parking lot. All that vast space might be easy to cross with a magic flying belt, but a bullet would be faster yet.

Then he heard Dennard call out, "So how do you explain this picture, of your boys with these bottles? I wonder who took that," he added, and real satisfaction throbbed in his voice.

Angie. It had to be; of course she'd spot the Blades first and stay hidden, she'd got the picture and sent it to her father's phone, and she was safe, safe, he knew it even as he heard the startled curses below. But the sniper, if there was one, where was he?

"So, are you guys ready to clear out?" the cop said.

"Back your ass off, or—"

But the shouting didn't grow, didn't escalate. Mark didn't need to lean down to know Rafe was reining in his punks. Rafe wouldn't really risk a shooting right in front of the police, even to avenge a gang war, would he?

"What is *this?*" Dennard's roar cut through the conversation, a barely-leashed scream that chilled Mark more than falling out of the sky had.

"What's what?" Rafe answered in perfect, shocking calmness.

"This!" Dennard was shoving through his friends, Mark saw now, not fighting through them but thrusting out his cell toward the Blades. "My Angie, tied to a tree!"

No, there's no way. Angie was safe, she'd just sent the picture of the Blades—or had she? Was this new picture the "shot" the Blades had muttered about? Mark stared down at them as Griggs and the rest held Dennard back. How could they even have caught her, here in *her* park?

"Let me see that," one of the police was saying. "That's all it has of her face? Was it sent from her cell?"

Dennard growled "No, but—"

"Sounds like a fake and a prank, then," Rafe said. "Or a promise, if you've got an enemy somewhere," and his oh-so-reasonable tone made Dennard push harder toward him.

Mark's fingers tightened on the edge of the roof. *Of course that's a threat, why can't they* do *something?*

The officer in front turned back to Rafe. One of the other Blades stepped toward them, and another reached in a pocket.

But the cop stopped and grabbed for his shoulder radio. "What? Repeat?" A moment later he said, "We have a report of a fire in the park."

Mark's head jerked up, and his hand slipped on the roof's edge. He scrabbled a moment, heart racing as he started to slide forward, before he braced himself again. Looking around he saw no glows up ahead of him, but down to his right the walkway had enough trees to block the horizon. Would he even see smoke against the night sky? What had Rafe *done?*

"It's still just starting to spread—come on! All of you!" the cop was saying, with a glare at Joe Dennard, while Griggs stared, frozen, at them. "And you—"

"Hey, we're gone!" Rafe said, and the whole gang bolted for the parking lot.

The cops stared after them a moment, then spun away to their car. One of the park officers—not Griggs—shouted to his team to move, to find the fire. With scattered curses they broke into a ragged dash down the walkway. The police siren howled to life.

Mark clung to the edge of the roof as the siren faded away behind the wind. A fire? Had the Blades really started a fire? And the picture of Angie, that *had* to be fake—what was Rafe up to?

Mark's body against the tiles felt like ice, and the wind was only growing. He heaved himself up on his hands and knees, ready to climb down.

Something moved, off to his side. A handful of Blades ran in from the parking lot... just as he'd pushed himself up into view.

He froze. If they gave one shout, one glance up... but Rafe and the rest didn't look over, they only dashed past and slipped into the shadows of the big patch of woods in the park's center.

Mark let his breath out, slowly. So they were doubling back into the park, despite the cops? Maybe that explained the fire, other Blades could have set it to draw the police off—all to let Rafe stay within striking distance of Dennard? And Angie, somewhere out there.

His hands were moving to yank the belt out of the satchel and buckle it around his waist, almost before he muttered, "I might need this."

Then he had the satchel over his shoulder, and swung his legs over the roof's edge.

And felt himself slipping.

Too much of his weight swung over—he had misjudged, after too long riding the air—and he went tipping, scrabbling for a grip, and swinging down to *bang* off the wall. His fingers pulled free, and he *slammed* down on his back on hard stone.

Lights flashed. Pain burned, warring with shouts and the thought that he should know who was shouting at him—

He stumbled to his feet as the Blades closed in. They spread out as they moved, predators closing in faster as they saw weakened prey.

Mark's hand went to the belt—*no, can't let them see me fly*—

"It's the bike-boy from the docks," the skinny one in front laughed over the wind. A knife moved in his hand.

Then another shouldered past him, and Rafe's low, hard voice said "Mark? What were you doing up there?"

The other Blades were circling, hemming him in. *There's no good answer here.* Then he heard a sharp voice fling back, "One guess," and realized it had been his.

"Spying for Dennard? *Stupid* bitch."

That voice came from the left, just at the corner of his eye, and it was all Mark could do to keep from spinning round to look. Where were the cops, the park guards, anyone? The fire couldn't be pulling them *all* away!

Rafe edged closer; not as tall as Mark, his folded arms gave him extra bulk, and without his do-rag, the part up one side of his black hair gleamed like a scar. "Think, Mark... this can be easy, or hard. Easy means you walk away, and then you bring Joe Dennard to us."

"What?" The word burst out on its own, shock lashing out at the cold faces around him. "You think I'll sell him out?"

Another Blade snapped, *"Bring* him? Fuck! We fake one picture and the old man's ready to come begging to us—"

"The hard way," Rafe went on—he never raised his voice or looked over, but the thug fell silent—"is we keep watching. Everything Dennard cares about, that's another chain we've got to drag him in, and those people go down first. Ten years ago? That's *nothing,* that stunt of his cost us brothers, and blood."

"My brother," hissed one of the Blades at Rafe's side. "I say we carve off a few bits to send the old man."

Rafe half turned toward him. "You call that a plan? No, if he don't want to help, we send his pieces to Dennard's girl, and when she—"

Mark never felt his muscles tense. One instant he was staring at Rafe, the next he was twisting away and racing across the grass, one shoulder slamming a startled Blade out of the way even as he turned.

Two steps away, four—how many seconds did he have? *Can't let them use me! One way out—*

"No guns!" he heard Rafe shout. Six, seven, eight steps.

Mark felt for the phantom pressure in his mind again, whispered "Zha-Daruath," and sprang up.

And he dropped back again, his mind struggling to find the power, only catching one instant that let him float. His feet kicked once in the air before they met grass again and let him dash on.

Trees loomed ahead, shapes of wind-tossed shadow. Not the thick groves he'd floated away from, but the wider wood toward the park's center.

He pushed his heaving breath harder—if he could just *reach* the wood and try to lose the gang—a roll of thunder drowned out the shouts behind him.

Then the thunder faded and the wood swept in, closer, closer. Suddenly the first tree loomed up and he raised his arm to keep from slamming into it. As he slid past it, he risked one glance back.

The Blades were turning away. Mark saw one stepping into the wood, back near its corner, and the others scrambling away around that corner, out of sight.

They gave up? Mark slumped against a tree, gasping for breath and stunned by his luck. *Two* times lucky; if he'd gotten the belt to work where they could see him fly they'd have torn the whole city apart to get it.

His eyes snapped open wide. The gang couldn't be giving up; he must have seen them chasing off after someone they wanted more than him. Angie, or Dennard himself.

"No, no…" He lurched forward in the dimness and his foot caught a branch and sent him staggering. Branches lashed in the wind, crowding what light got through with madly spinning shapes.

It was the Blades' voices ahead that made him slow, as much as his own stumbling. *They can't see in the wood either—and we know the place better than they do, if I stop crashing around.* Mark forced his breath and his steps to slow, and felt his way through the trees.

More voices barked out in the dimness, but he edged to the right, away from them. If Angie or Dennard were here, they'd head for the deeper parts of the wood. When the ground sloped downward, his stride shifted on its own, as he began to match the dim ground to the land he knew.

The wind was so loud Mark missed the footsteps, but he knew the outline, the slim shape of Angie falling into place beside him. She didn't say a word, just led the way, away from the Blades.

You're alright! Do we make a run for it? Mark held in the questions, certain she had a plan. Thunder rolled again. Through the lashing branches, he thought he could see open ground ahead.

Then he heard a muffled shout, back behind them.

Angie glanced back. Then she spun and scrambled after it, and Mark moved after her. How close were the Blades? He stared through the trees, trying to make out what she saw.

Two figures on the ground. The smaller one wore leather, and the hint of a blue uniform made the other one Joe Dennard, and so did his hand clamped over the Blade's mouth, and his other hand jabbing a gun at his prisoner's face.

"—where is she—" The low growl barely reached Mark's ears through the wind.

The thug waved in their direction. Dennard glanced up, and started to rise.

The next moment the prisoner's hand moved. Mark yelled, but the knife was already plunging in. For a moment, the winds were drowned out by the blast of Dennard's gun.

The voices, too many Blades, too close—

The Blade jerked from the impact, but his hand was lashing out again, and Dennard slumped. Mark saw a glint of metal dropping from his hand.

In another moment Angie had reached them. Mark could barely make out what she did, but her move left the Blade toppling over, his feet swept from under him as he was starting to rise. As Mark reached them he saw Angie searching for the dropped weapons.

"You're dead!" A shape stepped through the trees, bringing up a gun.

Angie fired first, and the Blade dove backward out of sight.

"Here! Down here, all of 'em!—" his voice came, and Mark heard the others closing in.

Angie only crouched, weapon ready, like she'd grown up with guns. Not moving an inch.

"No, no, get away..." her father gasped as he stared at her stand, his weakening voice fading in the wind.

Mark crouched to reach under Dennard. In the dark he could see mocking blotches spreading over his side and up his shoulder. Being moved was the last thing he needed.

The last thing, except for the killers reaching them. Mark gasped, "Angie, come on!" and he tried to haul Dennard up. *The belt. If it can make me float, can it make him lighter?* He felt for the power, and heaved upward.

The injured man barely moved, and his weight almost toppled Mark forward. Off to the side came another shout, closer.

"Come *on!*" He heaved again. Somehow Dennard came up, and Mark lurched forward, gasping, "Come on come on—"

He ran, he stumbled, he struggled to keep his balance as Dennard shifted in his arms, or was that their weight changing in mid-step? *Don't lose the power!* He nearly hit one tree, heard a gunshot behind him, another right at his ear—that was Angie running with him, shooting back at the Blades.

Then they broke through into open ground. The wind slammed into him.

Don't look back. He couldn't think about the shots behind them, couldn't notice the metallic smell coming from the burden he carried, he just filled his mind with his steps. One springy too-high leap that threatened to tear Dennard from his grasp, then a twist to put a tree behind them for cover, even as the weight seemed to grow heavier... He struggled to push on and hold the energy and keep balance no matter how the power shifted, until in midstride the last of it drained away and he had to catch himself, stumbling forward, slower and slower, swaying on his feet and starting to tip over, until Angie stepped in front and caught him.

So many people, staring at them. The spread of blackened ground ahead, the people watching. The flash of lightning, the flashing lights, the firefighters coming forward to take the weight from his arms.

CHAPTER THREE

DESCENDANTS

The ride to the hospital was a great winding haze. Mark remembered them loading Dennard into the ambulance, and Angie saying he was "their" father Mark could squeeze into the front seat with her and the driver. Somewhere along the way the rain began, turning the drive into a halting slide through darkness and thunder, windshield wipers beating back glimmering sheets of water that slid aside only for an instant, before pouring back over the glass.

Mark's head kept spinning with how much of the night couldn't be real. Dennard had looked so gray, so wrong, with the great red stains blooming on his shirt and the surreal words of the paramedics around him. And Angie... he'd never seen her sit so still.

Even when the streets stopped blurring past them and the paramedics wheeled their patient into what felt like a single long tunnel, past shouting figures, the shape on the stretcher never stirred.

"...wait here." Suddenly one of the men in green was blocking Mark and Angie's path, then turning away from them, toward the doors that Dennard was already disappearing behind.

"How long?" Angie asked, so faintly. "Can we stay..." But the man was already gone, and the voices were fading, swallowed up by the doors and the echoes spilling through the hospital walls.

They sank down onto a bench; a worn-out old man huddled on its other end. Mark shucked off the satchel and his coat, both of them streaked with Dennard's blood. Then he yanked off the belt to shove it back in the satchel, just useless old leather now. It had made him *fly*, and then made Dennard weightless enough to carry halfway across Rosewood, until its last tingling ebbed away on him in mid-stride. But all of that couldn't be, couldn't *be*... if that had been a dream, came one wild wish, could he take back the stabbing, too?

Angie stared up the corridor, looking away from him, back the way they had come. He could barely make out her words: "Damn, damn them... why would Dad leave the group? He knew he was safe with them... could he really hate the gang that much? He's *not* like that... if I hadn't gone off, or made him look up right when he was fighting—"

"No! It wasn't your fault—"

She rounded on him and snapped *"You* carried him out of there! So if you say that if you'd kept quiet about him and the Blades he'd be okay, I swear I'll..." She shook her head. "Please. Let's just sit here."

Then, despite her own words, she jumped to her feet and settled to pacing up and down the corridor. It was only sparsely lined with late-night visitors, most waiting quietly. Occasionally a doctor or nurse would race by, or shamble past them in exhaustion. As Mark sat, he saw a woman leap up from her seat and rush toward one of those doctors, her movement so sudden that Angie, still pacing, had to spin on her heel to keep from crashing into her. Each time the doors to surgery opened and a patient was wheeled out, worn, worried men and women would stand, tears in their eyes, waiting to hear the prognosis. There would be sobs, or sometimes, shouts of joy.

The longer they sat, the more Mark would have joined Angie in her pacing, except that sheer exhaustion and a tangle of aches and bruises kept him in his seat. *I fell off a roof and I crashed around the forest— after I fell out of the sky. I was flying, I didn't just hit my head and mix up the whole night?* At least none of the passing doctors and nurses seemed to notice his own condition. More important, neither did the restless, reckless woman he was with.

His phone said 11:03 by the time he remembered to look at it, and he returned a call from Lucy. Even speaking in a waiting-room whisper, he hated having to say the words aloud and make them real: "I'm sorry I never made the date. Angie's father's in the hospital."

"Who's Angie?"

He barely knew what he answered, but he could hear the anger in her reply. None of that mattered tonight.

As he put his phone away, he saw a husky man with bushy eyebrows walking toward him. Not one of the uniformed doctors, not someone's relative; when he met the man's gaze he felt the same probing look Dennard might use. A cop? Mark rose to his feet, suddenly thinking he should be feeling taller after making that rescue— *hold on, I can't tell him I think I was flying over the park—*

Footsteps broke into a run. He looked around to see Angie dashing up to a doctor who must have just emerged from behind the O.R. door. Mark rushed to join them.

"—has stabilized." The man looked young, and so exhausted he slumped in place worse than the desperate visitors on the benches. "But..."

"But what? *Tell* me!" and Angie leaned almost right into him, her hiss low and unstoppable.

The doctor edged away. "The procedure went smoothly, and his vitals are certainly strong. It's only... well, does 'can't fly' mean anything to you? He started to come to on the way in, and I'm not sure it was just shock. You might have to prepare yourself for some bad news."

Mark forced his face to stillness. *Fly?*

But Angie said "You mean, his brain might have..." Then he saw her draw herself up, and move back a step to a calmer distance from the doctor. "Or it's just shock. Who can I talk to about staying here tonight?"

"Well, I doubt there'll be any more news that soon. But the nurse at the desk would be the place to start. If you'd like to call your family—"

"Who, my mother? I don't know if she'd gloat or hang up," Angie snarled, but a moment later she softened enough to say an earnest, "I'm sorry, that's not your problem. Thanks. And, thank you *all.*"

She turned away and started toward the blonde aide tucked behind the little window. Angie's stride looked almost steady again, with her eyes locked on the woman.

Then the aide turned away and stepped out of view, answering some call from the room behind her. Angie sagged where she stood, like a scarecrow cut halfway-loose from its frame.

It was too much. Mark took her arm and led her a few steps back to get some privacy, his mind still telling him, *Not here, not so soon, I can't start talking or I won't stop,* as he told her, "I said it's not your fault."

She kept looking back as she followed him, her eyes still on the empty window. "Of course it was. My father admits he had set off a…" She broke off, leaving the bloody, shameful rest hanging unsaid between them. "And I insult him and run off, never mind that the Blades might be closing in. I never think what that could make him do *now,* and—"

"But he *didn't* go off alone. You saw him out there, right? He was safe with the park crew, and then with the cops, until the Blades pushed him into chasing them on his own."

At those words, Angie turned around, her eyes wide with surprise and rage, and he realized he'd barely guessed how tightly coiled she really was.

He added "Um, I overheard some of it, but it doesn't matter now—"

"Doesn't it?" Suddenly it was her hand clutching his arm, hard enough to make his bruises burn. "Tell me!"

"Uh…" He tried not to look away, but if she heard it all now—

Just then her head turned to look past him. He glanced around, following her gaze.

"You were saying?" Up stepped the bushy-browed man who had been approaching before. He pulled back his soaked coat to show his badge.

Mark swallowed. Now? While Angie was poised to go do God-knows-what to the gang?

Worse—*what'll he think if I talk about flying? That I'm out of my mind, or covering something up.* He could barely meet the cop's eyes, and he already saw interest sharpening in them.

"I'm Detective Lee. I know this is a bad time, but I've found the best way to get to the truth is to get people's statements quickly." His face was cold as he said it; not hostile, but without any of the sympathy that could have guided his words. "So you're Joe Dennard's children?"

"His daughter," Angie answered. "And a friend. Please, do you think the Blades will keep coming after my father?"

"'Keep' after? So they've got some kind of grudge against him?"

"Just rumors—about the night the war between the Blades and the 66s started. But all that talk was years ago."

To Mark's ear, her voice barely wavered as she covered up her father's sins. "So why come after him now? *Will* they be back?"

"That's why we're trying to put the picture together," the detective said. "Were you there when your father was attacked?"

"Right there—but, you want the story from the start, don't you? Did you get the word that the Blades threatened him today, through us?" When Lee nodded, she began, "I was talking with Dad about them, and then I went out for one last look at the park where I grew up, because I'm leaving town, and I saw they were there. So I stayed hidden, and once the park team came to chase them off I sent my dad a picture of them, drinking on Rosewood grounds... drinking, like that'll put them away," she added bitterly.

"And what then?" The detective leaned closer.

Then Rafe caught me, Mark thought, but kept silent.

She went on. "That was at the Nature Station. I saw Dad and the park staff and the police run the gang out of the park, but then they all went off to fight a fire. That must have been why they went; we saw the ashes later. And that must have been a distraction, because I saw the gang come skulking right back into the woods and I had to pull back out of sight. And then I ran into Mark."

"You too?" Lee turned and his eyes locked onto Mark. "How'd you get there?"

"Looking for Angie." He'd known it was the simplest, most natural answer he could give, and it bought him a moment to skip past the unbelievable part. "I was still with her father when we heard the gang had shown up. I went to warn her, and I saw them clash at the Nature Center. They were yelling about a picture of Angie, tied to a tree."

He tried to keep his voice natural, to brush past just how close he'd actually gotten to their clash—and how—but he heard a faint hiss of breath from Angie beside him.

"I didn't believe it was her, and I heard one of the other guards say that the picture didn't show a whole face. But I guess just the chance or the threat must have been too much for her father."

"Go on."

"Well, that shows how much the gang wanted to get at him. That and when I blundered into them, and they said they'd make me bring him to them, or they'd use my body as a warning, or..."

Mark tried to rush through that part too, but each word brought back more of the moment when the Blades had been closing in around him. His breath caught.

Then he pushed on: "Anyway, I saw it was Rafe Martinez leading them, and they could have killed me right there. Except when I ran, they must have seen Mr. Dennard and gone after him instead. Then I ran into Angie, and we heard her father and one of the Blades fighting. He was stabbed, he got a shot off, but the shot drew more Blades, so we carried him out."

"You did? Where was this?"

What followed was a hammer of questions, everything from which Blade had threatened Mark with what in the afternoon, to how many shots Angie had fired—all warning shots—before giving the gun to the police at the park. Mercifully, Lee seemed to have missed Mark's vagueness about how he'd gotten near the Nature Station, but he asked again and again just how far they'd had to carry Dennard on their long run to safety. "All that way, and you're still on your feet?" he said.

Finally Lee glared at them both for a long moment, then growled, "So nobody saw who drew a weapon first, Dennard or this boy you can't identify. And Rafe Martinez is the only one of them you know. Well, it's a start."

He muttered something that might have been *be in touch,* and whirled away to march off.

Mark watched him make his way to the far door, feeling wrung out and dazed, and grateful, once he finally stepped from view.

"Okay, that's enough!" Angie stepped in front of Mark, grabbing both his arms. In a low, fierce voice she said, "Lee couldn't have believed you weren't hiding something there, and he doesn't even know you."

"What—"

"*You're* hiding things from the police, with the gang after us? That's almost as wrong as hiding it from me. What did Dad do?"

Mark swallowed and took a breath.

"—Oh God, what did he *do?*" Angie gasped. "Or, what did you—"

"No! Or..." He shook his head weakly. "It doesn't matter right now. And you wouldn't believe me anyway."

And Angie actually smiled, a small, reluctant grin. "You were right about Dad, all these years. After that—me, not believe you? *That* is the craziest thing I've heard all night."

His lips twitched into an answering smile, and he felt some of the tension loosen from his muscles. Keeping her calm had to be easier than keeping secrets from her... if he could just make the belt work again to prove his story's craziness. His eyes went back to the bench, where he'd left it in its satchel.

The satchel was gone.

He blinked, stared at the coat he'd left it next to, and cursed himself for letting it out of his hands. He looked around frantically; could a thief have just walked through, while they'd been busy with Lee?

He dashed down the corridor, slowing for an instant to grab his coat and check that the satchel and belt hadn't fallen behind something, then bolted on down the way. Angie ran at his heels without a word. He burst through the swinging doors, dodging doctors and patients and staring down the corridors, left and right, hoping there would be something to see—

One movement caught his eye, the rushed way that one figure dashed around a corner and out of view. Not a Blade, or any kind of young man, but a woman, a figure in gray with something familiar about her.

Out of nowhere, a sudden idea struck. He shouted, needing to be overheard, "If she makes it to the roof we'll lose her!" then flung himself after her. His legs burned, not with the aches he'd felt a minute ago, but with the strain of not being able to close those six running steps *faster*.

The woman was gone. His eyes swept over the doorways, the scattered staff and the way one startled-looking doctor had turned to look toward… an *Exit* door, stairs? Trying not to think how long he might have before orderlies closed in around them, Mark scrambled for the door.

Nothing. Even as he froze and held his heaving breath silent, he couldn't hear any footsteps going up the stairwell.

"The elevator!" Angie said, at his elbow, pulling him back into the corridor. She waved at a pair of metal doors, as if she'd just seen them closing. "Heading up! Mark, that looked like—"

"Come on!" He pounded up the stairs.

When he passed the next floor Angie slowed behind him, reaching for the door out; of course, what if the woman had slipped out at one of these floors? But instead of opening the door, Angie spun away and rejoined him in the charge upward.

The roof, we have to gamble on that, or else there's too many other choices. If she heard me, if she fell for my trick and went for the roof, she'll be trapped when the belt doesn't work... unless she knows something I don't. Faster, faster, how many more floors are there? Can't think about what Angie must be thinking, she trusts me enough to follow my lead, but we're chasing a woman who pounced on a split-second opportunity and might well pull it off... just like...

Angie had pushed ahead of him by the time they reached the roof. She was the one who wrenched the door open and led them out into the storm.

He stared through the rain and the night, across the pools of water lying over the open space that must be a helicopter landing pad. For a moment he couldn't see, but then, shading his face from the water blowing in his eyes, Mark spotted the figure standing near the edge of the roof. She was reaching into the satchel.

Angie rushed toward her. Behind her, Mark found himself comparing the woman across the roof to Angie's old pictures. The rain-soaked suit that had been gray before was an all-out business suit, not the simpler clothes she'd favored then, and the hair plastered around her face looked shorter now, but if he were closer he knew he'd have seen the resemblance.

Angie shouted, "Mom!"

The woman's head jerked up and she looked toward her daughter. Mark thought he saw her head turn right past him in the rain to lock onto Angie ahead of him. She yanked the belt half out of the satchel.

An instant later her head dropped again to stare at the belt. *Can she feel that it's drained now?*

Then she took a step and stood at the roof's edge.

Angie screamed out, "What are you doing? Dad was almost killed, and you're—why?"

Instead of speaking, the woman—Katherine Fletcher? Kate Fletcher Dennard? Kate Woodward, Angie always called her—drew the satchel back, poised to fling it away somewhere so that it would be lost in the city dark. Then she paused.

Why'd she show up tonight? Mark wondered. *Did she have some kind of watch on her daughter and her ex for signs of trouble, or—*

"Let me guess," Angie hissed. "Are you working with the Blades? Paying them to kill Dad and get you the belt? You've got enough money."

She took another step, but her mother raised the satchel a little higher, and Angie halted at the warning.

—Why is she stopping? It should be just an old belt to Angie, and she never, never *told me one word that it was more…*

"That's a good theory." Her voice was nothing like her daughter's, less fierce, with a kind of solid resonance that pushed right through the wind. "Except that it would mean I'd involve those kids, or bother attacking Joe."

The contempt in her voice sounded real enough. Mark tried to catch any other emotion in her tone, but came up empty. So if she wasn't out to get her ex… then did she want the belt herself, and she was only pretending she'd throw it away?

Her eyes seemed to be solely on her daughter. Mark took a slow step backward. Could he edge around, behind her, hidden in the rain? *Concentrate,* he told himself. *Don't stop to wonder why Angie never said anything about the belt.*

"The orderlies will come up here soon," Angie warned her mother. "We made enough noise. Or, in this weather, the hospital might even need the helicopter space. And they all saw you running from us."

"You'll try to arrest me for purse snatch—" Lightning and thunder cut her off, blasting almost over their heads. When the booming had echoed away, she went on. "How much would that hurt me, when it's only your word against mine that this was ever yours?"

"Whatever keeps you from trying this again." Angie's voice rose a fraction.

"And you think that's worth the attention it'll get you?"

Was that surprise in her voice? Mark couldn't see clearly enough in the darkness, with maybe ten paces of heavy rain between them. He crept toward the roof's edge, wincing when his shoes splashed in the puddles, telling himself the wind must be swallowing any telltale sound.

Angie shouted, "The Blades are after Dad's blood, and I'm not letting that happen! I can live with some 'attention!'"

"But which of us are people going to believe? A resentful, abandoned daughter attacks her mother? All that will start is a circus. It won't stop me."

Circus? Even with the rain tearing at the edges of their voices, Mark thought he'd heard an extra ring of conviction in that one word, one thing that rang truer than the rest to him. Was *that* why she was here, for fear of a whole other kind of exposure? Was she trying to get the belt for herself, or just keep the world from finding out its secret?

And, would any of that be so bad? came the thought, even as he continued edging toward her, praying some flash of lightning wouldn't reveal him in the night. *As long as we survive the Blades, does the belt really matter?*

"Do you think hanging onto this piece of trickery can keep Joe alive?" she said.

He was five steps away from her now, and she was still glaring at her daughter.

"Or that the police can really protect him? They can line up all around him, and there will still be dozens of Blades watching for the moment they look away. That dance has been going on for as long as bitter children stopped caring what it cost them to lash out at someone.

If you want to keep him alive you need to face those facts. Or do you think you're so clever you're going to change it all?"

"If I have to," Angie flung back.

And Mark thought, *'Bitter children'? Is she* trying *to make her daughter hate her?*

"I have to have that belt, *Mom.* Or I'll tear your life apart, I'll use every story I can make up that anyone will listen to."

But she didn't tell me, all our lives. Mark shoved that can of worms back down in his mind. Another step closer.

Her mother shook the belt's slack that dangled from the satchel, out of Angie's reach. "If it's gone, you have no reason to make any trouble for me. And you wouldn't bother me, or drag a child like my James into this—you want protection from your enemies, not revenge on me."

"Are you sure? You think I'll worry about *your son* if they get *my father?*"

The woman smiled. "I'm sure."

Wait, why is she talking at all? Does she really think she can back Angie down, or is she ready to toss away the thing she's afraid of, and just stalling...

Angie snapped "Damn you, Mom, what *happened* to you?"

And as she did, Mark lunged.

His feet splashed and slipped a moment, but he leaped forward as Kate started to pivot, winding up for the throw, her move bringing the prize toward him as his fingertips raked out and struck, caught, closed around canvas and leather and dragged them down.

She staggered a moment as her lesser weight pulled against his, then caught her balance and let the prize go, backing away. Her face might have been a mask for all the emotion it showed.

Angie stepped to his side, glaring at her. "Still think we don't have a chance?"

Her mother returned the glare, then glanced at Mark and back to her. "So that's your decision. You won't give the thing up."

Mark swallowed. *I guess it is—but what's Angie going to* do?

Her mother pressed on. "And if those street punks find out what the belt does? At least tell me they don't already know."

"Know what?" Angie said. "Why *is* an old belt worth stealing?"

Mark's jaw fell open, and he stared at Angie and the small triumph in her eyes. She didn't know what the belt did, she'd never known—and never hidden it from him—but she'd still been ready to face her mother down for it… He felt his knees going weak.

But the older woman's mask didn't crack. She only said, slowly, "You… don't know. But you played along, all through that, only because…"

"Because you showed us it was important." Angie smiled tightly.

Mark looked from mother to daughter, and felt a wild laugh trying to well up: *you thought you could outmaneuver* this *girl? This is how fast she learns.* But still, underneath, in his stomach, lay the fearful memory of the Blades chasing them down the park, bullets flying.

Kate Woodward shook her head, slowly. "Poor, poor girl," she sighed. "What the belt 'is,' is not worth having. You won't listen to me, so ask your father about the Fletcher house—"

"*Hey!* You want to tell me what that chase was?"

A man splashed toward them, a plump figure in blue, shouting like the outraged guard he had to be.

Angie stepped closer to her mother. Mark followed, to hear her hiss, "What? Why isn't it?"

Her mother glanced at the approaching guard, then gave Angie one long, probing look. "Ask your father. Or ask your friend," and she nodded toward Mark, "how he knew I might head for the roof."

And she actually started to turn away. Angie grabbed for her shoulder, calling "Oh no you don't—"

She broke off as her mother looked back at her. If her face had been hard to read before, now it was the picture of stone-hard will, giving back nothing but echoes of its silence.

The guard reached them, and she pulled away from Angie to meet him. "I'd like to apologize for the commotion inside. I wasn't ready to see my daughter here, and… it got out of hand."

"Out of hand? You tore through the ward to get away from family?" The guard folded his arms and tried to block her, but Mark could see him starting to back down from her gaze.

Angie said "We should never have let it happen. We didn't knock over any patients, did we?"

"Her father is in surgery," Kate continued, and she moved past the guard to the door. "We're not at our best right now. But do you really think you can press any charges for this?"

The guard looked from her back to Mark and Angie, and the two followed her lead in moving off the soaked roof. The moment they reached shelter and the guard closed the door behind them, she started down the stairs.

"This can't be the worst disruption this place has seen…"

She kept talking as she went, forcing the guard to stay with her, though he kept trying to look over to Mark and Angie as well. They brought up the rear as the four of them moved down.

She's not just defusing this, she's taking the blame on herself. And Angie had to know that, though it didn't soften all the fierce glares she was shooting at her mother.

When they reached the next floor and another guard caught up to them, Mark and Angie were able to step away with another apology. As they did, Angie caught his arm and half-pulled, half-dragged him down the corridor, until they reached a turn and found themselves alone.

"You!" she snarled. "What happened there? Are you still going to lie to me?"

"Are *you* going to charge off after her, or maybe the Blades?" It was the first thing he could think to say. "The way you've been seething, and after how our talk at your dad's went—"

"You really think I'd run off *again?*" She glanced around, and brushed soaked hair out of her eyes. In a controlled, less carrying hiss she went on "I lost my head once tonight, and Dad got stabbed, and just as I'm trying to face what he confessed to, I find my mother's fighting us over some old satchel. So not another step; talk!"

"Okay…" He swallowed. *God, if she laughs—*

"First," and he met her gaze, "I just found this out tonight, and I wasn't even sure—until your mother made a grab at the belt," and he grinned weakly—"if it was anything more than me hitting my head in the park.

"But, well…" Then he remembered one thing that would support his story, one sign he wasn't talking nonsense. "Well, when they brought your father in, remember the doctor said he was talking about not flying?"

She nodded.

"He wasn't hallucinating. You see, after you left us tonight, I saw him try to go after you."

She nodded; that much she'd clearly figured out already. But then…

"But then, he stopped, and he went back to the house and took out the belt your Fletcher grandparents had. I could see like he desperately wanted to take it with him, but instead he took it out back and shoved it under the grill and lit a fire. It was so strange that after he left I ran to save the thing, before I tried to find you. And I found out…"

He tightened his grip on the belt, clutching for the power it had had. Nothing, of course; he could only look up and face Angie's waiting frown.

"I found that if I said the words on the belt—well, I think it was just for the first time that I needed the words, and that was after they led me to maybe just the right place in the park… I started *floating.* Right over the park. And I drifted over some of the Blades as they were clashing with the park staff, trying to control it… me control the belt, I mean, and they were trying to control the park too, of course. I think it even helped me lift your dad, made him lighter—" *I'm babbling, when I need to make her stop and think.* "It almost got me killed, again and again, and I guess it's all used up because it doesn't even work now, but the belt did let me fly."

The words left him out of breath, and worn out from unloading so many secrets. The sounds of the hospital pressed in around their sudden stillness—muffled voices, the clatter of some cart—all of it still seeming like a world away. But why didn't she move, why couldn't she just…

He must have held the things out to her, because she slowly took them from his hands.

She stared at the belt, felt within the satchel.

"If… the Fletchers had a belt that did that, why are these bits of leather in the bag with it?" She held up one of the finger-sized strips, and passed the satchel back to him.

"Mmm." *Was she really* listening *to him?* Mark pulled out the other scrap. They must have been inside the satchel ever since they'd first seen it, years ago.

It tingled against his hand. Weaker than the belt had, but still—he hadn't thought of it, but the scraps had been in the woods with him too. They even looked like pieces from the belt, or some of the same stuff. And the corridors still looked empty.

He gripped the scrap harder, tightened his will around the tingling.

His body shifted, releasing upward—for one long floating moment before his control slipped away and dropped him sprawling on the floor.

I was right, the words and the place just prepare them, and then I used up all the belt's power…

When he got to his feet, Angie was staring at him, open-mouthed.

"So they really… but the Blades, if Dad had this he could have shot them… but we could fly down to Dad's window if it works—"

Her words stumbled around, and Mark could hear some of the rhythms he used himself when he had too many facts for his thoughts to keep up. He'd *never* heard her struggle like this before.

All at once her voice broke off. She raised the bit of leather up, and clenched her eyes shut to concentrate.

She didn't stir. She waved the leather around as her face twisted with strain, but still nothing. For her, it didn't work.

She broke off and dashed back around the corridor, Mark behind her. But her mother was already gone.

CHAPTER FOUR

RUINS

You just *feel* it?" Angie whispered as they crept through the dim brush.

"It's not a feeling, or a touch either. It's..." He couldn't find the words, even though he heard the need in her voice.

Instead, his sensation of that one place in the woods drew them both over the mud-washed ground, bringing down showers of raindrops from each branch they pushed past. Up the next slope... and then he stopped and drew back a step.

"Here."

Angie took a slow, deliberate look around the dim trees, with the same intensity she'd used watching for Blades all the way into the park. In the still moment, the hollow sounds of the mostly-sleeping city beyond the park pressed in.

Angie gripped a branch with one hand, and slowly raised the belt up. *"Zha-Daruath."*

The still night *lurched* to life, blinding, staggering Mark, like a giant's breath had been drawn in—all through the leather strips in his pocket.

"Wow," Angie whispered. "Like lightning... now the belt's just tingling. So now I can..."

He saw her face clench in the shadows.

"Nothing. Still nothing," she said softly.

"But it worked!" Mark reached out to the invisibly throbbing shape, gripped one end, and felt for the power.

For long seconds his thoughts fumbled for the right pressure...

A surge of force yanked him upward, so suddenly his legs jerked at the same moment he let the pressure drop and sent him sprawling into the mud below. His eyes went to Angie as he scrambled to his feet.

"So it's not that I couldn't use it because you said the words before," she sighed. "It's just me. Even though the belt was my family's."

"If you call what I did using it. And you *did* feel it." He knew it was too little to soothe the ache in her voice, and he wished he could *give* her a sense of what it had been like in the air—and of when each slip had nearly killed him.

"But you made it work. And my dad must have used it before. And this is what it gets him? Stabbed?" She didn't even sound angry, only hurt. "He already gave up being a cop. Instead he worked here, we lived right *here,* all these years beside this place, like he was keeping watch over the secret. He *has* to wake up soon—"

She broke off, and her head turned in the darkness.

"What is it?"

"Was that... a siren?" Her voice was hesitant.

They listened to the wail as it drew closer, somewhere in the night. But then it snarled once and came to rest, and *not* from off across the park, not from down where the Blades' decoy fire was long out. This had come from somewhere up ahead, toward the park's corner. Close.

Angie led the way through the mud, clattering up the chain fence. As they passed the corner parking lot, the flash of lights came into view across the street.

Mark saw two police cars, and a few people out that the police might have been warning back. But where was the Dennards' house? The silhouette was wrong...

Only the frame was left, only the burned bones of the house.

For one mad instant, Mark thought of the fire Dennard had set for the belt. Had there been any embers left burning? No, and they'd never have spread through the rainstorm anyway. This had to be something else.

"We have to get away." Angie's mumble barely reached his ears.

"Sure…" Nobody, nobody, should have to look at the place they grew up in like this.

"The Blades could have stayed, to watch for us, after." Her voice broke on that word. "And we're not ready."

Ready? For what?

The word echoed with him as they gathered their bikes and rode across town. It took all the strength he had to remember he was too worn out to argue, to keep from shouting when his fear grew louder with every block.

*   *   *

He knew the voice. The scratchy voice speaking his name, the broad, bearded face bending over him. He wasn't at his own place, but back at Henry's…

His cousin stepped back, and Mark sat up on the couch, feeling his bruises flare. *The falls, the killers, Dennard stabbed… the flying and all the rest, it's all real.* And they'd dragged themselves to Henry's place to stay hidden from the Blades.

Now full daylight shone in through the window, and he could hear the shifting drone of morning traffic.

Henry leaned against the wall to ease his injured back. "Mark. It's not that I mind your crashing here again. But who is that in the guest room?"

"I… Angie needed help," he began, and he saw Henry's mouth twitch down.

Like I'd never moved out last year. Like we're still the kid and the cousin in his twenties stuck with each other. And every time Mark thought he could show he'd gotten his life together…

He shook his head. If he started fighting with Henry now, he'd never get through to Angie.

"Look, I'll talk to her. I'm sure she has plans for somewhere else to go."

"I'm sure she does." Henry took a slow breath. "Mark, I know you don't want to hear this. But some people just can't stay out of trouble, and the best you can do is not be dragged into it with them. Even if it's your girlfriend."

"She's not a girlfriend, and she's *not* stupid," Mark snapped; how could Henry not know that by now? "She's just… got a lot to deal with, that's all. But none of this is her fault, and she listens to me." No matter what he had to tell her.

A click sounded up the stairs, a door unlatching. They *had* wakened her.

Henry glanced up toward it. "I hope you're right. Anyway, I have to get to work."

He headed for the front door, faster than he usually moved. Was that an act of trust, or just running away from confrontation? Henry paused to pat Terry the terrier once, and then the door thumped closed. The dog padded away, ignoring Mark just as he always had.

Mark got to his feet and stretched his still-aching muscles. The pains helped him think past the mustiness of the clothes he'd slept in, and how much sleep he still needed. He had to picture Angie shooting that gun into the face of a dozen killers, and her father so close to death. She couldn't talk about being *ready* for the Blades.

Angie came downstairs fully dressed, the belt and satchel in her arms. How long had she been awake?

She glanced around at the landscapes on the walls. "Are these paintings your cousin's? You used to draw too."

I'm still trying to. Did I not tell you that? "That's right. Commercial artist, he is."

"I called about my father, and they say he's still out." She paused at the foot of the stairs. "The police have a guard on him. But when you make *that* many enemies…"

She stopped, shaking her head. Mark tried to catch her eye as she turned, but she swept into the kitchen, pulling open cupboards until she had two bowls and some cereal on the table. But instead of eating, they both paused, Mark sitting and Angie standing by the wall with her eyes drifting to the window. Mark swallowed. *Think of those gunshots. Make her listen.*

He glanced at her again, and this time he found her eyes just flicking toward him too.

She cleared her throat. "Funny. We used to wonder where Sha Ta Ruath was, and now it might not be a place at all."

"It's not even the right words. When I said it that way all I got was my… sense… that there was something out there, but that those words weren't quite right." But the belt, all of it, didn't change how many Blades were hunting them.

"So they put the wrong words on the belt, and then they even disguised those as a country of origin label—that's what it's called, I looked it up," she added, with a small smile. "All to keep it hidden. But they still had to record that hint. I think if they didn't, someone could die and they could lose the secret and *never* find the right words again. The magic would just be lost."

"Hide it in plain sight?" Then Mark's eyes went wide. "Wait, what? You know something about 'magic'?"

"I don't mean I remember anything about this—but you see what I mean about losing the secret?" Her smile flickered on again. "Anyway, it's this one belt and some pieces that only power themselves up when we bring them to those particular woods, and say just the right magic words. *Words!* So what else could we call something that works like that?"

Mark could only stare. Was this what Angie had been thinking about, after a night of almost dying?

"My mother said their old house would show us why we shouldn't use it at all, but—"

"Angie—" Mark managed to break in, and he saw her start. "You're talking about all of this like there's nobody trying to *kill* you. Your dad almost died, they burned your house—"

"All of it?" And she took a slow step toward him. "What if they pulled out everything that looked like a family record first, and burned the house to cover that up? What if all of this is the Blades looking for clues about the magic?"

Mark opened his mouth, but no sound came out. If that was true, if the gang had guessed that there was something that could make one of their killers *fly,* they'd terrorize everyone Dennard had ever met to get it, no matter how far away he ran.

She went on, "That's why they still care about this, ten years after what Dad did to them. Some kind of old clue about it got to them. And now that they know, they'll chase us anywhere—"

"Except that's *not* what they're doing. They just stabbed him—" He saw Angie wince, but as his thoughts fell into place he had to push on, "They don't want power, they want blood; I heard some of them talk about relatives they'd lost in the fighting. And something else: I got a birds-eye view of how they kept a lookout for him last night, and they looked in every direction *except* up."

"So they don't know—"

"I, I think they don't know how he made the gangs kill each other. Sure, something set them off again now, but it doesn't have to be that, if they just know he *did* it. This doesn't have to be them chasing some world-changing secret, it's worse than that. It's them wanting you *dead*—your father and anyone who gets in their way…"

He saw her fists clench.

"…Because he got *them* killed. And it's dozens of them saying they'll *never* stop looking for that moment that you let your guard down. Everywhere, every day—don't you know that's what we'd be up against?" He was on his feet now, leaning across the table toward her.

"Of *course* I know that!" Angie's voice was louder than his, but her gaze was focused on the wall past him, not looking at him. "And I know the police won't guard Dad forever. So we have to talk to him. He can tell us if the magic can fight them—"

"He already did." The words were out before he could think.

Her eyes went wide, the sudden hope in them stabbing at him. *"When?* Did he tell you—"

"He didn't say it, he *showed* he'd rather burn the belt than use it against the gang. No, it's that he wouldn't use it on them *again.* He did once, and it only fooled them for so long, because now here they are for their payback. This time, he knows there's no way."

Her eyes clenched shut, but not before he saw the anger in them.

Am I trying *to shock her? But maybe I have to.* More gently, he added, "There's only one good thing here: if they don't know there's magic they could get hold of, they'll still target you forever—but they won't *hunt* you too far, if you and your father disappear. You were going to do it yourself anyway; now you just have to take him with you, somewhere the Blades have never heard of, and don't look back."

"So that's it?" Her eyes flew open. "We let the gang win—"

"You don't let them *kill* you... and," hating himself even more for grinding her spirit down, he finished, "and your father will say the same thing. Are you going to risk yourself for him when all he wants is your safety? And, do you even *think* you could get him to go if you stayed in this town? Leaving is the only thing you can do, and it has to be both of you. And you know it."

She turned away again, looked toward the window.

'Both of you,' he realized he'd said. *I never asked to go with them.*

"So," and her voice was almost normal, "I'll see when he's able to travel."

"Weeks?" *One week, ten weeks, we don't even know enough to guess at this yet!* But he couldn't leave it at that, not after hearing that strange, brittle courage in her voice. "We can… still talk to the police. Maybe they *can* round up the whole gang, somehow. Or they might have ways to get you out faster. And help me keep my own head down."

"If they don't lock Dad up for starting the whole feud," Angie sighed. "But, we can try."

She turned away, walking to the next room. Slowly, stiffly, never looking at him. But alive.

Mark slumped against the table as all the breath sagged out of him.

* * *

"Mr. Winton, this is Mark Petrie. I wanted to thank you for buying a couple of my drawings this year." *Even though I never got any better.* "And, you remember when we met, when a gang smashed up your store, and you were the one who believed I wasn't one of them? You said you trusted me because you supported some of the police anti-gang task forces." Knowing it was reaching, he went on, "I was hoping you could put in a word for me to someone there. A friend of mine's in real trouble."

Not "trouble," they'd almost been *killed.* Mark finished the message with his number and managed to set the phone down gently, despite his fingers wanting to clench on it.

The sky was too bright a blue. Washed clear by the storm, the sun shone through the window like it was mocking him for having taken all morning to get the police gang experts to agree to see them later. Mark could still hear the guarded, weary tone in the officer's voice; he'd sounded like a man with too much work to do to stop and bring strangers up to speed. To explain why the fight was endless.

Staying inside Henry's place might keep them both out of sight, but every minute that passed while they were holed up there only tightened the truth that they might *never* be safe again.

Angie's pacing footsteps on the floor below never stayed at one speed for long. The shifting, frustrated patterns drummed through

Mark's head, but that was still better than going downstairs to see her face or relive how he'd had to force her eyes open to the truth.

"Are you saying he's conscious or not?"

He caught her words, another call to the hospital. At least this wasn't one of her barely-calm conversations with her mother's office about whatever "business trip" she had retreated into.

And, between focusing on one call and the next, he missed the text from Lucy.

It was her first since her call last night, and he'd dated enough girls to know what *"This isn't working out"* meant. Leaving the break-up to a text stung—but, came the tired feeling, the two of them had never had enough of a chance to deserve more.

Better that than anyone else being dragged into this madness. Angie's losing everything and I'm not much better, because of a tangle of one treacherous miracle *and Dennard's abusing it when we were kids, and now she has to leave and I can't even say—*

"What's there to say?" he growled to himself, in the softest voice he had. "I'm sorry I'm making you think of your own life?"

He could only go back to rummaging through his last year of jobs and projects for some glimmer of an idea, a contact, anything that might lead somewhere different. Back to struggling with his memory for details, and not staring too long at the mostly-empty screens of the phone he'd only just got for his courier plans. Even his *notes* were back in the apartment he couldn't go near.

The bike courier job was long gone. His thoughts of joining the police? Just an idea he'd kept putting off; no leverage in that. No use calling Winton again, and struggling with sketches had never done any other good. Waiting tables? No, none of the places he'd worked could help.

* * *

"Still our last chance, isn't it?" Angie said quietly, eyes on the police station ahead. "If they could stay with Dad permanently, or they know some other plan besides disappearing?"

"Right." Mark nodded. When she glanced at her phone, he asked, "Still no visitors allowed?"

"I *know* I set up the HospitAlert app right—what are the doctors doing? Never mind. Ready?"

"One last thing." He grabbed his own cell phone and tried Roger Winton's number one more time. He hung up when it went straight to voice mail. "Okay, we're not getting any special introductions to the police, I guess. You know," he added, "before this, I was thinking of becoming a cop. Just for a chance to, well, do more. Maybe I'll try it soon."

That brought a smile, but just for a moment, before Angie looked away. "I see. Now, we can tell the police whatever we need to that'll help Dad, except admitting what he did back then, okay?"

"Glad there's no pressure," he had to say, and at least that got a wider grin. He added, "You know, if I could float up to their ceiling just once, they'd give us all the protection we'd ever need."

"And lock you up in a lab. Or send Dad to prison, if they reopened the gang shootout case. If the police can't *help,* I'll settle for a clean escape."

"That's what I thought." Mark squared his shoulders, thinking through the pleas he meant to make.

The central Lavine police station stretched higher and wider than he remembered, a broad shape with rounded white edging along the bricks' corners. The inside was the same, though, civilians and uniforms, and all the voices with that same tight, edge-of-shouting tone.

Even without the guidance of the officer who led them there, they could probably have spotted the anti-gang section. The walls were covered with everything from photos of bodies to a poster for GED certification, labelled *"The way out."*

Officer Peters looked older than his voice had sounded on the phone. The weathered cop waved them straight into chairs as soon as they came near his desk. "Let's keep this quick; you said you had something on the Blades?"

Angie took a moment to study the battles plastered over the walls, then said "When they invaded Rosewood Park last night; how much do you know about what they wanted?"

"You tell me. We know the usual." He tapped a set of pamphlets on his desk. "Kids looking for trouble, or the gang's old warhorses making a statement about getting their drugs in anywhere they want."

"That's not it," Mark said. "Last night a man named Joe Dennard was—"

"Dennard?" The cop held up his hand for a pause, and his fingers dove into a stack of papers and pulled out one sheet, then a second, right from the middle of the pile. He glanced through them, then looked up, waiting.

Mark went on "They were looking for him. And they'll try to come after him again."

Peters looked down at the pages. Was he avoiding Mark's eyes? "They might. This says one of them might have been wounded, but… well, we're keeping Mr. Dennard under guard at the hospital."

"But for how long?" Angie asked. "Does that file say how the gang was *hunting* for my dad?"

"And you saw that?" The grim voice came from behind them. They looked back to see Detective Lee, scowling under his thick eyebrows. "You never said how you managed to get such a good view of the gang."

"Lee, are these yours?" Peters asked.

Mark stood to meet the detective, gathering his best smile; if they'd come to the wrong cop he wanted to smooth things over. "Perfect; we were hoping we could talk to you both. Last night we told the detective we'd been watching the Blades when they came in." *Do I offer to be bait for some kind of trap, or just go straight to begging?*

He pulled out his phone as he went on. "We had to pull back when one of them came near—"

"Right, because when they showed up you went out *looking* for them," Lee growled. "And Rafe Martinez? Minutes after he got ordered off the park, your 'ringleader' was seen up at a bar by a dozen people. Nowhere near the real attack."

"What?" Mark tried to think. "They're lying, he *did* come back. Hell, he could have *bought* that alibi."

"Probably, but he sure set it up well. And you're the only one who saw him in the park. Why don't we have a talk without your girl?" And his hand closed on Mark's shoulder.

Mark's first reflex was to shake off the detective's grip, but one glimpse of Angie's startled expression stopped him. And Peters… he was turning his head, and his eyes flicked away from Mark's, as if he were… embarrassed? Or worse? There'd be no help there.

As Mark stood up he set his phone down on Peters' desk, in front of Angie. In case she'd remember what he'd said about Winton's connections and try him again.

Lee didn't drag him. His firm grip guided Mark down the corridor, past desks and windows and on by face after knowing, muttering face that seemed to follow them as Lee *led him along like a criminal—* Mark fought down the fuming in his stomach, telling himself it was worth it if he made Lee listen about Rafe and his threats.

They stopped at a set of small doors, and Lee motioned him to one of them, and into the room behind it. Mark saw four chairs, and not much else. When he turned around, he saw the detective had stopped in the doorway. Not even bothering to follow him in.

Lee folded his arms. "So they attacked Joe Dennard over ten-year-old rumors. You think anyone believes that bullshit?"

Even knowing he needed Lee's help, Mark couldn't keep from snapping, "You're talking about a man lying in the hospital."

"I'm talking about people in the *ground* long before then. The gang took the time to chase *you* yesterday, before they went near Dennard's home. Then you wind up out there in the attack, and yet you 'never got a look' at the punk who stabbed him, only the one with the alibi—what were you out there doing for them, what deal did you make?"

"It wasn't like—" He stopped, caught his breath. "I guess I see how you could think that, but that's not what happened. Like we told you last night, Rafe Martinez brought them around Angie's home, and when he saw me, he knew I knew them both, so I ran. Then in the park he said he'd use me as bait for Dennard—and I broke away, it *wasn't* a 'deal.' Angie and I saved Dennard, so now we have to be on the gang's list too, and if there's any way you can use that to catch—"

"You mean Martinez had you, and you just got away."

"Yes! I told you, I got lucky—"

"And that wasn't a deal? We'll see what your friend has to say."

"She already knows—" But even as he spoke Mark saw Lee's heavy brows rise in disbelief. And then he shut the door on him. The lock clicked.

That was the last sound Mark heard except his own fist on the door, a low thump swallowed up by what had to be soundproofed walls. He was stuck here, and the great detective would be heading back to bully Angie next.

He glared around the tiny gray room and tried to think. Did Lee really think he'd sold out his friends? No, no, it couldn't be more than just one of several guesses Lee had, and this was only the nastiest way he could use to prod Mark about any secrets he was keeping. And an easy theory to check. All he had to do was shove around a longtime thief's son.

And I was thinking of joining *the cops!* Mark kicked the nearest chair away, refusing to sit and wait. He'd told Angie he trusted the police, and yet at the first sign of trouble he'd panicked and slipped his cell to her. Clearly he'd panicked for nothing; with Lee ignoring him now, he could have called Winton himself. Or used the phone for *something,* anything but waiting sealed away in here.

He leaned against the wall, trying not to imagine hopeless scenarios; Lee the vengeful partner of some cop killed in the gang war Dennard had provoked, the Blades murdering Dennard in his hospital bed while Mark could only wait...

He couldn't bear to check the time, but it felt like at least an hour had crawled by when at last the door swung open, letting in a rush of sound and a grim-faced Detective Lee. Behind him, Mark saw Angie, glaring, and Roger Winton, overweight and squeezed into what might have been the same rumpled but expensive suit he'd worn when they first met.

Lee scowled at Mark, but now his tone was firm rather than harsh: "Alright, now let's hear your—"

"Let me save you some time." Mark knew he should be generous, polite, try to get some leverage from Lee's overreaching, but all he felt was anger; he moved to block Lee at the doorway. "Rafe Martinez and his thugs *did* chase me yesterday, and they did hint about some kind of overdue revenge on Joe Dennard—you must know the old rumors better than we do. And *yes,* Angie snuck some pictures of the Blades when they invaded the park, and she ran rings around them. *I* blundered into the gang, and I got out alive because they spotted Dennard instead; I helped pull him out, and I *thought* you might understand that they'll keep coming after all of us, and I get it, you people can't be a lifetime bodyguard service for us, but I thought you might have *something* to keep us alive—are we done?"

Mark was almost shouting by the end, or at least the other voices outside had hushed enough for his words to fill the corridor. He didn't let himself look at the other witnesses to his frustration, only at Lee.

Lee's teeth were clenched and his overgrown eyebrows had burrowed down along his forehead, but he held his anger in; his eyes flicked toward Angie and Winton before he gave a long sigh. "We *are* trying to help, you know. We'll watch Dennard while he's in the hospital, and we might be able to scrape some protection together for you as well if we can confirm you were targets. But everything you say shows that the gang has a long memory, and our budget doesn't run forever. If you want real advice, see how soon Dennard can be ready to travel, and then keep going."

"We'll see," was all Angie said.

Lee stepped out of the way and Mark headed out with a quick stride, keeping his gaze forward, avoiding all the eyes that might have seen his humiliation. Angie and Winton followed behind him.

When Mark was almost at the entrance to the station, he slowed to walk beside Winton. "Thank you, really," he began. "You barely know me, and—"

"You *should* thank me," the businessman glowered, speaking in a low voice that barely carried as they walked. "I was two minutes from a meeting when your friend called." His tone softened. "Still, I've seen enough young people railroaded when the police get sloppy."

Mark turned to Angie. "I don't know if you remember, but Mr. Winton owns that store those Blades hit when we were in high school. All those rumors that I was there almost got me arrested before he stepped in, and he also works to hire people away from the gang life, so I thought he might have some pull here."

"Guess you were right." She turned to Winton. "We're really sorry to—"

"Look," Winton cut in again, eyeing them each in turn, "I'm glad I could help, but I do have a business to run—several, actually. So please, try not to call me again unless you're in real trouble. I almost thought this was about your drawings after all." He gave Angie's hand a quick shake. "A pleasure to meet you, Ms. Dennard."

He pushed forward, closing the last steps to the exit and leaving them behind.

For a moment they walked on silently, Mark wondering what Winton would consider "trouble" enough to be worth his time.

"You never told me you were still drawing," Angie said quietly, as they stepped out into the open air. The afternoon was almost gone.

Mark looked away. "Sometimes. The things never got much better."

"Anything else you haven't been telling me?"

Her tone was light enough, but he found himself taking a moment before he answered, thinking of how few chances he'd have left to see her. "Not really. But thank you for calling him."

"Like I'd let them push you around. But they'd never have tried to hold you. I was raised on police procedure, and that was just a cheap trick."

"Well, thank you anyway. I'm just sick of..." *Of being judged for* my *father, or trying to prove I'm not another petty crook. Even when we're fighting for our lives.*

Angie only nodded; she'd know how it got to him sometimes. Then she sighed, and squared her shoulders. "So, their best advice is what we already knew. Then... we should look at what used to be the Fletcher house."

Mark's stomach fell.

"Hold on, you mean try and find out more about the belt?" He felt his voice rising, fought to keep it calm. "You just agreed, the only thing we have left is getting you out of danger. All of your 'family history' doesn't change the fact that the Blades could come at you anywhere. And you want to spend *more* time on the street?" He motioned around the sidewalk, at the people walking by. None of those faces looked interested enough in them to be gang informants, but how would he know?

And the sun wouldn't be up forever.

Angie took a step toward him, and her voice dropped to a sharp whisper. "I thought you'd *want* me to see my grandparents' place. For one thing, you say the gang only wants revenge for what they know about, so they won't be watching there the way they might be, say, the police station you brought me to.

"Second thing, Kate said it would show me the reason *not* to use... this." She touched her waist, where the belt was hidden under her jean jacket. "I know a little about what happened, but I never really looked at the place before.

"And—" She spun around and kicked at a coffee cup at her feet, but it only sent the Styrofoam hopping into the air to land near where it started. "If I sit in one place for another day I'll be ready to shoot someone myself. I need to *do* something."

* * *

North of downtown the crowds thinned down, as Pollan Street began boasting more upscale shops, then sloped uphill toward the start of one of Lavine's nicer, tree-shaded neighborhoods. The emptier streets and later hour had Mark looking around more nervously, but his main effort went into pumping the pedals to keep his bicycle from dropping too far behind Angie's motorcycle. Then when they neared the shift from commercial to residential, Angie waved Mark to pull over, beside one of the dull chunky buildings on the last block of business-related buildings .

With a small smile, she said, "You're the one with the eye for the street layouts. Did you ever notice this is too industrial to be so close to the houses ahead?" She motioned to the parked truck behind them as it brought a ramp banging down at the front of a shop.

"It can happen—" Mark began, but broke off as she began walking her motorcycle to the building's side. She parked it a good ten feet in from the street, so when he dropped his own kickstand he asked "Why pull over here? The old house is somewhere we have to sneak up to?"

Angie shook her head, a slow, weighted gesture, before she answered "It's not a house. Not anymore," and she nodded to the fenced-off space in front of them.

The screen was all Mark could see. Gray plastic sheets hung on a seven-foot chain fence surrounding an area that might be sixty feet across. He stared harder, but no equipment peeped over it from inside, and no workers orbited the site; it was simply a closed-off gap between the properties around it. Somewhere behind them a truck rolled by with a low, heavy roar.

Angie led him farther off the street, walking along the fence. "This used to be the Fletchers' home," she said softly. "Part of a block of Crescent Hills houses."

As he heard the name, the memory fell into place, a moment of Lavine history that had stuck with him. Something about upscale territory turned industrial, decades back… and something had happened to push that change through? Something was tightening in his throat as he said, "This *all* used to be homes—and they, what, all got abandoned?"

"Bought out, I'm sure. Not that the vultures seem to be doing that well," Angie added, with a certain grim pleasure. "And they still can't find a use for this one site. The Fletcher family crater."

Crater? Mark blinked, staring harder at the fence and the stillness around the lot. Even after using the belt, and seeing how Angie's parents had both fought to keep it secret, the word spilled the mystery out onto a whole new scale. What had *happened* here?

Angie moved to the fence's edge and reached inside her jacket. Mark realized she must be gripping the belt when she said "Can you… feel anything? Feel any magic, or any signs that there might have been some used here to make the house collapse?"

"It… collapsed? And you think that was because of *the belt*?"

"Kate said this would show us something, didn't she?"

Mark felt a shiver rush through him as he looked back to the fence. He drew out the leather strips from his pocket, but instead of some ominous force emanating from beyond the barrier, all he felt was the faint throbbing within the scraps themselves.

They continued walking, circling the rusty fence. Mark studied the gray sheeting, trying to find any cracks that might reveal what was inside, but even the chained-up gate at the front was screened off. He looked at the telltale gaps between this lot and the next, the wide unpaved stretches that lay empty, still muddy after the storm. A whole upscale residential block, abandoned to struggling businesses that couldn't even pave over the ground around it—what did it mean?

"There's nothing," he sighed, not sure if that was good or bad. "In the park I could feel the magic, sort of concentrated. I figured somehow the power was drawn from the location—I mean, that's how I found it in the first place. But there's nothing like that here."

"Or nothing you can sense from out here." Angie strode forward, following the fence away from the street again.

Mark moved after her, wishing he could drag her thoughts back to keeping Dennard alive, to keeping herself alive. Subtly, he kept watching the truck parked at the shop next door, and the few people on the street, each of them knowing this spot belonged to someone besides themselves. If two trespassers came back here, it was all Not Their Problem.

Angie stopped at the back of the fence. "Nobody will notice, if we climb fast. Or, climb with a little…"

She gestured toward the strips in his hand.

Go inside? Mark wanted to draw the line there, but then he remembered that this might be Angie's only chance to learn more, or even to *feel* the power at work, before she had to leave it all behind. He couldn't keep that from her.

Another car rolled by on the street, but still nobody seemed to be looking their way.

He twined the strips between his fingers to secure them, stepped to the fence, and cupped his hands, ready to boost her up, trying to remember how he'd used the belt to lighten Dennard and carry him out of the park. *That must have been the magic, not just adrenaline,* he thought. He could make this work, right?

She smiled and moved in, and he tried to make it all work with one motion: when she stepped on his palms he braced and heaved up and carefully tightened his will, trying to squeeze just enough of the power from the leather strips to fill both of their bodies. He felt tingling seep out from his fingers, but only weakly; he was still supporting most of her weight. With his boost, Angie climbed to the top of the fence.

Then she reached down and took his hand, and he *pushed* the magic as he leaped—and a surge of power swept him up, carrying him and Angie half over the fence before they caught at its top, dangling half-weightless over the other side. He froze for a moment, trying to keep the energy steady in his mind, and then they twisted around to bring their feet down and dropped. Almost gracefully.

He felt his face flushing even before her teasing words came: "So is *that* how it works?"

"Hey, that's the best control I've managed so far. And it's my first time using these little scraps, or almost," he added, before he remembered he was protesting to someone who still hadn't worked the magic at all. Embarrassed, he turned around to face the area the fence had hidden.

What greeted him was a riot of weeds. Rough grass and tangled undergrowth stretched knee-deep and higher, and it all sloped downward, following a broad sinkhole, a green-choked space forty feet across that dipped probably five feet into the earth. All overlaid with shadows from the slope and the fence behind them.

He walked slowly toward the sinkhole through hip-high rustling grass, trying to ignore the grinding sound of a truck passing somewhere beyond the fence, and his feeling that this undergrowth and maybe even this hole could be no more than any patch of rough ground at the city outskirts. Angie moved through to his side.

Coming closer didn't help. Or... what if there was power here like the park, and it needed the actual unlocking words to be felt? He squeezed the scraps tighter and whispered *"Zha-Daruath."* Nothing.

When he opened his eyes, Angie was already marching down the slope. He picked his way after her, sliding a step on the wet grass before he reached her. She was poking through the brush with her shoes as if expecting to find old ruins still buried underneath. When he reached her, she looked up and held out the belt to him.

He closed his fingers only lightly around it—the actual, full-sized belt, at the very center of the hole—and breathed *"Zha-Daruath"* again. Then he let the belt go and shook his head.

"So this site isn't like the source," Angie said. She stopped prodding the growth and motioned with the belt around the sinkhole's rim, and the fence beyond it. "But there was a family's home here, my family's home, and all these years later, after the city cleared it away, they still don't know what brought it down. And they're still spooked by it." She moved a step nearer to him, close enough to whisper. "Kate meant *this* is what the magic can do."

"It could be. If the traces are only from the source, not just some place the power's torn up." Mark shook his head, glancing around the fence. He'd told her and told her, with the gang at their throats it was just too late to care about this mystery.

"Next we go to Kate," Angie said suddenly.

What? Next? *You told me this was one stop!*

She went on "Her whole office says she's on a business trip. The day after we met her! I bet she's hiding out at her home now. So we go there and we tell her we've seen the crater, and it's time she told us the rest."

"The rest? And *then* what? What are you—"

Before he could finish, Angie moved another step closer. Wide blue eyes right on his, she said, *"Please,* Mark. We still don't know what we can do, or what happened to this place, or if we can use any of it... Think of those pictures on the police wall, little kids, everyone those animals go after! I'm not talking about coming up with some reckless plan, and I get that you want me to get out of reach, out of danger, but we haven't even *talked* to Dad yet, or Kate—if either of them said there was a way we—"

"Are you trying *to get killed?"* Mark stumbled back, away from the heat of her words on his face. His fingers itched to grab her and shake the madness out; why couldn't she *listen?* "You just... you think you can... why..."

The words choked each other trying to tumble out. He took another step back and waved at the ruin around them.

"You think this is just a riddle? Something *flattened* this place, and your answer is you want to dig deeper? Why, because a few dozen killers out for your blood aren't enough for you? What your mother said was that it wasn't worth—"

"You want to walk away? I saw you save Dad, you can't just be scared—"

"Don't you—"

Something moved, a pale streak dropping almost straight down between them, making them jerk backward as it *thumped* into the growth. Mark caught his balance and stared at the white shape, half-hidden in the weeds. A tiny bundle, made of what looked like a piece of paper.

From *above?* Mark's eyes darted upward, but he saw nothing but clear evening sky. From their position, down in the sinkhole, even the next roof over was barely high enough to show over the fence. But someone had dropped this down to them.

He reached into the weeds while Angie stared around the fence. The bundle only took a second to unwrap; it was simply a pebble with a half-sheet of paper twisted around it. The paper had three clumsily-scrawled words:

"Don't fly. RUN!"

As he said the words aloud, Angie stabbed her finger outward— just her finger, held close against her body, and only bending her hand at the wrist—in a secretive gesture up toward the fence. Where a head in a black do-rag was showing over the rim.

CHAPTER FIVE

FROM THE EDGE

"Go, go!"

An instant after she said it, Angie was racing up the sinkhole slope and the far side of the fence. The Blade dropped back beyond his end, yelling, "They're here!"

Mark dashed up after Angie. As he reached level ground he saw her fling herself into a beautiful runner's leap to grab the top of the fence, a move that flowed perfectly into hauling herself up and dropping beyond it.

Then he was leaping and clattering up it himself, up and over and scrambling down to bolt toward the street.

He'd picked that direction by instinct, but now he couldn't catch sight of Angie up ahead. Instead he ran, staring past the wall of tarps and the brown warehouse at his other side, searching for a glimpse of anyone in view that might make the Blades hesitate. One man stood on a ladder against the chunky building across the street, his back turned, but the sidewalk lay just ahead.

He spun around the corner toward their bikes and froze as Rafe and a grungy hulk of a thug advanced on him. For an instant Rafe seemed to be catching at his enforcer's arm, but then he let go and the big man charged.

Mark whirled and scrambled up the street. He heard a harsh, "This is for my brother," behind him and then his eyes registered the young couple ahead, a whole forty feet away, but close enough for the man to call out a warning shout.

Witnesses. Mark turned and glared at the Blades. The brute was just pulling himself to a stop barely ten feet away, with Rafe catching up behind him. Another shout came somewhere near the ladder across the street, and out of the corner of his eye, Mark caught a glimpse of another punk in leather closing in along the fence.

A motorcycle roared. The two Blades on the sidewalk spun around as Angie sped out onto the street and rode past them, veering just close enough to rev her engine at them in one taunting howl as she rushed by. The big thug stepped into the street after her, and as he did Mark slipped away, behind him and Rafe. As he did, he thought he heard Rafe mutter something, but he didn't slow, just rushed on to the wall where he'd left his Raleigh.

They hadn't left a guard on it or smashed it, but two motorcycles stood right next to it, almost pinning it to the wall. As he stopped he turned and saw Rafe and his man arguing, the couple and another woman advancing, and other Blades closing in while Angie's echoes faded up the street. A moment later he wrenched his bike up to lift it over the others and took off down the street.

She's leading them away, he realized, as he found himself steering the bike in the opposite direction, dodging obstacles and listening for the roar of engines behind him. It never came.

As the sun dipped lower, Mark twisted his way through the streets, trying to choose routes that would be open enough for him to move down fast, without being so obvious that the bikers would think to glance down them. And as he pedalled frantically, he had to beat down his fear that Angie might not keep ahead of her own pursuers.

How did we let this happen? He should have *made* Angie go straight into hiding, or begged the police to take them in, not wasted time and exposed themselves poking into the history of her family magic. *How'd the Blades even find us?* Angie had said the old site was one place the gang wouldn't think to look—did they really have eyes everywhere, or had they guessed something, somehow?

And someone else knew, someone had dropped that warning note right out of an empty sky, maybe someone like Angie's mother, who'd sent them there in the first place—but would she really be looking out for them after their clash? Trying to guess made his head hurt. And now the belt was off with Angie somewhere, and she couldn't use it, and he'd barely tested the scraps of power he did have, had no idea what they were really good for. Not much, if Rafe found him once—

His phone started ringing.

Angie! He took a quick look around the street and braked, realizing as he came to a stop that it wasn't playing Angie's tone. The name on the screen was *Henry Maes.*

Still, that icon in the corner—he flicked the screen over and found a text from Angie: *i ok. keep running*

Mark frowned at the words. How safe could she really be, if she didn't have time to tell him where to meet her? Or she didn't want to, because she was chasing her own schemes of stopping the Blades herself? No, *no!*

The phone tune was still sounding. He dragged his thoughts back to his cousin's call. "Hello?"

"It's Henry. Mark, I saw you and your friend didn't come back to my place. So I thought we could talk at yours. If we can."

Mark felt his head spinning as he tried to focus. He knew that worried tone of Henry's, the sound of him afraid of what Mark might have done now—and he used it about Mark's apartment? *No, we* weren't *crashing with you because I destroyed my place!*

But the Blades could be watching for him there, right now. "No, don't go there!" he gasped, then pulled in a breath and struggled for less suspicious words.

A young man in leather stepped around the corner and turned straight toward Mark.

"—need to tell me—" Henry was saying before Mark hung up and cycled away.

The Blade didn't follow him, but Mark still threw his bike up a side street, dodging out of sight, then across another street to get clear of the area where he'd been seen. Every push on the pedals only hammered home the sick feeling: the faster he shook them off, the sooner they might move on to check his home.

After one more turn, he grabbed the phone and called Henry back… and got no answer, while it rang and rang… *He thinks I'm hiding something over there, and I deny it and then hang up?* The voice message came up, and Mark could only say "Henry! We were cut off, I'm sorry, so sorry. I'll tell you everything, but I'll be at the burger place we ate at on the next block up, just please *please* don't go near the apartment. It's not safe, nothing's safe."

That had to be enough to stop Henry walking into a trap—wasn't it?

He tried a call to Angie and got no answer from her either, so he had to settle for a simple text of *ok too, be safe,* hoping she'd be able to read that much. Her GPS app was off again; what was she doing now?

He headed home, watching the street corners he passed and finding a side street that gave him almost a beeline back. Maybe, maybe he *could* have memorized Lavine's twists and turns well enough to have been a top bike messenger… or fugitive…

Knowing his cousin, Henry would have gone straight to his apartment in spite of his message. And he had his own key, he could let himself in, be there right when the Blades came.

If they came. "Maybe not, maybe not," he gasped, but he kept pedaling, as the sun sank lower.

Block by block, the shops grew fewer and then gave way to apartment buildings as he drew nearer to Beekly Street, and the scattered crowds grew thinner and the streets dirtier. He paused at the Burger Box and ducked into the alley next to the diner, feeling a rush of worry that someone would lunge out of the shadows at him—but there was nobody there. He chained his bike to a railing and dashed into the Burger Box, staring around at the early evening crowd. No Henry, and still no messages on his phone.

Mark could only move back into the street, his tired legs all too eager to slow to a walk. If he could just spot the Blades and draw them away, or be sure Henry hadn't gone to the one place they'd be sure to look… but, when he passed the last dirty brick building before his and looked up at his own window, he saw a light on. "Maybe it's Angie," he sighed, but he knew better.

Tired though he was, he pounded up the cramped metal stairs hard enough to make them ring; he found himself wondering if a touch of the magic might quiet his step on them. At least nobody jumped him when he passed the second floor. A block away, a train screamed by uptown.

When he opened his door, Henry was waiting. His cousin sat stiffly in the chair, supporting his bad back. He was still wearing his suit—he must have come straight from work—and the tired look on his face wiped away all Mark's scattered ideas for how to begin.

"You hung up on me." Henry frowned as he set down the book he'd been reading. "But, I owe you an apology. I was starting to think you were hiding, oh, something awful here."

"It's… fine…" Mark panted.

Henry's eyes flicked over him, taking in the dripping sweat. "Please tell me I only got you in the middle of deliveries."

Right, I was a bike messenger… just yesterday… Stalling, Mark moved around toward his one other chair, but he stayed on his feet, so he could watch Henry while keeping an eye on the blinds and an angle on the street out beyond the side alley. What were the right words, how could he ease Henry into leaving?

"And I didn't mean to intrude—"

Screw it. "Look," Mark said. His cousin's eyes widened at the interruption, but he pushed on. "I want to tell you the whole story, really, but right now we don't have *time.*"

"What has that girl done?" Henry's voice rose.

"She didn't *do* anything!" It was her father and the magic, not her, and now she was out there alone... He struggled to keep his voice calm, to hold on better than he had with Angie or Detective Lee. "Please, *please.* We're trying to keep her father alive, and that's made us targets, but I wanted to keep *you* out of danger. Please can we go somewhere else to work through this—"

"Are you out of your *mind?* If he's still in danger why haven't you called the police? And don't try to avoid talking to me, I won't let you shut me out! I told you the Dennards are trouble!"

I beg him to save his questions for one minute, and he spits out more! Mark took a slow step forward, raising his hands as if he could just drag Henry away. "Please, can we just move this—"

Out the window, he saw motorcycles glide up the street.

Not now, not now, not fair... he wrenched his thoughts out of that futile loop to focus on the one thing that mattered: how Henry would never be safe once the Blades became aware of him, and how the distance that hid him from the gang was shrinking by the second.

And once they start up the stairs, they'll have us trapped. Please, let this work.

As the bikes rolled out of view toward the front of the building, Mark grabbed the window and *click-wrench*ed it open. Electronic dance music flooded in, and he stared down two stories at the shadowy gap between his building and the next. Nobody seemed to be in view.

Henry was just lurching to his feet with a *"What—"* when Mark swung a leg outside. He yanked the leather strips from his pocket, hissed out "Don't let them see you!" and then he dropped into space.

The moment he felt the air sweep by him he remembered he had no idea how much magic the little scraps had left. Fingers and his control squeezed tight, *tighter, falling faster, too close—*

He slapped down on hands and knees on the rough concrete, but he jumped right up with only a small stumble. A middle-aged woman passed by out front and looked at him, and he tried to draw himself up to walk with the tight dignity of someone who'd been caught stumbling, nothing more. She hurried on, and he didn't hear any shouts from Henry above; he'd find some explanation for his cousin later. Now, he needed to draw the gang away.

With that thought he rounded the corner onto the street, just twenty feet from where five Blades were climbing off their bikes.

He froze. They hadn't seem him, they went on setting down kickstands and removing helmets, two of them joking together and the others ominously silent. They weren't looking in his direction, they'd just go on inside anyway and… then one of them looked up. Rafe.

Mark bolted back up the alley. Shouts erupted behind him and he strained to wring more speed from his tired muscles, a part of him wondering why he'd run *away* from the street and whatever witnesses it had. He dashed around the back of his building, his steps echoing as he swerved around a dumpster and glimpsed the leather-clad horde at his heels, led by the big thug Rafe had barely held back before. Too close for them to miss if he leaped for the sky, but if they were really out for blood now—

And I am so sick *of running away.*

He broke through onto the back street, and spun left. Only one man was in sight at the corner, plus a family across the street; as he glanced back at the gang he saw the Blades notice the onlookers and slow to a quick trot.

But Mark's lungs ached, his feet thudded awkwardly on the pavement, his legs were barely able to hold the pace to stay ahead. Witnesses or not, Rafe knew how much the gang could get away with here, and they were all too close to getting a chance to test that.

Then he saw the overpass, the narrow footbridge over the broad road below. *Of course, that's why I ducked back here.* He scrambled forward, squeezing what felt like the last measure of strength from his legs and then sagging over just at the start of the bridge. The magic, was that a tingle left in the leathers? So hard to focus…

"You're coming with me." Rafe's voice was calm, certain. Glancing at his men, he said, "All of you keep watch. No interruptions."

Mark straightened up as two other Blades, stocky boys who might have been brothers, moved past him to block any more running.

"You want to drag me away?" Mark fought the urge to edge backward from them all, and kept the hand that held the leather scraps motionless at his side. With his other hand he made a warning gesture at their surroundings—but he could only spot one distant man turning toward them, and his gait held none of the urgency that might hint he'd call the police. Still, Mark challenged the gang, "The cops already know some of you put Dennard in the hospital. You sure you want to do this out here?"

The biggest Blade moved up beside Rafe, a sneer forming against the tangled tattoo on his cheek. "You keep saying that. I'm gonna make you scream—"

Rafe was stepped in front of him. "I said I've got him, Monster."

Of course his name would be Monster. But it was the still look on Rafe's face that made Mark clench his fist tighter around the bits of leather, too tight. How could Rafe's eyes always look so normal when they should have been dead as a shark's?

Rafe leaned in, inches away, to whisper:

"You'll tell me. Why the Eel thinks chasing you is worth screwing us all."

"What?" *It couldn't be, what did Rafe guess about what they could do?* Mark managed to spit back a low, "Who? You're the one who's chasing us."

But Rafe just smiled faintly and drew back, as if his point was made. He folded his arms and pitched his voice for the whole pack to hear again. "Time to choose, Mark. You still want to die for them?"

Then Monster rumbled "Shut up! He's mine!"

He shoved past Rafe, and his arm stretched out, about to draw Mark's shoulder into what would look from a distance like some "friendly" grip. The huge body moved with practiced smoothness, already angling to conceal how his other hand was slipping into an inside coat pocket.

Now! Mark twisted backward, his palm slapping down to vault him out beyond the bridge's handrail as though it were a simple turnstile… and in the instant that the Blades froze, his right hand caught the big thug's outstretched arm. For one more instant he fell through space, and then his weight slammed the thug down against the rail with a delicious crash.

The lurch jarred Mark's fingers from the thug's leather-coated wrist, and he dropped away, triggering the magic just before his feet hit the concrete at the edge of the road, the safe spot just below where he'd stopped on the bridge. He sprawled there for a second, shocked that the magic had *worked,* again, then stumbled to his feet.

"Shit!"

"Howdidhe—"

"C'mon!"

Mark ducked under the bridge, out of view, and glanced around. One car and then another sped past the shoulder where he'd landed, but nobody seemed to have noticed him so far—and the enraged gang would already be scrambling for the steps down.

He leaped upward. The bridge's underside was almost lost in shadow, but he squeezed at the magic and floated up and in among the dim gray beams, bumping his head before his arms caught at the metal and he steadied himself.

Birds blasted out of crevices, what seemed like an explosion of pigeons, before he realized there were only a handful. As he tried to brace his hands and feet in place, the gang reached the spot where he'd landed.

"Dead, dead, he's so dead—"

"Which way?"

Rafe's voice cut through the rest, speaking as fast as any of them, but steadier: "You head up there, but if you don't see—"

"Fuck that, he's gone! And *you* went soft on him, again!" The giant thug nursed his injured arm.

Rafe rounded on him. "Soft? What do you care? And as long as we get the old man—"

The roar of a truck drowned out the rest. Its echoes resonated in the beams Mark clung to… was his body getting heavier?

The big man rumbled, "Did you even meet my brother, the one that got his head blown off? The Eel said they pay, big, and when he hears how you—"

"I heard him." Rafe motioned to his gang to follow him, and started walking away. "But if jumper-boy had wanted to live, we'd have got right to Dennard without losing one…"

His voice grew fainter as they moved on. Mark held his breath, straining to hear more, even as his arms and legs scrabbled for purchase, trying to brace his increasing weight between the beams.

As the gang turned up the steps, he did hear one of them say "…bet they finish it all tonight."

'It'? Tonight? Mark clung to the bridge, muscles trembling, as panicked thoughts raced through his mind, alongside the fear that the Blades could still look back and see him. *Tonight?*

With a gasp he let his legs swing down and released his hands. The magic almost didn't answer this time, but the last tingling he'd hoarded did let him come down softly enough to stand and trot down the hard shoulder of the road.

The hospital. He had to get back there! He pulled out his phone and tapped 911 while his eyes swept the half-empty street for a cab or police car. With his free arm he waved wildly at the next car coming down the road toward him, but it drove straight past.

"—what is your emergency?" came a woman's voice in his ear.

"Gangs... about to kill... at Watkins General Hospital, kill Joseph Dennard, I *heard* them!"

The phone went silent for a long moment. Mark saw a cross-street ahead and rushed toward it—was that Green Ave, or Gold Ave? Anywhere up there had to be better for catching rides than this.

"This is the police," came a new voice. "Sir, what's the threat against... Dennard? Joe Dennard? His file says he's already under protection."

A battered old Chevy slowed and began to pull up beside Mark.

"Tell them it's happening *now!*" he snapped, and then lowered the phone to run the last steps to where the car came to a stop.

The window slid down just a crack.

"*Please,* can you get me to Watkins General Hospital? Fast?"

The middle-aged black man at the wheel frowned. "Hospital? Accident or baby?"

Murder. Mark bit back the word and said only, "Please!"

"Okay, okay." The driver reached for the door switch.

Mark tumbled inside and slammed the door shut. As the car started up he heard himself gasping an automatic, "Up to Garcetti would be—
"

"Hey, I know where Watkins is, alright?"

"Sorry. And thanks, seriously, thank you."

Once Mark settled in his seat, he looked at the phone again. His call had been cut off.

He stared at the phone a moment, trying to remember if he'd hung up by accident as he'd run to the car. Shouldn't they be calling back?

First he dialed Angie.

Still only the voice mail! He told it: "It's about your father, it's... happening tonight." He glanced at the driver, and bit back the sinister details that might have gotten him thrown out of the car. Instead he gasped "Was that note—can you at least *talk* to me? Anyway, sorry."

He shook his head as he hung up; he had to hang on, keep his cool. One mistake could finish them all. The Blades were on the warpath—what had Rafe guessed, what would he have said if his men hadn't been there? And Angie could be anywhere in all this.

If she wouldn't listen to his voice, maybe she'd at least read a text. He tapped out: *sorry sorry sorry they hitting your dad tonite*

The phone rang in his hands. With her song.

Mark slapped the phone to his ear, thoughts spinning—and a hideous *crash* blasted from it.

No! His stomach dropped in his gut as he clutched at the plastic. Then his ears stopped ringing, and he heard a voice. A male voice, young, tight and hoarse and barely coherent. "What the fuck did—akk!" The voice paused, then came louder and clearer: "Everything's alright, don't need any *HELLLLP* —oh-shit-oh-shit..." and the voice dissolved in terror.

Then a gunshot.

The blast in his ear almost made Mark drop the phone even before the car swerved and the driver yelled "What was that? Was that a gun?"

"Please, I'm trying to hear..." Mark begged, trying not to flinch as he brought the phone back to his aching ear. But no more explosions smashed at him, there were no clear voices at all... except that the babble sounded like people, shouts blending together; how many people were there?

The hospital. The Blades were already at the hospital, that had to be it, and Angie's call meant *she* was there too—

The line went dead.

Mark shook the phone, stabbed Callback once, twice, hearing two rounds of the familiar *"Angie Dennard is right in the middle of something, but..."* He saw the shaken driver look at him and open his mouth, then close it and lock his gaze on the darkening road ahead. The engine's roar swelled.

What was going on? Gunshots and crashing, and that man on the phone—a man's voice, for all that it kept breaking like a little girl's. Not Angie. But it was Angie's cell, she'd called him to let him hear she was in trouble. Or else the Blades had her phone, and wanted him to know what they'd done. But who was shooting, and who was hit? Who?

When they pulled up at Watkins, he gasped out a thanks and flung himself onto the pavement. The driver sped away in a squeal of rubber, no doubt all too glad to get clear of Mark's troubles.

At the entrance he stumbled into an exiting family, but he ignored their protests and rushed on to the wide door. Inside, the place was already buzzing, three uniformed police and twice that number of hospital staff gathered in a knot.

"—can we send more—"

"—not terrorists, just the—"

"—I need to hear—"

"—how soon before—"

Mark grabbed a doctor at the edge of the group. "Please, is anyone hurt?"

The doctor ignored him and kept arguing with the others; a tangle of voices talking about rooms and floors, searching.

He tried again. "Was someone shot?"

That made the doctor look at him. "Please, let us handle this!"

He didn't say no... Mark fought down a roar of frustration and tried to think, to listen.

"—think the fourth floor's clear—"

Fourth floor? Hadn't Angie mentioned her father's room was four-something? Mark went for the elevator, remembering not to run this time. More than a dozen people were circulating between the entrance and the first corridors leading inward, and to his glance they didn't look panicked; they might not even realize what had happened.

The elevator opened smoothly, and he punched *4,* surprised that the way didn't seem guarded. Were they stretched thin, or just afraid of trapping killers in with their patients?

When the doors opened on the fourth floor, he saw more of the kind of confusion he'd expected. A group of visitors was pressed around an orderly, repeating *what happened*s with raised, half-controlled voices. As Mark strode past he saw that other staff were moving around slowly, looking uneasily at the corridors around them.

One doorway, then another... he glanced into each room he passed, wishing he'd taken down Dennard's room number, and thinking, again, *where is Angie?* He saw an old man, a couple, a nurses' station—shouldn't he be seeing more people gathered where the shots had been, or seeing damage from whatever that crash was?

Then as he moved past one room and its blaring TV, he heard voices echoing up the hall that sounded sharper, more urgent. He turned up that way just in time to see four men in staff blue rush by at a trot.

Mark fell into step behind them, wondering how long it would be before they noticed him. But they were busy searching ahead, and he heard one man say "—somebody in green scrubs, trying to hide a gun."

Gun? And, scrubs? Mark glanced around at the people they passed and tried to remember: how many people had he already seen wearing scrubs? Not that many, but a killer in that uniform could blend in, even use a surgical mask to hide his face. The men barely glanced into the rooms they passed, but when they passed one little man in scrubs they paused a moment to take in his face and check his ID badge.

"There!" one of the men shouted, and Mark looked up a side corridor just in time to see a shape in pale green dart across to another corridor and out of view.

The group charged after him, Mark at their heels, even as one of them waved for him to stay back. Dodging around a nurse and a rolling table of supplies, they reached the corner and headed after the likely Blade in the scrubs—but that runner was already far ahead, leaving a corridor of startled people in his wake.

"Attention hospital staff, patients, and visitors," the announcement came over the tinny sound of the PA system. *"There's a disturbance on this floor, and we ask that you all stay in your rooms until it's been resolved."*

Mark halted. The way that Blade had left his pursuers behind, he must be the fastest runner they had. But even if they couldn't catch him, he'd still be focused on getting to Dennard.

Or drawing everyone else away from the target.

Mark turned back to his own search, walking faster now and barely glancing into the rooms. They'd put protection on Dennard, so shouldn't there be a guard he could look for? And Angie, maybe she was with her father? It was all he could think of to find her. He had a sudden image of a gang so vindictive they'd crowd the whole floor with camouflaged killers.

Was that… blood?

Ahead of him he saw a room, door open, with a ruddy stain on the white floor. He rushed toward it, hearing the TV within just as he entered.

"Hold it!"

Mark froze, eyes on the shaking gun the cop had leveled at him. *Careful, careful.* He slowly spread out his empty hands, looking past the pistol to the face of the man holding it. Young, blond as old paper and with a face that was tight with tension, but not panicked yet. Mark felt cold air hit him and realized the TV wasn't on here; the sounds he'd heard were the city outside, wafting in with the night air through a shattered window. He shifted his foot and something clattered, and he glanced down to see medical tools and bottles scattered around the floor.

But what mattered most lay behind the cop—Dennard, in his bed. He was unmoving and stuck with wires and IVs, but the machines still beeped out proof of his stubborn survival. There was no sign of Angie.

"Stay where you are!" The officer raised the gun a little higher, knuckles whitening.

What happened *in this room?* Mark took a slow step back, into the doorway. "Easy; I'm a friend of his."

"*You* say. A cop was shot here!"

"I'm a friend of Joe Dennard's, I've known him all my life! Listen, you got a 911 call, before the shooting happened, right? That was me." The words gathered speed as they came out, but Mark managed to keep his tone level.

Something in that seemed to reach the young cop, and his fingers eased their death-grip on the pistol. "Maybe. We stay here until they sort this out."

"Fine with me." Mark took another look at Dennard, still but alive, and then he had to ask. "Is Dennard's daughter Angie here? Has anyone seen her?"

"Just wait."

"But her phone was—"

Something stirred at the corner of his eye. Out in the corridor, a shape in green moved at a full run straight toward them.

"The killer!" Mark jerked his head toward the corridor and took a step in.

"Don't move!"

Mark froze again, stuck right in the doorway. *Now I can get shot from either side!* The cop kept his gun up, while from the other side Mark saw the suspect in the scrubs—surgical mask and all—barreling right at the room. *If he doesn't see the cop behind me, maybe at the last moment I can step aside...*

But the Blade didn't turn toward the doorway, he swept right past. Mark took a step after him, but the cop's "Hold it!" froze him again. The thug was already gone.

Mark sagged in place, hands trembling in the air. Maybe the sight of him there with his hands up had been warning enough to send the assassin running, or… did it matter that the thug hadn't had a gun in his hand? Maybe he *had* been a distraction.

"Okay, you were right," the cop said, and he lowered his gun.

Mark let his hands drop, but then he looked at the cop again, having a sudden suspicion that the earnest young cop could still be a Blade in a stolen uniform… *no, this must be getting to me, suspicious of everyone and everything.* Still, his voice quavered as he said, "I got a strange call from the hospital. What happened here?"

"Wish I knew. We don't even know how many punks are here, but we got the first one. The officer here was shot just outside the room, and his gun's missing. It was the shooter's own gun we found Mr. Dennard holding him under—with the old man staying conscious just until the cavalry came." He gave a respectful glance to the *old man* in the bed. "Don't know how that happened, and Lord knows how the kid got pinned under…." He stopped there. "The sergeant says I talk too much. He'll figure it out when he gets back."

But Mark's mind raced. That could have been what he had heard coming over Angie's call: the voice of the Blade getting caught. Except, *"pinned"*? What did that mean? He looked around the room again, but saw nothing large enough to pin anyone down except Dennard's bed and the undisturbed banks of sensors, and a sizable metal desk along one wall. The desk was too huge for someone to have heaved it on top of anyone, but… its top *was* bare, and supplies *were* strewn across the floor, and it *could* have made a crash just like the one he'd heard, if it had been… been *what?* He put his head through the doorway again, peered around outside. "Are you sure you didn't see—"

The words died in Mark's throat. Two young men had stepped into view further up the corridor, not in leather or do-rags, but the anxious looks they shot around them had Mark reflexively ducking back inside the room. But he knew they must have already seen him.

He hissed to the cop, "Two of them, sneaking—"

"Shh!" The cop had his gun up again, covering the doorway. Mark tried to step farther away from it, but the cop motioned him to stay, keeping the gun on him and the entrance together. *He still can't trust me, but there are Blades coming right toward us!*

This had to be the quietest back corridor in the hospital: over the murmuring voices from other rooms and the street sounds from the open window, Mark thought he could hear footsteps coming slowly closer, maybe a low mumble. The cop raised his weapon higher, held almost straight out.

Then other footsteps pounded up the corridor, several together, with shouts of "You there!" Mark caught one "Shit!" before he heard the Blades dash forward, a headlong run right by the doorway.

Mark slammed into the kid's side before he even realized he'd lunged. The punks' footsteps had been so clear they'd made an easy target for his own coiled frustration to track, and so Mark crashed into a tackle that swept one Blade down and carried through to drag the other down as well. They slammed across the floor together, a tangle of limbs and curses.

One long, bruised moment later, the police pulled them all up. The one from Dennard's room waved the others back from Mark as he heard the Blades yelp, "We didn't do it!" and one uniform snarl back, "You shot a cop!"

His head ringing, Mark looked at the two prisoners. No wonder they had gone down so easily, they were *kids*, barely fourteen but swearing like demons as the police pulled guns from their pockets. *Baby-faced killers.* He remembered reading how sometimes gangs raised the youngest and most vicious boys to take risks no adult would ever get out of prison for. He shook his head weakly.

"Where's your pal in the scrubs, kid?" one cop asked.

Another added, "It could have been one of these—"

Mark glanced back at Dennard's room. The first cop wasn't even near the door now, he was busy with the others. Mark stepped back toward the room again, looking back at the boys and wondering if he was still paranoid; maybe the runner in scrubs *had* been thin enough to be one of the ones they'd already caught.

Except the runner hadn't tried to get at Dennard, he'd only run on past, toward where the other Blades had come sneaking from… in fact, he might as well have *led* the cops onto their trail… and thinking back, why had his scrambling feet made so little sound… no punk could run like that…

Outside the shattered window of Dennard's hospital room, something moved. A blurry shape he almost missed as it ducked down into the darkness—but then, a moment later, a surgical cap and mask peeped up again to let the familiar eyes between them meet his gaze.

—How far away, the cops and everyone in the world outside sounded far too close, surely they'd notice if—

But still she moved, she *floated* gracefully into the room and into his reach, where he could catch her and help her settle to the floor. Where his body could hide her as she yanked off the mask and cap, the last of the disguise she had used as she'd run down the hidden Blades and led the police to them.

"You crazy—" The words hissed out of him, none of the things he'd wanted to say, but all he could do was grab Angie's shoulders ready to shake her for what she'd put him through.

Except, he couldn't let go. Not when he touched her, not when she stared back at him, not when they caught at each other in a ragged embrace where their lips almost missed each other, then met, bruising and burning and blazing up in the kiss as they clung tight.

A TEXT

—No word from our other two soldiers either. You think we can keep throwing Blades away? I can still shut this all down if you don't convince me it's worth the cost.

No more games. We need to meet.

CHAPTER SIX

GONE

"So, well, I tackled them." Mark flushed as he said it, and he felt the heat creeping farther up as he stole a glance toward Angie standing *just two feet away*, but his moment of courage didn't earn him the smile he'd hoped for. "They were running right past me, and it seemed like the right moment."

"It worked, anyway." The graying police sergeant chuckled, then broke off and cast a wary look around at the others in view—the doctor working at Dennard's bedside, two newly-assigned guards, and the chattering staff and onlookers their glares were holding back in the corridor. The sergeant dropped his voice even lower than Mark's, to ask "But all that was after the first shooter got caught. And you have *no* idea who shoved that desk over at him?" He glanced at the bulky metal shape, now pushed back to the wall as if it had always been rooted there, and as he looked back, his eyes turned toward Angie. "I guess there must have been someone else with Joe Dennard who was desperate to save him."

He thought a daughter's hysterical strength had helped her throw the desk? It was close enough to the picture Mark was putting together, and if the idea kept the cop from thinking of wilder theories, that was just fine by him. And this cop actually seemed to appreciate their help.

Still, Mark said, "I wasn't even here then. Maybe it was the officer that was here first, before he passed out from his wound. I hope that Blade doesn't end up suing him for any broken bones."

The officer grimaced, and stepped closer, whispering now. "Never say *sue* in a hospital unless you have to." He glanced out at the people in the corridor again. "Listen, this could get ugly, and you don't have to stay. The detective in charge is on his way in, but I can give your statements to him unless you want to wait."

Wait for Lee, after our last clash? No thanks.

Mark kept his face straight as Angie said, "Thanks, we'll be going. You'll keep watching over Dad, right?"

"After a gang shoots up a hospital? Damn right we—"

"*Angie!*" The voice was hoarse and tired, but it still cut through the room and drew everyone's eyes to where Dennard was now sitting up in bed.

She was kneeling at her father's side before Mark was halfway across the room.

He caught Dennard's low "—can't tell anyone! And don't, *don't*—" and then his glance up, as the others pressed in around them. Whatever Dennard was going to say faded on his lips.

"All… right…" Angie said, the frustration in her voice almost a match for the look on her father's strained face.

Her pain drew Mark's hand to her shoulder—then he snatched it back as Dennard's eyes flicked toward it. *That kiss! He's got to know what changed between us, it's got to be written all over me!*

"Please, all of you." A tiny doctor swept into the room, the woman who'd been at Dennard's side before. "He needs rest. Do I have to call Security about your security?"

Angie looked at her a moment, and said "No, we're done." She turned back to her father. "You get that rest, we'll be fine. I love you."

As she started away again, Mark gave Dennard a careful nod, trying to look supportive, protective… trustworthy. Dennard's face was unreadable, but he let them go.

They squirmed their way through the thickening, muttering crowd and turned up the corridor. As they did, a visitor called after them, "You see that huge desk? Did it *hit* a kid?"

"Hit him? No, I heard he was *hiding behind* it. Anyway, that 'kid' came to kill someone." It was the first thing Mark thought to say, but it made the woman pause and frown, and he hoped it might help quash any rumors of someone making desks weightless. At least they made it past the corridor's bend without more delays, to a quieter space, out of sight of Dennard's room.

At last, he was able to lean in to Angie. The words caught in his throat as her face drew close—*you really did kiss me.*

It was too hard to say. Instead he whispered, "What happened? Did you see who warned us? Did your mother show you how to work the belt?"

"No, no, I just—"

She broke off and looked down at the main corridor; husky, scowling Detective Lee was pushing through the people there.

She sighed. "Do we need to stay?"

"Not for *him.*"

Mark answered without thinking, then realized what he'd said. Had he really just dismissed the police, when their security was still what was keeping Dennard safe? But... it was too *late* to try fending off questions from officials when they had so many of their own.

He felt those unknowns press around them as they moved through the hospital, and it slowed his pace—and even slowed the light, normally restless footsteps beside him that made his eyes want to follow her every move.

At one point she asked, "How'd you find the gang was coming here? Did you catch them coming in?"

Me? When I was alone I never thought that of course they'd come for Dennard here. And she'd come straight here too. "No, they caught me," he confessed. "I heard that when I turned their trap around."

She didn't answer, but this time he saw her smile as she looked away.

When they reached the ground floor, he asked, "What was that I heard when you called?"

"Not me. The first kid had just shot the cop, and he was coming at Dad and me. But right when I needed a distraction, my phone rang with your message. The little fiend grabbed it and called back to gloat at you, so I grabbed the desk and made it light enough to throw at him. I think it broke my phone. Once I saw the cops pull him out, I ran around until I found his backup, and led the cops to them."

Just like that, she ran *to* more danger. *And it still surprises me?* But all he said was, "And the belt? How'd you get it working?"

Her eyes shifted away from his. "Call it… guilt, and getting past it. Dad did a lot of harm with this belt, but I don't have to be like him— and we *are* going to stop the Blades, aren't we? If we can."

She said that as they drew near the entrance doors. And her steps slowed again.

Angie was making it a question, even after everything she'd done tonight. And none of that changed the fact that they were facing a whole gang, that they could *die*... The thought of her meeting her father's fate, or worse, made Mark's knees tremble. He could barely deal with the idea before, and now that kiss had scorched open whole other fears of losing her.

Or holding her back.

They'd barely stepped into the night air when a cab pulled up in front of them. And Mark heard himself say "So, you wanted to face your mother."

They climbed inside.

Angie called "Nine—right, it'll be Nine Hundred Heath," to the driver, and the cab lurched forward. She leaned back against Mark's shoulder, her breath in his face as she explained "That'll still be a few blocks from Kate's place, in case they try dragging our destination out of the cabbies. You think she's the one who warned us at the Fletcher house? Or, someone *else?"*

He managed to say "Well, she is the one who knows about... all of it, she even sent us to... there." They shouldn't even be whispering about it now, and he ought to be watching whether the driver had overheard their ominous words—but he couldn't look away from Angie. Her face was so close, and her eyes were so wide... she must be feeling something too.

I can't go back to pretending, forcing myself to notice every other girl, fearing I'd never catch up with her—

He dragged his gaze away. Wasn't there something else he'd been afraid about?

"Henry!" God, he'd left his cousin with the Blades almost on his doorstep! He pulled out his phone, praying he'd been right that the gang wouldn't go back to check the apartment after they'd seen him run away from it.

Henry's dry, shaken voice came on at once. "Mark! What—what *was* all that?"

He shot Angie a relieved smile as he answered, "Just tell me one thing: are you still at my place?"

"No, no. What are you doing? You just ran out on me, and you almost broke your neck!"

Mark slid the phone's volume down before his voice could blare all over the cab. Dropping his voice lower, he answered "Like I said, I wanted to keep you out of... this."

The car turned a sharp corner and Mark was swung over and tipped, sprawling, half into Angie's side. His elbow almost burned at the contact. Her wide eyes locked on his—

"Keep me out of what?" came the voice in his ear. "I saw you jump out of... why would you do that?"

Henry couldn't even say it, as if he still couldn't get his head around the glimpse of magic he'd seen.

Mark pulled back from Angie. If his blood would just stop racing, he might find some words for Henry that would work, that would re-assure him for now, without spilling the whole crazy story from the back of a cab.

"We're... I... was just trying to keep everyone away from the gang. I did have a way down from there, I know it was dangerous but I couldn't let them find you. I wish to God I'd told you this morning you had to stay away from me! We're talking to the police now, and anyone else who can help; we're doing whatever we can, to make this right. And we're going to win." His throat had tightened, each evasive word he said growing more intense, more fierce. *Almost like I believe it.*

Crazy thoughts. His eyes were edging back toward Angie, but he forced them away to stare out the other window's cool blackness.

"The police. And... 'anyone else.'" He could hear Henry weighing the evasive words, but this time his cousin sounded more natural, less shocked. "I see. So, where are you now?"

"I, well, I can't tell you that, I'm really sorry; I only just got them away from you, I don't want you in danger again. And this simply... isn't something you can help with."

"I see," Henry said again, slower. "I wish you'd... well, I guess there's nothing I can say to change your mind. I hope you're right." And he hung up.

Mark let out a slow sigh; *who knows what he thinks I've gotten in-to, or if he'll ever trust me again.* But... Mark blinked, and realized his stomach didn't have the usual queasy feeling it should have, at the thought of disappointing his cousin. Like it no longer mattered.

Neither of them spoke as the cab drove on through the night. Mark tried to follow their progress, past neon landmarks and towers of light, stealing glances at the still-silent Angie next to him.

When they finally got out of the car and started walking the last few blocks, he decided that the gang probably couldn't have followed them anyway, not onto Heath Avenue's elegance; they'd have stood out worse than he and Angie did.

Halfway up the third block, Angie motioned her head forward."The tall one's hers."

Mark had to crane his neck to take in the tower Angie had indicated. It rose over all the others, boasting dozens of rows of lights. And yet—*funny how having a flying belt makes heights look different.* "Thinking of 'dropping in' on her?"

"I wish. But we're trying to bury the hatchet, not show off, right?"

"So it really wasn't her who got you flying." The words came out as a question, even though she'd already answered it once.

"No, that was all me. Anyway—" did she rush those words out a little fast? "—if you could talk Henry down from that call," and he could hear the smile in her voice, "maybe we *can* get her to help."

"You think *that* call counts as making peace? Half the time I don't have a clue what to say. I can't even guess what your dad's thinking about us…" His voice died away. Of all the clumsy ways to mention it—

"Does it matter?" she said. "It's my choice, my timing, my risk who I go for." She didn't look at him; he could see every muscle in her jaw tensely *not* turning toward him as the words came out.

The flush that started in his cheeks could have gone down to his toes, warming him, loosening, even lightening, his step.

"I've… jumbled so much up," he said at last. "I was trying so hard to treat you like a sister—I don't know why, maybe I couldn't stand losing anyone else, just keep it the same and date everyone else to prove it—I think I fooled myself. You?"

Instead of replying, Angie kept walking, her footsteps tapping a bit faster. The distance to the tower's lit entrance shrank and disappeared.

They held their pace even after they ducked through the revolving door and into the quiet lobby, sidestepping a graying man with two little boys. The elevator stood just ahead—

"Excuse me." A little man in a security uniform trotted from a side door, motioning them to stop.

Mark walked over to meet him, wondering how many alarms their sweat-soaked clothes and quick pace had set off here. "Can I help you?" he tried.

The guard looked past him, to Angie. "Ms. Dennard? We were asked to watch for you, and to give you this." He held out a key.

She stared at it a moment before she took it. "Then, did she say anything else?"

"No, miss."

Angie's knuckles were white on the key as they walked to the elevator. The boys and the man they'd passed before were already inside, so he couldn't trade more than surprised looks with her as the car rose. *Her mother warns us away, but now she's ready to help?* The elevator stopped to let the family out, but a tired-looking young couple joined them before he could speak.

Eventually the doors opened on their floor, and Angie all but dove out, Mark at her heels as she strode down the corridor. He swallowed. *Can I really keep the peace between these two, with their whole tangled history, and now people almost getting killed?*

Angie halted at a door, and rapped the brass knocker.

Silence. Mark counted all the way through four slow breaths before she knocked again, slower but even louder. Still no response. She slid in the key and swung the door open, and he heard her voice waver faintly as she called "Mom?"

The only answers were echoes. They gazed past a wooden railing to a wide room stretching below that was lined with bookshelves and held a huge TV, plus a curtained-off section that Mark imagined was probably a French door out to a balcony.

"So she's not back yet," Angie sighed. "Or—"

She broke off, and Mark followed her gaze to another shape at the side of the room: a fish tank at least seven feet long, but drained and empty, with fresh tarps all around the plumbing, as if it had been cleared out just hours ago.

They marched along the railing to the next rooms: an elegant dining room, then a kitchen with a long string of onions dangling above a broad shelf of varied cookbooks, spotless but just as deserted. Mark trotted down the corridor ahead while Angie dashed back toward the balcony. He heard her slide the door open.

Behind the first door he came to Mark found a study—a computer, more walls of books, and more pictures of Kate standing among other suits; was that the mayor? And there and there, more of Kate, this time with her son, a dark-haired boy, at various ages—James, wasn't it? The most recent shot of him put him at around twelve years old. No shots with a little Angie, or her father, or the other man Kate had been married to for a short time.

He also didn't see any giant book conveniently titled *Secrets of the Fletcher Magic*. And he realized the place was deathly silent, the only sound was their footsteps; not even a heater running, even though the air was warm enough to start him sweating again.

By the next room he'd slowed down more, while he tried to piece together what had happened. This had to be James's bedroom. Mark walked past the video games and *Casablanca* poster to slide open the closet. The rest of the boy's room looked lived-in and almost orderly for his age, but here he saw great gaps in the clothes rack.

A door slammed. But an instant after he whirled around, heart pounding, he realized it was the other bedroom—where Angie had gone—and he could already hear her stomping away.

He caught up with her in the front room. She was just sliding open the curtained doors for a second time, glaring out at the balcony as a night breeze wafted in. She didn't go outside, just slammed the door shut again and turned to kick at a plush beanbag sofa opposite the TV.

"Gone, gone, gone," she muttered.

"I think James is too, even though it means dragging him away right at the start of school. And if you're going into hiding, why not empty the fish tank too?" *I should stop before it I make this worse.*

Angie flopped down on the sofa with a slam of her fists. "Even when she lets me *in,* it's only because she's run off!"

He eased down next to where she lay. "But she did arrange to let you in, and I don't think it was so you wouldn't kick in the door. And even if your mother's out of sight, she's still the most likely one for dropping that note—"

"Her name's *Kate.* And she could have *sent* us into that trap and someone else warned us... oh, okay, I know I'm reaching," Angie ended with a sigh, then looked at the balcony curtains again. "But we don't know!"

"We don't," he said gently, stretching out beside her. "I mean, I was thinking someone must have had another belt, to drop a note like that straight of the sky. But now that I remember... when Kate was on the hospital roof, we thought she was trapped there because our belt was drained. So how could she have had her own way to fly off anyway? That would mean that *all* the time she was standing there arguing, she was just playing along—why, to use the time to warn us?" It was too much like how Dennard had tried to tell them something when he woke up.

Angie shifted where she lay. There was a faint rustle of fabric under them.

"Hmm."

She said it softly, but he heard a thought in her tone. "Angie?"

"Keep the magic secret, if hiding it protected someone?" Now she glanced over, and a small, reluctant smile tugged at her lips. "I can see how someone would get to a place like that."

"Oh?"

"Mark, I didn't figure the belt out in the hospital. It started working this afternoon."

What? His mouth fell open. He felt like he couldn't breathe.

"At your cousin's. While you were upstairs and I was downs," she went on. "Like you said, it's like working a muscle in the back of your head, if you can only find where the thing is. So I kept trying and poking and telling myself I wouldn't be like Dad all day, until I got it. As if I'd caught up with you again. But all you kept saying was how we couldn't fight back, so I spent the whole day waiting for you to see we *had* to do this but pretending I hadn't changed so you'd never have to come after me, but I just wanted to tell you—"

She broke off, and his hand froze in mid-air; it had been reaching for her face almost on its own. She stared at it, then shut her eyes, but he could see every line of tension in her face, the trembling in her shoulders. They weren't talking about belts any more.

He leaned back, heart hammering. He couldn't touch her. *This is* Angie, *this is the girl I didn't even dare show my idiot sketches to!*

Still, still, he tried a soft, "I wish I hadn't taken so long—"

Then she opened her eyes, and her hand closed on his. "It's *us*. What else is there to say?"

He leaned closer, then drew back a moment. "You never answered me: did *you* ever think we'd wind up here?"

"You really want to know?"

The kiss stretched on and on, but they couldn't lose themselves in it, not this time, knowing what they'd begun. He'd just started to explore her face when their shifting weight rolled them off the beanbag sofa, jarring and awkward, no time to laugh.

Mark reached under her shirt and felt the lean strength of the muscles at her waist. She was so different from that little girl he'd first met all those years ago. She kissed him again, and they struggled out of shoes and clothes, still hesitating over where and how to touch.

Then, understanding, and they pulled off the rest and drew together, knowing that even this one time couldn't be more than a start in discovering each other.

It was.

* * *

They finally found the air conditioner controls the next morning, and brought down the muggy heat in the air. What they couldn't find was an address, or any clue to where Kate had gone, or if she'd been the one to warn them at the Fletcher site. No way to get answers from the evasive phone messages they'd left her the day before.

Even with all the plush chairs in the place, in the end Mark and Angie found themselves most comfortable sitting barefoot on the carpet, surrounded by mostly-empty pages of half-formed plans. At one moment the mood felt almost nostalgic; the next he might find her hand edging over to his.

Now he floated, with his head brushing against the ceiling, looking down to where Angie stood by the TV, reassembling her cracked phone and watching the news.

"—*may be a street corner brush between the 66s and the Blades; two young men are reported wounded. In other news—*"

Mark waved the remote to flick it off, still hovering. "It's just one rumor, not the gang war restarting," he said. "Besides, 66th Street barely runs a block—if that bunch wanted to be called the Devil's 666s they should have—"

"*Now!*"

At Angie's call, Mark released the magic, then *squeezed* it again immediately. His drop halted and he began rising again, but not before he bent an ankle to confirm he'd come close enough to tap the floor.

"Not bad," she said.

"I think the tingle in the belt faded a little. I can actually feel how fast it's using up its power."

"Using it up," she said slowly. "And what then? Then it's just a belt until we get it to that one place again… or are there dozens of the right places?" A slow, shining grin began to spread over her face. "The right words pull more energy into the belt and the strips. After that, if you can just *make* that magic lift what you want, you're back to floating in the wind, jumping, running… you even made Dad light enough to carry out of the park. It's *magic*—and we've got it." She laughed aloud.

"I know. And if these 'brakes' keep working like this, and we can sense how long we can stay up…" Mark felt an answering laugh rising in him. "Hey, that's our whole safety net right there."

"That's right." Then she looked straight up at him, and her grin faded. "Against falling, anyway. But Dad was talking like he had something more to warn us about. And then there's Kate saying it wasn't worth—now!"

He dropped again, watching the floor rush up and squeezing out another midair stop. His toes didn't quite reach the carpet this time. He released, and dropped down the last foot to the ground. "Enough?"

"I pronounce you cleared for flying—and landing, and walking away. So, no wasting the rest of the power with the Blades between us and getting more."

Mark nodded, but Angie turned away, glaring at the balcony curtains again, at the gleams of morning sun glinting through them. Feeling shut in.

To change the subject he said "So they really let you grow up without this, how your family never had a secret bigger than the whole city. Why do you think your dad did that, or she did?"

"It could be anything! If they'd just given Dad five more seconds to tell us…" She sank down to sit on the carpet.

She only answered about one parent. Mark settled beside her, saying slowly, "What he did say was not to tell people. And Kate warned us about being noticed too."

She turned toward him. "You think it's all about that? Keeping the magic hidden?"

"Well, I wouldn't want Detective Lee to catch us flying," he pointed out. "But that doesn't explain your grandparents' house."

"Or Dad attacking the Blades, way back then. That started a *war,* it got dozens of… of people killed." She forced the words out, her eyes clenched shut.

Mark lifted a hand to touch her, uncertain what to say.

She shook her head. "I hate to think we still just have to get out of town. The gang will go on to kill someone else; you saw those pictures at the station. But there are too *many* Blades, we can't stop them all, can't expect the police to watch us forever—there's always a way, but now I just don't see it. How do we stop them?" She glared at some of the notes around the floor, too many pages all but empty.

"It might be more than that," Mark said. "Rafe was trying to ask me something last night; he said that 'the Eel' must have some reason for chasing us."

"Reason? We could float outside their windows *forever* and not overhear that." She looked up at the curtains again, then sighed and pulled her gaze away. "I guess it comes down to getting the cops to lock them up, and being sure they get all of them."

Angie's alarm chimed.

10 AM. They'd set it to remind them when to check on her father. She sat up straight, giving Mark a strained, eager look as she dialed the number. The phone did seem to be working again.

Then she sighed. "Sorry, Dad. I bet you'll be up soon; we'll call back."

Silence hung in the air, edged against by a distant sound down the hall like a couple quarreling.

Angie flipped through a few screens on her phone. "They still list him as okay; why won't he answer? If we could *go* there—"

"He could just be having visitors, or another call. You know, Kate's firm has to be open by now."

"You're right. We can't keep waiting here. Someone's got to know something!"

He watched her dial, and listen, and just for a moment her eyes lit up, before her face fell again.

"Yes, I'm trying to reach Kate Woodward. This is her daughter— and yes, she does have one," Angie added, then stopped, listening to whoever was on the other end. She glanced at Mark. "Good. Then, just be sure she knows I appreciate her help, and I need to talk to her soon. Please."

She hung up and set the phone down. Softly, she asked, "You think I should have said it was life and death? I figured a big legal office would just take that as a teenager being panicky."

"Maybe," Mark mused. "You never really know, I guess. If she wants to call, she'll call. And I think there wouldn't be any clues to her plans at her office, any more than there are around here—"

"How does she do it?!" Suddenly Angie was on her feet, a barefoot kick sending notes flying up from the floor. "Just run out on us, *again!* You know, Dad still won't tell me why she left us, not one hint. I used to think it was for the Fletcher family money; all that money was suddenly gone, along with the house, and for a while Kate thought she could live with Dad, then she dumped us to try to earn it back on her own. Look how that turned out—just fine." She waved her arm around the condo. "I could handle that; it was just what my family had always been."

Mark looked across at her, wanted to go to her side, but something held him back. "Yeah," was all he said.

"And when she remarried—well, she told us about the wedding just to be sure I *didn't* come. She spelled *that* much out to my face, when I was *six.*" She was looking away as she said it, but she couldn't hide the pain in her voice.

"Sure, but look how that marriage turned out," he joked.

She gave a strangled little laugh.

He looked at the floor then, and went on, "But then, that man gave her the child she *did* keep, and the last name too. One way or another, she keeps hurting you."

"But all of this time—we had *magic?* What's that mean about losing the house and my grandfather—or maybe having the fortune in the first place? Is it connected at all? Or her being with Dad, even having me at all and then leaving... how am I supposed to know which of those was just her, and how much was what keeping the magic cost us, and why can't anyone *tell* me?"

"I wish I knew." He thought, again, of Angie's mother on the hospital roof, and the idea he hadn't been able to shake since then. Carefully he looked up to where Angie was pacing, and said "Did you ever think that maybe… she *wanted* you to hate her? To stop you from coming after her, and all this?"

He expected a shout, but she only nodded. "Of course I have; these days I think I've tried on every idea there is." She walked over and sank down to sit beside him again. "So what was it Rafe said?"

Mark had to laugh at how her mind jumped back. What *had* he been saying before the timer went off? "Okay. The Blades thought they had me trapped on that bridge, but Rafe still stole a chance to ask me what 'the Eel' really wanted with us. Like he didn't know, and like he needed to know, even when the other Blades almost turned on him for being soft on me."

"Rafe Martinez, *soft?*"

"I know," Mark said. "But he said the Eel was screwing the gang over this vendetta with your dad. Please let it just be a vendetta, not wanting the magic," he added.

"So it's the Eel that runs the gang, not Rafe. So we drop a battleship on *his* home—"

She broke off, and pulled her knees in tight against her stomach. Her face looked pale. "Now I'm joking about mass murder, because we've got a bit of power," she breathed. "But, do you think that's why Dad tried to make the gangs kill each other? Because nothing else would slow them down?"

He leaned toward her. "You just made a joke. What I think is that you aren't your father. Or Kate."

When he added that, she winced, and shook her head as she looked up. "Smooth."

Great. All these years of just sharing his thoughts with Angie, and now he was trying too hard. Last night had mixed up all his instincts.

"So, if we don't run away," she sighed, "that leaves using Rafe and the Eel and everyone somehow, I guess, to get them all locked up. There, it's half solved." She forced out a smile.

"Sure, arrest them, when I get along *so* well with Detective Lee. Maybe if we had more to tell him…" He reached for one of the pages Angie had kicked around. "Roger Winton made him listen yesterday."

"Anyway, we can't do it all staying in here. I was thinking…" Her hand caught his arm. "When I lightened myself to help me run around the hospital faster, did it *look* like more than fast running?"

"No," and Mark felt a smile spreading on his face, a match for the one she had. "It didn't. If we can do that the next time some Blades come at us, we could just outrun them and our secret weapon's still secret."

"What secret?" Angie smiled back.

Crash!

He jerked his head up—where was that sound, beyond the curtain? the balcony? it was too muffled to be the window breaking—and felt a chill sweep through him. He slapped his waist to be sure he hadn't taken the belt off; it was still there. Angie was already lunging across the room, putting a wall between herself and the balcony. For cover.

She thinks they'll shoot *at us?* He flung himself after her.

A moment later they reached the front door together. Mark remembered to look through the peephole first; at least there were no attackers waiting out there to cut them off.

Angie caught his arm then, and they looked back toward the balcony. Nothing had moved, and the sound hadn't been the window itself breaking.

Something *twitched* in his head. A motion, out there, a little like the tingle he sensed as he readied the belt's power. Like something *resonating* with the energy.

"There's magic out there," he breathed. "I can feel it—and it's pulling away."

Silently, they made their way back and peeked past the curtain.

Nobody was there. The French door stood intact, but he saw shards of pottery on the floor of the balcony—from one of a stack of empty planters, now shattered. And a sheet of paper tucked under a wire chair, fluttering in the wind.

They yanked open the door and stared out into vast open air and bright daylight. Angie flicked a pottery fragment to the side and walked to the rail, looking up at the balcony just above them and then the one below, and for a moment Mark thought she'd have floated right off if she'd had the belt.

Instead she sighed, "More notes, and smashing that thing to get our attention, but she still won't stay and talk!" She bent down and pulled out the message.

Mark leaned over to see the same odd, shaky lettering as the last note: "When you understand how the Fletcher home fell, you will be ready to know about little gangs."

He blinked, blinked again. *"Little" gangs? Are there bigger gangs in this—or are all crimes petty things?*

"I don't get it." Angie looked up at the sky. "It's more secrets, more games, when we're just trying to stay alive—and now it turns into a test? There's no way all this just got this simple."

"Simple?" Mark moved to her side, the wind catching at his hair. "Figuring out that crater?"

"Compared to getting into killers' heads and stopping them all without more blood? Letting us *do* something? Yeah, it seems too simple." She shook her head. "And we still don't know a thing about who really left this here."

"Yeah." The last note had saved them from the Blades, but... "Then again, we've got no reason not to try and figure it out, either. We sure don't have a lot of choices now."

Angie's slow nod showed that she knew that all too well.

CHAPTER SEVEN

FASTER

The streaks of sunlight faded so teasingly slowly from the clouds, seen from the condo's vantagepoint, too high above the streets. But when the last glow sank beyond the western hills, Mark and Angie shut down the computer and put their sheets of frustrating, dead-end research away. The only way to learn about the Fletcher magic was to gather up its energy again, and then find a way to reach Dennard—or make sense of the collapsed home itself.

"Keep 'looking' around as we go," Angie said one more time. "You never know when you might sense maybe-it's-Kate watching us again."

"I could use the practice anyway. If I'm going to get anything more out of the ruin." Mark smiled gently, knowing it must hurt her restless nature to let him wear the belt again when the leather strips were still drained. But none of her tests had let her sense the magic as clearly as he did.

Just stepping out to the corridor made them walk faster, needing to stretch their legs after a whole day shut inside. They marched past potted ferns and doors echoing with children's voices, heading for the elevator.

Mark's phone vibrated.

He glanced at the screen. "It's Roger Winton." Angie moved closer to listen as he picked up. "Mr. Winton. Thanks for calling."

"Well, you were right," came the gruff voice. "A friend of mine at the station says the detective's putting a lot of pressure on your friend Dennard."

"Did he charge him with something?" Angie asked.

She raised her voice so that Winton would hear her, and up the corridor they saw a young woman's head turn toward them, and they drew back a few steps.

Winton answered, "No, sounds more like he's got the hospital juggling papers to keep him there while he interrogates him. He can't do it forever, but he's probably got other tricks lined up."

"Thank you," Mark said. "We really appreciate your help."

"*Someone's* got to watch the police, any time they try something like that. I'll keep you posted," the businessman said. Mark could picture the tight grin he would be wearing.

Angie was already trying her father's number again, shaking her head. "So Lee's in the way again. Just when we *need* to talk to Dad—think we can get in past the..." She didn't say *guard* aloud, and she gave a warning nod toward the woman lingering up ahead.

"With the right tool again? Easy."

They reached the elevator and rode silently down, Mark checking his planned route against his phone's map one more time.

The night breeze was already ruffling the little trees along the sidewalk. To Mark's eyes, the street looked almost like a tunnel through the night, lined with different walls and fences and populated by the night-going people he and Angie stepped around.

Heath Avenue roughened and flowed into less fortunate streets, glass and steel thickening to Lavine's more common brick, and casual strollers giving way to sharper-eyed pedestrians walking alone or in knots. Mark's eyes flicked from one passer-by to the next as he led the way westward, watching out for any glimpse of the Blades.

"Anything?" Angie would whisper now and then, and he would concentrate on the belt's energy and search for any of the resonance around it he'd felt at the window. *She'd rather think our mystery visi-*

tor mentioned the Fletcher ruin to warn us of some enemy out there who has his own magic—or that our protector has her—or his—own agenda. Angie hates the idea that the note might just mean the belt's caused more problems than the gangs, a dead end.

They worked their way along, eyes and other senses watching for trouble. Here a car pulled up for someone to whisper with a little man who might be selling drugs... there a street singer seemed to be watching the onlookers as much as playing for them. Was it someone like that who had tipped the Blades off that they were at the Fletcher house?

They passed a knot of seedy-looking punks, and from the corner of his eye Mark saw two of them snap around to watch them pass. They didn't make a move after them, but still Mark and Angie started walking faster.

Half a block further, they risked a glimpse back and saw the two punks had started to follow them. *And only my belt has any magic left; Angie's scraps are empty.*

But Angie gave a grin of sheer joy like a little girl. "Now?" she asked. He nodded, and her hand closed on his.

Mark tensed the magic just a fraction, then a touch more, and felt some of their bodies' weight slip from them. The two kicked out together into a long step, and he felt the lightness launch them along the sidewalk, stretching one pace into a pace and a half before they came down, her landing a bit ahead but still holding onto his hand. As they flowed into their next step he sprang forward harder, to catch up.

By the third step they'd found their stride, in time to dodge together around a man and his barking dog. Each spring melded into the next, carrying them along like they were riding on their own momentum, or swinging on a rope while hopping along stepping-stones. Every move needed its own balance; one too-vigorous step bobbed them upward higher, and Mark had to stiffen up his stride to keep his motion from bouncing him up like a rubber ball, though the shift nearly dragged him back out of Angie's grasp before she slowed to match him.

Behind them their pursuers broke into a dash, but he and Angie kept speeding along, moving as fast as if running all-out, but at a gait that tired him no more than a quick, wobbling walk. Not floating, not even jumping, just lightening their steps enough to give each that extra spring. *It works!*

Up at the corner, the streetlight turned red, and a thin stream of cars started across their path. Mark glanced at Angie, then eased the magic away so that they could catch their balance and separate. They sprinted around the corner, Mark catching one glimpse of the punks, now far behind them.

He reached for Angie's hand again, but then stopped and waved toward the alley down the street. A dozen clumsy-feeling steps brought them to it and let them twist into the shadows there.

For a moment they halted in the alley, glancing around for anyone who might see. Then they drew into a crouch, clasped hands, Mark tightened the magic once more, and together they leaped, soaring up-ward past the bricks, past the gutter, and dropping down to flatten themselves on the roof, out of sight.

This time Angie didn't let his hand go. He looked over and saw her smile in the moonlight. They waited, watching as the two informers ran blindly by in the street below.

"We did all that," she whispered, "with just you carrying me! Once we power up the scraps too, either of us can get away from anyone we see coming—any street, any time. If they don't shoot us on sight," she added softly.

"Yeah. And you know, I think we must be far enough south to be in line…"

A moment ago he'd barely noticed the breeze brushing them here above the street. Now that he thought of how the wind angled along the city and which blocks would lead to the park, the soft pressure flooded his awareness. He stepped them back from the edge, to face across the flatness of the roof while he thumbed on his phone's map to compare. Yes, the next blocks on the grid matched the ones he saw off behind that ragged ridge of taller buildings, along Horst; they had already reached the right upwind "road." He considered the breeze a moment longer, and finally motioned almost due east.

Angie squeezed his hand. He tightened his other, internal grip, drawing the magic out and over them both. They pulled up and away from the roof almost before they kicked off it.

The breeze began melting away, its pressure slowly absorbed into bending their leap's course into its own, carrying them on its path. The city's dark shapes and lines of light *moved* around and below them as they arced upward. Even the sounds shifted, the hum of cars and occasional voices clearer and more evenly spread through the air without walls blocking them off.

They drew their legs and their free arms in tight, curling almost into joined balls. That had been Angie's idea; if someone did glance up, there'd be no telltale human outlines in the moonlight, only tight lumps riding the wind like a pair of balloons.

The first block passed below them, and he tightened the magic to lift them up past the Horst rooftops. Beyond, the dim stretch of the park itself drifted into view. Everything fitted into its own place, all of Lavine, from the gleaming eastern lake to the farthest shadowy hills to the west; every corner Mark had ever seen stretched out before them.

He looked at Angie, her hand the warmest thing in the autumn air. Were her eyes shining? *She doesn't have one second's worth of magic herself, she's just hanging up here, trusting in my control...* He wanted to speak, but he couldn't find a single word.

Rosewood drew nearer. He loosened the pressure to let them begin descending, and tried to feel for the energy waiting for them up ahead, but he couldn't make out its presence yet. Instead he watched the gray concrete shapes of the tiny factory that pressed against the park's north edge, slowly separating from the black wood beyond them. Soon—

What's that?! His head jerked up, up and left, toward the flicker he'd sensed. And the flicker *turned,* veering up ahead of them now, *how far away is it, dammit why can't I see anything against the dim sky—*

Beside him, Angie hissed "Got something? Go!"

His fingers tightened on hers and his will pulled them upward. Maybe they could get a look before the magic swerved out of their path; just a glimpse of Kate, or whoever it was.

But the presence vanished. It didn't turn again, it winked out from his head as though it had never been there. He reached further, trying to sharpen the sense of magic; there had to be *some* tingling, like the belt, a ghost presence, where could it go? He craned his neck, saw Angie doing the same.

Nothing. He saw nothing but streaks of clouds over the moonlight above, and the sprawling city below, felt only the pulsing of the belt itself... as the streets shrank away.

"What is it? Do you see *anything?*" Angie asked.

Mark shook his head, hard enough to jolt his attention back. How high had they already gone? The black-beside-gray of the park's edge had blurred below, and its factory border might be behind them already. Locking both his hands on Angie's arm, he took a deep breath, and she must have guessed what was next, because she did the same.

One thought started them plummeting down, for a few stomach-wrenching seconds before he flexed the power to slow their fall, then drop again. The dim shapes sprawled outward below them, and he had to take one hand back to wipe wind-stung tears from his eyes to see the distance clearly. Drop and catch, drop and catch... until their shoes thumped down on asphalt.

So *heavy!* Mark slumped to the ground as his full weight pressed on him again. He saw Angie stagger against a gray wall; the hum of an electric generator filled his ears.

"Sorry," he said. "I think I sensed magic up there, and then it was gone. It might have been nothing, but—"

"But whoever they are, they're still *hiding* from us." He saw her frown in the dimness.

He nodded. It left the same questions as before; the watcher could be Angie's mother keeping back and testing them for her own reasons, or it could be someone else. They still had no way of knowing.

Footsteps echoed, under the engine's hum. Mark and Angie looked up at the factory corner and saw a watchman coming, then dashed for the fence screening off the park. This time the leap over was nothing.

They slid into the shadows of the thicket, putting the fence behind them. For a moment they looked around the dimness, trying to guess which way the magic's center was, then Mark felt for the power and found it, following it like a beacon in his head.

"At least we started upwind of the right block," he grinned.

The little hillside looked the same as ever, one spot partway up the overgrown slope. Mark could feel Angie's satisfaction as she whispered *"Zha-Daruath"* and at long last drew in magic to fill the strips of leather in her hand. He did the same and felt the belt's pulsing—that had become all too thready—surge back to full strength.

It was still all they knew about this power. Not why he sensed the energy only in this one place, or how these words and these objects could store it up as tools, or what all of that meant about gravity and all the rules of the world they'd taken for granted a week ago. No matter if that message *had* been from Kate, Mark knew it had a point: they needed to know more.

They didn't speak then, only glanced up the thicket and then at each other, knowing they'd had the same thought: nobody could see them leave here. They drew together again and lifted up on a shorter arc toward the buildings beyond the park's eastern edge.

As they floated over, he saw Angie looking around below, and he picked out one, then two scattered figures here and there lingering at the edges of woods and buildings. Too many visitors for Rosewood at this hour; how many of them were Blades looking to find them, or to sell drugs, or bully people, or anything to show they controlled the park now?

The thought pushed him to walk faster when they reached the streets again. Watkins General Hospital was closer than the destroyed Fletcher house, and it only took a few words to agree that Angie had been right: a few answers from Dennard could change everything about solving the ruin's "test." So they headed uptown again, saving their power by keeping to the street, eyes watching the figures around them for more Blades as they moved into the aging Grayton shopping district.

Then Angie's phone rang and she gasped, "Dad!"

They finally let him call? Mark grabbed out his own cell, and she forwarded him into the call just in time to hear Joe Dennard's harsh "Angie? So you're okay?"

"We're fine, Dad. You too?"

For a moment Dennard didn't answer. In the stillness Mark could hear two drunks on the nearby corner stumbling through a country song.

"I'm healing. The detective's just throwing his weight around— thinks I'm keeping secrets," Dennard added.

"Don't you worry about us, Dad, we're being careful. Listen—"

"How careful?"

The sudden interruption had Mark trading frustrated glances with Angie. She tapped a finger on her ear, and he realized her father was afraid someone might be listening in.

Mark ground his teeth, then settled into a reassuring voice. "All we're doing now is waiting, and studying the old Fletcher house."

"The... house?"

Dennard said it slowly, uncertainly, and Mark sighed. *Does he think the word's some kind of code?*

"Old *family* issues," Angie said. "We've gotten some quiet support from, I guess it's a friend of Mother's. Or maybe it *is* her, I'm not sure."

"But…" Dennard stopped, and began again, slowly. "Kate said once that she'd never get involved in our lives again, and I don't know what 'friends' she's got. But, Angie… while I'm stuck in here is *no* time to *dig up old business.*"

The intensity in Dennard's low tone almost choked the words now, reducing his euphemism to a bare gasp. And yet, Mark had a sudden sense that this fierceness wasn't just from speaking in hints; that those words would have stuck in Dennard's throat even if they'd had all the privacy in the world.

Angie only said, "Don't you worry. Besides, we can come see you as soon as they let us in." She gave that the briefest pause, and Mark remembered her floating through his window before; they had their own ways in. "Then we can all work out the best way to deal with this."

"'The best way'? That's the *problem…*" Dennard's voice died away, the drunken voices on the street half swallowing it.

"Dad." Angie met Mark's eyes a moment, then said slowly, "I get it, I know, I almost lost you—but there's always a way."

Dennard's words came as a hoarse, heavy wheeze in the ear. "I said that's the problem! You don't know, *it…* the more you get into all this, and try to get *above* it, the more you won't want to get out. You won't *want* to!" he hissed.

"But we—oh *God!*" Her face went gray, dead gray.

Does he mean… suddenly Mark could almost see the ground dropping away below him again, how easily he'd lost track of time while he chased that flicker of magic. And when it all began, when he'd first looked through the window, he'd seen Dennard struggling with his own desire to use the belt…

"You mean," Mark forced words out, hammering stress into the coded words that had to carry his real meaning, "like some old rag *you want to burn* because you're afraid you *can't resist* wearing it *again?*" If Dennard meant the magic itself made you want to keep using it… was that what had sent Angie's grandfather mad?

"*Exactly* like that," Dennard said grimly. "Think about it. Angie, think about what that means. What it leads to."

For an instant, the world went still, only the drunken singing still echoing somewhere at their back. And Angie's horrified face.

"That's not true! It can't be, Dad—"

Mark caught at her free hand, but she didn't notice, only stared numbly at the phone.

"Please—say there's some way around—"

"No! Stop thinking about ways to cheat it, or beat it, or anything. Besides, nobody's going to let the Blades get me now. All you can do is walk, *walk,* away. That's it, don't you see?"

"I get it, alright?" Angie snapped, and she hung up.

Mark saw her knuckles going white on the black plastic. Her shoulders were tight as iron when he put his hands on them.

"Angie? It doesn't mean—"

"I get it." Her face was clenched tight, her eyes only half-open. "The Fletchers' house. It wasn't an enemy attacking them, or an accident, it was the magic, getting to my grandfather. Sure, if the belt can make things light enough to float up, it can smash whole houses down! Just pile on more weight until they fall apart."

She laughed weakly.

"It was all him. That was Kate's lesson, how it's all a dead end. The magic is more dangerous than the gangs. And Dad, when he saw me playing with the belt that time years ago he tried to explain that Grandpa had gone out of his mind... Dad tried to tell me, and like a stupid little girl I ran away, and we went right into the Blades territory and he had to go after us... that's what started all this and now they're back..."

Mark stared at her tormented face, his thoughts scrambling to catch up. He had to say something, but it all fit... *God, are we going to end up dead like my mother, rotting our bodies away while we scream after the next fix?* But they didn't know, couldn't be sure—*but the times he'd used it so far... when the Blades got near Henry, did I* have *to jump out a window?* Every thought they *had* about the magic just might be part of its pull to use it again.

It couldn't be that bad, it couldn't put its hooks in them in a day, surely… but wasn't that what addicts always said?

He could feel the belt's throbbing at his waist, like a living thing coiled around him.

And Angie, *she's the one who lives by rushing right in, because she's smart enough to make that work for her. If the magic's influence means she can't even trust her own will to act… could anything be a worse trap for her?*

All he could think of was to draw her closer, to pull her slowly against him. Her whole body went rigid, and he thought he'd stepped wrong… but then her hand settled over his on her shoulder, holding it there even as she stumbled out of his embrace to turn and look back at him.

—Her eyes cut *past* him, behind him. "No!"

Mark twisted around, saw the huge Blade Rafe had called Monster charging up the sidewalk toward them, not close yet, but—

As he spun away to run, Angie's hand caught his arm. She was pointing toward the man in the ragged clothes up ahead, with the low hat over his face, just now scrambling to his feet. Another Blade? A trap?

The next instant, Angie said "Run, *or* get through to him!" And she was dashing away *toward* Monster—no, an alley lay between them, if she could reach it before the Blade cut her off—

She was leading him away. That was the only thought Mark could make sense of, in that mad, scrambling moment. What did she mean, *run or get through to him?*

"Him" must be the other Blade. Mark lunged toward the man up ahead, letting his feet chase the idea his head couldn't catch up to. The man was standing now, his hand moving inside his coat, then pulling back out, empty, forming a fist. And now Mark recognized him.

Rafe. And if he hadn't pulled a weapon, he *must* want them alive, he *could* be their chance to break the gang out of its vendetta—*if I can face him down, find a reason that can* get through to him.

Mark stumbled to a stop in front of the gang leader, and one other thought stirred in his mind: when Angie had spotted this one desperate chance to influence the Blades, she'd given *him* the choice.

As Mark looked at him, panting, Rafe's hand dove back inside his coat. His head nodded toward the alley he'd positioned himself beside, just the place to march a prisoner into. "Your girl up there was fast, but don't you start thinking you're outrunning bullets. And I *will* shoot if you don't come with me."

"'The girl' knows there are three easy exits out of where she went. I bet Monster only knows one." In the face of Rafe's sneer that lie was the first words that came to him, making up street knowledge as an excuse for what Angie would—had to!—use to keep ahead of her own enemy.

Rafe's face didn't change. Instead he reached his free hand out to give Mark a push toward the alley.

Mark forced himself not to shrink away, only shucking the push off, then sliding his hands into his pockets—was one somehow still clutching his phone? With all the arrogance he could muster, he said "How many times are you going to keep trying this? You never do catch us."

"Didn't you hear? We only have to win once." And Rafe *smiled.* "And we only lose if we give up and let you walk around saying you beat the Blades. So yeah, we keep trying."

"Is that you talking, or the Eel?" Mark flung the name at him, and followed it up with, "Throwing kids into a raid on a hospital, and shooting cops, all for revenge? How long can the gang survive getting that kind of attention? You know where that's headed. Hell, you *told* me that, back on the bridge."

Rafe's smile dimmed, just for a moment.

Then his eyes narrowed again. "Tell that to the Eel. Not that you'll get the chance—"

Just then his features twisted in rage, his head twisted, his whole body twisted in a wild spin away. In the instant Rafe moved, Mark followed his glance up the alley and saw a hulking shape that had to be Monster in a ski mask, with a gun trained on them—

No, its sight was moving, tracking *Rafe* in his hopeless attempt to dive clear before—

Then a small shape dropped from a roof onto Monster's back, and the big man began to bend, his body folding and buckling and crashing down, forced down by little Angie with a sickening *slam* of bone on asphalt.

How did she do that? Why *did she do that?*

Mark could only stare, watching the fallen the gun slide away from the killer's hand. It was only when he saw Rafe stand and start walking slowly toward the two figures that he managed to move himself, falling into step behind Rafe.

His phone was still in his hand, and Rafe kept his gaze on the felled assassin ahead; Mark brushed *record* and slipped the cell back in his pocket.

Monster was still squirming, but he couldn't rise, not with Angie on his back. As he moved closer, Mark realized what she held him in only looked like a pinning grip; the brute couldn't seem to lift his arms even an inch from the pavement she had flattened him against. She hadn't knocked him down or pinned him, her magic had *added to his weight* to leave every inch of him trapped and helpless.

She looked up at Rafe with a challenge in her eyes.

Then Rafe pulled his hand out from his coat, and Mark saw the sinister, elongated shape in his grip—a gun, with silencer ready.

Mark tensed, ready to lunge if the weapon was turned toward Angie. But Rafe didn't raise it, just moved closer to Angie and Monster.

Angie didn't flinch, or pull back from her prisoner as Rafe came in. "I just saved your life, so tell me, why did you need saving? What would you like to ask your 'friend' about his orders from the Eel?"

"Same as..." Monster's voice was a groan, fighting to lift his head to stare at Rafe, "for any traitor..."

Rafe said, "I know."

And suddenly his arm swung up and his finger moved, just enough for a sharp, high *poof.* The impact sent a single tremor through the head under the mask. The giant's sluggish thrashing ceased.

Just like that.

Angie stumbled back, off the body, mouth open, hands brushing frantically at the blood spatters that had reached her.

Mark locked his eyes on the gun. He'd thought he could *stop* Rafe before he used it...

Somewhere, far away, cars rumbled down a street.

Rafe walked on, past the body, gun staying down at his side. "Squeamish? That's nothing to what your dad set off."

Mark saw the fresh shock in Angie's eyes, and he dashed past her to throw his words at Rafe's back: "So the Eel's answer is to attack a *hospital*? And he just tried to have you killed—for calling him on it, right? He doesn't care *how* far he goes, or how it drags your people down. For a grudge that's ten years old!"

Rafe glanced back at him as he tucked the gun back in his coat. "You haven't seen the Eel."

"We can't." Angie caught up to walk beside Mark. "Because he keeps sending all of you to take all the risks *for* him."

Rafe looked at her a moment, then laughed. A cold, hollow laugh, nothing like the calm voice he spoke in then:

"No, you haven't *seen* the Eel. He's still got the scars from when he was a young Blade. Some old-timers still talk about how they saw him hiding, crying like a baby, long after the 66s and *your* daddy stopped shooting that night. 'Cept they don't talk about it, they *whisper*."

Mark slipped, stumbled a moment over some trash in the alley. *Please, no... is that what's driving all this, a gang lord with lasting scars and humiliation, an enemy Dennard's attack* created? *Someone who'll* never *stop?*

Then he heard Angie's voice, as clear and calm as if Rafe had been talking about a stranger instead of her father. "And that's *it*? You just let him run your gang into the ground—and chase you out of it too? I guess the Eel's *not* the worst coward in the Blades."

Rafe stopped walking then. He turned and gave her a long, slow look, and then turned to Mark, before saying, "Go on, say the rest of it. How you're 'enemies of my enemy' and that makes you my friends, right? So what is it you think you can do about 'our' enemy?"

Angie laughed. "Besides save your life, and survive every move the gang throws at us?"

"So you're *quick.*" Rafe's voice seemed to twitch for a moment as he said the word, but then he started toward them. His finger stabbed toward Angie with every question: "What are you going to *do* about him? Hunt down Little Sammy and make him say he *didn't* see your dad running away from the shooting? Go begging to the *cops* again? After he's had your dad *stabbed, chased* you, *burned* everything of your dad's that his boys could get their hands on?"

Mark felt his lips twitch, and forced the odd smile off his face. At least burning the Dennards' house was one sign the Eel was only out for revenge, not clues for the magic... *I hope.* He forced those thoughts away and countered, "You talk so tough. But now you're just another victim on the Eel's hit list."

Rafe shook his head. "A victim's some loser who doesn't know he's in too deep. Now that the Eel's stopped playing he trusts me, I know enough not to let his boys near me. But you, I'd give you about two nights left to live."

Then his smile widened.

"Or one night, if you get near Whey Street."

And he turned and walked to the alley's end, at the street.

Was that a hint?

Mark ran after him for only a few steps before he stopped, with Angie beside him. They'd given Rafe all their warnings, faced his threats, stood over the bloody evidence of how far the Eel would go—and Rafe had only dared them to go after him and walked away. And told them *where* the Eel was tonight.

He reached in his pocket. The phone was still recording; he shut it off.

Angie's voice was soft. "Y-you *recorded* all that? Not bad."

He heard the tremor in her voice, thought he could still smell the blood from the dead Blade behind them. The smell twisted his gut. "Did you really just do that?!"

Angie lowered her eyes. "The magic must be able to drag the Fletcher house down, so I thought I'd try pinning—"

"Not *how* you caught him." He grabbed her, and pulled her against him; so small, so tight with muscle and tension as she nestled in. "You charged right in, you led Monster away from me and Rafe. and then you jumped him again. You risked everything, with just seconds to figure it out. And you got it right." *Of course she did. I thought nobody could keep up with how fast the Blades come at us, but she can.*

Her voice buzzed against his chest. "We needed some kind of edge. And if anyone had tried to shoot me, you were right there."

He hugged her tighter and bent down to kiss the top of her head. He couldn't smell the blood now with his nose buried in her hair...

Eventually he lifted his face enough to blow the strands back.

Angie pulled back a half-step, but remained within his arms. "So, do we send your recording to the police now, or try to get something more? Because..."

He saw her pause, just for a moment, before she went on.

"Because now Rafe needs the gang shut down too. His tip might be good, I get it. And I think we have to take a look at this Whey Street place. Record what we can, if there's a chance to stay back safe. Just... just see if we can get what the police really need before someone else gets caught in the crossfire. A way to get them all." Her eyes couldn't quite stay on his, but they didn't blink.

"Is that what you want?" he whispered.

"I want to do *something.*" Her fingers tightened on his arms. "Besides just leaving it to the cops, even with what we have for them. And now we know the magic's worse the more we use it—so we have to make the most of a few jumps at the right time. Except," and her voice grew thin, "if I want to rush in and finish it before the magic gets to me, is *that* already the magic talking?"

"You're asking me? I'm the one who's used most of it since last night—" He shook his head, tried to remember what they'd said when they'd discussed the belt's history. "You think your family had it for years before your grandfather lost control, right? And your father did hang on to it all these years. I don't think it can ruin us in one night. And... I think the Blades owe us at least one chance to do them some damage."

Her smile was better than a kiss.

"Oh..." He remembered, and lifted up the phone that was still in his hand, dialing Kate Woodward's number one more time. Her voice mail didn't even give her name, just asked for a message, but he said, "If that was you leaving us riddles, we solved it. Angie's grandfather must have done that damage himself, when he was addicted to the..."

He left the word "magic" unsaid. The thought came: *It was Kate's house as a girl, too; had she been there when it came tumbling down?* If that had been her own father's work, if he had gone mad, then no wonder she hated the magic—but would *she* be the one to take a belt and watch over them now?

She might, for her daughter.

He added, "I hope we're right, and you do want to help us. If you do, we'll take what we can get. But we won't be waiting."

CHAPTER EIGHT

FALL

Narrowing down the location on Whey Street was simple. Even without the research they'd already done that day, digging through news reports, they would have picked the sprawling auto salvage yard as the obvious site for stolen cars and the gang that chopped them up.

Whey sloped upward, to the city's dusty outskirts. Mark and Angie had seen one open gate in the tall chain fence around the yard, and glimpsed the guard on it. But now, looking down from a ridge above the property, the moonlight gave them a fine view of endless lines of cars that formed a shadowy maze around the central garage. They watched the pool of light at that center, as well as the four entrances spread around the tall chain fence, and they tested the wind blowing toward it, before Angie made the call.

"Hi, Dad."

"Angie? You're alright?" Mark could hear the uncertainty in Dennard's voice, after the way they'd broken off before.

"Fine. In fact, better than we've been since this whole thing began. Sorry we didn't take your warning too well."

"Doesn't matter. As long as you know why we have to back away."

Mark saw Angie swallow once before she answered. "We get it, Dad. But not yet. We do have one chance to do something."

"What?" Dennard's voice began to rise, swallowed up by the trees around them.

Mark jumped in. "It's what I've known for years—your daughter always sees a way out, because no matter how massive the problem looks, there's always a way—I know that because she's always right *there,* in a heartbeat. And I can—" He broke off, and looked away from Angie, his face burning at what he'd spilled out. Every word of it was true.

"What are you saying? What are you going to do?"

She said, "Trust me, Dad. We've already survived plenty—we're just taking a look, and we're only making moves we can keep control of. Anyway, you can tell the police the gang might be stepping up its plans against you; we'll tell them what we saw once we're back in hiding.

"Or if we can't... you stay safe." Her finger pressed down and sent him the recording Mark had made.

They had to dial down the volume on their phones as Dennard's voice started rising, to keep it from carrying through the late-night road. They hung up before he could ask any questions.

Angie looked at the street. "He'll pass that on to the police, 'Whey Street' and all. I don't know if that means we have to find everything before the troopers show up, or if we let them take over, or what. But we did have to get that evidence out there, right? And I owed him the truth."

Honesty between them now. While Henry and I can't even talk without him suspecting the worst, came the unexpected pang. But all he said was, "You mean after you saved his life twice, maybe three times? He ought to trust you."

Angie sighed. "It's bad enough *I* know what Dad did to the gangs. What really gets me is them waging this vendetta on him and saying he's just a killer down at their level. Better than the Eel knowing about the magic, though."

"Your father wasn't on their level, he was floating way over their heads…"

The clumsy joke made her mouth quirk in a smile. But as he made it, another thought took shape: "You know, he *would* have been in the air when he went after them, or we'd both have seen him. But didn't Rafe say their witness saw him running?"

"So he only flew partway—or," and Angie's voice darkened, "do you think this 'Little Sammy' is only telling the Blades what the Eel lets him, and the Eel knows there's a real secret worth keeping from them? He *has* guessed about the magic?" She shook her head slowly. "You think we'll get to meet Little Sammy?"

"Either way, the Eel's the problem. Besides, with a name like that, 'Little' Sammy's probably bigger than Monster."

They looked down at the yard again, their phones vibrating with Dennard's attempts to call them back. Just one more reminder that he'd have the police here soon.

"That's one big yard, with four gates to get in," Mark said. "They can't watch the whole fence; one hop and then we'd have all those cars to lose ourselves in."

"And only risk a bit of magic? Seems simple. Except, that'd still mean starting down there at eye level, where anyone might still see. What if instead, we…" she held out her hand to him.

He nodded. "We change the rules," and his fingers closed on hers.

She had taken the belt back again, since he'd used most of the magic tonight. And he'd expected she would have her own style in controlling it, but even her warning smile didn't brace him for how they exploded upward.

In a few shocked heartbeats the ground shrank to a mottled surface in the dark below; anyone glancing out a window would have had to be looking right at them to see them, in the bare moments they took to leave eye level behind. She slowed their rise, and they tucked their arms and legs in as the wind arced them toward the yard. He watched it as it drew closer, some hundreds of feet below; a huge rectangle of dark shapes walled off from the lighter patterns of the city, with a few gleaming corridors of cars radiating out from the lit garage. With its four entrances in the fence, the pathways looked like arrows pointing out through the space.

Even though Mark and Angie couldn't feel the wind they drifted in, the high cold air made them shiver.

Somewhere in the night, an owl screeched. Mark thought of clicking a few birds-eye pictures of the yard to help guide them through the maze once they landed, but then realized the central building lay straight ahead, drawing nearer as he watched. *Were we that perfectly upwind of it, or is she starting to fly instead of float?*

However she did it, Angie dropped them squarely onto the building's roof, cutting off their speed at the last moment to bring them down, cat-soft.

They lay flat, waiting for the first sound to hint that someone had seen their drop. The wind they'd just pulled out of buzzed around them now, raising whispers off the fleets of broken cars, and the weight of rust and metal in the air pressed at Mark's nose. Voices rose up from the building under them at differing volumes, magnified or muted by the irregular echoes of the garage.

"—course we'll have time... don't remember, but... 66s don't want war either. They're all talk."

"Cut up cars or cut up them? Cars pay more," said a louder voice.

"...got the truce once..."

Silently, Mark and Angie drew out their phones and began recording, sound only; Mark knew better than to crawl to the roof's edge now. He wondered if they'd come too soon, or too late, wondered whether the Blades were making new plans for Dennard or for them at all.

The voices went silent.

Mark froze at the sudden hush. He saw Angie catch her breath.

Then, from below, "You say something?"

"Nothing."

"I heard 'scared,'" someone said, and this was the same deep voice that had been talking about the 66s.

"Uh, yeah. The 66s, I mean those fuckers are scared, of *us*—and still scared of that shooter back then. And *he's* gotta be more scared'n any of us he had ducking down—'cause you got up and you handed the 66s their asses then, and you'll get him now…" The voice grew faster and shriller with each word., until it choked itself off in its own fear.

Metal clattered, like something tossed onto concrete. Something loud; Mark pictured a tire iron that had been poised to smash bones, flung aside for the moment.

"Right. Them," another voice said, and Mark could *feel* people start breathing again.

He edged closer to Angie, not sure what to whisper to her. Just like Rafe had said; there had been one Blade at Dennard's ambush who was still beating down rumors of how frightened he'd been that day. And years later, that man knew it was Joe Dennard that had humiliated him—and maybe how he'd done it, too. The Eel himself.

Later, Mark would remember the moment it all began to change.

As the voices below muttered, he thought of the leather strips in his hand, and tested the sense they gave him. And somewhere in the sky, he felt magic flicker.

He reached over to nudge Angie and point upward, and they twisted their necks up, searching. The sense was still just a stirring at the side of his mind; faint or not, their watcher had to be somewhere nearby… but his eyes couldn't make out even a dot in the thin moonlight.

"…the right doctor, we'll get to him…" said a voice below. *Doctor? To get to Dennard in the hospital?*

"…what Rafe said…"

"But the 66s can still—"

"Hey!" came a shout from out in the yard. Mark looked across and could just make out a black van pulling in the main entrance.

Then the roof masked it; the position Mark and Angie had taken, hidden so far back from the roof's edge, blocked their view now. Mark heard the punks in the garage moving out to meet the newcomers—there were maybe half a dozen of them here tonight, judging by the different voices he heard muttering.

He caught one other sound, almost covered by the voices: feet moving around in the other direction, behind the garage, then stopping at the back corner.

He heard the van engine cut out and doors slam open and shut. He couldn't tell how many people had been in the van, but the two groups met, and lingered, staying out in the yard. They were exactly the wrong distance away; not far enough that Mark and Angie to see them over the roof without crawling too far forward, not close enough for their low voices to carry clearly through the breeze.

Angie's hand squeezed his shoulder, too tight. These didn't seem like more of the gang in the van, not when the Blades had sent a man to lurk behind the garage. If he was their insurance against trouble… maybe these were the 66s meeting them?

"Time," he breathed, quiet as he could in her ear. "They were just saying they needed more time to do this, and to stop the 66s from starting the war again—like they're more worried than they'll admit. You think the 66s know about your dad too? I mean, his trick did pull both gangs in, so are they ready to go after him, and will they start in on the Blades too if they don't make up for their mistake themselves soon? By killing him themselves, I mean," he added, trying to sort out the rush of thoughts.

"You mean the Eel's going from brutal killer to *desperate* killer?" Her mouth twisted in the dimness.

Mark strained his ears, trying to make out anything from the sounds below. Mostly one voice, that might be the Eel, but he couldn't *hear!*

Then he saw Angie looking around the yard, her gaze moving from one pathway to the next. She crept forward on the roof, but stopped herself; they already knew it was too risky to peep over the edge. Her look back behind the garage was longer, but he saw her turn away from that, too; the hidden Blade had already taken that cover. Then her head turned toward the labyrinth of cars beyond the clearing, offering all the ways they could have asked to creep closer unseen. Did she think it was worth risking the move to get down there?

The gang voices weren't moving, hadn't grown any louder. He watched Angie as she weighed the odds, then nodded and slid her legs in under herself, looking over at him and nodding for him to do the same. Just enough for a quick jump across to behind a stack of cars before anyone saw, he hoped. He drew on the magic—

Power surged, but it wasn't their power—the surge came from above them. Was it Kate? He froze as magical energy veered around toward them, sweeping downward. He thought he felt it pull up from its dive, but he couldn't be sure. He caught Angie's arm and pressed her down again.

Where was it, where had it gone… he felt for the sense of the magic's motion again. The burst had already dwindled, but something dark was swinging through the gray air, some shadow already rushing away in the night. Dammit, why couldn't he *see* it?

He held his breath and, somewhere between his heartbeats, he picked out the magic turning again and swinging away, up the valley. And there it turned again, circling over one block.

Without drifting, or floating up and down…

"Our watcher… *flew* right over us," Mark whispered to Angie. "So fast I couldn't see, like Kate owns the sky—or whoever it is, they're that good. And, swooping over just before we jumped? Was that a warning to stay down? And now… the way she's moving, I think she's watching a spot uphill."

"About where we were looking down at the yard before?" Angie said it at once. "Someone with binoculars—like we should have brought," she sighed, "could be watching all this from there now.

Cops, Blades, or who? But they almost saw us float away, except for our friend."

They flattened themselves lower still, staring around the night. Voices murmured across the yard, and still they could barely make out a word… but one of the voices spoke faster now, more urgently. The bright lights below and the Blade back behind the garage kept Mark and Angie from creeping down closer—and now it could be someone up the street was watching them too? *We can't move, we're* treed *up here.*

The voices growled, faster and fiercer. Mark caught one fragment that did carry: "…bomb them…" Angie heard it too; he heard her breath catch.

Long, long seconds later, the voices stilled. For a moment Mark thought he heard footsteps, but they didn't move any nearer to the garage, where he would have been able to hear them speak. But, he thought the sounds were splitting apart, like two groups forming and muttering within their own ranks.

What *were* they planning? And if their flying watcher was trying to warn them that someone was up on the hill, who was it? It could be the police, or just another gang lookout. Not that he and Angie could risk moving in any case.

"We have to follow them," Angie whispered. "Stop them."

"And if they see the magic? Or someone's watching with a gun?"

Her eyes clenched shut, but he saw her nod.

She reached down, digging out her phone. Mark leaned close to make out the hurried text she threw together:

thanx

u rite

it ALL worse if they find out

they said bomb

"For Kate. If she's listening up there. She's *got* to help," Angie whispered as she sent the text.

Mark heard the pain in her voice and wondered how many kinds of regret and hope were tearing her up inside. His hand closed on hers, and he felt an answering squeeze.

Around them the breeze rose, swallowing even more of the night sounds. Mark reached for the strange magic again but felt nothing; it had pulled out of "sight" completely.

The breeze dipped a moment, and he caught a voice from the gangs: "...got one day." A firm voice, a confident tone, like the Blades weren't an hour away from charging into mayhem. A good sign.

He saw Angie stare at her phone, and flick open a text:

are you there at the yard?

keep quiet its almost over

The text was from 'Det. R M Lee.'

Mark felt muscles unknotting, all up and down his body. So Dennard *had* passed their recording to the detective, and sure enough, the cops knew what "Whey" meant too. This had to mean they were closing in with enough force to finish the threat.

"So that's it," Angie sighed. "We find nothing, but with them here we may not have to. We don't even have to move again. That's a good thing, right?"

He nodded, and shut off his phone's useless recording. They could still give the police that evidence too; maybe something would be audible. The cops knew they were here; thanks to the fly-by warning, he and Angie had stopped short of showing them how they'd *gotten* right into the lot. Mark hated to think of a bully like Lee getting hold of the magic, or how fast its influence might seduce him.

Kate, the magic's secret, the two gangs, the police... running through the pieces in his mind, he saw one thing as the most urgent unknown: who was that on the hill, was it someone worse than the cops? He looked at Angie, and gestured for her phone. She handed it to him.

Squinting in the faint light, he worked out a reply to Lee:

is that 1 of u looking down, the corner north on Whey?

Lee didn't answer, and another minute ticked by. The gangs held their ground out in the yard, their words still too low to hear. Mark wondered if the police had brought listening devices that would catch all the plotting he couldn't. They would have *something,* some way to stop the Blades now.

Long minutes later, Mark glimpsed a figure uphill, edging toward the shadowed slope he'd asked Lee about, and wondered if the tip from them would get a Blade captured after all. The night grew colder, the hard roof drawing more and more heat from his body.

When the van engine started, he heard a loud sigh from whoever was hiding behind the garage. He squeezed Angie's hand again; it felt half-frozen. He could just make out the Blades heading back to the garage.

Angie gasped. Mark whipped his head around to follow her gaze. There, trotting down the hill from the north—from the spot he'd asked Lee about—came a figure in black. He was *waving.*

Rafe.

Mark knew it before he made out the face. Rafe didn't run, he didn't shout any warnings about cops; he just stepped calmly through the north-side entrance and strolled in to join the Blades in Mark's blind spot. He just walked right up to the Eel? what was he after?

Angie began crawling toward the corner of the garage nearest to the confrontation, and he started moving with her. *They* might *not spot us peeping over, not when the garage light is more out front than on this side—and we have to see more.*

As Rafe neared his gang, Mark saw some of them shifting in place, beginning to edge away from each other, like the start of battle lines forming. The other man the gangs watched was the broad-shouldered Blade in their front, the one with the gleaming pale skin, whose gaze rested on Rafe. And off to the side, a different group—the visitors?—stood back and watched.

Rafe's voice cut through the air. "Surprised to see me alive?"

The pale man glared back at him, and Mark pressed lower on the cold roof, tensing for the bullets to fly.

Rafe went on "Or are you just too busy getting bombs?"

"Not for a hospital," growled his rival, and he spoke with the deep voice they'd been hearing all night. He had to be the Eel. He added, "Don't need mad dog moves like that."

Angie tapped Mark's shoulder and pointed back along the roof. He looked, and thought he saw a glint in the distance. Was something moving at the south end of the yard, on the side street across from the gate?

"Tough talk," snapped the tallest of the five men around the van. The 66s had hung back in their own group, content to watch the Blades feud, but now their leader went on "So what *are* you gonna do? That fucker Dennard killed us too. If you're going soft we can settle up with him and you both."

Small things shifted among the gangs: a hand reaching nearer a weapon, a man edging back from the comrade at his elbow to give them both room to attack.

The Eel only folded his arms. "I told you, I got plans, I just need time. And I need that *rat,*" and he spun around, back to Rafe, "to stop signaling his own pets to sneak away. Like he knows something's coming down on us right now!"

Mark stared as the yard erupted into shouts and accusations. But the way Rafe recoiled at the words, something about how far spread out some of the Blades were… if the police were closing in, like that motion on the far side, *could* Rafe have seen them and walked right in to sneak his own followers out before the net closed? *He's got nerve—* but it was also him who told them the gangs were here, and let them tip the cops off at all.

The cops. Lee needed to know. Mark brought up his phone.

A new text had popped up on his screen, but not from Lee. Mark's blood ran cold.

What are all these messages? I dont know who you think youre talking to - Im just getting into town. From Angie's mother.

Mark nudged Angie with a shaking hand. The letters blurred and swam in the dimness as they both stared at the message. It had fit so well that Kate seemed like the one to find them at the crater and then give them another message at her own home—but if it hadn't been her, who was it? Someone who'd known all of Kate's secrets... no, she or he had only known the Fletchers *had* secrets, and *asked them* to solve them, mixed in with warnings about danger. And someone who'd always stayed out of sight... He saw Angie's face next to his, paler than the moonlight. The magic—he tried to reach past the sudden wave of chills coursing through him to feel for something, any sign, out in the endless night...

"Leave you to the cops?" Rafe's words broke through the babble of voices below. "You think I can't pull my own trigger?"

"Why not?" the Eel flung back. "Calling me soft on Dennard wasn't getting you shit."

It was Rafe *driving the vengeance against Dennard? But he pointed us right at the Eel, and we believed him.*

"Getting me shit? The man who spilled our blood—and yours," Rafe added, with a nod to the 66s, "is still breathing, Little Sammy saw it all, but you—"

"Who d'you think you're bullshitting?" snapped the 66 leader.

The Eel took a slow, heavy stop toward Rafe. "Spill it. We all know Sammy would say anything for his next fix, and you bought his 'memory.' So who'd you bring down on us tonight—was it whoever aimed *you* at Dennard?"

"You're losing it—"

"*All* those secret calls you got, right before you and Sammy made Dennard your reason to show off how much better you could run the Blades? Yeah, I saw them. Sammy's bought and paid for, but what hand is up your ass?"

But Mark stared, stared, couldn't breathe. The Blade leaders were competing to get Joe Dennard, and keep the 66s off of them. But if Rafe had bought Sammy, because someone had told *Rafe* about Dennard, turned them all against him… and meanwhile someone was watching Mark and Angie fight back…

He croaked, "Someone sent Rafe after us, someone who knew what your father could do—and whoever's up there, that was never Kate, ever—"

"Someone else, watching us…" Angie added.

"If they're the same manipulator, if someone's playing all the sides—"

He saw a flash of fury in Angie's eyes. But he struggled to hold back the rush of rage; *why* would anyone do all that? If Rafe's hidden ally was even the same as their own; all they really knew about their own supposed "helper" was that someone could fly, someone who wasn't Kate. But they both stayed in hiding to pull strings…

Now Mark fought to shut out the voices of the "little gangs" below, trying to find that tickle in his head that could warn them of magic out there. Instead he sensed only the pressure of their own magic, and the breeze that whispered across his face and through the rows of cars around them, shifting the clouds over the moon, and thinning the moonlight. Sour fear stung his mouth.

Somewhere below, the gang was still shouting, but there was still no sign of the person who had guarded them—or used them all—

Magic stirred.

He looked up quickly, but lost the sense almost as soon he had felt it. Shutting his eyes, he reached for it again, caught a fleeting impression—the sense was moving, rushing downward, somewhere behind them. Not toward the gangs; he looked around.

Clear across the yard, something moved toward an open gateway in the fence, a dim human outline Mark could barely make out. As he watched the figure, he felt the magic blaze into strength again, felt it diving down; this time he could just see something flicker through the air.

The flying flicker reached the earthbound figure and the magic's pulse… skipped a beat. For an instant, Mark lost the sense of it. The figure halted. No, was it *falling*?

Mark squinted harder. He could just see whoever it was, sprawled in the gateway, but he couldn't make out his attacker except for sensing the magic staying right by the fallen shape. It settled there for endless heartbeats before—

A gunshot smashed the night. The blast rang off the walls of cars, banished the wind's whisper, launched a swarm of "*fuck!*" and "*what are you doing?*" and "*not us!*" shouts from the gangs that all ricocheted into each other to become, "*RUN!!*"

Far up the street, a car's lights flared on as it swept toward the yard. Mark saw other figures outside now, heard a shout of, "Police!"

Then Angie's hand pressed his head down to the roof. Mark lay low, blind to most of the spectacle, listening as gang shouts tore through the air below. In his mind's eye he could still see the glimpse he'd had of the police and their cars. The cops had the exit nearest the gangs blocked, but had there been any lights next to the other three gates?

He felt for the magic again, reaching through the roar of engines and the shouts of the pursued. It wasn't by the far gate anymore, but… there! Somewhere high up. Not attacking again, so far.

In his ear, Angie said, "That cop…"

She was staring back, toward the fallen figure. *Right, it was probably a plain-clothes cop that had been moving in… maybe even Lee… and the watcher struck him down with magic? There had been a flash from right there, too, had it been the cop's gun that was fired, by his attacker? Had he done it to finish him, or for the noise to rouse the gangs…*

Engines roared, some of the gang cars and bikes… and Mark snuck a look again at exactly where the cop lay. Not out on the street, not among the steel stacks inside, but squarely *in* the fence's gateway, dropped right in the path of any escaping cars.

Whatever else this watcher wanted, he'd set someone out to die.

Mark scrambled up, and even without glancing over he could hear Angie rising beside him. Squeezing his scraps of leather, he ran to the roof's edge and flung himself into space.

Too high! His burst of power swept him up in too steep an arc. He caught a glimpse of cars wheeling around, away from the front entrance, heading for the gate where the fallen man lay, helpless. He released the magic, plummeting and then catching himself as his path bent again, sending him into a running landing, feet crashing on the dirt.

Stacks of cars loomed around him; he was in a canyon of shadow. A twist of the magic lengthened his steps to a bouncing run, but he could already hear an engine growling somewhere at his back. He couldn't look away from the fallen man, too far ahead. From the little he could make out, it seemed to be Lee himself.

He's here because of us. We showed him glimpses of how we used the magic, all our escapes and lifts and spying, and now someone has dropped him right here *where his death would look like an accident—*

The motor swelled to a roar, and he could feel the car, ready to barrel right at his back, but then came a sound of—

A giant's groan, a growing cataclysm of metal on metal, wrenched his head around. A stack of cars toppled and cascaded outward with ear-shattering force—a dark one under a black one under a white one under a doomed pale convertible at the crest—spilling and smashing across the path behind him. The avalanche swallowed his sight of the van, swerving to a stop beyond it, but he could make out the small figure at what had been the fallen tower's base, just now lowering her arms.

Somehow he remembered to spin around and charge forward again, away from the sound of gunshots and engines revving. Two more hops brought him to the form lying in the gateway, and a flicker of his tiny strips' power helped him lift the man and bound away across the street. *Here I am making another single rescue, while Angie can cancel enough weight to* topple a pile of cars.

When he set the man down he finally had a moment to check his face, and felt the odd confirmation of seeing Detective Lee's thick eyebrows in the moonlight. And, he could feel him still breathing, and he couldn't see any blood… he really had been left to be "accidentally" ridden down in the confusion. Lee's lips were moving slightly, mumbling, as if being wrenched out of danger could only make him stir in his sleep.

A siren screamed somewhere down the hill, forcing its way into the chaos, the sound warring with the shouts and engines and scattered gunshots within the yard. Mark turned back, looking for Angie.

Running. She was running from the gateway toward him, head tilting skyward. Leaping, she rocketed up, the shocked look he glimpsed on her face sending him searching upward for signs of the other magic. There it was, that other force, diving, streaking down *at him.*

Attacking him. And she burst up to cut it off, the two energies meeting and soaring up together into the night.

Where, where? His eyes raked the blackness above for any hint of solid shapes moving, but found nothing. But the magic, that he could still sense…

Energy *smashed* through the sky, not a sound, not a flicker of light above, but a wail of power twisting inside his head.

Where? Blink back the tears, try to stand, where—

Something fell, above. He pushed at his power, jumping, and staggered down short. The shape fell, fell, starting to turn in the air before it hit.

When Mark reached the spot where she lay, her jean jacket was stained as dark as the sky she'd flown into. Gone.

CHAPTER NINE

THE LOST

He caught her up—so light in his arms. His head turned, gaze drifting over the street, the dark scattered buildings outlining it. The wind was freezing.

Stumbling, swaying on his feet—the flicker of power ahead drew him forward, the thing he had to reach now. It hung low, faint as a shaft of the moonlight around them, somewhere behind the building ahead. Voices shouted somewhere up the street as he plodded forward.

Have to find it, get to it... his feet crunched on earth, leaving the hard asphalt, and he knelt to set her down. *Have to* stop *him, get him, save them all, it's what she'd want.*

The presence had shifted to the right, not so low now, but still slow-moving. He started after it, drawing on his power to hop to the building's corner and search around. Somewhere ahead, but he still couldn't *see* the thing.

Faster now, he scrambled past the back of a squat wooden building and jumped a fence. Where, where? The magic wrapped around his hand was barely stirring now, and the belt at his waist was drained. *Belt? When did I put that on?*

The thing that attacked them had turned in the air again, swinging back toward the street—no, along it, back where he'd been. Toward *her.* Mark sprang around a corner and leaped over a jumble of trash to stumble onto pavement again. There, yes, something moved in the air high above where he'd laid her down.

He rushed forward, gathering his remaining strength. The presence turned, flickering in the moonlight as he felt it starting down toward him. *Yes, yes, he wants this finished too—*

"Hold it there! Police!"

He drifted to a stop, as the enemy swung away. A cop was trotting up the street, to crouch down next to where she lay. *Why's he keeping his gun on me? Why did he stare when he saw me?*

Then the bald officer looked up, studying something in his face, and the gun dipped a few inches. Almost gently, he said, "Son. Did you see… how she was…"

"Did you get the Blades, and the 66s? Rafe?"

"Some…." The cop halted then, and started again. "Sure. We rounded them all up. But, you do know that the girl is—"

"Of *course* I know she's dead!"

The words rolled out into the night, freezing the cop in place but only gone, gone, swallowed up without an echo in the darkness.

The cop sighed, loud enough to hear from where he stood. "Yes, she is. Now, you just come over here with me."

Mark sagged on his feet, looking around again at the hillside, spotted here and there with police lights, but still abandoned. The cop started toward him, then looked back.

A car was gliding up to stop beside them. A door opened, and another uniform climbed out. From inside, Mark heard a hoarse, weak voice: "…help him."

That was Detective Lee in the passenger seat—*right, at least we did save him.* Mark watched, silent, his dwindling magic holding him up on his feet.

A flicker, a tingle, somewhere in the moonlight. *He's still here!* Mark spun away, following the trace in a dash up the street and twisting into the block where he felt the killer. Voices shouted somewhere behind him, but he only ran faster.

Another fence. A surge of power let him leap up and spin over it. His feet pounded in the dirt as he twisted around a corner. His target was somewhere ahead, not yet out of reach. And there were cops behind; he could hear them clambering up the chain fence at his rear.

A thought came: before the cop saw him, had the enemy turned just when Mark had made the jump out to the street, because he'd sensed Mark's power? Mark squeezed the magic to spring himself forward, to behind the next wall—then he let the energy drop and dashed back around it without any surge of power, and crouched behind a stack of tires.

He pressed himself low, fighting the urge to even feel for his opponent's magic up in the blackness. Please, just let his bursts of power be enough to draw the enemy to where he'd been, and give him his chance to hit back. If he could only get one real glimpse in the dark!

One clean shot.

Where, where… he saw motion in the sky. *Did ducking back here actually fool him?* He craned his neck, heart pounding in his throat. There, that *was* something, angling toward him.

It came toward him—straight toward his hiding place. His fingers tightened on the tires, as he stared through the night for the descending shape. Just a movement, an awkward flapping, that he could barely pick out in the dimness…

It swept out of the night, small and pale as the moonlight, the shape coming clear around the uneven flickering of power that had been the only sign until it swooped in close enough to see. An owl. A gray owl, pulsing with magic, angling down toward him.

One frenzied heartbeat, then another, and his muscles tensed, hands tightening on tires, ready to throw them as his magic gathered. But then, on his next heartbeat, the bird twisted away and spun off into the night.

"No—" He scrambled after it, flinging himself into a long leap, feeling for its energy. It was somewhere ahead, already climbing up, heading out of reach.

But… the last of his power trickled away, and his sense of the owl's presence vanished with it. Blind, drained, gone—he toppled down, palms slamming into the dirt.

Can't stop, can't slow down, or I'll never start again! He lurched to his feet, one step falling into another, a heavy jogging rhythm. His feet led him across the block, careening around another fence that sprang out of the dark, then finding the hill's slope and following it down. But… somewhere below was the park, and more magic.

One back street and then another slid into view. He'd turn a corner, then look up, always up, wondering if he'd even see the enemy if it came at him again. No, he'd never make out an owl up in the night, not without magic… the skin between his shoulder blades shivered helplessly.

He tried to hold his pace; the ache in his feet was nothing if he only kept going, it kept him from thinking. One block after another fell away, and the dusty city outskirts thickened around him into fenced yards enclosing better and better houses.

Still nothing when he looked up. He found himself winding through side streets more to avoid any chance of a late-going observer on the ground than his real enemy, though once he saw a pair of young men—too clean-cut to be from a gang—falling back from him.

Cold air seared his lungs as he panted on, all part of a deeper chill. How could anyone escape an owl in the dark, an owl with a killer touch, when all he had left was only normal flesh and blood? *Blood—* he finally placed the salty smell that had lingered around him ever since he'd picked her up. Too much on him to go near people.

This is between me and that thing hiding up there in the night.

He stumbled against walls, glancing off and moving on, his footsteps echoing in the alleys. All the familiar street names were gone from his head, leaving him only a sense of which nameless way led further downtown, and which turn kept him out of sight.

A bird, an owl… *what kind of magic could turn someone into an owl?* Or create something that looked like one?

Same power, it had felt like the same energy as the one that left the note at Kate's—

But then it tried to murder Lee—

And dived at Mark—why him, was he just the easier target? He certainly was now, with no power to track it. *But it had been diving at me, not Angie, until she—*

Until she... to save me... because I saved the belt and let her stay in the city, she...

He stopped, slumping against a wall as his ragged breathing tore through him. Lights moved up the street; cars still wending along the artery. Someone would wander down his way in time, someone he could wait for, police or gangs or owls... did it even matter who? If he only stayed where he was and let them do whatever it was they wanted to him, it would *end*. But, he staggered on.

Somewhere on Summer Street he remembered the enemy had tried following him to Rosewood once already, high in the sky. The thing might be waiting for him, or trailing him now, in some diabolical game of wiping him out right at the edge of the magic. That thought pressed on him as much as the lead weights that were his clumsy limbs, but he didn't care, not as long as he made it *to* the center of power before the thing attacked...

Then, finally, he entered the park, reached the thicket and its tiny hillside, and gasped the words.

Energy flared. It crackled up from the ground to sweep though him, and even the miles of heavy exhaustion seemed to melt away as he stood, buoyed up on tiptoe. Power burned around his hands and his waist, and his sixth sense sprang to life again. He clenched his fist, magic at the ready to chase down a killer and crush it to the ground.

But... he couldn't feel it out there. Only the air, that had been so cold a moment ago. He heard the scattered engines and voices of the night-time city, but he couldn't feel one touch of the other magic resonating against his. *I still have nothing.*

How do you find an owl in the darkness? Mark whispered *"Zha-Daruath"* again and felt even more power flood in. Ready to hunt.

He paused, remembering the Blades… "little gangs," the killer's note had called them all. He dug out his phone with clumsy fingers, flicking through screens to find the searches he'd made so long ago. There it was, the number of the biker shop that had stood out as most likely connected with the Blades… during all their research… today, *before*— He shoved that thought away and hammered out the command to send them the record of Rafe revealing his gang's meeting place. *If that snake is still on the streets, he should have* everyone *hunting him.*

Then he was free to tuck the phone away, its last use against simple enemies finished. He sprang into the air.

He let himself settle into the wind, balancing in the air and arcing outward over the park. The sky was pitch black, with some dark gray clouds for variety, offering no light a human eye could use to find an owl. Below was black as well, crisscrossed with slashes of white or yellow, forming the lines of the streets.

But drifting on the wind had no speed—if he even had a target, or a weapon. Struggling to think, he sank down into the noises again to settle on a waiting roof. Cars moved here and there, and peering over the edge showed him one small figure hurrying away from a bus stop. Up the street, the silhouette of a man walking a dog. *And none of them knows what's lurking out there, what I have to kill.*

If he could *find* his enemy. His gaze followed the breeze eastward—yes, toward Watkins General and Joe Dennard, one man who would be all too eager to share anything he knew about the killer.

Leaping up again, he could just make out the complex of lights that ought to be the hospital, blocks away, but slowly drawing closer. He could drift a while longer in this direction, slightly off course, then he'd land and jump to angle across to it.

The lights below blurred a little; he wiped his eyes, wondering if the air up here had trapped a layer of the city's smoke. Watching and feeling for the enemy was useless, and nothing he could do in the sky would draw it out. He needed real answers.

Except, thinking about it more clearly, he knew Dennard wouldn't have them. If that man had ever guessed there was a magical enemy out there, *nothing* would have kept him from warning them. And to face Dennard now...

No, *he* wasn't the one who'd kept the worst secrets. But the real Kate had said she was getting back to town. Finally.

Moving north was harder, against the wind, so he settled in to long, low jumps that moved him a roof or two at a time. Dropping down to run along the wind-sheltered streets would have been faster still, but he couldn't bear to spend long on that level now. Instead he zigzagged a block north, then west, then north again toward Heath.

Long before he saw the tower he was *sure* there'd be a light on in Kate's apartment, and there it was. From the roof across the street he gauged the wind, then leaped across, pulling himself onto the balcony, right by the stack of planters their enemy had used to draw them out to that treacherous note.

The curtain behind the sliding door hung half-open. Mark paused, realizing he could have gone up from inside and knocked on the apartment's front door. That might have been more diplomatic. *Whatever.* The glass door slid open at his touch.

He blinked, stepping into the light—so bright, the same TV and sofa and drained aquarium they'd paced around when—

There was nobody in the room. A quick brush of magic found no power around either. Mark scanned the room for any signs of change other than the light being on. Was the air warmer? Had their notes been moved? He didn't see them.

A sheet of paper lay on the coffee table. Yellowing, maybe decades old, with stark block lettering slanting at an odd angle... he couldn't look away as he walked toward it and bent down to read it:

Don't trust the words—you have to see deeper to claim what you are.

Don't turn your back on the greedy—they'll never stop wanting what they see.

Don't look down—look up, when the wind howls or the road is blocked.

Don't forget your friends—but anything I leave you, they can still take for themselves.

But don't trust yourself—your instincts are the first thing you can lose.

And don't trust me, for writing this warning. But Katie, I wish I could let you see it.

A footstep moved at his back. *Too close, how'd I get so careless?* He spun around.

There she was, just moving down the steps toward him. Kate. The woman who'd run away, who'd left them to their enemies and kept even this message from them—she raised a finger for silence, but he advanced on her, reaching for the words that would drag everything she knew out of her.

Another footfall, up the stairs, and a boy in pajamas stepped into view behind her. His delicate features and blond hair were the same ones Mark had seen in pictures around this home. He flashed a twelve-year-old's smug delight at having caught two adults in his living room… then the smile faltered and the face went white.

No wonder, to see his mother facing down a stranger wearing a bloody coat—

"I couldn't save her." The words wrenched themselves out of his gut, and they carried all his strength away with them. He sagged where he stood, barely able to keep his head up to face the mother. "Angie."

Something moved behind Kate's eyes. Pain, shock, just for an instant, before her eyes slammed shut.

"My *sister?*" the boy asked, voice cracking. "Is she..."

He didn't finish, and Mark felt a whole new pain as he looked at him. Her brother wouldn't even know what he'd lost, not ever...

Kate took a step toward Mark. "Why don't the two of us talk outside?" and she motioned to the balcony.

He muttered some kind of agreement and stumbled back toward the door. Somewhere behind him he heard the boy protesting, and Kate sending him away. He stepped through the open door and crisp open air washed over him again. Cleansing him, calling to him.

The light dimmed behind him as the curtain closed, and then Kate stepped out, bringing the glass door whispering shut behind her. She walked right up to him, motioning to him to back away from the door. "Alright—"

"You never told him either!" he snapped, in a low tone that slashed through hers. "Does the kid even know what you all are?"

She didn't back away, not an inch. "James is safer if—"

"If you keep more secrets?! Not this time! This time you're going to talk."

His hand closed on her arm, and he flung them up, outward, dragging them both over the railing and into open space.

They lurched to a stop in midair. Looking back, he saw her hand sliding off the railing and realized she'd caught at it and broken their momentum. At least his leap's force had torn her grip free, so they'd been left dangling, hanging in place some five feet out from the balcony. Smoothly, she turned her head to look him in the eye—not rattled at all.

Damn her! Mark floated them upward, past the next balcony and rising. His fingers clenched on her arms, hard. "Someone, someone with magic, killed Angie. And you *never warned us!!*"

"*What—*" For just a moment her face's steadiness wavered. Then, "Keep your voice down," and she nodded toward the apartments nearby. "I... was afraid that's what you meant. And we're next? Me, and my son?"

"So that's all you care about? Maybe you *should* worry." Mark felt a certain fierce pleasure at stripping away her sense of safety. "Whoever it is was right here at your place once, watching us—it's all him, it has to be! He knew about the Fletcher ruin too, so you're on his radar alright. I think he's been watching us for days."

"Watching, here," she repeated slowly. "So there is 'someone with magic'? He's floating around too?" Was that fear in her voice, real fear?

He hesitated, one part of him grimly amused to see her start to unravel. A hint of breeze brushed at his face even in the shelter of the building.

Then she said "I'll make you a deal. I'll tell you whatever you want to know. The sooner you tell me about the danger we're in and I tell you what I know, the sooner we can go back inside and keep anyone else from being pulled into this."

"You mean, before someone gets *hurt?*" he spat back.

He thought he saw her twitch in the darkness. *She ran out on Angie, then kept pushing her away... to keep herself safe? Or could it have been to keep her enemies from finding her daughter?*

He gritted his teeth. Why she kept her secrets didn't matter, they just had to point him toward the killer. "Fine. Now, what do you know about him—if it's a him?"

"I'm the one who wasn't even in town a few hours ago, and you're the one who saw what happened. You tell me first."

Even hanging in mid-air, she stayed in control... for a moment in the dark, he saw Angie's face instead of hers. He had to close his eyes to answer.

"An owl," he sighed. "Or it looked like an owl—and that's not its only trick with the magic. He can just zap you into unconsciousness, I think that was what he did when Angie was flying, he made her *fall—* " He bit the word off. "Whoever he, it, is, he's been watching us, he made us think he was helping us; we thought it was you. And then we found out it wasn't you, and that someone was pulling strings with the gangs to go after Dennard, and we saw it, and it looked like some kind of owl, and it set a cop up for an 'accident'—maybe it went after Lee because he was learning too much. But whatever he, they, it, wants, he kills for it." *He made* fools *of us... but I let her die, but we never knew, and part of it's because you ran out on us again...* His fingers wanted to tighten, crush, on her arm.

"An… owl. What else did you see? What do I have to watch out for?"

"I don't know." He glanced around the night they still rose through. At least he didn't feel the thing out there. "But 'watching out' won't cut it. The thing's too fast and too small to see it coming at you, unless you're *her*. Still… when it knocked Lee out, he woke up a few minutes later. And the owl had to swoop down on him to do it, and at least I could sense it by its power—but that was while I was controlling magic myself. Do you even *have* any of your own to spot it?"

"No, I don't," she said flatly. "But, you're saying that you *sensed* his magic?"

Was that surprise in her voice? "That's right, the same power when it dropped us notes and then turned around and started killing—and by the way, no, he's not out there watching us now. And your daughter was strong enough to levitate tons of cars to save a life before the end, if that matters to you. But that's all I know; it's your turn to tell me—"

He made them *skip* upward in the air, the nearest balcony dropping a few feet further below. He felt his grip on the magic start to tremble, and paused to steady their rise.

"*How?*" he hissed. "There's a killer out there, who somehow turns into an owl, and he's watching us. What do you know—and how *dare* you not tell us?"

"I never knew. Any of it."

She said it calmly, not flinching when his hand tightened on her shoulder. She was *bluffing*? Her whole bargain was a *lie*? But then she continued.

"What I know is that the belt controls gravity—not birds, or sleep, or anything else—if you charge it at that one place in the park, and I know that using it can distort your mind. That was the family secret my parents shared with me when I was young, but that was all we ever knew. And then, as I gather you discovered, my father lost control and a high-gravity wave crushed our house—" Just for a moment, he thought he heard her voice catch in the darkness. "Then, before he died in the institution, he wrote that message on the coffee table; I wanted to show you that. Since then, I've wondered whether he was trying to warn me that there were enemies out there. But mainly I thought our own magic was dangerous enough."

"But you never warned us!"

"Warned you?" She shook her head. "I just told you, there was nothing to warn you about, except the belt itself. If there had been even a hint that there might be someone out there he could fight, do you think Joe Dennard would ever have stopped hunting for him?"

His daughter didn't. Mark felt them wobbling in the air, and clamped his will tighter on the power.

She went on "I never thought there was anything else to find. And the belt's own dangers… I'll only say that by the time I left Joe, I was living proof of how it can nearly destroy someone." She looked down, just for a moment, before adding, "I would have destroyed the belt, but he said he had to keep it in case he needed it some day. So he hid it from me, and I had to leave."

"He saved our *lives* with it, when Angie and I ran into the gangs. That's what a parent does, not run off and *leave*—" He broke off; was he talking about Angie's parents or his own?

Not that Kate's desertion was any better.

"I told you, keep your voice down," she said, and her words hardened. "Yes, I left them… and then I found that in keeping myself away from the magic, and Angela away from me, I'd pushed her away to the point that she never listened to me again. I told you both at the hospital, Joe would give you reasons enough to leave the belt alone."

"You mean, you trusted Angie's life to her half-dead father waking up in time to stop her from using it."

But Dennard did wake up, except then there was Lee keeping him separated, and us not listening, and the killer was already making his move—

He shook his head. "So what you've got is excuses, and fears, but not one thing that can help me!"

"Not in chasing your enemy, no. But, Mark, I know what the magic can do to you; even after my father's example, I couldn't leave it alone and it ended up costing me another family. And even then Joe couldn't leave it, and I couldn't be around it, or him." Her voice softened again, mingling with the hints of breeze brushing at them. "In the end, all I could do was keep myself away from them."

Something in that softness twisted his stomach more than ever. "And look how that worked out."

"I know. But, just listen to me. I couldn't control it; my father always thought he could, but I know why he stopped fighting it—"

"Why? *Why?* That's easy."

He released the power. He caught one gasp from her before they plunged down, down, whipping through the cold air with just his hand on her arm while floor after floor streaked by them.

The single light swept up along the building, the balcony of the apartment they'd left, and he snapped the magic into place to halt them there.

"Easy. He couldn't handle it, because nobody out there gave him a *reason!* Well, I've got one: that 'owl' is DEAD!"

One motion tossed her away, outward, to land on her balcony below. And the pushback from his throw sent him drifting backward, beyond the building's shelter, and he felt the wind catch at him even before he flung himself up, up, the rush of the passing floors swallowing the shaken figure below as he arced out into the night.

PREY AND HUNTER

The wind had to be rising. He couldn't feel it, riding within it, but the lines and clusters and pillars of city lights that stood out against the darkness drifted by at a quicker pace than they had before. The wind's speed made it easier for him to just keep still, to let the pulsing magic in his body hold him up. To try to simply wait and *feel* when he drew near the killer.

The sounds that did reach him through the air were faint. His phone vibrated in his pocket now and then, but when he glanced at it he saw it was just Kate, no doubt wanting to make more excuses. He had to keep his mind on the other vibration, the enemy power he knew he could sense if he could only get close enough. Even if he had to crisscross all of Lavine to find it.

What is *this thing, and why is it after us?* The thoughts kept churning. It had manipulated them, warned them, then suddenly attacked them... and now it wasn't showing its feathered face again? Or whatever his, her, its real face might be. *I can still find its magic. I have to.*

The wide blackness of the lake crept nearer, no more lights cutting through the black, and he knew the wind had brought him to the eastern edge of the land, across most of Lavine—and no trace of the enemy yet. He touched down, into the silence of a sleeping suburban street, and as he landed he felt the wind again, its coldness softened now, and it swept away the metallic smell that had hung in the air with him. He flared his power up, more energy crackling out from the belt, into him. He sprang up the street, back westward, with fast leaps along the pavement that ate up block after block until the rooftops became dense enough to let him step upward again.

He'd thought to cross back to the city's western edge to let the wind bear him back on the next southeast sweep, but the scattered hum of the cars at night began wearing at his nerves, and somewhere in the streets he soared up again. Easier for him to feel for the owl up there, or let it come to him.

Then his phone sang—not the standard tone that rang for most callers; what split the air now was the tune he'd set for *Angie.*

His fumbling fingers brought his phone to his ear.. but he heard a male voice, a tired, nasal sound: "Please… come back in. I'm so sorry about your friend, but if you—"

He hung up. *The police.* One of them had taken her phone, maybe the one who'd seen him beside her. But the distraction hadn't even made him bob in the air, and he smiled. *—I'm smiling? That shouldn't be right...*

The energy continued throbbing through him, but still nothing else stirred against that other sense. Focus, don't see the lines of light receding below, just...

There! But as he dipped, ready to land and leap after it, he felt the touch slip away. Cursing quietly, he steadied himself. It wasn't quite at his feet, not a pulse passing below him, but more a faint presence…

He dropped again, settling on a flat roof, his weight dragging down on him as his shoes met the asphalt. Were those traces nearby, some thin cobwebby presence that his straining senses couldn't detect clearly? Even closing his eyes and holding his breath didn't reveal anything more than a faint hint.

Not the killer. Just some dusting of energy in the dimness.

Belatedly, he looked around, noticing that the roof held a jumble of machinery. It overlooked a tiny square of brick buildings squeezed in around benches and a single working streetlight. The pool of light seemed to blur, like it was behind wet glass. *My eyesight is changing.*

And nothing in it got him closer to the thing that had killed her. To break away from that thought he leaped up, flared up, flinging himself out of the shadows, past the roofs and into the clean air again. The scattered sounds of the night streets reached up to him as he moved into the open, then began falling away below him. His skin throbbed with the power, a match for any chill.

The light and dark shapes were dimmer now, and he knew he should stay above the lights if he wanted to keep his night vision, but staring down at the streets did him little good anyway—the killer could be at any light or in the blackness between them, and even feeling for magic wasn't clear anymore. *I have to make this work, I have to.*

The silence of the sky wrapped around him. Noises faded, the wind became only the lights' motions below and the motion of his coat's corners. He still felt the faint threading of magic somewhere beneath him, or was it actually running all through the land? And above him, was that another layer? He tightened his grip on the power to cut through the air toward it. *Find him, find him!*

Something buzzed against his skin. He yanked out his phone and grabbed a breath of soggy air to say, "What?"

"Mark? You're there?" Joe Dennard's voice sounded hoarse, desperate.

"I..."

"Angie isn't answering her phone."

The name, from *him,* set Mark's heart thundering in his ears so loud he could barely hear his own answer:

"She won't. The owl killed her."

He felt the last two words come out as a choking noise that ended in a gasp. When he heard the first piercing sounds of a reply, pain pushed his hand back from his ear.

Let him talk, face what I let happen? Or—

He let power rush into his hand like blood into his head. When he opened his fingers the phone shot upward, falling up and gone into the night. Just like he should have done himself, the first night.

No more distractions. All that's left is finding the killer.

He dropped downward, surprised to see the city lights had drawn so close together, so far below him. In the rush of free-fall, with no ground to brace him or magic to hold him up, he could feel the distant layer of power below, and the other layers above. So faint, so different from the burning in his belt. His eyes blurred.

The owl had dived at *him,* like it had set Lee up to die. Instead it had gotten the one person it hadn't gone after.

The roof loomed up below. Through the haze in his eyes, he pulled up, and stumbled down to scrape his ribs falling across some ugly lump of machinery.

"Damn, *damn!*" The rage bounced him up and slapped his hand down across the humming cowling of a vent. For a moment the magic only *lifted,* until he found the right *push* and heard metal begin to grow heavy and creak, groan, flatten under the crushing weight…

What am I doing? Reeling back, he jumped away from the wreckage. *I needed that energy I just wasted!* And he'd only thought to test his weapon, not ruin some stranger's vent… such a small thought now.

He shot a glance around the ragged outlines of the buildings, glad he could still feel the faint power in the land, and flung himself back up into the search.

Just as he settled in to catch the wind, the other magic stirred.

It was clear and firm, like a pebble against his tensed skin, but this touch was far out in the night. Mark twisted his head around. Not high, it was somewhere down toward the streets, below and off to his side. Winging toward him. The same small twist of power that had come diving out of the darkness once before.

Mark sucked in a breath. How close was that sense; was the owl a block away, half a block? His eyes raked the slowly-passing streets below for any patch of motion against them, and saw nothing. But he felt it when the presence swung closer, and started to glide around *behind* him.

He caught himself before he turned his neck, forcing himself to keep looking ahead. *Mustn't let it know I can sense it. Let it think it's hidden.*

Teeth clenched, eyes watering from strain he didn't dare wipe away, Mark felt the enemy's presence moving, weaving back and forth somewhere at the back of his head—while he could only drift on in the same slow direction as the wind with nothing to jump from. *Trapped.* Shapes edged by below him, and the hums and rumbles of the distant streets filled his ears.

Still it hung back. Mark fought to keep his breathing slow, and let himself begin to shift downward toward the roof ahead. The patch of cluttered, moonlight-dappled grays drew closer, closer.

When his shoes reached the surface he let his breath out at last. He scrambled forward, staring around at the tangle of vents and heaters; there had to be *something* in the mess that wasn't bolted down, something he could use as a weapon.

The bird moved. In his head he felt it swerve around and dive straight at him, *just like when it got Angie.* He froze.

The next instant a shadow formed, a blur streaking in at the corner of his eye just where the magic was, small and dark and *real* enough to send him twisting away in a dive. The bird swept past him and rushed on into the darkness.

"No!" Mark leaped headlong after it, outstretched hands clenched.

He felt the open air rush by him; the enemy pulsed in the night ahead, right in his path. The magic that had given steel the weight to crush itself surged into his grip, and his leap brought him closing in—

The bird swerved away. Mark glimpsed its wings lashing in the dark as it spun clear and he shot on past it.

"No, dammit!" Mark stared back toward where his enemy had been; his fists flailed uselessly in midair with nothing to pound. *I can't turn while I'm up here, I can only jump and then float, and the killer's got wings.* Had the owl been that fast before?

A moment later he forced his rage back from his senses, and found the bird was diving at him.

Trapped in the air with nothing to jump off of, all Mark could think of was to let the magic go. His stomach lurched as he dropped out of his headlong lunge. For a moment he felt the bird still closing in at his back, but then the wind rushing against his face gathered strength. The killer began to slow, to pull back, as he fell faster.

The ground! Through wind-teared eyes Mark saw lights rushing up at him; he threw out a surge of magic that wrenched him back like a giant fist. Breathless, head ringing, he let himself drop again onto the concrete.

He broke into a run as the shapes around him resolved into cars; a half-empty parking lot. The sound of other cars moving on the street pressed at his ears, but he only had time to run, his feet stumbling on the ground and his head staring around low for something to fling while still looking up at the sky. *There, it's diving right there!*

A wire trash can was the best he could find. He caught at it and wrenched it up, making its weight vanish in mid-motion and sending it hurtling toward the attacking bird.

The can tumbled through the air. Mark watched the dim shape spin toward the tiny presence in the night, upward… and *floating* up as the bird dove under its path. The can sailed on by until it crashed into the next building's wall and suddenly dropped, clattering, to the ground.

As car alarms began shrieking, he felt the owl flap away and begin climbing. *It's getting away!* He flung himself up after it. He could sense the bird moving more slowly, fighting its way up against gravity this time. Vulnerable?

Mark burst upward in its wake. It rose in a simple, steep arc, up between two buildings, and for a moment Mark thought he'd caught his enemy in a blind spot. *If I and my magic can strike before it touches me, if it doesn't dodge—*

Then the bird twisted around and dove at him.

Spitting a curse, Mark cut power to drop again, but he could feel the enemy already tilting its dive to keep on him. *It knew, it's got its own touch ready, and it's too fast!*

With all the strength he had, he blasted himself upward. For one instant he felt the bird above him just short of where he'd pass by… then all his senses blurred as the flare of power shot him up, hurtling upward as sheer speed rattling through his limbs, cold flesh warmed by burning nerves and *free…*

The other magic shrank away. He wrenched himself to a stop and looked down, to the tear-blurred shapes below—the enemy had slipped away down there. He gasped in a breath, and his joints ached.

Something inside in him whispered that he'd let the joy of the power take control. But that only lurked behind the broader, driving need: he could be *losing* the owl every second, he'd let the enemy chase him out of his sense's range. Failing Angie.

He dropped, and the wind shifted from pushing against his face to rushing up along him as he fell.

—Was I bracing against the wind up there? Did I use gravity to hold *me in place, to stay above where we fought?* But with the lights rushing up he had no time to question that either; he could sense his target below again. It wouldn't get away this time.

No more fighting in his enemy's element. He stared around the growing shapes of the blocks below, looking for a way to knock the bird out of the air. A broad pale space stretched off to his right—a construction zone, downwind, within reach, and he slowed his fall to ride the wind over toward it. The bird flew after him, but he'd already dropped past it to near the ground first.

His own magic felt thinner now, like a weaker pulse against his pounding heartbeat. But, he was luring the bird in.

He slid over the painfully white lights shining at the perimeter, and his feet hit the earth. The construction grounds were a light-washed haze; fence, looming building, sawhorse barriers, and an outline walking toward him.

"Okay, how'd you get in here?"

His vision cleared enough to make out a man in a watchman's cap. Mark only walked past him, staring around. Was that some kind of metal bin?

The bird glided closer.

With what ragged control he had left, Mark didn't run, didn't dodge, only held his stroll toward the four-foot-wide bin of gravel ahead.

"I'm *talking* to you—"

Straight at the watchman, the magic struck. Mark felt it dive, felt the faint twitch of power as the bird brushed against the man. Then the thump of him crumpling to the dirt.

Asleep. Like Lee, asleep—he saw a hint of the man's chest still moving. Because he'd only had a few feet to *fall*...

He lunged the last two steps and snatched up the bin with a surge of power. The bird was flapping upward again, and Mark whipped the bin around and sent the gravel in it cascading out in a shower of not-quite-weightless stone, a shotgun wave too wide to miss even a bird in flight. *It* can't *escape, it* mustn't!

The wash of power and rage blurred Mark's sense of the magic. For one heaving breath he could only see the black storm he'd launched... then he saw the slender shape lurching away in the air. Still flying.

He was dashing forward with the empty bin in his hands, spilling out power like blood to keep it held high, but he was too weak, too weak. The bird pulled upward toward the corner of the building, he flung the bin at it, but it crashed off-course into the night before the bird even reached cover.

Move! He sprang for the corner after the bird; he could feel it drawing further away. Confused voices echoed somewhere behind him, and he flung himself up for the rooftop, but by the time he reached it the enemy's presence was already growing faint.

He ran and leaped for the next roof—but as he did he felt the bird heading off to the side. Trying to shake him off, when it was already hidden from sight and almost beyond his range. All he could do was dash across the rooftop—

His foot caught on something in the dark. He crashed down, bounced up and leaped the rest of the distance to the roof ahead, and he could feel every twinge of magic that the move wasted.

When he reached the next roof, he couldn't feel the bird. He could only jump again, a long, desperate glide down the block hoping it would bring him into reach again... but when he thumped down on the tiles, the streets around him were still empty of magic.

Something moved in the sky, blocks away and too slow. Only a helicopter.

Left, right? His head jerked this way and that, trying to pick which way the bird might have gone. He started left, his movements feeling heavier with every step.

The killer had outflown him, outwitted him, and it was even outlasting the belt's supply of power. Mark ducked under wires and scrambled on. Through his sweat, he noticed the same coppery odor he'd been carrying half the night—from the stains on his coat, *from when I tried to carry her...* he hurled the coat into the night.

The helicopter's distant whine faded behind the rooftops.

Magic. He needed more magic. Wasn't the park in this direction— a mile, half a mile, how far? If he just had enough power left to make it to the park, he could still fight.

Then he felt it again: the killer bird. Somewhere in the dim shapes behind him, a block away and already veering to begin closing the gap with him again.

Mark thumped down on a ledge along the side of the next building, already half-turned to spring after his enemy again... but the power along his nerves was fainter now. Too faint.

Dodge the bird, get to the park—

No, can't show it where the power comes from—

He flung himself in the bird's direction with a roar of rage at his weakness. He let the wind push him toward the dim shape of some kind of sprawling, crowded roof below. The bird closed in slowly, slowly, as he angled down.

He *dipped* in the air. Tremors went through through his gut; he squeezed his will tighter around the magic and felt far too little of the burning left. But solid ground lay just ahead.

A gust of the wind tossing him along the roof, clumsy feet clattering to catch himself—and he tumbled into a wide shape that lurched out of the dark. He jumped to his feet and blinked against the haze; he'd hit a wall of glass, with what must be trees and plants beyond it, some huge greenhouse garden covering most of the roof.

He scrambled alongside the glass wall. The space between it and the edge lay wide open, but he ran for a rounded shape ahead, barely big enough to cover him. A vent, he could see that now, and the sky was growing paler.

In that first hint of sunlight, he saw the bird streaking out of the sky at him.

Dive! He flung himself for the asphalt ahead and crashed down hard. Head ringing, he looked around and caught a glimpse of the killer swooping on past him.

Into the dark, coming from out of the light. Struggling to his feet, he watched the bird circle around in the sky. His hands clutched for a weapon, but something about that outline stirred a thought in his head...

Its lean, deadly lines, not like the owl he'd glimpsed before? No, it had been the same nimble shape all night, the killer must have changed from an owl to his fastest hawk... he'd only dodged it because it had struck from the daylit side where he could see it...

No, no, get after it, no matter what trick it's playing! He lunged forward; some kind of scaffold loomed above him, and his fingers closed on it to heave.

It didn't move, only rattled in his grip.

"Not now!" He couldn't be that weak yet—but he could almost feel the burning seeping out of the belt now. A thready sense of the enemy magic still circled above.

He clutched the metal tighter, and felt two stories of metal frame grow light for an instant, then thump down again. "Come on, come on!"

But the bird didn't strike again. He fought to sharpen his sense, to slow his breathing and focus, but even the belt and the scraps barely tingled in his mind. He craned his neck to stare beyond the roof, up past the greenhouse glass. Where *was* it?

Slowly, along the higher buildings around him, shafts of sunlight began to creep downward. The wind still whistled around him. Even without his coat he didn't feel cold, just emptied out as the power dimmed and his ragged breath rattled in him.

Once a shape moved beyond the edge and he lunged toward it, but the scaffold's weight in his grip yanked him to a stop. What magic he had showed him it was just a simple, powerless bird drifting through the air. He glared helplessly across the skyline.

Somewhere out there was the park, the energy he needed to keep fighting… he took a step toward open space.

Useless! With a moan he tore himself away and crouched back behind the humming vent, for what little cover it gave him. The killer had flown rings around him, flitted clear of every move he'd made—while he'd barely kept himself alive…

Or the bird had been *letting* him escape, every time. The thought burned deep in his throat, growing sharper as the sunlight stretched lower around him.

And still the killer didn't come.

Angie would have saved her father, beaten the enemy, saved them all by now, and I'm still struggling... need power to make this right....

Something moved. Somewhere in the shrinking shadows of machine housings, he picked out a rat sniffing and hunting. *No magic in it... I* can *still know that, right?*

It was too much. He found himself scooting over, keeping low as he moved closer to the creature, waving his hand to shoo it away. "Get out! There's a hawk, there's a killer coming."

There *had* to be, the enemy had to finish him off soon... *I have to show Dennard I can do this much...*

"Not like her," he whispered, "she never tried to prove anything to anyone, so she never gave up..."

He waved weakly at the rat again, but it only huddled further behind the engine, away from the growing light. The east would be blinding in another minute, and Mark's senses were already dazed, the magic thinning away.

"Except, for Kate..." *Angie did want to impress her at the end—* but why was he muttering?

He stumbled back to the scaffold. His hands closed around it, wrenched the whole shape up in a clatter to wave it at the rat—why didn't it get away? But the surge of released power felt so *good.*

Sunlight stabbed over the horizon and blazed along the greenhouse wall. The scaffold tumbled from his tired hands and he pressed low, eyes watering, ears deafened by falling steel, knowing that the great wave of light was the perfect moment for the enemy to fly at him...

All he felt was the wind, tearing at him. Squares of gold flared along glass towers, and he could just make out the whine of the roof's machinery somewhere below the wind, more of it coming to life. But still no enemy.

He'll come, like he did for Angie. He pressed down by the vent, looking across the sky and trying to feel for any power. So weak, helpless. Down along the roof, the rat was still watching him.

"Too weak." Too slow, too drained of magic… but if he could just take the killer with him… He clenched a fist tighter, trying to find the rage again, not think about himself, left talking to a rat.

But the sun and the looming, blazing glass wouldn't let him blink his eyes clear. He stared past them to the clear sky, that he could still soar away into… no, there was some reason he couldn't… he had to stay here, to spot the enemy when he came. He moved, half-blind, to the raised edge of the roof, giving up what little concealment he had in hopes of catching a glimpse of something in the bright canyons below.

When he glanced back, the rat had edged out a step from its shelter, too. "He'll come, like he did for Angie…" But the magic was fading, he needed the power if the killer came… if? "He'll come, like he did for her," he said again, weak against the wind.

He leaned out, looking past the glass walls to the still-dimmer streets below. The killer could be down there… his fingers clenched on the masonry rim. *No, I don't have the strength left, I can't* stand *this!* He started back toward the vent, his body too heavy.

"He'll come, like with her, he'll come." A hand shaded his face to let him stare at the sky; he shivered in the wind; wind that hadn't chilled him all night, dammit. "He'll come… he'll come, like her—"

I'm losing it! He choked off a cry and tried to wave the rat back to shelter; *why can't I save it?* No good, no good, *forget waiting, I need more magic!* He stumbled back toward the edge.

"Don't you think you've made enough noise tonight?"

The voice, calm and cold, spun him around. The door to the building below stood open, and two figures were stepping out into the sunlight. For an instant one looked like Dennard, but when the silhouette came clear in the brightness, Mark saw it was just some uniformed watchman. The other, the one who had spoken, was Kate.

She went on "Even finding a helicopter took me—"

"You can't have it." The words slipped from his mouth, and he edged back until his foot touched the roof edge.

"Of… course," she said, slowly.

She turned back to the guard then. A whisper and some motion passed between them. Money, a bribe, came the distant thought. The guard nodded and went back inside.

When the door closed on him, Kate said, "Can't have what?"

"Just… you can't take the belt again." She had to see that much, she *had* to. "The killer's coming here, and I still need it. For her."

"But she—"

Kate broke off then, but he slammed his hands down on his thighs anyway, to cut off the thought. *If someone says she's dead one more time—*

"Remember?" She almost whispered it, but it still carried through the wind. "You remember the night I tried to take it? I warned you about my parents' house."

The ruin, all the tricks… "That… that *was* still you on the hospital roof, right?" The killer hadn't started all his games then— *but I need—* "I need the magic, she wanted to do so much with it, until he— she loved it—"

She was walking toward him, slowly, each word a little softer than the last. "Remember my house? Remember, my father destroyed it?"

"I know. Too much magic." What was she trying to say? "But we could have handled it, together, Angie loved… it…"

"My mother loved my father," Kate said. "They went all over the world together, and people thought they could do anything, without even knowing what that belt did. When he lost himself in the magic, it was after she died. He lost his anchor, in everything. And now here you are, leaving a trail all over town, after—"

Mark roared in pain, hands to his ears as he lurched away from the ledge. When Kate moved toward him he clapped a hand over the exhausted belt, holding on to the only thing he had left.

When she reached for him, it was to wrap her coat around his suddenly-shivering body.

Step by too-heavy step, he let her lead him to the door. His gaze still searched the sky for anything that might be circling there, though no enemy had appeared. Or… could the rat have been more than a rat?

They stepped inside, and the door closed behind them.

A TEXT

—Just in case you didn't notice: the Blades are in pieces, and there's a recording that says I sold out the meeting to the cops. You think you can FIX that?

CHAPTER ELEVEN

SOMEBODY

Mark sagged onto the bench on the subway platform. He couldn't remember if it was him or Kate that had said to travel underground, but one of them had thought to go down where birds couldn't follow them.

People pressed in tighter, louder, the buzz of the commuters making his head ache but reminding him that the right train couldn't be far away if it was this busy. He kept his hand on the empty belt, trying to believe there was something left to care about. His other thought kept him muttering "Soon, it'll be here soon now" aloud. He said it for Kate, he told himself.

When the train screamed up beside the platform it took all he had to drag himself to his feet again, but he made it to the car and found a new seat to slump into. The jolting and the flickering lights began beating at the haziness in his eyes...

Kate's voice at his ear told him they'd arrived. He pulled himself up and off the train, and stayed on his feet, barely, all the way to the station exit, but he didn't recognize the man waiting for him until he heard the gasp of shock and squinted harder at the face before him.

For a long, long moment, Henry didn't say a word. Then came the soft, "So. What did you take?"

"It's not drugs." He couldn't get Henry's face to focus, but the sorrow in his cousin's voice stung, in numbed parts of him he was just starting to feel again. "But I'm so sorry. I'm sorry."

They started toward the lot. Mark couldn't seem to get his eyes to work right; he could barely stand the gleam of Henry's silver car in the sunlight. But he found the front passenger door, stumbled in, and sank down into the blessed cushioned seat. He sensed Henry settle at the wheel and heard Kate take the seat behind them as his eyelids drooped—

Too easy. And… he didn't deserve to rest.

He forced the words out. "Sorry. I know there's not much left of me, but I should have made her leave, and I was too slow, and Angie's dead—"

"*What?*" The car swerved an instant, then steadied again. "Mark, what happened?"

"It's all gone wrong. The owl, and my saving the belt at all…" Except, *it's still my only weapon—but I didn't make my mother's mistake, I can't be an addict, I can't!* "Take it! Just keep these away from me, see if I get better. If I can."

He caught at the brass buckle, to peel the belt off his waist and slap it down above the dashboard, then dug in his pocket to put the two spare scraps of leather beside it.

Henry's face was still hazy. "But, if Angie—"

"These are what killed her, them and me." The words barely made it past his lips, but at least now he could slump back against the seat… *not yet, he needs to know why…* "The belt lets us fly… well, not now, I used all its magic hunting her killer. Now I can barely stand…"

Kate spoke from behind them, gently. "I wouldn't worry about how your cousin talks just now, Mr. Maes. Losing my daughter hit us all—"

"I'm not on drugs, and I'm not crazy! Henry, were *you* on anything when you saw me jump out my window?" *Wait, that came out wrong…*

In the mirror behind them, Kate shook her head. "Again, I apologize; I suppose we're all to blame for what Mark's been through. I do know several places upstate that can give him some help—"

"Stop telling him I'm imagining it—you think you can put me away somewhere and make me forget what really happened to her? Henry, I dropped three floors, *and walked away,* you saw me," Mark said, grabbing Henry's shoulder. "We caught the Blades tonight, we even saved a man's life. And the killer chased me all over town, but I wasn't worth finishing off." He tried to remember if he'd ever understood why.

"Killer? Mark, what happened to Angie? You're not making sense, and you're scaring me."

"I'm *sorry!* I just lost control for a while, that's what too much flying does to you." He leaned around to glare at Kate and her look of manufactured pity. "Stop saying I'm crazy. I tried to avenge your daughter, and it all went wrong. But Henry—" he twisted forward again, "Please, just trust me. Keep these things away from me—maybe I can still work this out, but I don't know what's left with Angie... gone..."

He stopped then, and Henry's and Kate's own silences held themselves at a distance from his own. When the car finally slowed, Mark thought for a moment that Henry had an answer for him, but then he looked out of the window and saw they'd only arrived at his cousin's familiar townhouse.

As they climbed out, another car pulled up beside them and a man stepped out. It took Mark long moments to match the blurry shape and the oddly hesitant voice with Detective Lee: "Mark? I know you were... are you alright?"

"I don't have a scratch. Lucky me."

Lee didn't answer, just stood there, letting the badge gleam where he lifted up his coat.

"Detective," Henry began slowly. "His best friend was just... she died... he needs rest."

"I understand. I just need to ask him a few questions. Mark, it was you who pulled me out when those cars fell over, wasn't it?"

"Right. We saved you." *Blocking the gang cars was the last thing Angie did before she looked up and saw...* He twisted past Henry and rushed over to Lee. "Are you sure nothing followed you here? You've got to keep looking up! You can't relax, I think someone tried to kill you—" *For knowing too much about the magic.* He froze. Why was he telling *anyone* another word?

He turned and saw that Henry had the belt in his hand. Mark's words must have made some kind of impression, for his cousin to bother bringing it along.

"Look," Lee said slowly. "We just caught some higher-ups from two of the nastier gangs in Lavine; of course I'm keeping my guard up for anyone left. And, I guess I do owe you some time to rest."

"Thank you, Detective," Henry stepped in. "Rest is just what he needs—and when Mark's ready to talk to you, he'll be right here," he added, with a warning glance at Kate. "We're grateful to both of you for your concern. But I'm his family."

Mark let Henry help him to his home, pulling the gate shut, then opening the front door. Lee and Kate stood watching on the sidewalk. Little Terry was already bounding up, yipping for his master and ignoring Mark. Just like it had always been.

He smiled, then stiffened. "Hold on, we can't stay here anymore! If the killer was watching Lee, he'll know I'm here—"

"Let it go, Mark."

Mark tried to raise a hand to shake at his cousin, but his arm sagged weakly in the air.

Before he knew it Henry had taken that arm over his shoulders and was half carrying him to bed; it was only when Henry winced at setting him down that Mark remembered how bad his back was. He ought to feel something about that. But the bed was warm, warm and soft as it had always been. Even the humming of the humidifier in the hall was familiar.

I can't—can't let Henry be caught up in my disaster. He tried to sit up, but his body was just too heavy.

*   *   *

When he woke, the sun was too bright, too painful for him to curl his aching muscles up against and wall out. Mark lay still, staring at the pale paint of the walls.

One image crept back to him: Henry leading him inside, and setting the belt down on a shelf along the way to the guest room. Mark shuffled to his feet—*he'd want me out of bed, right?*—and made his way down the steps, but when he reached the hallway he saw that the shelf was empty.

"Your things are in a safe place."

Mark whirled round, flushing, to see his cousin sitting in the lounge, enjoying one of his huge sandwiches. The *Lavine Chronicle* lay next to him; when Mark sat down he saw it was open at the police reports for the previous night. Had someone glimpsed enough of his rampage to make Henry take his talk of flying seriously? *Well, at least he's keeping the belt safe—from me.*

But they didn't talk about the magic, or the killer. Or Angie either; instead Henry stumbled through words about sketches and layouts and ad campaigns as if this were just another day of the many he'd tried filling in as Mark's guardian. But even his droning wasn't the right shade of awkward.

Eventually Mark roused himself enough to convince Henry to head into work for what was left of the day… and when Mark heard the front door close he echoed its gentle click with a sigh that felt almost genuine. He started back to bed then, but as he hauled himself down the corridor his head began filling with images of all the places where Henry might have hidden the belt.

To keep from digging through drawers and closets, he forced himself to take Terry out for a walk, but the cold air seemed more to sting his skin awake but couldn't rouse his muzzy head. He tried swimming in the complex's tiny pool, but found himself drifting, numbly, on his back. His skin was half blue before he realized the floating only reminded him of flying.

Angie was still dead.

* * *

The next days were more of the same. He told Henry his vision was growing less hazy, and it was mostly true. There was no point trying to tell him about the weight he carried around, the walled-in sense of Angie being *gone*. He still didn't dare call her father. Nothing made sense except for the *need* he felt, to catch her killer, but whenever that thought stirred he felt again how his best efforts had been worthless; they hadn't even made the enemy think him worth killing, and how badly the magic had twisted him up just to try. Now he didn't even know where Henry had put the belt.

Now and then the question came back to him: wouldn't *she* be doing more, if she were in his place? Wouldn't she be searching harder, even with no hope left—or would she step back and try to make more of the life she still had? The question always circled back to the same answer: now, she *couldn't.*

Somehow, Roger Winton knew to send a condolence card to him at Henry's address. It was a beautiful thing, of silk-smooth paper embossed with evening skies. The rough scrawl under the printed calligraphy said only, *And when you're ready, I know a few places with job openings.*

"He just adds 'when you're ready'?" Henry scowled. "If that's his idea of tact, what's the point of sending a fine picture like that?"

There is *no good way to talk about this kind of loss.* And Mark figured that him working would mean something to Henry, when all sitting around did was hurt. "Maybe it's just what I need."

Still, just going out… wouldn't that be risking his enemies would spot him again? Thoughts prickled at him, of staying in, or forcing himself to go home and leave Henry out of it all. But all he could manage now was the one step.

Winton's office sent him a list, and he picked the job he hadn't tried, thinking Angie might have appreciated that reasoning—cab driver.

That thought helped him push through an hour's studying, and he found the licensing questions easier than he'd expected. The first day on the job he got a simple burner phone and kept himself to a day shift; he still needed to make a conscious effort to keep his eyes from blurring. But once on the road, he found he didn't need to do much more than follow routes through the streets and keep the company car clear of the cars in front, for hours at a time.

"It's strange," he told Henry that night. "I just keep going, and my memory of the city almost leads me around the turns. There's a nasty smell in the front seat though. It's like someone threw up there and they never quite cleaned the last of it."

Henry smiled at that.

On his second day on the job, Mark began to appreciate something else: most of his passengers didn't want him to talk. But the stretches of peace would end when he'd remember that he ought to be thinking about what to do *after* that day, and the next. Or he'd drive past a knot of glowering young men who could have been Blades, and start when he realized he hadn't noticed them until they were far behind him, stick figures in his mirror.

Driving was something to do. He would look at the streets and remember how he'd zigzagged through them with Angie, or seen the paths through them from above. The thought of going after the killer again still made his fingers tighten on the wheel, but what was the use?

"One fare heard about the Blades being rounded up. He said they still don't know who gave the police the tip," he told Henry that night.

"You told me it was your doing. Part of what you did with that belt." Henry spoke dryly; Mark couldn't tell if he was humoring him, or starting to believe him.

"I told him I hadn't heard. I've heard some of the guys at the garage talking about it too."

"I'm sure you have."

Of course; Henry would expect him to talk to people, to build up connections the way he always had before. To try.

Sometimes, when he drove, he was surprised he even reacted when another car braked in his path; surprised that his basic reflexes still had more purpose than he could muster on his own. But he had no interest in truly ending his pain, knowing how it would have hurt Henry, and what Angie would have thought. He couldn't pull backward, he could only hold on, and hope, despite himself, that a magical bird would dive at his throat to force him forward into the one struggle that mattered. And every night, he told himself it was too soon to ask Henry about the belt.

* * *

Mark felt a moment's unease when he turned onto Beekly; he had just stepped into view of his home, where someone could be watching for him. He tried a glance up and down the street, picking out a stocky woman, a mother and child, an older couple, but he couldn't sustain the effort to guess who might be who, and he just walked on, right up to his apartment building. Better to take some vague risk than go to the funeral in clothes that didn't fit.

He grabbed the blackest outfit he could put together, his eyes skidding away from the rows of boxes full of half-formed plans that seemed to belong to a stranger now. Back outside again, the sky was not clear, not overcast; white clouds drifted to and fro past the sun. Were any of those birds up there waiting for him?

That plump woman walking behind him, had she been on the street when he went inside, too? Mark couldn't remember, and part of him thought he should test her, let himself be followed. But by the time he thought of switching to the subway to see what she'd do, the woman had turned away up the street.

Did it matter? Should it? Sitting on the bus on the way to the funeral parlor, it grew harder to hold his head up with every street he rode past. It would have been easier with Henry... but if there was going to be trouble today, at least he had made his cousin stay clear of it.

Once he arrived, he found several dozen people in the chapel, circulating among the billows of white flowers along the walls, some already sitting in the pews. Not nearly enough people to honor Angie. Oddly, Mark couldn't find a one he didn't know himself.

"I remember when she got sick as a junior, and she wanted on the track team? I tell you, I never thought she'd..."

Mark nodded and drifted on. He could see her father up front, pale as the flowers and propped up on crutches, with a hulking shadow of a man behind him that had to be a police guard. The black rage in Dennard's eyes was no surprise to Mark.

"My roommates wanted to come too—we were always sorry she'd moved out on us so fast..."

Did *all* of them know him, and think he'd want to chat? *Well, I've always been helping Angie with her friends.*

Kate stood in one corner up front, opposite Dennard in the other. A woman had ways to go to a funeral in disguise; she was wearing a thick veil, and Mark recognized her mainly by the boy at her side, the boy he'd met in her condo, twelve-year-old James. The two of them stood silently, keeping back from the other mourners' hushed chatter.

An arm like a python closed around his shoulders.

Mark froze, too late to twist free, *I've got no magic, but they can't have come here...* the swarthy face was only inches from his; a fleck of pale skin showed at the man's jaw, hinting at makeup. The shock of wild hair had to be a wig. The Eel himself.

"Now don't do something stupid," came the thug's low rumble.

"Like come here?" *But do I mean him, or me?* Mark couldn't manage to clench his fists, couldn't fight. *Didn't that cop on the scene say they'd caught them all? Of course it wasn't so simple.*

"I came to tell you I'm in a giving mood," the Eel said. "You and your friend—your recording brought the cops down on us, but you nailed how Rafe gave the place to you too. That and his secret deals, and his power play that we needed old man Dennard dead and him in charge to pull it off... the whole scam is as buried as that traitor will be. If..." he added.

"If what?" Mark growled, and his eyes turned to the cop over at Dennard's back. One shout would bring him down on the Eel.

"If, when, Rafe comes after you now, you call me. Not the cops, *me."* He tucked a scrap of paper into Mark's jacket pocket. And he let go.

That's it?

Mark watched the Eel walk away. Just like that, the gang boss had rewritten the history of their whole vendetta against Dennard as nothing but a lie Rafe had pulled them into, pardoning Dennard just to discredit his own enemy. Without one glimmer of regret for Angie, even *here.*

And Rafe was somewhere out there too.

He knew he should shout. One deep breath, one yell, and every cop in earshot would rush to drag down the Eel. Instead, he watched him walk out the door.

"Who was that?" came a light, male voice behind him. "I know I don't know many of her friends—"

"Nobody much." Had *any* of these people really known her at all?

"So she really got that job out at Spitz? She talked like she would have been a great pilot someday. Are you sure there won't be a wake after this? It seems like she would have wanted a wake—"

Mark just walked away, and the man's babbling broke off behind him. He glanced at the door where the Eel had left, almost missing the callousness the thug had brought to the room. That honesty was easier than facing how all these people felt compelled to *say* something, as if any words would change the tiniest part of what had happened. And all of them pretending they knew a thing about Angie.

He glanced at his watch; just a few minutes to the service now. He walked forward, dodging people and brushing past the masses of white flowers along the wall.

A casket lay ahead. To someone who didn't know what lay inside, it could have been just a box of blank, beige wood. His mind couldn't take in the huge photo propped up beside it, just that it had to be something pretending to be Angie, the way it kept so still.

I never once tried to sketch her, not even from memory. Now there's no point.

"So your name's Mark Petrie?" A young voice; Mark turned to see that James had approached him. His mother hung a few steps behind. "I'm James."

"I know."

With his finer features and blond hair, the boy barely looked like Angie at all. His voice had an earnestness in it that made Mark swallow any retort he might have come up with, about having seen his bedroom, his home--or whether the boy had a clue about the magic that had brought Mark to his balcony before.

Instead, Mark looked past him to Kate. "Her father couldn't afford all these flowers. They're from you, aren't they? Thank you."

"Of course." The veil twitched as she nodded. And this time, Mark did hear a hitch in her voice.

James took another step toward him. "Mom wants us to say we're just friends of the family. But there's been so much to… to take in, you know?" His eyes darted around the room, then stared harder at him, pleading. "All that, and I never even got to meet my sister."

Is he saying Kate finally told him their secret, and he knows how much he missed? A bit late for her to come clean now.

Slowly, Mark said, "She wasn't easy to know. You must have heard these people," and he glanced around, "talking about her spirit and hard work and all. The things people say about everyone who's brought in here. But that really *was* what you would notice about her. Or there'd be one more thing, if you were with her any time you might think she'd be afraid, she wouldn't be. Not once, not once in ten years, was she ever... not until, the time the belt meant she couldn't trust herself to help someone... or when she thought she'd lose *us*—"

He stopped then, surprised his voice was still steady. *None of it matters.* He twisted away from them and squeezed past the wall of white petals back down the aisle.

Still no tears, no anything, except the uselessness of trying to talk. He saw her father glaring down at him from the front, and didn't bother to flinch. If the service didn't get moving soon he could just about march out of the place and miss nothing. *I ought to care about these people here, about my life, but she's just* gone.

"Mr. Petrie? I'm so sorry, it was an awful way for anyone to go— um..."

At least this little man knew he was babbling. Mark looked at him and found he didn't know him, but the nasal sound of his voice was familiar—oh God. "You're the cop who tried to call me with Angie's phone?"

"Um, almost," the man said, and the eyes in his wrinkled face slid away as he said it.

From behind Mark, another voice. "Now why would you say that, Osborn? If you want to talk to Mr. Petrie, you should wait till this is over. Unless you're avoiding someone." Detective Lee.

"What?" Mark blurted out, his thoughts stumbling. *When did Lee get here? And what's it matter if I talk to this Osborn?*

"Mr. Osborn's not an officer," the detective told him. "He's on staff with our medical examiner."

Osborn cut in quickly, "It was nothing really. I only wanted to give my regrets. I just don't see how she could have taken a fall like that out in the open—" He caught himself again.

And then came Joe Dennard's growl: "You think *this* is the place to go into that?"

He was right at Mark's elbow. Mark had even missed the clatter of his crutches.

Osborn looked at the floor, his face almost as pale as his accuser's. "Sorry."

Dennard wobbled himself into a turn around, and his eyes moved right past Mark, giving him only a contemptuous curl of his lip.

Softly, Osborn asked, "That officer who called you on the victim's phone, did he give a name?"

"No," Mark said. The question felt odd, but what did it matter?

But Dennard twisted partway back around on his crutches, letting out a gasp of pain but keeping his balance. A few heads turned along the nearer pews as he shuffled closer to Osborn and hissed, "What are you saying? You don't know who it was?"

"Never mind," Osborn said. He started to retreat, sliding along one of the empty pews.

Lee added, "I think we can talk about this later—"

Dennard pushed after Osborn. "Then why did you mention it now?"

Osborn edged back, out of the pew. "Nothing. Just a mix-up I got some blame for, that's all."

His back touched a mass of flowers, and he leaped forward again, then stumbled down the aisle and out of the chapel. Most of the crowd missed the confrontation, having already settled into the pews up front.

Dennard moved into the hall after Osborn, and Mark followed.

"So why don't you tell us about this mix-up? Who made that call?" Dennard was keeping his voice low, but Mark could hear his interest sharpening.

"It's just... Ms. Dennard's phone was listed with her effects. But then, sometime after I processed everything, it wasn't there." Osborn kept backing away, trying to whisper, but his words kept slipping toward a whine.

Dennard stayed on him, Mark following at his shoulder, not sure what to do. The murmuring voices in the chapel faded behind them. When Mark looked over his shoulder he saw Lee still standing there, motioning one of the funeral staff to… back away?

Dennard had eyes only for the retreating Osborn. "So you lost evidence."

"Not me! Some cop, some cop must have taken it. Mr. Petrie said he got a call, and that wasn't me."

Mark found himself taking a step forward, to Dennard's side, to say "So it was someone else there. Can you just sit down—"

"*Out* of my *way,*" was all Dennard said to him, before closing in on Osborn again. "So that wasn't you? If you didn't do a thing wrong, what made you come to my daughter's funeral—for one break in the evidence paper trail?"

"I said I'm sorry. There's just weird things I wonder about sometimes, that's all. I shouldn't have disturbed you." With that, he turned and yanked open the nearest door and stepped quickly through it.

The more that nasal voice spoke, the more Osborn did sound like the voice on the phone.

Dennard blocked the closing door with a crutch, and moved right after him. "How weird? *How weird?*"

"Just… the deceased's injuries, out in the street with no place to fall from like that. And the missing phone; nobody ever found it."

—As Mark reached the door, as Osborn's voice paused, he heard the murmurs back in the chapel. From the corner of his eye he saw one old man moving up behind them, curious.

"And the body was moved."

Osborn's last words left a silence after it that all but drowned out the clatter of Dennard's crutches. Bitterness stung Mark's mouth and he felt his fists clench, as Osborn gasped on,

"The deceased was on a gurney, I found it had been wheeled half out of the room, and it had a sheet over it that wasn't there before—"

Mark could feel Lee behind him, listening.

"You mean, not only did my daughter's phone go missing, but her body was moved? And you call this just a simple screw-up?" Dennard challenged. *"Just a screw-up?"*

"Yes!" Osborn stopped then, holding up his hands as if to ward off Dennard, or maybe to beg him. "My shift went on forever, you think I'd see everyone? So I dozed off for a few minutes, but that doesn't mean I misplaced anything—I mean, I was right in a chair—look, it just means someone thought the body should go somewhere else, then realized they were wrong and left it in the hall—it was late!"

The voices were getting louder. The old man was drawing closer behind them, morbidly taking in the whole show.

Mark stepped after Dennard, his mouth opening.

Dennard spat "Someone? Like *him?*" and he twisted to nod back to Mark.

What? *He thinks I'd try to steal her body—well, I did pick it up at first...*

The traitorous thought must have darted across his face too, because he saw Dennard's jaw clench. *"You!"*

"No!" Mark flared. "Of course I didn't—what do you think I'd—"

"Not him," Osborn cut in. "I never saw him! I didn't see anyone."

Again, Osborn turned to escape and again Dennard thumped after him, eating up the distance between them. "Is there anything you *do* see? God, is that even her in there?"

"Of *course* it is! Hell, that's our *first* duty, we check everything, from DNA to birthmarks to..." The little man's outburst faded then, and he took a slow step toward his tormentor, speaking more softly. "I, I know you want this to be just one more part of a world that fucked up, but there's no way. I'm so sorry; that really is your daughter, she's really gone."

The word bit at Mark inside, like it had done so many times already. For a moment the hall was still.

Except for the old man in the gray suit, still shuffling closer at their rear.

Then a younger man in flawless black scurried into view toward them. With a tireless funeral director's patience he said "Please, sirs. You're holding up the service. If you want to wait a moment outside—"

"Gone?" Dennard ignored the pleas of the young man and lurched toward Osborn. "Sure, and for a minute, even what was *left* of my daughter was gone? Let me guess, you had her and her phone right there in front of you before your eyes closed for a little *nap*. Just where *anyone* could get at them, right? Right?"

Osborn staggered backward. His back hit a door and he stumbled into the room behind him, Dennard still pressing at him. Beyond them, Mark could see pale horizontal shapes dotted around the room.

Where Angie had lain.

Just like in the morgue, before. Where Osborn had fallen asleep. Like Lee had fallen asleep in the junkyard, like the watchman who'd interrupted Mark and the bird had too. Mark's thoughts whirled, and crystallized. People in the killer's way were put to sleep. *Even in the morgue, the killer had gone after the belt, he hadn't let Angie rest!*

Mark gasped in a breath, ready to roar a question at Osborn.

A hand caught his sleeve, and he turned, a fist coming up... to see the shocked face of the funeral director at his elbow. Behind him were Lee, and even the nosy old man.

"Stop it!" Mark heard himself saying, and two steps brought him to Dennard's side. Somehow he dropped his voice back toward calmness: "It's... just a phone, isn't it? Can't we go back inside? You want Angie's friends to remember today like this?" He reached for Dennard's shoulder, and the father turned a snarl of rage on him, but Mark could feel his weight trembling on the crutches; so precarious a balance. "Please, it's not his fault."

"Sir, please!" the mortician added.

Dennard's eyes didn't leave Mark's. "I *know* it's not *his* fault. But you—"

"I *know*! I let her die!"

The words ripped out of Mark's throat, taking the moment of calm with them. His pulse was smashing against his temples as his fists clenched, crushing away morgues and lies and everything but the pure truth that he had *shown* Angie how to get herself killed, and at last her father was there to s*ay it!*

A cold soprano voice cut into the room: "Is this all that's left of you, Joe?"

Every head turned toward Kate. Mark saw Dennard's eyes blaze up, but his mouth locked, half-open, finally still.

—Just like she had done to keep Angie away from her as a child. Kate was shutting the confrontation down by drawing all the hate onto herself.

Kate moved toward her ex-husband, not sparing a glance for the others. "You spent years raising that girl. And now, when it's time to say goodbye, you're back here throwing accusations around." She reached him and leaned in close, so close that Mark only caught part of her whisper. "...seen what revenge..." She stopped then, and her eyes flicked to Mark as she drew back.

Dennard spasmed in pain and slumped against his crutches, silent.

The silence hung over them all for one relieved breath, then another. Mark felt his own rage settling too, shifting back toward the the target he needed to point it at. The killer.

Then Detective Lee cleared his throat. "I'm sorry, this has been an inexcusable breach of procedure. I'm sorry for your loss, and that it happened while your daughter was trying to help the police. I'm in your debt," he added, with the slightest glance toward Mark. "But if this case takes one more wrong angle it'll take a whole fleet of sailors to undo the knots, *so* after we've gone back and paid our respects, then we need to sit down and—"

"And what?" Kate didn't raise her voice, but the detective froze where he stood. "Unless you honestly think you can arrest us, you can stop wasting your time asking for things we don't know. That's the only decision you get to make here."

Lee blinked. He didn't turn from her gaze, but Mark could see the moment he backed down, outmatched. Mark forced out a slow breath, trying to let his head settle from the whirl of secrets and pain they'd skated around. One breath, then another…

Osborn dodged around them and all but ran from the room. Mark felt his breath ease as he watched the little man slip away up the corridor. For someone who'd been brushed by the killer's tricks, he was getting off easy.

And the old man turned after him. He didn't stay to watch the rest of them, he didn't drift quietly away, he headed straight after Osborn, as if he hoped to catch up to him.

Either he was some sick funeral chaser, looking for even more spectacle… or he had come to see what Mark and the rest knew… and Osborn too…

Just then Kate moved, walking briskly by in a click of heels. Mark left Lee and the funeral director closing in around Dennard, to scramble after her, and beyond her he saw Osborne and then his pursuer duck through the chapel door.

"Watch yourself!" he gasped to her, and the voice almost tore through his effort to hold it to a whisper. "That old man might be with the killer. We have to—"

"'We'?" and Kate didn't even slow her pace as she hissed "I *am* staying on guard. But don't tell me you've caught this revenge sickness too."

As she finished, right at the instant Mark opened his mouth to answer, they stepped through into the side of the chapel.

He halted as the heads in the nearest pews twitched toward them. Kate ignored the minister's questioning stare and moved quietly forward to sit next to her son.

And the old man… Mark caught a glimpse of him in a middle pew, and forced himself to look past him and start walking to a seat in the back row. Back there, he could watch him—and, keep some distance from the minister up front who could never do Angie justice.

He thought he saw one or two frowns on the faces he passed, following his retreat to the rear. But they didn't *get* it, not her friends, not past acquaintances who'd wandered in; even Angie's mother couldn't face it. Angie's killer was still out there… unless he was right here.

Then the minister began to speak, and Mark pressed his fists on the cold wood of the pew to block the words out. He filled his mind with the images of the old man he'd glimpsed; not quite old after all, his face had only a few lines, but those were deep, haggard shapes as if he'd be beaten down by the years, and his ratty suit wasn't much better. Mark saw his head turn; he was watching Osborn make for the exit behind the chapel.

Take control of the moment; it was was what Angie would have wanted, he told himself as the minister's meaningless words rolled past him. He couldn't miss this chance, if this intruder—the stranger sitting alone, one of the few faces Mark didn't know—could be the one who'd sent the Blades against her father and *dared* to touch her.

He looked up at the picture of Angie, the life-sized figure frozen in place, gazing up at the sky. Concentrating on her killer was what she would have wanted from him. *Or else it's all I have left.* Find out the truth while he had the chance, and worry later about if he was only falling into paranoia, or guilt.

The tears on his face must belong to someone else.

When the casket finally rolled into the flames, he realized the old man had slipped away.

CHAPTER TWELVE

TRANSIT

Even from the back of the chapel, Mark had too many people to brush past to get to the door. But if he didn't answer any of the *sorry*s and *anything I can do*s, he wouldn't have to slow down.

It still took an eternity before he burst out into the sunlight. The sidewalk was crowded, too many figures blocking his search for the old man.

I only looked away for a minute, didn't I? I can't *have lost my one lead!*

Then he saw the stranger's slate-gray suit and slow gait, just ambling past the flower shop next door to the funeral home. Mark hurried after him, as quick as he could without actually pushing through the people around him. If this really was more than a nosy old man, it was no time to get himself noticed.

Then the man turned into the shop's parking lot, and Mark growled under his breath. If he lost him just for not bringing a *car*... he reached for his phone, thinking to call Dennard or Kate, but stopped. They'd never join him in time.

Instead he pushed forward faster. The parking lot had a thick sculpted bush by its corner, big enough to stand behind and try to catch the license plate once the car passed. Mark started running, wishing he had the belt.

Then a figure loomed out of the crowd ahead, and Mark froze.

Taller than the old man, disguised in mismatched clothes that might have been fished out of gutters, Rafe strode toward him, swinging his arms, ready to smash something. "Knew you'd show up here! You think you can use bugs on me and——"

"Threats? Cut the crap!" Mark pushed forward again with a sudden eagerness, and in moments his face was inches from Rafe's burning eyes. In a lowered voice, he added, "You've got the cops *and* the Blades after you, and you think you can start trouble right here on the street?"

He gave a slow, warning glance around them. As he did he caught a glimpse of the old man moving deeper into the parking lot, still in sight…

"I was a *leader* with the Blades, until you!" Rafe snarled. His hand slid inside his pocket as he added "Save it for someone who has something left to lose."

You think you've *lost something?* Moving on their own, Mark's hands slammed out and shoved Rafe back a step, and when Rafe hesitated, he lunged at him, hissing, "You did it to *yourself,* making secret deals behind their backs. And then I bet your new boss *used* you and threw you away!"

Just for a moment, Rafe's eyes flickered. "Deals? You think I'd screw around on my people?"

"I heard it! All those secret calls the Eel caught you at—*they* told you to keep the Blades pushing at Dennard and us."

Rafe flinched again… and Mark stole another glance past him, tracking for the man who might be his lead to the real enemy.

When he looked back, he saw Rafe had followed his gaze.

With a cold smile, the thug said "So, it's about that old man? Why him?"

"What, your boss didn't tell you?"

As Mark said it, a thought flared: *Rafe* doesn't *know about him, that's how cut off from the schemes he is. And he knows it.*

Fast as Mark could, he followed up with, "That's the killer's *real* spy, the one he sent to watch the funeral now that you're history. Take a good look!" He stabbed a finger toward the stranger's back, where he hunched against a battered car in the parking lot. "Ragged, wasted, he can barely walk—but you're learning all about dressing in rags now, aren't you? You have to, to go out without 'your people' gunning you down!"

Rafe's teeth clenched, but now he was looking around them, instead of glaring at Mark. More and more people were eyeing them, starting to gather around them. Their clash had gone long past whispering by now.

And Mark pressed on "Are you still covering for him? What did he promise you, that you'd take over the Blades? Look at you now... was it worth it?"

"You tell me," and suddenly the nervous look on Rafe's face split into a predator's grin. He leaned in close, and whispered "Just what *would* be worth pushing Dennard?"

Mark froze. *My God, he's playing* me! *He wasn't waiting here to kill me, he wanted to get me talking about what his boss was after.*

"I... wish I knew," Mark said, and that was true enough.

"Oh no. You're in too deep for that—"

Then, from somewhere in the crowd, came a harsh voice: "Alright, freak, leave the poor bastard alone!"

It was one man stepping out of the crowd, but Mark heard other rumbles from it. And the next moment Rafe was dashing away.

Part of Mark was registering the hostile or puzzled glares coming from some of the passersby—not just at Rafe but at him too—but mostly he savored letting his breath slide out again, letting some of the anger fall away. Rafe could have been a second away from stabbing him, and he'd barely *cared*.

There, walking out of the lot, the haggard old man came watching him.

Mark stared back, an instant too long, and their gazes locked. So much for tailing anyone.

If this stranger was even part of it. If he *was* just nosy, Mark had just given Rafe reasons to go after an innocent man…

Then the pale man gave Mark one slow, ominous shake of his head, and moved past him.

Mark watched him start up the sidewalk, trying to think what the gesture could mean. Finally he started after the man; it was better than just letting him go.

The old man walked faster now, wobbling as he did, fast enough that Mark had to weave and twist through the crowd to keep him in view. *Don't think about what the killer might do if he sees me still on his spy, or even if the old man's armed.*

A knot of corporate types in suits clustered on the sidewalk ahead. Mark saw the old man weave onto the grass to step around them.

Then, a stumble. The haggard man bumped into one of the suits, and staggered back, one step, that tottered into another—before anyone could reach for him, he toppled backward.

Straight into the oncoming traffic.

Screams ripped through the air. Mark's stomach clenched as he watched the impact, the body spinning away… it was already over.

The people ahead stared and shouted at each other. Tires squealed as cars tried to twist around the crumpled heap in the road. But Mark had to be the only one who knew enough to accept what his eyes had shown him: the old man hadn't tripped, hadn't been pushed, he'd *faked* that stumble. He'd thrown himself to his death.

To get away from me?

Mark whirled and twisted between onlookers, scrambling to get away from the sight. With every step he saw the dead man's last moments, and the chillingly calm look he'd given Mark. Before he'd walked away, to his death. What had the killer done to him?

A block later, the thought had formed: There could be no more standing around powerless, no more being *blind* to his enemy's powers—he had to get to the belt.

The crowds were thicker around the next corner, and he slid in among them, hoping they'd give him some cover if someone else tried to follow him back to Henry's. If *anywhere* was safe now.

Someone made that man take his own life—*without showing a trace of fear on his face.* And the killer had enough spies under his thumb to throw one away, just to keep him from being followed?

Mark stumbled down toward the subway, feet aching, risking one glance back up at the sky and wishing he could spot if there were pigeons on the ledges tracking him through the crowd. If that was even the same enemy… but sending a suicidal spy *felt* like the same same ruthless, manipulative touch that had sent Rafe and the Blades to target Joe Dennard… left notes they'd begun to trust until the same magic had turned against Lee… then Angie… and if its influence even stretched into the morgue and the funeral how could anyone fight it?

When the next train came, Mark sagged down onto a seat, a shell of gasping breath and sweat wrapped around one bitter thought: *Angie would be telling me there's always a way.*

It was all he could hold on to, as the train clattered past one stop after another. It pulled out of the tunnels' shelter onto onto too-bright surface tracks, and other passengers in the car glanced at him; he tried not to wonder if any of them had been sent by the killer, or if one of them would be the next to get hurt just by being near him.

His phone rang.

He stared at it for two rings before he took in the name on the screen. Roger Winton.

Mark fought down a shiver; this was no time to worry about bad omens. "Hello?"

"Mark? What's this I hear from the cabbies? Wrong information on your ID forms, and Johanson says you dropped *my* name as a way to excuse it?"

"Um." Mark blew out a breath, trying to push his thoughts back to his job. He'd had some fear traced from it back to Henry's home, so he'd faked some details... "I guess it was a moment of paranoia. I mean, I was hiding from the Blades a few days ago. You said the gang's pretty much broken?" Except for the Eel, and Rafe.

The woman in the next seat glanced back at him, and Mark realized he hadn't kept his voice low.

Winton scoffed "After all those arrests? Everyone knows they're finished."

So your friends on the police don't tell you everything. Still, a thought shot through Mark like a pang of sudden hunger; Winton had helped him once, even before the job, and with his money he could be a real edge in finding a hidden enemy.

The second thought slammed through him right behind that one: people searching for that enemy got *killed.* Or the schemer could already have gotten to Winton... or to anyone Mark reached out to. The middle-aged woman in the next seat was already shooting him another curious glance.

"Sorry." Mark's voice sounded short in his ears, but he did want some distance from his friends now. "I'll fix those forms; shouldn't be a problem."

"Well, don't throw my name around like that. Bye." And he hung up.

Mark looked at the phone a moment longer. Had he really been that close to dragging someone else into this fight? He still hadn't even warned Dennard or Kate about how their enemy could simply throw away lives.

The train drew to a stop. People scattered up and down moved for the doors, but the woman in the next seat was still studying Mark. He made himself look calmly away from her and joined the march out the door... and she stayed behind, in her seat.

Mark started up the platform, trying not to be caught looking behind him again. The eyes around him felt like prickles on his skin.

After two more trains and many more twists around the streets, he reached Henry's familiar block as the sun was setting. The wariness he'd stretched tight around himself seemed unnatural; the family next door was setting up a noisy autumn barbecue in their yard. He watched them a moment and tried to let the sound of their carefree voices steady his nerves. *I can't get the belt back if Henry thinks I'm afraid of my own shadow. Even if we all need to be.*

When he stepped inside he heard the sounds of more cooking from the kitchen. The overhead extractor fan was humming while chicken fried in a pan. Henry stood watching it, doing tiny bending exercises to help his bad back.

"Smells great," Mark called over the fan, although he couldn't really smell much, with the fan roaring away. "Sorry I took so long getting back."

"You said you wanted to face the funeral alone." Henry sighed, and tried to hide it by looking away to turn the chicken. "I knew it wouldn't be easy for you."

"It… wasn't. But I found out I'm not on the Blades' hit list anymore." *Now there's just another dead man and a fiend who breaks into morgues and might be watching us now, and Rafe—don't say that—* Carefully, he added "Anyway, I think it's time I took the belt back."

"The belt?"

Henry had been turning to face him, but with that, he froze and looked away, as if he were hiding his reaction. Then he slowly turned back to Mark.

"You really think," Henry said, eyes narrowing, "that old belt was what had you running around wild. And that it lets you *fly.*"

"You saw me drop out my window. You've read about some of the rest." Mark nodded at the dining-room table, where he'd seen Henry poring over newspaper reports of the scattered "vandalism" he'd done chasing the killer. "I'd show you, but I used up all the belt's power until I take it back to the right place. And really, Henry, why would I come up with a lie that crazy?"

"I don't *know* why. First you say a few pieces of leather are so dangerous I have to hide the from you, and now you want them back." Henry scowled. "Mark, I don't know which half of that makes less sense."

The part where the enemy kills people I catch watching me, but he let me go that night?

Mark forced his frustration back, trying keep his voice even. "What I asked you to do was to keep it and see if I got better. The thing is, that was what Angie and I had started doing for each other with the belt: spotting each other, making sure neither of us used it too long." His voice didn't even break as he said her name. "This time, I'll be trusting you, and you won't have used the magic at all. So: you can see I'm doing better than I was. And you have my word I'll hand it back to you after one night, and let you decide if I'm still in control before you let me use it again.

"And," he added quickly, "I *know* that's just what addicts promise. But we were working out that the magic's grip does fade over time. And the only way to really know for sure is to see if you can trust me, for one night. Or do you really think after what Dad's stash did to Mom I'd let *anything* turn me into her?"

The last words rushed out on their own, tightening his throat. He kept his eyes on Henry's, searching, looking for something else behind that suspicion.

Smoke stung at his nose. Henry turned away and scooped charred chicken pieces out of the pan, drops of fat spattering everywhere. Even after he'd fumbled all the cutlets over to a platter and set the tongs down, Henry took his time before turning back to Mark.

"Trust you, you say. Mark… why don't you take me to this place that lets you fly? If it works, we can talk right then. Or if you see it doesn't," he added, "then I think we *really* should talk right then."

Mark forced himself to hold eye contact, to not reveal how much of the secret he'd been glossing over. "Mmm. I don't think that'd be safe for you. I can show you some when I come back, so you don't have to get too close to—"

The doorbell rang.

Mark froze, and saw his own frustration mirrored in his cousin's eyes. The bell rang again. Henry sighed and trudged out to open it, Mark watching from behind him, trying not to assume the worst.

Beyond the door stood Detective Lee.

Mark swallowed. *All that work to get back without being followed, and Lee just drives up to Henry's door.*

A woman in an apron, from the cookout next door, was tugging at Lee's arm and chirping, "If you're throwing a party you should all join us, there's plenty for everyone, and Henry never—"

"I won't be staying. Please..." Lee looked almost embarrassed as he waved her off and pushed inside.

Mark stole a glance out the door as Lee turned to close it—and the detective caught it.

"Last time you said I could've been followed, right? I'm not stupid. I was careful. And we need to talk, both of us. Or all three of us." His gaze moved to Henry, then returned to Mark, and one huge eyebrow lifted upwards ever so slightly.

Mark saw the threat; Lee was ready to dig up the worst he knew about him right in front of Henry, if Mark didn't tell him the whole truth in private. *But if we split off and Henry doesn't trust me with the belt, we could all be dead.*

Henry cut in. "Detective, please! Mark just got back from his oldest friend's funeral—"

"I was there too, Mr. Maes. But I'm here to talk about Jerry Tate." He looked back at Mark. "That's the old ex-con who ended up dead today, an hour after I saw him at Ms. Dennard's funeral talking to our medical examiner. But why was he there? And why is he dead of an apparent 'accident', when he was thirty years too old to have any ties to a gang, and he had no connection to Ms. Dennard, either. Unless that was the point: use someone with no connections, and nothing to lose."

Mark kept his gaze on the detective's, and his face still.

Lee went on "At least I got Osborn, the M.E., to a safe house. And he told me what had happened that night in the morgue. That one moment Ms. Dennard's body was in order, and the next he must have fallen asleep, because when he woke up he saw it had been moved."

Mark heard a faint gasp from Henry. He didn't look over; kept watching Lee's face.

"And, well, I could tell you the rest, if you stop treating me like an idiot. One thing is clear: you're the only one who knows what's going on here—or are you in on it too?" He looked over at Henry again.

"Um." Henry's face was pale, but he stepped in front of Mark. "Detective, you're talking about our friend's *body*. This has to be some kind of harassment—"

"*This* is harassment? I've let you alone for days, ever since her death. I don't understand how she took a fall like that, I don't understand the other injuries on that Blade Rafe Martinez shot, as if he'd been pressed under weights, or how you always escape—" This time he sighed as he broke off, and his big frame seemed to deflate. "Mark, I know you saved my life—and that's saving me from what sounds too much like a murderous case of Osborn's dozing off. I've given you time, I've tried to think it through myself, but I can't wait forever for you to trust me.

"Because if you don't, someone else in the department won't be as nice. And if it comes to that, we both know whoever killed Angie is going to go free. Think about it."

He walked away. For a moment Mark could hear the sounds of the barbecuers outside, then the door swung shut. The detective was gone.

"Trust?" Henry turned to Mark, a scowl tightening over his face. "You were just asking me to trust you, and all the while you're keeping secrets about… murders and, what, something about Angie *in the morgue?"*

"Hold on, I just found all that out today!" Mark countered. "Up to now there's been no sign of the killer since… *that* night. I was starting to think he'd given up on me. And I wanted to keep you away from the danger. *And* I couldn't run in here and give you more reasons to think I've lost my mind—"

"So you look right at me and lie? And you let me find out from a detective—you don't even tell me there still *is* a danger?" Henry shook his head. "Why are you keeping us in the dark like this? What are you really hiding—are you even trying to come out of this alive?"

"What?" Mark stared at his cousin. "You think I've got some kind of death wish?"

"I… no, not that. But, you never did tell me about the place this 'magic' comes from."

"The power site isn't…"

Mark stopped. He looked at his cousin, thinking of how he'd seen the killer's man calmly take his own life—nobody who knew the magic's secrets was safe—

Henry's right, I have *been hiding it all. Thinking like an addict, anything to get what I want. He's already involved, and it's time to start trusting.*

"It's in Rosewood Park, in the half-fenced-off thicket by the Summer and Fall Streets parking lot." The words should have been liberating, but instead they made him hang his head like a traitor, betraying what only he and Angie's family had shared.

Henry looked at him a moment, then turned and shuffled back to the kitchen.

Mark stayed where he was, calling after his cousin, "You're right, I've been letting this make me crazy. And you *are* in danger—maybe more than me; I've seen how the killer uses people. Forget about helping me with this, you should get as far out of town as you can go. And maybe I *should* talk to Lee, so he has some idea what's after him too. He might even be able to help me."

Why was it so hard? Was it the magic, making him too jealous and greedy over it to share, or was it just this hard to open up to anyone besides Angie? He sighed; this was *all* wrong.

Henry slid open a kitchen cupboard, and reached deep inside. Then he set the belt and the two strips in Mark's hand.

"I'm not going anywhere. I'm making sure you bring the bastard down."

* * *

That evening—just long enough for the streets to grow darker but not emptier—Mark set out. He'd borrowed a trick from Rafe, collecting enough old clothes to wrap a concealing "homeless" look around himself. At the last minute he wondered if someone might try tracing his phone, and decided to leave it behind.

The cool roaring subway trains brought him most of the distance. He hated to use the same dodge so often, but as long as the drained belt left his senses blind, he meant to keep solid concrete between himself and any birds hidden in the sky.

Leaving the last train, he watched from the corner of his eye as one overweight man seemed to be keeping pace with him, but finally turned away. He stepped out onto the street.

What would a bird see from above? Mark moved along the thicker knots and currents of night-going people; the louder they laughed and argued and filled the sidewalk with their own worries, the more cover they gave him. The breeze ruffled his scarf, teasing him with how much open space, and seductive power, he meant to leap into again.

He found he'd gone a block past Spring Street and the turn to the park. *I'm stalling.*

He made his way back toward it. Not many couples or dog-walkers ventured into the darkened green expanse at this hour, but each figure he did see just might be one of the killer's spies.

All he could do was hope the killer hadn't guessed that this was the one place he had to come back to no matter where he flew. Restoring the belt's power was almost a worse weakness than its addiction.

No, it's more than that, came the sudden thought. *Anyone* who saw him at the hidden place, then got their hands on the belt itself and the words, could use the magic themselves, same as he had. He gasped, twisted his head to shoot a glance at two figures walking by the parking lot... still walking on by. And he was already in plain view, shuffling toward the thicket itself.

All he could do was keep walking, and hope nobody was out there watching.

Then he slipped in among the trees, moving quickly as he felt his way through the branches. Now that he was camouflaged, the anxious thought didn't fade, it gathered new fears onto it: *if what the killer wants is this magic's secret... no wonder he made me chase him all over the sky and then left me alone—because I still wouldn't go back to replace the power I burned up.* If the killer wanted the magic... sure, he could push Dennard into using it, trick Mark and Angie with fake tests from Kate...

Murder Angie to make me reckless...

The cold, hideous reasoning coiled around Mark like a chain. Each link fit, wrapping tighter around him with each branch he squeezed past in the dark. Until he reached the little slope at the center of it all... with still nothing but blind hope that the killer wasn't watching his every move.

"Zha-Daruath."

Power ripped the old world away. The blaze of energy surged around his waist and through his nerves, made him lock his knees to hold down the urge to *leap* straight into the sky. *Steady, keep control.*

Then, far out across the park, he felt the flicker of the killer's power in the air.

No! Mark crouched down in a crunch of bracken that sounded like thunder to his shocked ears. But... the resonance had to be halfway across the park.

He felt it drawing closer. But as it did, he could sense it swinging to one side, then the other, weaving in the air. *Is it out here searching for me, and didn't see me coming in?*

Mark's breath grew ragged, waiting. The bird closed in in a wide, lazy path that seemed *different* from the nimble hawk he'd chased before. Was this the owl again, was that the form the killer used to search instead of fight? Then it passed on by.

Gone. Mark crouched in the dirt as the sensation faded into the distance. He counted another sixty of the slowest breaths he could manage, as much to steady his nerves as to let the enemy go.

Then he tightened the magic to drift up through the thickest of the branches, and then hurled himself *up.*

Raw force snatched him through a blast of cold air. *Stay in control*—Mark felt his vision gray and eased back, and the screech of wind slowed to let him hear the city noises filtering up to him with the strange, balanced clarity of distance. The broad dimness of the park was already drifting away behind him.

"You missed your chance to spot me," he whispered to the night. "Looks like my magic's got better eyes than yours."

He levelled out until the wind seemed to melt away, as he blended into its motion. Then he closed his eyes and let his sense of magic fill him.

The park's center of power burned behind him, but even against that backdrop he could make out the other faint traces threading through in the air. Just as he'd felt on his last flight, hints of magic seemed to ripple out from the earth and the sky—could he catch a ribbon of magic leading back to the park? And then learn to find traces to whatever source the enemy used?

But the flickers were too faint. One brushed his awareness only to fade when he reached for another. There were no trails, no patterns.

And I can't risk trying this all night, I know what that does to me. Mark peeked out at the rows of lights passing below, and concentrated on the cold on his skin, proof the magic hadn't numbed him yet. *For Angie, for everyone, I have to make this work.*

The killer's magic moved in from below him. The bird itself.

Mark dangled helplessly, feeling the presence rising, circling up toward him. His teeth clenched at the truth that he could never outfly his enemy, could only duck away and let the killer win again.

Then one idea stirred. He had the speed for a sudden dive directly down at the killer, if he could *move* himself to that spot. If he could do more than rise and fall with the wind.

The bird drew closer, somewhere below his feet. Already closer than it had followed him before.

Before. Mark reached for the memories of that magic-crazed night battle, of his body hanging in the air with the killer somewhere too far below, the moment he'd feared he'd lost his target below him—how dazed he'd been from the rush of magic, the blind, instinctive way he'd reached power *around...*

He froze in the air, no longer moving with the current. Gravity balanced and held and locked him in place, and cold wind brushed past his skin again.

On his next heartbeat, the bird passed exactly below him and he slammed himself *down.* Mark heard the owl's shriek of surprise as his power poured out in a shockwave of a kick that dragged him earthward. Force wrenched up his spine—red filled his eyes—but he felt the owl slide clear—

The haze of red in his vision melted to gray as Mark let the dive ease. Dark and light shapes rushed up from below, too fast...

He tumbled down onto a roof and rolled, limp, over the edge before he trusted himself to float again. He drifted down to sprawl on his hands and knees, on shifting plastic bags. His nose told him the rest: he'd landed in someone's garbage.

Shaking his head to clear it, he felt for the owl again and found it still circling above. And then it turned and flew away.

"Scared, now?" Mark jumped to his feet, but he kept himself on the ground to dash out of the alley and up the street. The owl's presence had already faded to just a prickle in his mind.

But I can't just chase it, the moment it sees me I lose—think! He stared around at the dark street, trying to match the dim shapes against the taxi maps, the skylines he'd flown by. He needed to get ahead of it, unseen.

He bolted up Lansing Avenue toward the subway stop. The owl had faded out of range ahead, but if just this once it held its course long enough…

Then, as he dodged around a startled family on the sidewalk, he felt it again. The bird was heading back *again.*

How'd it swing around that far left? But Mark held his pace; a few more seconds of running brought him to the subway stairs, and safety. He trotted down into the cool underground, still too quick for the enemy to have spotted him—he hoped.

After running free so long, balancing his way down the stairs felt worse than standing still. He wove around one upward-climbing man who was bundled against the cold, catching a warning look from a pudgy transit cop. *Right, I've still got the homeless outfit;* he gave the cop a reassuring wave and popped a token in the turnstile.

When he reached the wide, echoing platform, he glanced at the map of brightly-colored routes on the wall. He'd been wrong, most trains crossed too many blocks to let him out anywhere near sensing range of the bird above. But at least he *could* still sense the bird passing by.

Then it stopped. And slowly, slowly, he felt it start down the steps.

Mark saw a woman up the platform back away from him, and he realized he'd spun around and was gaping at the corner still blocking his view of his enemy. The bird was leaving the open sky it ruled and trapping itself down *here?*

And yet, from the measured speed he felt as the enemy closed in, it didn't move like a bird any more. As if the owl, the hawk, had changed again.

But... there were no screams. Around Mark hummed the low echoes of the subway at night that swallowed the sounds of the few people to venture down there... but still, shouldn't there have been *someone* on the steps who saw a bird change into a person?

Mark stepped around the corner, knowing even as he moved that he was giving up his concealment; he tensed the belt's energy ready to pin and crush his enemy at a touch. His eyes locked onto the killer's magic.

There, that slight man that wobbled down the steps, pulsing with unseen power—but something about him seemed familiar—

The scarf. The orange scarf and the pale face made him the man Mark had almost run into on his way down the steps, and now that same stranger was weaving toward the overweight transit officer—

He stumbled, and the transit cop caught him. The magic *moved...* and the first man slumped over, abandoned, and the cop leaned him back to sit against the wall as if he'd simply fainted, now that the killer had possessed a new victim. His head was turning around.

Mark dove back behind the corner, afraid the killer's stolen eyes had seen him watching, then poured all his strength into a dash across the platform. He swept past the startled woman and heard her gasp at his bounding pace. The enemy's power lay well behind him, but all Mark could think of was to get away from that *touch.* One wild leap swept him over the tracks and onto the far platform, where he bolted for the opposite stairs.

When he reached the surface he twisted toward the emptier side of the street and kept running, anything to put more distance between him and that presence below, the power that could turn anyone to its use.

No wonder the killer could send old Jerry Tate to his death. And get past Osborn in the morgue... and use Osborn's own nasal voice to speak to Mark through Angie's phone. Even the birds could be more possessed tools... The killer had been slippery enough when it had seemed like it *became* an owl, but what if he'd never come near the enemy's real body?

Can I even find the puppetmaster?

Mark stopped running many blocks later, hands on his knees, chest heaving, next to an all-night diner. He slumped into the back booth, out of view of anything that might fly by the window. It took his best smile and most of his cash for coffees to get the waitress to trust him, but at least he had a place to think.

Mark put his head in his hands and broke off searching for magic, looking up only to check that the rare graveyard-shift workers who slogged in were no more than they seemed. Every second he used the belt might push him closer to madness again. But, that awareness it gave him was the only protection he had.

Track down the killer. Catch the enemy himself off-guard, don't keep chasing birds and body-hopping presences as if I could keep up with them. The magic itself might the only thing Mark could trace... if he made those faint, fragmented threads into some kind of trail... before he burned out his brain following vapors?

"I can't."

The words slipped out once, and he clamped his fingers over his mouth before they could escape again. But even to get justice for Angie, what did he have left?

I can't do this alone.

* * *

The first glints of gold were in the sky when Mark emerged from the subway. His eyelids felt like the heaviest part of him, but he still had the strength to sense that no magic was lurking over Henry's house. He staggered inside and to his room, set the belt on the nightstand and fell into bed—

A sound. He bolted upright, shaking away dreams of owls and Angie to find Henry peering at him from the doorway.

His cousin jumped at his sudden movement, but then he ventured an uneasy smile. "Good… reflexes, I guess."

Mark looked at Henry a moment… and then felt the belt dangling in his hand. *When did I grab that up?*

He felt for the magic, and a sigh of relief slipped from him to feel *no* enemy control over his cousin. Or anywhere else in the block.

He got to his feet, swaying, forcing himself away from the blessedly soft bed. "It was… a long night. But at least I know a little about what I'm fighting," he added. It was the best he could say.

"So you—did you…" Henry motioned to the belt.

The hesitant, awkward hope in his cousin's voice stabbed at Mark, like watching one glimmer of sunlight try to push through a raincloud.

But it was *one* worry that had a simple answer. Slowly, he tightened the magic, and felt his feet pull away from the floor.

Henry's mouth opened, a fraction at a time, as though Mark's ascent was drawing his jaw down. When Mark's head brushed the ceiling, his cousin's eyes almost popped out.

Mark grinned. He dropped, then caught himself in midair again. *Just like I practiced with Angie,* came the bitter thought, and his grin faltered.

"So, you *did* jump out that window," Henry managed to say.

"That's right. Like I told you. But here." And before he could hesitate, Mark slapped the belt down on the bed and forced his hand back from it, then dug the two leather strips out of his pocket and dropped one of them next to the belt. "If I still keep this," and he held up the other strip, "I won't have enough power to fly much, but I'll still sense it if the killer starts following me again."

"And you're actually handing the rest over to me?" Henry's face was calm now, but his voice was still shaky.

"I have to, for a day or so. One thing I've realized is that I won't catch the killer in one night. This could be a long haul, and I have to stay in control."

Henry nodded. He reached over, gingerly, and picked up the leather talismans.

"In fact," Mark added, as his thoughts crystallized, "I'm going to need more help. Detective Lee's already part of this—and he put together that Osborn dozing off was like what happened to him. And I think he understands that magic isn't something he can write up in one of his reports." He hesitated, hoping he was right. *The killer* possesses *people and yet I still want to trust someone—but the killer's already tried to kill Lee once. He needs to know.*

"You're probably right." For the first time that morning, Henry smiled cleanly.

Mark dug out his phone and Lee's card, and punched in the digits.

"H-hello?" answered a woman's voice.

Mark smiled at the thought of Lee with a wife at home. "Morning. Can you put Detective Lee on?"

"I'm sorry…" The voice quavered, and faded until he could barely hear the next words. "The detective's car crashed tonight, and he, he was killed—who is this?"

Mark saw Henry staring at him, knew the horror had to be written all over his face.

Lee was dead—of an "accident," when Mark had seen him just that evening. It might have happened while Mark was hiding out in the diner, being grateful the killer had stopped searching for him. Or maybe before Mark had even gone out, the enemy could already have caught the detective at the wheel and slipped into his mind…

Lee was gone—*and I never warned him.*

CHAPTER THIRTEEN

STILL NIGHT

Mark? What do you want?"

What was that in Joe Dennard's voice? It wasn't sharp anger coming through the phone, he just sounded… heavy. *At least he answered; that's more than Kate did.* Mark squirmed on the hard kitchen chair.

"Sorry for bothering you. But I've got news."

"So, go on."

Mark took a deep breath. He saw Henry nod goodbye at the doorway, then heard the door click as his cousin headed off to work, like a late start on any other day. Was that courage Henry was showing, or just blind optimism that the killer wouldn't go after him next?

"Detective Lee's dead," Mark sighed. "He crashed his car—"

"But you think it's the same thing that got Angie." Dennard's voice tightened.

He used to leave so much unsaid on the phone, and now he just blurts it out, no matter who might hear. The only way I can ask him for help is face to face. "The police say it was an accident. Or it could have been Blades still out there, or something." He took a steadying breath. "I hope you're still watching your back. Is there a time we could meet—"

Dennard cut in "I let Lee walk away with just a peek at what could be after us. And so did you. You think knowing more could have kept him alive?"

"Maybe." And Dennard could be next if they couldn't find the enemy, *soon*. Mark's eyes went to the cupboard drawer where Henry had put the belt, this time right before his eyes as a test for him. *I won't touch it today, I won't!* "I kept telling myself if he got any deeper in, it just made him more of a target."

"Or knowing the truth might have saved him. And you'll never be sure." This time Dennard made it a grim accusation, at Mark and himself.

"I'm starting to get that. Just... watch yourself," he added. No, Joe Dennard was too hurt and too worn out to help him search. *And this might be the last time I can speak to him if the killer does decide he's a threat.* "I think that's all we can do. Sometimes it seems like the 'gangs,'" and he made the word a warning for how much more they were actually facing, "will always be here, with no way to stop them."

"I could have told you that years ago. But, take care of yourself. For her sake, anyway," and Dennard hung up.

Mark set the phone down on his lap, scowling. He had a sudden image of Angie's father in a deep hole, slowly sliding further down into it and not bothering to try and climb out. Even if the killer let him live.

Or... the belt was right there, Mark could just grab it and *make* the traces of magic make sense. No matter what it did to him... anything would be better than sitting through all day and all night *waiting* for the magic's addiction to let him go. *I'm only guessing that the killer isn't setting up an accident for Dennard or someone else right now.*

But he'd tried searching for the killer just by tracking his magic, and he'd failed. "It's not being scared if I just *can't* yet. It's *not.*" He banged a fist on the cupboard drawer, hard enough to make himself roar in pain.

* * *

Taking a taxi shift was a kind of self-punishment, daring the killer to attack him the same way he'd caught Lee at the wheel. Mark promised himself he'd only use the strip of magic leather in his pocket for real dangers… or if his calls took him to some out-of-the-way neighborhood his searches might miss. Just cheating on his recovery from magic a *few* times, right?

What Mark wasn't ready for was the startled looks when he walked into the garage.

"Whoa!" Bill stared at his face, and laughed. "What kind of night did you have? And does she have a sister?"

"I wish," was the best answer Mark could give. The jokes, the playing off other people's leads, just didn't feel natural after what he'd seen.

Hamid was giving Bill a warning glare when Johanson stepped out from his office.

"Just one question, Mark: you think you can drive?"

"I'm fine." The words sounded real, anyway.

"Good. We had a call asking when your shift started. Willoughby Theater, now."

Somehow Mark kept the shock off his face.

* * *

At least he couldn't feel any magic around. Mark drove slowly up to the movie house's steps, scanning the thin queues there, and up and down the streets, for anyone he knew. His scrap of leather still held enough magic to pin an attacker, Angie had proved that—

The thought made his eyes fill. When he blinked back the sudden tears, he saw a small figure in a green Goshawks jacket step out under the marquee.

James Woodward. Kate's son. Alone.

He walked up to the cab, and the questions whirling around Mark's head started to settle. The boy looked too calm for something to have happened to Kate… but why was he risking coming to Mark? Wasn't Kate taking him out of town?

As James slipped into the seat beside him, Mark felt around for magic one more time—none—before he asked, "Where's your mother?"

"She's on her way. She wanted us to come separately." The twelve-year-old's eyes stayed right on his, firm, refusing to look away. "Mark, do you know what kind of games she taught me when I was little? There was one she'd do right in the middle of anything we were doing; she'd make me stop and point out the most ordinary thing I could see, and then the one that seemed most out of place. Just to make me notice things."

"Sounds like you were good at it." And as if he'd rehearsed that speech. Mark's answer brought a sudden smile that proved he had. *Why's he trying to impress me?* "Did you two get my message? The detective on the case was murdered."

"So was my sister. And I never even knew why anyone would want to, until it was too late." He leaned closer, staring up at Mark. "You want to get this guy?"

Mark swallowed the first angry answer to that. And James hadn't really answered his first question. "Look, when is your mother getting here?" he asked, and felt his heartbeat rising. *Did the killer get to her first?*

"I *said* she's coming." His voice rose, but he sounded more angry than shaken. "Don't you shut me out. This is my family we're talking about—oh."

His voice choked off.

Kate was walking up to the cab. A few yards short of it, she stopped and beckoned them both out to her. James hesitated just a moment before he clambered out.

Mark left the car at the curb and joined them, reaching them just in time to catch her low words to her son:

"—a good place to meet, I'll grant you that."

As if it was never her idea to come here.

Her faint smile faded as she stepped closer to Mark, letting a group of kids go by. She stopped only when she was standing almost against his ear. "And you're sure you didn't lead anyone here?"

That was the one thing Mark did know, and he grinned. "Don't forget, I could sense him if he was out there."

"And what if he hired a professional to follow you?"

Mark frowned, remembering the woman he'd seen on the way to the funeral, and Jerry Tate dying after it. Tate must have been possessed, but he'd never found out about the other...

"Or put a tracking device on you, or your cab? Or used your phone to track you, or hacked into your messages?"

Mark saw James flinch at the last words. Had she done that to her son? Had the boy snuck out to meet him, and that was how she'd found him?

Kate turned to look at James. "I've known about this enemy for just as many nights as Mark has, no longer, but I've thought of all those. I told you a police detective was just killed, and your response is that you want to get involved in this?"

"Um," was all James said.

"Thanks for the tip—" Mark began.

A family with several rowdy kids was moving up the sidewalk toward the line in front of the theater. When the noise didn't die down, Mark bent closer to Kate.

"We need a place to talk. It all fits—if you didn't know there was *another* out there who could do what your family can do, but he knows about you, he might not be sure about what secrets *you* have, and he's doing all this to find out, so he can take over our power. If we put what we know together, we can find the place he gets his power from—"

"Shh!" Kate shook her head hard, then leaned in to whisper, "I appreciate the information. But you've made my point. If there are 'others' who've lost track of each other, that's more proof the secrets *should* be lost."

James gasped, then pressed himself against Kate's side to whisper, "But… if we could *fly*—"

"*And,*" she added, with a fierce look at her son, "if he killed a detective, he could come after us any time he wanted."

James's eyes widened.

Mark opened his mouth, but waited while a young couple walked by, filling the air with chatter and the smell of too much perfume. He had to stay alert, *any* of them might be under the killer's control. "You really think—"

"I *think* it's not safe. You know I already took my son out of Lavine in case someone thought to use him against Angie. But," and she shot a cold look at the boy, "even without my telling him the background, he became suspicious enough to run away back here."

Mark stared at James, standing so quiet at her elbow.

"I don't want any misunderstanding between us." Kate turned back to Mark, her stern face close to his. "I appreciate your warnings, but whether you continue this search or not, I don't want you to contact us again."

"*What?!*" he snapped again. "You say we're all on borrowed time, but your plan is to shut your eyes and hope the danger goes away?"

"My plan is for James and me to leave this city, and this time we'll stay away." She looked at her son again, meeting his glare. "Where I hope the problem won't follow."

Because the enemy's magic may be tied to Lavine as much as mine is… no, because now I'm the one who has what the killer wants. And she doesn't care.

He steeled himself, embracing his anger as he leaned toward her to hiss, "And what if I don't let you run? I've been wishing I'd told Lee enough to stay alive. Well, Angie and I talked about how if we had no other choice we'd show the whole world how this thing works. She said if it's the only way to get help in hunting—"

"Unlikely. That would only mean trading one enemy for all the hundreds that would crawl out of the woodwork with a taste for a new form of power. I'm certain she knew better, and so do you. Please, *leave us alone.*"

"Fine, I'll track him down myself!"

"You think so? At least talk to someone who can get your phone protected." As she said that her voice softened, and her lips twitched toward a smile. "That's the last help I'll give you, for her sake. Good-bye."

Mark clenched his teeth, not trusting himself to speak again. But… she did have her reasons. He nodded a goodbye to James.

The boy was looking at the ground, different expressions shifting across his face—but then he drew himself up and held out his hand with deliberate dignity. "Good luck. I hope you're good at the game."

On the last word, he squeezed Mark's hand tight, then let go.

Mark kept his face stiff, watching as the Woodwards moved away. If James had meant *game* as some kind of clue… no, it had to have been a reminder about the story James had told him about growing up with Kate, and being trained to observe. As if still had a head start on Mark.

Does he still think he could help in a fight like this? He's twelve.

And he was one more of Angie's relatives who could get cut down if Mark didn't find the killer.

Kate and James were already out of sight.

*   *   *

The taxi shift stretched on and on through the day. Human spies, bugs, on top of possessed birds and people—Kate's list of potential threats gave Mark even more to watch out for, but the long night he'd endured dragged at his eyelids as the afternoon sun bounced off the passing cars. He promised himself he'd pull over if they tried to close.

But his enemy never made a move. Or not one he saw.

After his shift, he found himself on the bus toward Beekly and his own apartment, not the roundabout route to Henry's. *It's time I started keeping him at a safer distance.* And if someone did catch him at his place when he had only one scrap of leather as a weapon… maybe it would be better than just waiting. He sent Henry a quick text and staggered into his apartment, hauling his mattress over to block the door before he collapsed on it.

The night was still deepening when Mark woke. He hadn't missed any calls; not the police calling with more questions, not calls about work—and no change of heart from Kate or Dennard to help him track down their enemy. Just a whole night ahead of trying to do more than *wait* for the magic to be safe again.

He picked at a sandwich he pulled together with stale bread and watched the sky darken outside, knowing he needed to rest up while he could. Now and then he searched the internet for tips on how to keep a phone or computer from being hacked, and he read up on every legend he could find about possession, birds, and magic.

And again and again he looked at his silent phone, knowing who he should have called in a lull like this. But this new machine would never even hold Angie's number.

When he opened his eyes, it was daylight again, and he'd slept through a call.

The message was from Roger Winton. "Have you heard? Detective Lee is dead. So you might be right and there *are* still Blades out there with a grudge. Watch yourself."

Mark looked at the phone for a long moment. Something, *something* had to help him find the killer before someone else died—

And pulling someone new into the crossfire will help? He blew out a long, slow sigh and turned back to his keyboard.

* * *

By the time his next driving shift began, Mark couldn't get out of the apartment fast enough. Between the dead ends of his research and the sitting *alone* with his failure, getting out on the streets was a blessing. Even on a busy Saturday.

The strip of leather pulsed in his pocket, ready. He kept his eyes open, searching all sides as he walked for any sign of someone following him, for any reason to search for attacking magic. Once he settled into his cab, he drove faster and dodged through traffic better than he ever had.

The hours ticked away, with still no sign of trouble. The killer could have been waiting for the same thing he was, for Mark to start searching again.

If I'm right, he needs to catch me using my magic's secrets, and that's only when I'm ready to go look for his. So we're both trapped, watching.

When the shift ended, his knuckles were aching from gripping the wheel so tight, knowing he was finally free to go to Henry and the belt, and the search.

He made one quick stop back at his apartment, and his eagerness almost made him miss the new envelope tucked in with yesterday's mail in the lobby. But something about the priority markings and lack of return address made him pause and open it.

I appreciate you telling me about Angie. Here's what I've learned:
Our own power seems to be an old secret handed down through the family. If the other one is the same way, its owners may have used it like the Fletchers did to make their fortune. I'm sorry I don't have anything more, but here's a list of the older money in the city.
—James

The second page was a list of names, some of them familiar from the news.

Mark started upstairs, trying to think. Of course James would try to stay in the hunt, if he could get a message past his mother... and a simple letter was one thing she couldn't trace. Or this might not be from James at all; it could be another of the enemy's maneuvers—not that "follow the old money" was much of a trap to send him into. He tried a quick call to James, but the boy didn't answer.

* * *

There was no wind that night, even after Mark had collected the belt from Henry and renewed its energy in the park. The stillness of the air gave him one more reason to conserve power and move mostly along the ground; when he tested it with a leap from a roof, there was no wind to ride—and his jump had to push through the still air until he drifted to a stop and had to drop down in the middle of a parking lot.

The potential "suspects" on James's list lived mostly in the western neighborhoods of Lavine, some in towers like Kate's on Heath Avenue, others in grand houses in quiet suburbs like her parents had. But several more had estates in Orchard Heights, to the southwest—and, just that location put it in a corner out of the way of the usual diagonal winds from the northwest, a spot most of his searches would carry him on past. So tonight, moving on foot, was the perfect time to look there.

As he hurried down the street, he strained to make out the traces of power he'd sensed around him the last time he'd been out. Again, there were only faint threads; it felt like he was brushing against a drifting cobweb. But if he could just find a pattern, or a concentration of that magic, anywhere besides Rosewood…

He was almost surprised when he sensed the killer's bird instead.

Heading *from* Orchard Heights.

Mark's legs were tensing automatically to leap toward it, but he checked the reflex; the birds always outflew him, and now he wondered if crushing it would even hurt the possessing force behind it. He shot a hurried glance at the street around him and dove underneath a parked car.

The smell of oil filled his nose. He could sense the bird winging closer, but it was still far off in the distance; it couldn't have seen him yet, could it?

He stayed hidden, the cold of the asphalt seeping into his skin. Once the echo of footsteps stopped right beside him and he turned to see a pair of battered looking men's shoes, but a moment later they moved on.

The bird passed blindly by too. Mark stayed in place, a grin growing on his face. *Who's got the better senses this time? Your magic can't feel mine at all!* By the time it moved beyond his range, Mark was busy reviewing the Orchard Heights streets in his head.

Mark kept to the ground until he reached the estates. The winding streets lay quiet as he walked past their high walls and hedges; the few Saturday parties in progress were easy to avoid just by steering clear of the music they spilled into the night. Whenever he left a cross-street behind, he floated upward for a minute to watch for the headlights of the few residents—or security personnel—who were still out driving through the darkness.

From above, he could almost match the dark patches of ground and their borders with the maps he'd studied. But instead of searching out any particular address, he focused on avoiding attention and working his way south, keeping himself alert for any shift in the city's dim threads of magic.

He found only turn after turn of dark hedges and walls, and the same energy thinner than the faint smell of late roses that hung in the cool air. Apart from the few cars he dodged, he met nobody, just glimpsed one figure out strolling the grounds on one grand estate on one of his brief moves into the air. *I'm doing this wrong. I should have swung by here in my cab, then I'd never have to explain my presence.*

He heard another car on the road and darted upward to see a white Porsche heading away from what might be the same quiet grounds he'd seen the late-night walker on. Wait…

Was that it, a different sense in that direction? He dropped down and quickened his steps toward it. *Am I just feeling what I want to feel?* It wasn't a force or a shape within the energies, if anything it felt like there was a fraction *less* power there. Where a hedge gave way to the brick wall of the place he'd noticed, he felt the presence thin away even further. It was the first difference he'd found here.

And that departing car meant the house just might be empty. He checked the number on the gate, and his notes. The owner was on James's list, one Olivia Nolan.

He had to try *something.*

Mark stepped back across the road, eyeing the squat block of the house beyond the metal gate and wondering what sensors would be sweeping over the grounds. He took five running steps to build up speed, then flung himself at the gate and arched up high, soaring upwards with the wind of his jump pressing against his face and the building shrinking in the dimness below, then slowing, slowing, until it was near enough below him that he risked dropping down, and managed to catch the corner of the chimney before he coasted past

"Not bad," he had to chuckle. As he settled his feet on the angled roof, he could feel the slight dimming of the magic around him—

And a clearer power, of the enemy, far off in the sky.

Suddenly the tiles felt colder. How far away was that presence? Had the bird seen him leaping through space? He'd have to gamble that it hadn't, that the killer didn't know where he was.

He gripped the sides of the brick chimney, wondering how wide it was inside. He yanked himself up, twisted around, and dropped down… into empty space. The shaft was so wide he had to spread his elbows to stop from bouncing right down it.

Then he let go and clenched his power to drift downward. The sudden darkness sharpened the smell of smoke, but Mark told himself it had to be old smoke, absorbed into the bricks the same as their crushing coldness. Still, the blackness pressed in on him; to steady himself he closed his eyes and felt for the bird, tracking its pulse as it winged blindly one way and then another. *How can I be worried when I'm sliding down a chimney? Ho-ho-ho.*

His toes brushed the floor. He spilled out onto a cold floor as hard as the chimney, his reduced weight making only faint echoes in a house that sounded empty. Blinking in the dimness, he tried to make out the room using the moonlight around the curtained windows.

The bird faded from his sense, pulling out of reach again. Mark waited for its presence to swing back, wondering if the killer truly thought Mark had missed his house, if this was the killer's house at all… or if he'd landed in a trap.

Except, he'd never felt a house as *still* as this one. He let the magic lift him to a feather-light tiptoe, and began to explore.

As his eyes adjusted to the windows' slivers of light, each wall looked more and more like the hard smoothness his hands and feet already felt. One room after another was layered in hard tile and trimmed in stone or metal, rarely anything as organic as wood. The few tables and counters he passed were hunched shapes in the dimness, and the faintest brush of his shoes over the uncarpeted floor was the only sound besides the hum of a refrigerator. And he still didn't feel even the usual feathers of magic in the air.

Nobody was there, not on either floor.

Once he was sure of that, he began closing curtains—they were thick and heavy, and still almost the flimsiest things in the rooms—to keep anyone outside from seeing the lights he'd need to search through desks and drawers. But even those told him little; he found only a few papers, confirming the house's owner as Olivia Nolan, owner of North Star Events. He found a computer, but couldn't get past its password to discover its secrets. He couldn't even find a single *map,* aside from one chart showing Lavine's weather patterns for the year; he could barely imagine an enemy tracking gangs, or his own moves, without at least a few maps on the wall.

What the walls did display were a few photos of different gatherings Nolan had organized, all sealed away in glass. Twice Mark found a pair of crossed bamboo fishing poles, but otherwise those occasional framed photographs, and the windows, were the only things breaking the monotony of the walls, until he found a small library. Even there, the books sat within locked cases, and they looked too much like some generic collection for him to risk breaking them open.

Then his head jerked back to stare at the photo on the wall.

It was just a face, just the same stocky middle-aged woman he'd seen in most of the other pictures. But this time, the close-up shot seemed familiar. Was Olivia Nolan the woman he'd glimpsed on the day of the funeral? The one who might have been following him?

Mark looked harder, trying to remember the woman he'd seen outside his apartment. Part of him was sure it was only a faint resemblance; that this was just his own need to find a connection, to have the strange non-magic mean something. Still, he left the library and moved to the center of the great reception room, and tried to feel for any brush of energy around him. He closed his eyes and held his breath, knowing he was trying to probe nothingness…

But there was *something*, the faintest power, off to his right. He waited a moment, afraid it would fade away, until he trusted himself to take a shuffling step rightward and feel how—yes!—some magic *was* still there. Unlike to the left, by the pictures and crossed poles…

What *were* fishing poles doing on the wall in a home this spartan? He stepped left and felt the tiniest chill, as though a single faint draft had crept into this fortress.

Out in the driveway, a car engine purred.

The lights! He dashed left, his feet echoing on the hard floor, and snapped off the light, leaving himself in darkness.

In the back of his mind, he felt the killer's bird nearing—no, *turning* toward the house even as it moved into his range. It turned the *moment* after he'd shut off the light, as if he'd just signalled it he was hiding from the car's driver.

Mark stared through the dimness, toward the faint glow from the lights in the other rooms; why had he left *any* of them on? Idiot! He leaped across the room and his shoulder *banged* the doorway as he careened through it.

How close, how close was the owner? He clenched the magic to stretch his stride and quiet his footfalls, and bounded toward the staircase. At least this place didn't have much furniture to slam into.

He made it to the second floor and clicked off the last light, then stopped and locked his gasping breath silent. Below, he could hear steps moving around on the first floor; the casual sounds of someone who suspected nothing. And yet Mark felt the bird circling right over the estate. Had it not warned her yet? Or maybe Olivia Nolan *wasn't* the bird's mistress?

Mark seized the window frame, but stopped before he slid it up. If this place was the killer's base—and the strange magic he'd felt had to mean *something*—and he floated off and let the bird see he'd found it, what would they do to him later? Right now, if the woman below was still unaware of him, Mark could…

I could what? Sneak downstairs and attack her, for having an old name and a face I might *have seen before? This place may feel all wrong, but I don't know that the bird is hers.*

His breathing came faster. There was one way to find out—if he was fast enough to trick the bird or its possible mistress, and strong enough to test them.

He slid the window up, then stepped back from it to lift the blocky sofa and silently slide it out two feet from the wall, letting him crouch down behind it. With the lights out, that should be enough to set up the trick, but the test… his fingers tightened on the belt, heart pounding at the thought of even flirting with this much raw force. *Why did the place have to be solid stone?*

Mark let his thoughts stretch outward, pictured them spreading like unseen wings across the building, ready to unleash the magic over it all… except even his imagination couldn't keep from raising barriers against him reaching so far out. He'd never even tried this before; he only knew Angie's grandfather had, in his madness. But Mark only needed to manage a single squeeze of power, enough to rattle the house to see if the bird would fly in to defend it. *Now!* And he pulled.

But pain stabbed through his head, *wrong,* his magic twisted around by something and *wrong.* He stumbled as his weight lurched sideways against the sofa, tried the magic again, felt an explosion in his head.

Pain, pain, falling, no sound anywhere but a ringing in the floor... *not an explosion, but something...*

The window waited, open, ready. He heard feet clattering below, rushing upward. Fighting against the pain, he felt for the bird and found it, still circling. It hadn't made one move to defend the house. So what *was* this place?

Mark felt like he'd cracked his skull. He crouched lower behind the sofa that he'd planned to fling at the bird. He had to know, had to!

A plump figure ran into the room, fast despite her weight. Mark pressed himself lower, watching the woman turn to the wide-open window and stare out. It *was* her, the woman who had tailed him. He could tell, even in the dark, with her so close.

Now, now... Mark slipped to his feet, readying the magic despite the pain in his head. Nolan still had her back to him, muttering curses while looking into the night. Silent, nearly-weightless, Mark ghosted toward her back. *Closer, closer, and then my power can slam her down and squeeze the truth out of her.*

Nolan put a hand and elbow on the window. Her graying head glinted in the moonlight as Mark brought his hands up.

Then he saw her start to whirl toward him. Saw the hidden gun ready in her hand, levelled straight at him.

The screech that split the night then could only be one thing. Mark knew it, so clearly that he used the woman's instant of distraction to dive aside even before he glimpsed the shadow hurtling at the window. He hit the floor and rolled up to his feet, as the gunshot blasted out.

Olivia Nolan was staring back and forth, at Mark, and at the dark shape finishing its dive and twisting around through the dimness at the far end of the room, turning back toward her again. The owl.

Nolan took a step toward it, raising the gun.

One more thought moved at the back of Mark's mind, but what he saw was that both of his enemies were clear of the window, and that sent his feet springing forward to launch him into a headlong dive out into the open air, and a snap of magic yanked him upward, to leave the stone bunker of a house falling away below.

He saw a blur streak past the window below that might have been the owl escaping too—*after it* saved *me from Nolan's bullet. It saved me, impossible!*

The gray square of the window shrank back in Mark's view to merge with the dark gray of the building, that shrank back into the wider gray of the earth below him. He could just about make out a dark silhouette leaning out the window, and he grinned; let Nolan try to shoot him from so far below, aiming by moonlight! The figure raised an arm.

Then Mark heard a sound he'd almost forgotten on that still night: the howl of wind.

Air squirmed to life around him; he could feel it waking. For an instant it only tugged at his coat, before it swept, smashed, slammed him tumbling with a breath-crushing blast, downward—

No! Mark clutched at the magic, fighting to wrench himself up again. The world lashed and swirled, a sea of branches tossed in the gale, or was that himself spinning in his fall? He had to get control—

The strain felt like it was splitting his head. His lungs locked, his watering eyes slammed closed, but he kept fighting upward and away, huddling himself tight against the tumbling world, pushing, soaring, gasping for breath but never cold...

Not cold? A memory came back to him, of the warmed feeling he'd felt when the magic was seeping into his mind. *No, no, not now!* His head pounded, beating at him within the mad spinning of the world. Forcing his eyes open showed only vague blurs and dizzying whirls. No up, no down, no way to aim. *No, the* magic *leads up, I know that.* He let the power go and felt his stomach lurch. Blinking, he fought to see *something;* for all he knew, the ground could be seconds away.

Then the shadows pulled back to the dark constellation of city lights—so far below, with the smooth black of the lake beyond them—all rushing toward him again. He caught at the magic again, to slow his descent, and the world steadied again, and *ohh,* the joy it would have been to keep soaring forever; he felt it even now.

But down below still waited the one question. The killer's owl had saved him; when Nolan had been about to turn his ambush against him with her gun, the owl had attacked her. So… the killer wanted the belt's secrets enough to keep Mark alive?

Or else, he thought, Olivia Nolan and her wind magic were the killer's real target. And she'd just seen Mark attack her with the owl's help.

Nolan was ready to shoot me. And she still knows where I live.

CHAPTER FOURTEEN

WHO'S WHO

Was anywhere safe now?

Mark crouched on a low roof a few blocks from his Beekly apartment, the cold of the sky lingering in his bones, and holding down the magic-stirred drive to keep jumping, just *moving* through the city until he met something. Instead he shivered in place and kept his eyes and senses sweeping around for any sign of an attack... would it be a flicker of the killer's magic? Some human thug, if Mark dropped to the street? Or this power of Nolan's, that he would barely sense until the winds slammed into him?

Now and then he stared across the skyline toward his home. Nolan could be watching for him there just as she'd done before the funeral—but this time ready to pay him back for attacking her home. *Do I dare go back, or even go near Henry? But what's left, just stalking the rooftops until I lose my mind?*

By the time the dawn spread over the streets, he could see just how reckless he'd been. The owl's attack on Nolan proved she wasn't with the killer. And that letter with James's name on it could have been one more of the killer's tricks, to throw him off... or even to *put* Mark on her trail. And he'd fallen for it.

Again, Kate's phone went straight to voice mail. "Just call me! Let me talk to James, *please!"* The raggedness in his voice got worse with every message he left. Not the best impression to persuade her to check in—if she and James hadn't cut all ties with the city already. *If they have, and the letter was fake, at least the killer can't drag them in deeper.*

Again and again, he found his fingers brushing the belt as he picked over what had happened. "Sure, I can just sniff out his magic any time I can narrow the search down, *easy,* right? So the killer sees I can spot him and even turns that against me, he has me track Nolan down instead—and never once worries I'd join up with her. So why send the owl to save me? So he can watch us fight each other?"

He glared at the skyline again, looking toward his home and then back toward Nolan's. *She's out there, one enemy who does have a face... I can wait up here to let her come at me or go out and hit her first...* The logic was colder than the morning air, and yet he could only keep thinking, *I can't, she's never hurt me, maybe not hurt any-one.* Yet.

His phone rang.

He stared at the screen. Why was Dennard calling now?

"Mark? What's gotten into you?" came the furious voice.

An answering snarl formed on Mark's lips, but he forced it back. "What? I've been—"

"He's a *kid!* And you want to pull Kate's boy into this 'war coun-cil' of yours?"

"I didn't! He called me, but Kate and I..." Mark's eyes went wide. "What war council? The last time I saw him was yesterday, no, two days now."

"So who sent this text to meet you and him right now, at your place?"

Oh God no—

His words came out shrill and desperate. "It's *him* again, the killer! Or it's James and another trick on us—but if he's at my place now—"

Dennard's voice was steady. "Where are you? He's not picking up."

"On my way."

For five endless seconds Mark stared down the back of the building to check for anyone watching, before he dropped to the ground, free to dash up the street. He throttled the magic back to only lighten his stride into a skimming, darting run. The early risers on the sidewalk slid past him.

Why did it have to be broad daylight? Mark tried to picture his block up ahead, and what ways he could come at what might be there, waiting for him. Rush right in, in case James was waiting? Go back above eye level and risk sneaking up? He wracked his brains for a way to decide, but when his apartment came into view he was still on the ground.

He still caught no trace of enemy magic. He slowed and stared up and down the block.

Far up at the corner diner, a small figure trotted into view to meet him.

So James was waiting for me, out of sight of the street. Mark blew out a sigh of relief and rushed to the boy.

"I don't *care* if it isn't safe!" James said the moment Mark slowed. "You have to show me how—"

"So you did call us here?" Mark grabbed James's shoulders. James stared at him an instant, then nodded, and Mark added "And that 'old money' letter?"

Rain spattered on the street just as James answered "Letter? What old money letter?"

"So today's one more of your tricks, but that letter wasn't you, *he* sent it. The killer used your name, and he used me." The words came out hard and heavy, and he saw James's eyes slowly widen.

Mark took a deep breath to tell him how deep a hole he'd stepped in... but the air was stabbingly cold.

Startled murmurs were rippling up and down the sidewalk as the scattered people looked at each other, smiling, waving at the sudden rainfall around them. But their tones were only those of light surprise, puzzlement, not sharp with fear. Mark looked at the man closest to him, standing in the halo of the next streetlight, and saw he wasn't shivering... while shudders wracked Mark's sides.

Was she here, waiting for him? Mark felt around for magic, but of course Nolan's power didn't have the same clear pulse as the killer's. He swept his gaze around the street.

Across the road, sheltered just inside a doorway, a short, plump woman strolled slowly down the sidewalk.

So her weather magic means she doesn't even have to look at me to attack?

With stiffening fingers, Mark shoved James away from him, then turned to face the woman.

Behind him, James said "What happened? Where'd the cold go?"

Mark waved for him to back away; Nolan had to be wrapping the worst of her force tight around him, to freeze just one target on the street.

But she's not the real enemy, he tricked me! Mark took a slow step toward her and raised his arms, trying to gesture to her to stop and listen. The rain hammered on the pavement. He would have screamed across at her if any words had been good enough. She stepped out from the doorway and folded her arms as she watched him. Merciless.

His foot slipped on ice.

Mark toppled, slapped a hand down on the sheet of ice that had formed over the pavement. Wind beat against his side, starting him sliding, daring him to try to float away. While everyone could see.

If he couldn't go up... he pressed his magic down on himself. Weight crashed onto him like a sheet of lead, but it did what he needed: shoved his feet and hands against the ground and anchored him.

His eyes locked on his attacker. If he could just get to her, tell her about the real enemy and his schemes and losing Angie... his next motion dragged but he managed to make his hand slide forward. Hunched against the weight and the cold, he crawled closer.

Reach her. Push. Power burning, ready...

The honk of a car ripped through the wind's howl. Mark looked up, shocked—had he been about to move straight into the road? No, the car was a white shape well up the block, but it came barrelling up fast, right toward the opposite sidewalk like it had lost control in the ice storm. Heading straight for Nolan.

She flung herself backward into a doorway. The wind went slack.

And the car, the white Ford that could only have Joe Dennard at the wheel, veered back into the street and swung to meet Mark.

The car slowed before it reached the ice, and Mark saw a window sliding down. He flung off the magic's weight and made one joyous leap across to wedge his arms into the open window. The *lurch* of it yanking him forward cleared the last traces of the magic's haze from his mind and left him clinging to the side and scrabbling to keep his weightless feet clear of the pavement as they rushed away.

He stole a glance back when they swept around the corner—putting the diner between them and Nolan's view, he realized. Dennard didn't slow until they reached the end of the block.

"Hold on, there's James back there!" Mark yelled. But he saw the boy scrambling along the sidewalk behind them. The car slowed, stopped.

Finally Mark was able to let his feet down and open the back door to tumble in, with James climbing in behind him. Mark searched, but sensed no magic closing in on them…

What am I doing, using the belt again? The magic had had him ready to kill Nolan or push himself into traffic to get at her. Mark clawed at the buckle and stripped the belt off his waist, but found he still held it clutched against his lap.

James's young voice squeaked with surprise. "What *was* all that?"

"*That* is the magic you wanted to learn—" Mark broke off as he realized James didn't mean the belt, he meant the ice storm and their escape. "And back there, that was the other magic we never even knew about. Our newest enemy."

Dennard added "And this one knows where you live, and she went right after you." He shot the car forward in a squeal of rubber, and wrenched it around one car and then another to get them further away from Beekly. "This is no place for kids. James, where's your mother hiding?"

"Um…" For a moment James hesitated, then said "Right now she's at her firm. She snuck in to finish the arrangements for us to disappear. It was my last chance to get away."

"Where's that?" Dennard said.

James hesitated again.

The silence grew, and then Mark realized Dennard was looking at him too. Right, he and Angie had tried so hard to reach Kate before… and *Mark* was the cabbie with the headful of street routes, and he should have been the first to answer.

Is this *how worn out I am?* After gangs, and possessed birds, and frozen hurricanes, and fighting with the magic… He gritted his teeth. "Over on Harris."

* * *

Kate's law firm lay on one of Harris Street's older blocks, so deep downtown that even on Sunday the only parking was in the building's own attached parking structure. Even there, the spots closest to the visitors' entrance were filled, and they had to leave the car too far from the elevator. By the time Dennard finished hobbling to it on his crutches, his jaw was clenched in pain.

Everything in the offices *gleamed,* from the rich dark wood walls to the shining plastic on the waiting-room chairs, and young interns dashed down the halls like overdressed couriers on their way to their bikes. The sharp-dressed young woman who called Kate told James, "We're so sorry to be losing your mother."

Then they saw Kate leaning out from the overhanging upper level to wave them up the little spiral stair.

Kate's own office was more of the same elegance, and kept too warm, same as her home. Mark saw exactly three well-cushioned chairs set out along the wall, waiting for them. As they sat down, he noticed a thick suitcase standing by the side of her desk. He glanced at Kate's injured ex-husband and her subdued son, and thought of what a mismatched blended family they must look like. *But why does it have to be me, instead of Angie, bringing them together now?* Loss stabbed at him again.

Kate closed the door with a deliberate motion, and what little sound had been coming in from the hallway vanished. Then she rolled her desk's chair over to sit in front of James. "The truth now: why aren't you busy packing?"

"I… tried to trick them again," James said. "I wanted one last try to learn about the belt. And someone attacked us at Mark's."

"An enemy magician," Mark said, and as Kate's mouth opened he added *"Another* enemy magician."

Then, step by step, he led them all through the ins and outs of his hunt for Angie's killer. Not only the killer's power to possess birds and people, but that somehow he'd known James's schemes well enough to forge a letter to Mark—and how that letter had turned Mark's one advantage, his sense for magic, into his running up against the person they hadn't even known existed. He described Olivia Nolan's ruthless response, both in her house and then outside his apartment. Twice James broke in, but both times he cut himself off after a word or two, as if the depths of the danger they were in had just begun to sink in. The two parents said nothing.

At last Mark came to the end of his story, and had to admit "I'm not sure what my next move—"

"I take my son away," Kate said. "Not tomorrow, not after going to the hotel; we disappear *now*." She leaned toward James, and now Mark heard something softer in her voice. "You know it's the only response we can have. I don't care about the whys and wherefores. Just think of what that letter means: a murderer has put you on his list of bargaining chips, and he's never going to forget that he can use you. And now there are two of them after us."

James stared. "But… you mean, they could keep coming—"

A phone rang. Loud, jarring, and right in Mark's pocket.

With all three sets of eyes glaring at him, he pulled it out, glanced at the screen and took the call.

"Are you alright?" Henry asked at once.

"Fine. We got out safe, all of us," he added, though the boast sounded hollow to him. "No need to worry."

"Good. But Mark… you never brought the belt back. And you said," and Henry's words grew slower and more deliberate, "that you couldn't be trusted with it for long."

"I know." *And I just proved it all over again.* But with his eyes on James, Mark went on, "The problem is, Kate and James aren't out of danger yet, and his attacker's still out there. I can't give it back until they're safe. And it's almost drained anyway."

"So it seems like it's urgent. I can understand that. But Mark, *you said* you'd rather be dead than end up an addict."

"I… did…" They'd been easier words to say when he'd only thought of himself in danger. Risking the magic's influence was the treacherous key to all the other battles he'd been fighting—but Henry was right, if he gave it any more of a grip on himself, it might be too late for him soon.

"Henry, isn't it?" Kate said, and when Mark nodded, she walked over and took the phone. "There's a simple answer, Mr. Maes: I can take the belt and give him an hour to think clearly. Until we get to the plane."

No! Mark pulled back from the look on her stern, implacable face.

Except… she *was* the one who'd done the most to resist the magic, even leaving the Dennards to keep clear of it. He leaned back, wanting to roll his chair further away from her. He could already see the doubt growing in all their eyes.

I have to trust her. He handed over the tingling belt he'd still been holding, then passed over the two scraps of leather from his pocket as well.

He took his phone back from her. "It's done," he told Henry, and then he added, "Please, be careful yourself. We've got two different enemies that came at my home or used Kate's son against us, and when he's gone I'm betting they'll find out about you, sooner or later. Maybe you need to take a vacation too."

"Are *you* leaving?" Henry said, firmer than ever. "*You* aren't letting them push you out of your life; you're pushing back."

For a moment, Mark smiled, feeling his face warm and some of the tension loosen in his shoulders. "Thanks for the support," he said. "But it isn't that simple."

"Well, we can talk about that later, when you're home. So finish this and come home." And Henry hung up.

Mark looked at the phone a moment more. Then he tucked it away and turned back to the others, and their retreat from the fight Angie had died for.

Then James said, "Okay, I guess we disappear," and he shot Mark a look of gratitude as Kate gathered him into a one-armed hug.

Joe Dennard snapped, "And that's it?" He leaned forward in his chair, grimacing at the motion, but his eyes not moving from Kate as he went on, "Run and keep running, that's your plan? You talk like you've been waiting for this—how long have you known there's someone out there aiming magic at you?"

"I had this conversation once already, with Mark; I only knew after my daughter died. And this is simply the only way we can survive."

She met her ex-husband's glare without flinching. Mark could imagine how other exes would rush on into denial or old grudges, but not these two. Silence filled the room.

She just doesn't care? Mark found himself spitting out, "You won't even look back, will you? You save your son, and we never hear from you again, no matter how much we need your help? And the rest of your long, safe life you're okay with how Angie didn't just 'die,' someone *killed* her!" *Because the damn owl tried to get* me, Mark's mind added, and he felt his face twist in guilt.

"If there's anything safe about it," Dennard added. "This is an enemy who takes control of people like puppets. Remember Osborn 'napping' in the morgue? I've been trying to see if they had cameras running there, but now I bet there'd be nothing to see but him going about his work, and maybe whoever got taken over first and touched him to take him over. The bastard makes one grab at someone's mind and he has the perfect eyes in place to look for the magic, on the girl he's killed," and his breath gave the faintest hitch, "and even the M.E. himself barely noticed he'd been used. He could be *anywhere,*" and he stabbed a finger at Kate, "and you want to turn your back on him?"

Kate's voice didn't rise, it only grew slower, more sure of herself. "He could be anywhere—and your answer isn't to give him whole continents to search, it's to try to chase him? If this Nolan woman doesn't catch you first?"

Dennard opened his mouth, then shut it again, glaring in frustration.

Kate nodded. "James has already walked into that once. And you have to ask yourselves: has your fighting back honestly made anyone safer, Joe? Or you, Mark?"

No it hadn't. But still, Mark glared back and said "Safer than what? None of us knew there *was* a killer before, so who knows how long he's been at this, and how many deaths he's covered up? Or what he'll do next if someone doesn't stop him?"

Kate stood up then, and took a single step toward Mark's chair. Gently, firmly, she said "But you didn't answer me: tell me one thing that you've won in all of this."

"Besides exposing Rafe and making the Blades back down?" Mark shot back. *But, that was only Rafe's way to flush us out, and it fell apart on its own; the real enemy never lost a thing.* "Look, once James is out of reach I'll be free to keep looking for the killer—"

"What were you just telling your cousin?" She shook her head. "This hidden enemy *already* tricked you once, no twice, just with notes from myself and James. Who do you think they'll pull into this next?"

Dennard groaned as he slumped over in his chair. "I *know* we're playing with everyone's lives here. But the only options we have are to run or take the fight to them—" He looked up. "We could have one lead. You think Rafe was in the enemy's pocket. What does he know about him? How he got his orders, or just what he made him do?"

There's an idea... but Mark felt his doubts only press tighter. "If we could find him. Besides... I tried that when he found me after the funeral, I told him his 'friend' had dumped him, and he turned it around and almost had *me* spilling my guts about the magic. And the way the killer pulls strings, the thing he's best at is keeping his secrets, so who knows if Rafe ever knew much? But maybe Olivia Nolan, if we could..."

Mark was ticking off points on his fingers, a part of him grateful to have someone to hear the list, even when he couldn't decide what the different sides of the puzzle meant.

He said "Nolan was watching me, but she never made a move until she found me in her home sneaking up on her. She could have put the pieces together from our fighting the Blades, she might even have been an ally against the killer once. But—"

"But you *did* attack her," Dennard sighed.

"Yeah. And now she's blasting me on sight. Maybe that's another reason I got sent out that way. The killer just keeps running rings around us—hell, why run, he can just possess people all around us— and we can't even find him." It always came back to that, and how much blood and sanity it cost him to keep looking.

"So you see?" Kate reached down and settled her hand on his shoulder; it felt oddly warm. Gently, she said, "You've tried everything, and you simply don't have any other choices left. If you want some kind of revenge, it can be to see that the killer loses his chance to get the magic he wants, and see to it that you survive—because you choose to, right now. There's nothing wrong with that." She turned back to James.

So now we're talking about all *of us running, this minute? I never agreed to that.*

He called after her, trying to make her look back, to change *something.* "But who else dies if I give up? And Angie..." *But what* can *I do?*

"Come on," was all Kate said as she picked up the suitcase by her desk and led James out the door, Dennard limping along with them. Mark trailed after, trying to think of what else to say, trying to hold on to his mission.

They walked out of the office in silence, with barely a wave to the clerk, one more part of leaving no sign that Kate was pulling out *now*—and she wanted him and Dennard to cut their ties even faster?

The next words spoken were from James as they reached the elevator: "We left Mr. Dennard's car at P2. Since we're riding together, could we go in his one more time? I mean, we won't need any of the cars again since we're all getting on the plane, aren't we?"

Dennard sighed. "Let's just get you there, okay?"

Mark nodded to himself as they all started down. He'd see them off safely and take the belt back... but why couldn't he say anything better about staying? That he'd catch the killer, and then hand him over to Nolan and somehow it'd make peace between them? Or find another cop who'd help him the way Lee might have, without taking it public and panicking the whole city? *Even panic about magical killers would be better than leaving the city wide open to this enemy... or would it? I don't have the right to light* that *fuse.*

I'm trying to keep going for Angie, but it never gets easier.

The doors opened. Maybe a dozen cars sat along the concrete on each side of their path, and after those there'd only be the roads to the airport and then—

"You see that woman up left, the one that *almost* got out of her car?" Dennard muttered, right at Mark's ear.

What? Mark's eyes swung toward it, toward a movement he hadn't quite registered. In the scattered fluorescent light he could just make out a head behind the glass, but a woman climbing back inside just as they approached didn't mean…

Wait. The car was a slim white Porsche, like the one he'd seen in Orchard Heights. *Her* car.

The sound rose somewhere out above the ceiling, a muted shrillness anyone would know, but this was louder, stronger than natural— and even after the second it took it to press into the building, it didn't ebb back at all, instead the wind's howl only went on.

Then the wind blasted into them. Just for an instant Mark heard it whistling in through the horizontal, sunlit gap that ran along the far wall, and tried to brace himself. The next moment he spun away, trying to twist his fall into a crouch and a dive behind the nearest car.

Joe Dennard toppled down beside him, groaning. Mark pressed against the steel body of their shield, feeling it faintly shifting on its tires, and peeked over the top. Nothing moved near Olivia Nolan's car, but he did see Kate and James huddled behind the car just ahead of theirs.

As he looked, Kate turned back and spotted him. She hissed, "How strong can she make—"

A car alarm blared, and then another and another, drowning out all other sounds even as the lashing wind blurred Mark's vision into tears. He turned his head, blinking back toward the elevator and stairs they'd left behind them. It would be a thirty, forty foot run…

Something spattered on his head. The air darkened, blurred, as a spray of sleet tore across the floor. Mark could feel his teeth chattering, and the car rocking against his shoulder. As he twisted forward again, he saw a security camera perched in an upper corner of the garage wall, twitching and turning pale with ice. *What did she hit it with? What's she going to do to us?*

Leaning into the gale, he stretched a hand across his car toward Kate, flexing his fingers as he shouted, "Pass me the belt!" Not that he could think what use floating might be now. Kate looked at him and slowly shook her head.

Dennard caught his shoulder. Mark glanced down to see him motion with his left hand toward Nolan's car. His lips moved and Mark *thought* he mouthed, "pretend you think she needs help." With his right hand, he gripped a gleaming, short-barreled revolver.

Leaving the car's shelter meant sliding, clinging with numbed fingers to its bumper, and dragging himself over ice-slick concrete to the next handhold. As Mark tried to keep his eyes on Nolan's car he saw a fluorescent light beyond it spark once and go out. And he had to play decoy, blind ignorant decoy, with no magic at all.

Five cars between him and Nolan… then four, then one. He shielded his face and leaned toward the Porsche, into the teeth of the wind, toward the woman slouching low in its seat, to scream, "You okay?"

The wind *twisted* and slammed into his back. He stumbled forward, past the car, but even as he stumbled the pressure swung around to his side and flung him down along the ice.

One sound smashed through the madness: a sharp *ba-bang* that barely registered as separate shots. Mark looked up to see the Porsche's window collapse and in the same moment he finally felt the wind slacken. Down the row of cars, Kate and James sprang up and ran back past Dennard for the stairs.

They had just reached them when Mark saw Dennard dive for cover again. A wave of freezing gray *something* flew toward where he'd been standing. Then a whirl thickened in the air, and the space around Dennard began to darken, like some barely-visible hand tightening to crush him with deadly cold. And with his wounds weakening him—

Mark was on his feet, lunging through the gale-force wind around him to dive straight at Olivia Nolan's shattered window. For an instant he dared to hope she would be too fixated on the gunman to notice him, but then he saw her head twist toward him.

He gasped "Please, we don't—"

This time the wind smashed right at him, a simple reflexive shove… but Mark was already throwing himself sideways to let it kick him away up the corridor. He barely felt the impact as he came down hard on the ground and rolled further away, scrambling for the only escape—the ramp beyond.

Dammit, somebody *out there's got to guess there are people caught here in this "storm" and come help!* Mark slipped on the frozen floor, but he let that motion drop him into a low crouch. The wind was still tearing at his face. No cars were lined up out here, so there was no cover, but at least when he pressed himself low enough to the ground he found that the wind couldn't snatch him up. He crawled forward over the open concrete, yanking each hand up after an instant of contact, trying to stop his skin from freezing to the surface. Ahead, he felt the roar of air down the ramp. It must be coming from the open roof, so much fiercer than the winds he'd been battling… was that open air what *fed* her storm?

Sure, I just kept running the way I got pointed, because one path should have been as good as any other. Wrong.

Before he could turn back, the air smashed at him harder than ever, twisting around again and trying to tip him over. Nolan couldn't risk him getting outside, where he could fly away through the winds like he had last night.

Except he had no belt now. He was trapped—but she didn't know that. And as long as she kept after him, the others could use their chance to run.

He reached the ramp and caught at the icy railing alongside it, hauling himself upward. Just turning the corner brought him out of the concrete cave into weak sunlight, under blocks of roiling clouds crossing the sky. Somewhere on the climb he'd left the wail of the car alarms behind, enough that he could hear the beating of the hail on the garage roof ahead even through the shrilling wind.

Pulling himself out into the hail, he found the wind was actually *weaker* in the open. Through the fingers he held up to protect his face he saw that the walls and skyline of the streets around him were blurred in the hail and sleet—but one downhanging shape on the opposite wall that could be a flag showed that the rest of the city wasn't lashed with the full gale that raged around him. Mark turned back toward the ramp. *This is when I should be flying away, and hoping someone comes to help Dennard. And I can't.*

The pressure twisted and spun him and pitched him onto his side, and even as he hit the ground he felt himself sliding over the ice. The raised rim around the edge of the garage drew near and he pressed himself as low as he could, until he managed to slip under the wind's grip. He scrambled back toward the roof's center, not wanting to find out if Nolan could force him over. There were no cars on the roof for cover; even the concrete block encasing the far stairs lay a world away on the roof's other side.

Nolan's graying head peeped around the ramp.

Mark shouted "Now can we talk—" but wind slammed at him and snatched the words from his mouth. Cold stabbed into his lungs.

Trapped on a rooftop. Just like when he and Angie had caught Kate at the hospital—*and I deserve it, letting the magic out of my hands again.* At least Kate had gotten her son away, and now maybe Dennard was out of danger too.

He pressed lower on the ice, but the wind wasn't dragging him anymore, instead it beat down at him with soaking sleet and hail, cold worse than the ice against his cheek. How long could he take this? How long would he *have* to before someone out there reacted? If just one security camera was still working surely someone would have heard Dennard's gunshots or seen Nolan running out *into* the storm! They'd see someone needed help…

"I never wanted this!" he shouted, fighting to catch a full breath in the cold. "I was looking for the owl's master, *he's* the killer—"

Nolan didn't move, didn't respond. Mark couldn't make out her face, and doubted that his voice could even reach her. His hands felt like fingerless clubs of ice. Why hasn't anyone seen—

Nolan's head turned to look past him. Mark followed her gaze, to see the far door to the roof's other stairs catch a gust of wind and crash open, and there was Kate, already ducking behind the concrete hut that housed those stairs. *She came back.*

In the moment's lull after the gust, he heard Kate shout "You want this to be over? You want our power?" And around the corner she dangled a long band of leather, like the thinnest white flag anyone ever waved.

Mark saw the air darken around Kate's shelter, felt the hail resume its pounding.

Kate waved the belt again. "You want to disarm us? Take it? It's all right here, just let us go!"

Of course. The thought burst through Mark's mind; of course Kate would give the magic up, she'd never wanted it at all... *but then the killer gets away...* Mark tried to shout but his words came out as a frozen croak. "Get out!"

"Just touch it," Kate yelled to Nolan. "You'll know it's the real thing."

Nolan started toward her.

Mark pulled his feet under him and started toward Nolan, but she turned as he advanced, angling to watch him as well as Kate—and to watch the ramp behind him too. Was this alertness what years of controlling magic had taught her?

Another yell faded in Mark's throat as he saw the deadly blankness on Nolan's face; this was one person who was ready to finish an enemy. *Come on, where's the rescue crew? There* has *to be someone coming!*

As Nolan drew closer, Kate stepped into view again and waved the belt. "Touch it. This is all the power we have."

And Nolan stopped. She folded her arms and laughed. "All? You think I'd believe that?"

Kate stepped back out of sight. Of course, even she would hold the spare strips back… and yet Nolan had *guessed* there'd be some trick like that. Mark tensed for the next attack, hoping he could reach Nolan this time.

The belt waved into view again, and this time it had two thin shapes tied to it. "Here, both backups too. Just let us go."

Nolan reached the bunker, hand outstretched.

Mark remembered the belt's magic could crush with a touch; when Nolan touched the belt, could Kate use its power to pin her?

Unless Nolan takes control of it first—

Mark threw himself forward. Nolan didn't turn, didn't see him, only reached out—

Her fingertip brushed the belt, with Mark still long yards away. And, nothing happened, only Kate pulling the belt back and Nolan turning to watch Mark, still alert. Mark staggered to a stop.

Nolan edged to the side, eyes flicking between Mark and Kate. She smiled. "So, do we have a trade or not?"

Mark realized what Kate's answer would be an instant before she said it: "No."

It had to be. For Kate, this was the only thing she'd want, Mark knew it. His heartbeat seemed to slow as he saw her hand open, as the shape stirred and moved and shot upward to fall into the sky.

Nolan gestured after it, but Mark read the frustration on her face even before he saw the shape buck in the wind and vanish to the left. Too small, too far off; had it been impossible for her to focus on?

Mark could only watch his last glimpse of it fade from his sight. Lowering his eyes, he saw Nolan stubbornly making pulling gestures for her winds to flail after it, and heard Kate say, "So now you can either finish us, or hunt down the puppetmaster who's our real—"

"What in hell?"

The shock in Nolan's voice sent Mark's eyes skyward, and then he saw it too. Just a shadow in the storm, not even a shape, but it was a shadow that streaked against the wind through just that side of the sky. There was only one thing it could be: the killer's bird, in a flight that scooped in and then spun triumphantly away from where it must have snatched up the belt to let it twist away between the rooftops. Gone.

"Played me," Nolan hissed. "He *played* us! Huh!"

She turned away then, walking right past Mark for the door down, as if he and Kate no longer existed. Under her breath she grumbled what had to be something savage.

"You said 'he'?" Mark yelled after Nolan as she swung the door open. "Do you know who—"

"I will," was all she said before she let the door slam shut.

Mark couldn't move. One part of him felt the winds still shoving at him where he stood, and that part was able to think, *sure, she can't let the storm fade too fast or else* nobody *could explain it away.* But with a bit of care, Olivia Nolan had the perfect, untraceable weapon, so much safer than the belt.

The belt.

"It's gone. Can't fly, can't track, can't find Angie's killer—" Another part of him remembered to look toward Kate then and ask, "Is Dennard alright?"

"I don't know." Between one word and the next, Kate's voice fell into its usual brisk force. "We need to get to him. Because now we really *do* have to disappear." And she strode for the door.

Mark moved after her, numbly trying to grasp what she meant. Without the magic, what did it matter what they did? Why was she in such a rush?

His frozen body was tipping before he realized he'd forgotten the ice under his feet. Numbly he glanced off the stair's door, landing on his side—

He saw the shape above him. Not a streak this time, only a single dot in the air, growing larger before his eyes. He tried to roll away, but he was far too slow. He had only an instant to wonder what the owl could still want from him.

He heard the burst of wingbeats by his ear, right before the touch. The touch *inside*.

Torrents of force pouring into him, through him… him trying to push back, thinking wildly *get out, get out*… the force flowing past what little guard he could make from sheer willpower, raised too slowly… fighting, fighting, the intruder pulling back, then a feeling of something familiar… throwing his will at it no matter what it cost to drag the answer out of it, the presence already darting away in his head like a bird—no, nimbler than any bird—ready for him before he struck, leaving him only a taste of its strong certainty threaded into all the strangeness… tearing himself to reach, *reach*… as his eyes opened—

His eyes opened, his hand stretched out, but the owl was already flapping away. He started up, and felt something lying across his body that hadn't been there before. The belt.

Somewhere in the corner of his eye, Kate was starting toward him, bewildered, but he could only stare upward. He drew in pain like breath, drew in all the slashing risk of accepting that hope, knowing it was more than hope. Because of what he'd sensed, somewhere within that owl. Angie.

CHAPTER FIFTEEN

BIRDWATCHING

Joe Dennard huddled in the passenger seat, under the blanket. The emergency crew had pronounced him healthy enough, but he wasn't speaking—he'd barely said a word after Mark had told him that Nolan had gone and Kate and James had headed off, safe. Still, his eyes had the same hard set they often did, sweeping around the streets they passed for danger.

But he was awake, he was fine. Mark kept glancing between the road and his passenger, bubbling with the need to *say it*—

At the first light they stopped at, he began. "You were saying… you'd been trying to talk to that morgue man, Osborn, again?" Dennard's eyes swung around, surprised, and Mark went on, "I've seen our enemy possess people. One person touches another, and I sense his control jumping over to the other."

"Makes him damned hard to find," Dennard said softly. "I was thinking his magic was making people sleep, that and the birds, but he can just grab control of people to do his work. That's nothing like our gravity power, or that weather—"

"It all fits!" Mark slapped a hand on the wheel. "He moves part of his mind to the victim, get it? But when he went after Angie it back-fired—did he really think she wouldn't fight back? The mind's touch that I felt on the roof, it *is* Angie! Maybe she's buried in the owl's head, but she took control to—"

"WHAT?"

Breathe. Breathe. Mark forced himself to pause, and let the evidence line itself up on his tongue. "It's Angie, she's in that owl now. Look at the facts: that owl is the one magic bird that hasn't attacked me since the change, and it defended me from Nolan last night, *and* today it caught the belt and gave it back to me, and when it did I'm sure I sensed her inside it! The killer's been sending other birds after me instead of the owl—because he can't control her! I've got to find her—I can't whistle up a crazy storm like Nolan's to get her attention, but I'll find her. Someone has to know where owls den, at least narrow it down, so we can start—"

"Shut up!"

Dennard's voice rang off the windows.

"She's *dead!* Stop babbling, stop denying it—I killed—dammit, we both got her killed, so stop trying to wish it away!"

"Wish? So who brought the belt back? I just told you I *sensed—"*

A horn blared behind them; the light must have turned green again. Mark ignored it.

"I sensed *Angie* when that bird touched my mind, it was *her,* it had to be! Here I thought the killer made it save me from Nolan because those two were enemies, but it was just Angie protecting—"

"Stop!" Dennard's hand reached halfway into his coat... for the gun he had kept before, the one that Mark had tossed away to cover up his shooting up the garage. Dennard could only glare at Mark, as the cars honked around them. "Just stop it. I've heard enough." He reached for the door.

Mark pressed the gas once, to jerk them forward and throw Dennard back in the seat. He had to make him understand. "But... I sensed her," he tried again. "She should have come to us days ago, maybe she has some kind of problem staying in control. We have to find her, and then get our hands on the enemy's magic, it's the only way to help her..." His voice faded away.

"Ghosts." Dennard made it the bitterest sigh Mark had ever heard.

Mark watched him in his seat, still shivering in the blanket. *I really was babbling, I should have broken it more gently. But I need help, I need something.* Kate had at least had the excuse of getting her son away, but Angie's father needed to be helping him, if only he'd listen.

They pulled up outside the park management office. As they climbed out, another thought touched Mark: should Dennard even be coming in to his old job, when he could barely stand, and anyone from the mystery killer to the Blades to Nolan might still decide to finish him off? Was he hoping they would? Mark opened his mouth to ask.

Dennard saw the movement and cut in. "Ghosts," he said again. "Not even a ghost; you think there's a ghost inside an *owl?* First you're chasing a murderer, and now you think you can—can't you let it go—"

Mark spun on his heel and walked away.

Sheer frustration swept him along the street, glad to be out of the car and away from those doubts. If Dennard had at least *seen* the owl returning the belt…

But Kate had, and she hadn't listened either. She'd only waved a smartphone full of web alerts at him, and said *"This* is all the magic someone needs to find you. If you have to keep doing this, at least learn to cover your tracks." Those were her last words before she and James had disappeared into the airport line.

So *how* many tricks and contingency plans had Kate had taken away with her into hiding? *She lost her father to the magic, then she said she couldn't control it either, and then her ex used it to pick a fight with a gang; yeah, Kate would stay that prepared.* And now she'd deserted him.

Mark glared at the skyline. Human plans and tools wouldn't track an owl anyway, but he could lift himself up and keep searching until he sensed Angie again… but he knew that trap.

Damn, I'm tired. Instead of floating away he squeezed past a chattering older couple to slump down on the corner of a bus stop bench.

Hours of sleepless worry and pain crashed down on him. But this time, *this* time, he had Angie out there.

He looked up at the bus line and realized what had drawn him there. He could still head back to Olivia Nolan's home again, beg to join her in hunting their enemy, and trust that her letting Mark and Kate live said more about her than how ruthlessly she'd come after them did. At least she'd *been able* to track them down.

Still, Mark pried himself off of the bench to step back from the growing crowd and call Kate before he headed into the lion's den. No answer, but she and James were probably in the air by now... When he turned back, two men had already taken his seat. "Of course," he sighed.

Mark sagged back on the edge of the bench, looking up at the clouds sliding by. Was Angie up there somewhere? Owls hated daylight, but it might be different for her, whatever she was now. She'd come to see the windstorm during daytime...

Through flickering, grayed-out sight, he saw the bus roll up and sweep away again without him. *I can't be that tired, I have to find her, find a way to help her.* The bench was clear again but he kept himself on his feet, running though his plans. He'd face Nolan this time and make her work with him... or she'd freeze him to an icicle...

Am I getting reckless again? If only these people at the stop— when had it filled up again?—weren't battering his ears with talk about the storms... he had to make Nolan find Angie, or else he'd jump past every street in the city until he found her or lost his mind—

Storms?

The conversation around the bench finally broke through to him.

"They say autumn storms don't do this—"

"First downtown, then all along the—"

"Not a tornado, but—"

Mark yanked out his phone to check. His weather app announced another "freak micro-storm" on the west side, and from the talk he heard around him, scientists were already trying to explain the phenomenon away. The screen showed one, two more pockets of wild weather had flared and faded in the last hour. Sleet. Ice. Branches cracking windows.

Nobody hurt enough to make the news. So far.

Mark stared at the map screen, trying to connect the dots into a pattern. Could it be Nolan sniffing out and hitting the killer's strongholds? Did the killer have more than one stronghold?

Or is that Angie, flying, trying to keep ahead of Nolan's attacks?

His fingers tightened on the screen. But no, the spots were miles apart and they looked almost random. He forced himself to breathe again.

Hell, the randomness might be intentional—so the "freak weather" could be seen at more places than the ones where she'd actually fought them. Mark swallowed; if that destruction was Nolan's idea of a cover story, was she really someone he wanted to look for her again?

* * *

In the end, he called it research, but he knew he was stalling, and bleeding away what time and strength he had. So when he reached the garage and saw two of the cab drivers huddled around a cab's dented window, he tried to hurry past them. Just trading smiles with them took too much of his strength.

"You're late." The burly dispatcher barely looked up from his computer, but his voice echoed through the room. "What's this 'explanation' you couldn't give me on the phone? You think you can ask for my afternoon shifts and then skip Sunday?"

"Sorry." Mark tried to steady his voice; to sound reasonable, helpful. "It's two things. One, with all this talk about the weather today, I was thinking there'd be calls from people needing rides to check the damage. Or sightsee, the way they're talking. And all that's going to change traffic patterns—change them a lot if it keeps happening. And that changes business."

"If a whole blizzard socks the city in, sure." Johanson pursed his lip. "Right now, it's just weather."

"But it's still creating patterns in the traffic. I tried plotting them, but you've got the pro software there."

Mark held up his phone, and Johanson took a long look at the app and started clicking on his own keyboard.

This ought to tell me something *about how Nolan's moving, and maybe even a guess at why.* "I need a favor. Can you send me the findings as you get them—"

Johanson twisted back to face him, and Mark knew he should have worked up to it better. His boss said, slowly, "A 'favor'? Sounds like you're leaving. Are you going solo and want to steal our leads too… no, not that, I think. You don't look fit to drive a tricycle right now."

Mark held his gaze, fighting the urge to flinch away. "It's a family emergency. The last thing I would have planned on, believe me."

Johanson turned back to his screen again. "Go on, then. And I'll *see* about sharing that data. At least you did some good work while you were here."

"While he was here?"

Mark spun around. *I'm so worn out I can't hear someone Roger Winton's size behind me?*

As Winton walked up, Mark gave Johanson a quick, "Thank you— and thank you for introducing us," to Winton. "I hope I'll be back soon." If not, at least he'd said one goodbye right.

He ducked around Winton and slipped out the door, leaving the business partners to their conferring. With each step toward the street he pushed faster; the sooner he got clear of the garage and the chatter there, the more strength he'd have left to decide what to do about Nolan.

Then he heard footsteps echoing through the voices behind him. The awkward running steps of an overweight entrepreneur, and Winton's panting voice: "Hold on, Mark—"

Oh no, just when people are safer away from me…

The words mingled with the drivers' voices; Mark pushed on onto the sidewalk as if he hadn't heard. Once he'd turned out of sight of the garage entrance he dodged around a pair of deliverymen and kept moving.

But Winton's footsteps were still behind him, and now his voice was louder. "What are you doing? I *got* you that job and you blow it off?" Winton broke off for a moment, and Mark looked back to see him scrambling closer and closer. His wrinkled suit looked ready to pop a few buttons by the time he caught up. "I'm… I'm trying to help, and you run?" he wheezed.

"Sorry." But Mark only slowed, couldn't let himself stop. "If you're thinking I'm in trouble, relax. I just have a friend who needs—"

"And that *friend* has you looking like… like you haven't slept in days? What have the Blades done to you now?" Winton was getting his breath back fast, and he caught at Mark's arm.

"It's not…"

Mark paused and took a slow breath. Roger Winton had known him on and off for years, of course he was worried. *And he's a community leader in his spare time; if he thinks I'm losing it he may* never *back off.*

"It's not the Blades at all," he began again. "If you didn't hear, I was asking Mr. Johanson about today's crazy weather—"

"The weather? At least find an excuse that makes sense!" Winton shook his head. "If you can't say what the gang did, at least tell me what you're taking."

Too much flying magic. That truth sucked some of the strength from his denial: "It's not drugs. And it's not the Blades. These storms have been giving my friend a problem, that's all… and that's all I can tell you about it. But can you let me—"

Mark froze. A big man was walking up behind Winton and he wasn't simply wearing a heavy coat against the weather, he'd wrapped his scarf around to cover half his face. Hiding it. Mark opened his mouth—

The man took one more step, and stopped behind Winton, his hand, concealed in a pocket, pressed against Winton's back.

"That's a knife against your left kidney," Rafe said. "You know what that means?"

Winton's lips twitched. Then, softly but steadily, he said, "It means I keep quiet."

The words burst out of Mark's throat. "Rafe, please! You don't have to hurt—"

"Not here," Rafe cut in. "I'll bring him to you at one. By the pond in the park."

The tightness in Mark's chest clamped down like an iron claw. *What's Rafe doing?* If he was desperate enough to take a hostage in public... and he wanted to meet in the park, where the magic was... *how much does he know?*

Rafe guided Winton up the street. Mark's eyes measured how many steps it would take to jump on Rafe with the magic; pleas and threats rushed through his head. But Rafe's warning glance back held him off.

The two reached a battered car on the sidewalk. Rafe made Winton climb in first and squeeze across to the driver's seat, and Mark thought he saw the glint of a gun before the two drove away.

* * *

The killer knew everything.

Or almost everything. It was the only answer Mark could think of, as he walked up Summer Street toward the park. He tried to push the thought down with every tired step... but it had to be true. The killer had sent Rafe to trade Winton's life for Mark showing him the rest of the belt's secret, that was why it would happen here. And then they could all be dead.

Just think of Winton—Rafe only got him because of me! *Don't think about how long the enemy's already been letting us live, don't think about how I'd just started to hope Angie's still out there.*

At twelve thirty a tour bus pulled up at the park's edge, letting out a pack of passengers to stream down the sidewalk, waving books and smartphones. A few of them even had binoculars. A gray-haired woman led them along the side of the park with a flurry of eager gestures, and Mark realized they were there as birdwatchers.

The irony brought a grin to his face, and it widened as he scanned the area and sensed there were still no enemy birds here watching for *him.* The group even seemed to be moving toward the pond; Mark slid in among them, hoping the crowd would hide him from sight. This could be his one chance to look around the meeting place before Rafe or his boss arrived.

But then he saw two men sitting against the stone rim that encased the pond, the fatter one leaning his head on the other's shoulder. Rafe and Winton were already here.

Mark edged back in the crowd. People rustled around him, opening guidebooks, pointing ahead at the ducks drifting on and sometimes diving below the water. The group would pass by the pond soon... perfect witnesses that should keep Rafe from harming Winton.

From the other side of the pond, a young man marched toward the group, calling out, "Will you be ready when the Lord calls? When the righteous are—"

Mark saw Rafe turn and look at him, straight through the crowd.

With a swallow and another brief scan for enemy magic, Mark moved up to meet the two men.

Winton sat slumped against Rafe, as still as if he were asleep, but his eyes were open and darting around in fear. Mark readied his thoughts as he closed in; Rafe had to know he'd never get away with hurting Winton outside, in plain view of witnesses. And, if Mark could start by making Rafe think he barely knew Winton, surely Rafe wouldn't risk much for what leverage a "random acquaintance" gave him.

Winton's voice was low, but it reached him through the noise of the tour group. "I'm not hurt. So far."

Something about the background hubbub made Mark glance to the side. The group was starting around the other side of the pond. His witnesses were drawing *away*.

"This could have all been different, you know."

Rafe's quiet words snapped Mark's eyes back.

"Back in school," Rafe went on. "You could have been one of us. The boys hit a shop, some of the blame splashes on you—and you end up with nowhere to go but the Blades. It worked before… but no, you, you got the big boss over a dozen stores to come down and listen to you. And Winton's *still* kissing your ass?"

For a moment, the street preacher's voice broke through the crowd noises behind them: "Will you still turn away, have you not heard the word…"

Winton whispered, "Not everyone's as far off track as you, Rafe."

"Is that a line from your youth center?" Rafe chuckled, and then his eyes locked straight on Mark. "So don't you forget, this is one throat I should have cut years ago."

Mark felt cold sweep through him as Rafe patted his prisoner's shoulder; the crowd was moving further away by the second. *I've got to distract him from killing—he did have doubts the last time we met—*

"But you *lost* the Blades, Rafe. Because you let someone use you—"

Rafe's other hand crept over behind Winton's back, silent as a snake. "You know what I came to get, Mark."

But did the killer tell you *what the magic is?* Mark snapped back, "So you're still taking orders? And now he's got you taking hostages? Didn't you see how his other spy—"

He caught himself before he said *possessed* or *suicide* right in front of Winton's shocked face. But in the moment his words died away, he saw Rafe's smile widen.

Scrambling for words, Mark tried again. "You can't think you can stab him and get away." He nodded across the pond. "God, they've even got *binoculars* over there. What are you really after?"

Instead of answering, Rafe turned to look at Winton. "What were you saying on the street, about the storms?"

Mark felt his stomach drop. Was there *any* piece of the magic puzzle Rafe didn't have?

"What?" Winton's voice rose in surprise. "You grab me off the street, you threaten my life, and now you want to know about the *weather?*"

Rafe reached around Winton's shoulder, eyes never leaving Mark. "I think I asked you a question."

Mark snapped "Stop pretending! He can't tell you anything, and you can't hurt anyone out here—"

Rafe's fingers pressed into the side of Winton's throat. For one instant Winton's eyes went wide in shock—

Then his head lolled against Rafe's shoulder, his breath wheezed and caught and went still.

"You can't!" Mark gasped it, ready to scream it. The crowd across the pond wasn't shouting, how could they not *see?*

But then Rafe pulled his fingers back, then settled them lightly against Winton's pulse. "Hmm. He went right out." Rafe's lips moved in a tight smile.

His fingers pressed into Winton's neck again.

"Show me!" Rafe snarled.

My God... Mark's mouth worked helplessly, as Winton's face began darkening to blue. "Let him go, stop it! That's what *he* wants, he wants you to push me, to make me use it. It's about why I keep getting away from you—"

Rafe's fingers only tightened.

Mark clutched at his waist and the belt buckle came free all too easily. He held the length of leather up and let it sway in the air.

Rafe... stared. His jaw fell open, and then he shook his head. "You're shitting me."

His grip on Winton relaxed, and the choked color began to fade from his skin. The confusion in Rafe's voice sounded so genuine; the brutal schemer was simply a pawn, in over his head.

"Your 'boss' still didn't tell you, did he?"

He watched as Rafe drew his hand away from behind Winton, and he saw something glint in the sun. Was he putting away a knife, or was that a phone? *I'm getting through to him. I have to be.* Mark drew the belt back and slipped it on again. He leaned closer and let the hushed, sharp words tumble out, each one helping him pick the next:

"He only strung you along with hints, right? Or maybe some tips that have you still trying to figure out how anyone could know so much—so you tell yourself whatever it is he wants, he can still make it pay off some day? Well I saw what he did after the funeral: his spy threw himself into traffic just to scare me. And, he killed Detective Lee just for guessing there *was any* kind of secret. And now he's got you grabbing people and demanding the secret, and not even telling you what it is. What did he tell you, that this time you'd earn your reward? It must have sounded better than 'you've got an hour to live.'"

Rafe's eyes narrowed in warning. "Fear my 'boss'? I knew you'd try that one again. You think *I'm* in danger here?"

"I think you're playing every side against each other—*still*—and you don't see that you're taking orders from someone who could wipe you out the moment he needs to? He's done it before! You're trusting someone you never should because if you don't you've thrown everything you had away for *nothing*?" For an instant Mark thought *did I mean him or me,* but then he saw Rafe's scowl loosening and had to rush on. "He doesn't have to give you a thing if you keep letting him win. But *I* need everything you know about him, and if you tell me, I can stop him and fix what he's done!"

"So what're you trading?" Rafe said.

The words brought Mark up short. It *was* what he'd led himself to. The only way to free Winton and get to whoever was giving Rafe his orders—

If there's anyone else. The thought slammed through Mark's head, and made him stare harder at Rafe's cold eyes, at his hands that had nearly killed Winton. What if Rafe had only *pretended* to have a boss, what if *he'd* been the killer puppetmaster all along—

Mark clamped his jaw shut and banished the thought. Even magic couldn't make Rafe *that* devious, there had to be another mastermind behind it all.

So where was he? Mark realized it had been too long since he'd scanned for magic. He felt for it…

The magic glided by above and to his left. Mark's head swung up to spot one among the several ducks circling the pond, a shape that made his skull prickle.

A moment after he stared up, he saw the bird twist around and drop toward them… heard Rafe saying "Still holding out on me"… glimpsed the tour group on the far side start to point—

"Look out—" Mark tried to yell, but Rafe was already twisting and starting to roll away, but he looked *back* first instead of looking up as the bird struck.

In a flurry of wings it swept by Rafe, barely brushing him. But Mark felt the magic jump.

Then the duck pulled up and settled clumsily into the pond, abandoned. In its wake, Rafe slowly turned back to face Mark… with an expressionless, *empty* look that could never have been Rafe's.

"What was that? Did that duck attack you?" someone yelled. Some of the birdwatchers were running around the pond.

"We're fine!" Mark called back. "Near miss, that's all." *I have to keep them away,* came the wild thought, *or he'll start threatening them too.*

The crowd slowed. Mark saw a commotion in the back, saw the woman who'd been leading them arguing with the street preacher, still in their midst.

But the killer… the body that had been Rafe's moved so slowly, hands drifting like clouds on the wind as they reached down and drew Winton over to rest his head in his lap. He didn't say a word.

Mark's fingers clenched and his muscles tensed, ready to fling himself at the enemy—if he even dared rush something that possessed with a touch. But just looking at the stolen face made Mark's pulse thunder in his ears.

He took a step closer. "Murderer!" he hissed.

Rafe's dark eyes looked away… but they slid down toward Winton, and one hand settled on the man's shoulder. The other hand reached out to Mark.

Mark stumbled back away from that touch, but the gesture was no attack. The killer simply held out his palm, ready to take the belt.

Winton's life for the magic, again! Mark fought down a snarl of rage and grabbed for something to say, anything to distract him.

"So Rafe *did* see too much. Did he really think you'd trust a thug like him with what you were after? You never show your moves. I bet if he knew, if he got greedy and made one slip, he'd let the secret out and they'd be hunting for magicians everywhere."

"Everywhere."

Mark started. The cold, hollow voice made him wonder if this creature had ever been human. It had Winton's and Rafe's lives at its fingertips, and all it wanted was the belt. That and all its tracks covered.

Somewhere back in the murmur of the crowd, the street preacher's voice rose into a shrill, "Too long, too long have we walked—"

Mark could only clench his teeth and say, "So you used him and now you kill him; it's what you do. Of *course* your magic is about controlling things, what other power could a trickster like you have?"

("Can we only *crawl—*" the preacher shouted, from worlds away.)

The killer only motioned with his stolen hand again, waiting for the belt.

Mark's pulse thundered in his ears, louder with every word he said, with every second that he couldn't find a way out. "You think you're invincible because you don't show your face? You twist minds, you turn gangs against each other, you kill and you kill... you killed cops, you haunted Dennard, you couldn't get at Nolan so you tricked me into finding her... but when you touched Angie she *beat* you—"

The possessed face *twitched.* Mark's fury exploded and he leaped.

He was flinging himself at the killer even while in the corner of his eye he saw Rafe's hand lift away from Winton's head; a wrench of the belt's magic ripped away Mark's weight and then Rafe's an instant later as they crashed together and tore past Winton's still form and hurtled over the pond.

In midair the world went gray. Mark's sight and touch went dull as he threw all his strength, all his rage, into a surge of crushing weight at the body that was readying its own twisted power to flow out at him—

Waves of magic crashed together inside his hands. His avalanche of force slammed into a fanged storm, a hunger ripping inward through his bones—

Another surge hit him as the pond swallowed the sunlight. He pushed back harder with his own power, whatever it took to force them all down toward the bottom, but all he felt was the tearing power in his skull.

Bubbles of air brushed by his face. The killer couldn't hold onto his breath.

Does he care? Did I grab a breath when I moved? Mark ignored those thoughts and tightened his hold on the pain where the magics fought, one pushing back and down as the other forced deep *into* him.

Then, one more sensation reached him through the pain: Rafe's body had been thrashing in his grip, but now it stilled. Fainter, slower... and like thorns sliding from Mark's soul the killer's magic drew back and released him. Mark felt it shift and let Rafe go too, and caught one sense of it flitting *away* somewhere. Gone.

He's afraid of dying in a stolen body. And I'm killing Rafe.

Mark blinked in the murk, power still pouring crushing weight into the form trapped under his hands. *One more threat... almost gone...* no, that was the magic in his head again... *chest burning...*

Something moved. Something wrenched upward, he felt it pushing through the fields of energy as much as against his waist. Rafe's finger brushed against the belt.

Thrash. In his skull, something churned and lashed and strained against his control of the power but he clamped down again—but too late, Rafe had squirmed free.

Mark reared back to splash his head up past the surface and gasp in air. Standing chest-deep in the water, he saw that the air was roiling more than the depths, with flocks of panicked mallards struggling into the sky; far-off sounds began to sound like human voices. Blinking, he saw a hunched, heaving shape against the water's surface that had to be Rafe trying to breathe.

And Roger Winton on his feet at the side of the pond, eyes wide.

CHAPTER SIXTEEN

THE DIVE

Men splashed through the pond toward Mark. One shouted, "You let him go, now!"

The words cut through the haze of magic and rage from the—moments?—below. Mark watched them close in and his only thoughts were *I almost drowned Rafe. I wanted to.*

Two more men were moving to Rafe. Mark saw him wave them off and stumble away before the hands closed on his own arm.

"Not him!" Winton's voice slashed through the voices and the water. "He was saving me—it's the other one who kidnapped me!"

The man's grip on Mark went slack, but Rafe was already climbing over the stone rim of the pond, and bolting across the grass.

Mark gasped in a breath to call after him… but what could he say? *Come back and help me catch the killer who possessed you, betrayed you?* Even if he did, Rafe would turn on him, too, the minute he got a clear shot at the magic.

Instead he watched as Rafe cut past the edges of the tour group. All of them only stared, too slow to react to the changes in who was endangering who. They weren't the police.

But the police *would* be here soon; Mark saw phones coming out here and there in the crowd, and he knew the park guards would notice the noise soon. Finally the man holding him let him go, and Mark waded toward the side of the pond, trying to think. None of the killer's magic flickered nearby, but he could be back any time—and if he took over a cop while they were questioning Mark—

Winton was waiting at the pond's rim, but Mark brushed aside his attempt to help him over. "I'm so sorry I dragged you into all this."

"Mark, what is going—"

"Please!" He glanced around; his would-be rescuers were already nearing the edge of the water, and the rest of the crowd was too close for him to say much. He leaned closer. "All that matters is that he could come back for you, and the police can't stop him—he's already killed a cop, and the rest of the police never knew. You have to hide! And, talk to Joe Dennard."

Winton's widening eyes narrowed. "So... Dennard can tell me what—"

Wait, I can't pull him into more of this! Mark glanced around again; the bustling, pointing ranks of people were already closing in around him and Winton. "Listen! They tried to use you once, and the cops can't stop him. Just... assume he's *everywhere.* And you can't risk talking to me again."

With Mark's every word, he saw Winton's eyes filling with a look of pity. But Mark didn't care how crazy the words came out, as long as Winton took some of the warning to heart. He spun away and twisted through a gap in the crowd.

A flick of magic lightened his stride before anyone could catch at him, and oh, how he ached to skim forward three, five feet at a step and run *free*, but he clamped down on the urge and locked his movements into a brisk, earthbound jog toward the sidewalk.

One step at a time; the magic was the one thing he could still try to keep controlled. He reached the Winter Street corner and waited out the light before he trusted himself to a run. Still nobody shouted after him, and he sensed none of the enemy's magic around.

His phone buzzed, but he saw Winton's name on the screen and didn't answer, just kept loping and weaving past the people around. The man wanted some real answers, like any sane person would, and the fact that he thought Mark could give them to him was almost comforting. At least one thing hadn't been totally turned on its head.

And… Angie was still out there. She had to be.

Mark came to a stop and ducked inside a tiny bakery. Squeezing into a corner, he looked at his phone again and tried to sort out the pieces on the shadowy game board:

Winton was safe so far, and he'd had his warning. The force that had possessed Rafe had fled, for now, and Rafe knew his boss had betrayed him—*and that I almost killed him, too, and he's had a taste of using the magic!* But Olivia Nolan… he dug through the news and weather apps and found that the outbreak of "freak icestorms" had ended. So Nolan had done all the damage she needed.

Or she chased Angie down and killed her. Mark felt his throat tighten at the thought, but… he couldn't know, he could only trust Angie wouldn't go down easily.

He sent Dennard a text:

be ready for ANYthing

the killers taking hostages

he tried to use Roger Winton

have to stop him & get Angie back

He looked up from the screen, picturing the disbelief that had been on Dennard's face again. The baker behind the counter was giving him a curious look, and Mark took a step for the door before the smell of bread hit his empty stomach.

* * *

He'd loped and twisted through so many streets to hide himself, he could barely remember where the dirty little row fit into Lavine at all. Mark was too tired to fight, barely strong enough to hold his feet down on the ground… but he still hesitated a moment outside the hotel's door and boarded-up window.

Did my father sell his drugs out of a place like this? Did my mother die in a place like this? It couldn't matter. This was what he could afford, and he had no strength left to find anything else.

Two men sitting in the corner of the filthy "lobby" eyed him as he paid for a room. He walked on past them, closed the door on his tiny refuge, and used magic to slide the bed over to barricade it. And at last he could strip off the belt and its feeble, aching tingling, and toss it the too-short distance to the corner and hope its influence would fade from his head soon.

The smell stung his nose. A baby was crying down the hall. When he stretched out on the bed a clump of springs poked him in the ribs… then he felt his muscles melting and his eyes drooping…

Not yet.

He dragged out his phone and called Henry.

"Mark? Are you alright?"

"Fine. But *you* could be next—" He broke off and lowered his voice to slide under the noises around him. "Our enemy's tried taking hostages to get at me. Even if he never saw me with you, he can find out you're my family."

"Forget it. I'm not leaving you alone in this. But Mark… *are* you alright?" Henry said again.

"I told you." Mark shifted on the hard bed, hating the worried, insistent tone in his cousin's voice. "And, I'm better than alright. She's alive! Angie is, I saw her!"

"But…" Henry began, then stopped again.

"Okay, it's not that simple. I have to find her. But there's this other magician, Nolan, she tried to kill us but then she let us go. Maybe her magic can track down the killer's better than mine can, or find Angie, if there's a way I can trust her or get her to trust me. Or use Rafe for something, I don't know. Angie's the owl, Henry! There has to be some way to find her."

He stopped for breath then. Out in the hall, a man was shouting about the baby's crying.

"The owl?" Henry stopped a moment, then began again slowly: "Mark… the last I called, you said you'd give Kate the belt."

"She gave it back to me." *Hell,* Angie *was the one who did that too.* But Mark kept that to himself; the doubt in Henry's voice was thicker than the stench in the room.

"Mark… Angie's gone."

"She should be, I know. But people shouldn't be flying either, should they? And I am. It's the truth." He took a slow breath and tried to make his words steady, smooth. "I'm not losing control again, I promise. I've fought for my life three, no, four times since the sun went down, and now I'm making time to rest. But Henry, I *felt* Angie in the owl. I know her. And you know that if I'm right, if it is Angie, I can't leave her out there."

"But, you've still *got the belt,*" Henry said. "We agreed that you'd never keep it two days in a row. We *agreed* you'd let me decide when you could start using it again."

"We did." A pale stain on the wall drew his eye. *Do I really have to argue this in a place like one of my mother's dives?*

"So, it's time for me to take it back. You can sit down and explain all this to me, and I promise I'll listen, but first you need to hand it over."

"You want me to come to you when the killer's taking hostages? And I *said,* I have to find her. And I've got to be ready for the killer, any time. I'm not even touching it now." Except for the spare scraps in his pocket, he realized.

"That's not the point." Henry's tone was firm. "You always made it back here before. And Mark, as long as you have it you *could* decide to use it just one more time, and then again, until you don't come back at all."

"But I'm not using it, I'm being careful. And I *need*—" Hearing the addict's word made Mark flinch, but he stared harder at the stain on the wall and went on "I'm putting in my time without using it, I swear. And Henry… can you really say you'd do this any different, if you got a second chance like… like *this?* I thought she was *gone.*"

For a moment Henry didn't answer. The noise from outside filtered into the shabby room.

"Mark, what would *she* want?" he said at last.

Damn. Mark sighed, and said, "If I stop looking, I'll never get to ask her myself." And he hung up.

Damn, damn, damn it all…

He saw a text on the phone then, from Winton:

I'm safe. Talked to Dennard. He said you're in danger, and unstable.

The last word burned his eyes. Dennard, Winton, and now Henry, they all thought he was losing his mind…

And the way he'd babbled about Angie and run off, what else *could* they think? Mark groaned and shifted on the bed.

Think! Angie could be anywhere, and the puppetmaster never had to show his face at all… unless Olivia Nolan could track them, but saying one wrong word to her might freeze him solid. Every other time they'd met had gone so wrong.

And how warm is Angie in those feathers?

The last thing he did was pull out the strips of leather from his pocket that were still tingling, urging him to fly, and tossed them into the corner by the belt. Then he closed his eyes and tried to sleep.

* * *

The sleep wasn't enough. When darkness let him take to the streets again, his head wasn't quite clear, and his steps itched to float away. But the routes he'd planned through the town offered only a few bare chances of telling him about Nolan or Angie, and racing through faster would only push the magic's hooks deeper into him.

But the first storm site Johanson had found looked much like any other, untouched location now. It was just a block on Mulwray, its shops mostly closed up for the night; no windows shattered by hail, no lines of police tape staking out some suspicious accident, not hours after the pocket storm had faded. He stared at the spruce trees in front of the landscaping office, and thought they did look a bit ragged… but nothing he saw or sensed told him this could had been some hidden base of the killer's that Nolan had tracked down.

He looked up the street, west, toward the co-op that Angie had crashed in for a few weeks, but no, that was five blocks away. And the "freak storms" Nolan had thrown up were scattered so widely around Lavine that some of them had to be near some of Angie's haunts. The storm had never come within five blocks; that ought to *prove* Nolan hadn't sensed Angie nesting at her old home and chased her, and he didn't have to peer through the blocks' back corners for the frozen body of an owl…

Stop it. Concentrate. There has to be something I can use, somewhere. Mark turned and marched up the street, wracking his brains for what he might be missing. Had he really thought visiting what people were calling the "Stormday" sites would give him a glimpse into whether he dared to trust Nolan? Every site could be no more than a random target, to keep weather experts from looking too closely at how they'd all begun at Nolan's house. Rattling the whole city for her cover story.

And the other "hopes" left him with the same emptiness. There was no glimmer of Angie at her first childhood home, or at the airfield where she used to watch planes fly; and no way to turn what little he'd learned online about owls' habits into a sense of where she might hide in the city. Not even a hint of her when he slipped back into the park and renewed the belt's magic. All he passed were scattered pedestrians, individuals and groups on their own private missions, and dark buildings that didn't hold a flicker of Angie's tiny form or the killer's invisible power.

With fresh power but fading hopes, it took all he had not to run through the blocks praying he'd missed something.

He could feel the truth pressing in around him: only magic could find either Angie or the killer, and he might search forever before his dim senses stumbled across them. And if Olivia Nolan *could* do better… *everything I do except begging her for help is just stalling. But if she can't, or I go to her and she turns on me…*

"When the wind howls," Angie's grandfather had written in that old warning. As if Nolan's magic had been their enemy, even generations ago.

Do I have a choice?

His steps blended together into a path of fatigue, surrounded by shadows. The shadows only held themselves back, skulking, none of them willing to offer up one hint more to his senses. Once a police car slowed as it passed him, but he gave a nod and the cops drove on by. *I'm not a threat, I'm not a druggie, no matter how much power's coiled around my waist…*

For a moment he stopped, leaning against a hotdog shack, trying to hold together what options he had left. Keep stumbling around searching for Angie, or a line on Nolan, or ask…

"Mark? Come on now…"

Someone was *shaking* him. He looked up, and staggered back. Why was Roger Winton here?

Because I fell asleep here, and he owns half the food stalls in Lavine—but still, why is he here *when I told him to stay out of sight?*

Mark stumbled to his feet. Winton had a younger man behind him.

"That's him alright." Winton motioned with his head, and the other man backed away to let them talk. He must be the vendor who'd first reported a stranger slumped over in his spot.

Winton stepped closer to whisper, "Mark, what are you doing out here? You told me to stay out of sight, and you're just sitting out here?"

"I was looking… listen, I don't have to explain, I'm the one who saved *you* today," Mark shot back. "After *you* got too close to *me*, and they went after you to get to me—so what part of *stay away* did you not hear?"

"'They' went after me?" Winton peered closer. "You mean Rafe Martinez and the gangs, these people you said are 'everywhere'? Mark, I talked to your friend Dennard—yes, you do still have friends. You can't keep pushing us away when you're in… whatever this is."

"And I keep telling you—"

Something moved around the corner. Mark saw two glowering young men in leather stepping toward them.

Off to the side, the hotdog-seller wheezed a frightened "Boss…"

Mark heard himself say "Easy now," and walk over slowly to meet them. As he did, he dug out his phone and called Joe Dennard, though with Angie in hiding somewhere, trapped as an owl, and the belt throbbing, ready, under his shirt, a pair of punks hardly seemed worth the time. Holding the phone up as a warning, he asked the taller one in front, "Problem?"

"*Problem*?, he says," and the thug's lips tightened to a sneer. "We hear you *almost* caught the traitor today."

"Rafe?" So these were Blades. "He tried getting some kind of revenge on me today, but he missed. And he ran off." That should explain it enough, without bringing Winton or magic into it.

"You should've given him to us. We're looking, and we think he's still on the street somewhere. You think the Eel gave you that number for a joke?"

Winton's voice came from behind him: "What's this about?"

"Back off—" the Blade growled.

Mark tightened his will on the magic, ready.

Something flickered above them, magic circling above, and Mark's head almost jerked up despite the long days he'd spent learning to keep his face still. *That's not one of the other possessed birds, it feels like* her—

"Saint Winton, right?" jeered one of the Blades. "What'd we do this time? Get too near your stall, or your bitch there?"

Roger Winton looked right back at the two thugs, not flinching, but not saying a word to calm or warn them either. Mark stepped between them, trying to show them a reassuring face, not showing how his head was throbbing with that pulse of magic above, still circling, still watching.

"We're done here," the Blade said. "Next time he shows, you tell us first."

The two walked away then, a swagger in their steps. One was saying "You see that, he almost pissed himself—"

"Mark, what are you *doing?*" Winton demanded.

Mark froze. *Winton* doesn't *see me straining to go after Angie...* unless he had sensed her too, unless his rumpled suit and gruff kindness were masks for a killer—it could be anybody—

"What 'next time' are they talking about? Mark, what are you getting yourself into?"

"Nothing you can help with," Mark said, fighting to keep the moment of paranoia off his face, to answer normally. He sensed no magic in Winton, but above them he felt the bird moving, already swinging *away, dammit,* even as he went on, "The Blades aren't after me now—"

"So who is? Rafe grabs me and now you're hunting for him instead? And what else?"

"No! Look, it's for Angie, they took her *away,* and I have to do *something.*"

"How, by—"

Faint, tinny, and furious, Dennard's voice came from the phone in Mark's hand. "What was *that?*"

"Sorry," Mark said as he slapped the phone to his ear. "I thought it was trouble; it wasn't." He looked at Roger Winton again, seeing the stubborn glower he'd kept up while the Blades advanced on him, and thought *I'm paranoid again, confusing honest concern with spying,* even as he felt the magic curving further away above. Hoping to calm both men, Mark added into the phone, "Another friend was just telling me not to take risks—"

"Winton again? Put him on," Dennard snapped.

"But—" Mark couldn't find more words, he needed to get *away* from the two without making Winton more suspicious—the bird had slowed in flight, was it coming back?

A hand grabbed his wrist and pulled the phone over. "Yes, this is 'Winton again.' You told me not to get involved with Mark, but did you know he's still meeting with gangs, even after they killed his friend?"

"They killed my daughter," Dennard corrected bleakly. "Nothing Mark does surprises me anymore. He saved my life, but now... there's just no making sense of how he'll deal with all the crap. You'd do better to cut your ties with him."

"I see," Winton said slowly.

Dennard means, stop meddling, because all I am is in pain. And Winton hasn't seen how much deeper this goes. Mark let his voice crack a little as he said, "Haven't you ever lost someone, really lost them? I'll be okay. If I was trying to die I'd find better ways than talking to people who've already given me a truce."

As he finished, he felt it: the owl was pulling away again.

Winton said "But, you said there were enemies everywhere—"

"Look, thank you both, but I'm *fine!*" and Mark pulled his arm free and hung up as he strode away.

Behind him he heard a shocked huff from Winton, but nothing more, and guessed the real pain in his voice had finally scared him off. He sprinted down the dim street, eyes locked on the brick corner ahead and praying the bird wouldn't fly away any faster. Once he was out of Winton's line of sight he brought up the magic to break into a floating run of pure *joy.*

As that first step arched up he caught himself and shifted to a simple run: *don't think of flying yet, get nearer to her first.* He dashed down a sidestreet, then leaped upward to settle on the roof.

She was somewhere up ahead, further along the street. He moved across the roof and to the next one in three easy jumps, then to the roof beyond, staring through the dim air above, trying to match where he felt the magic pulse; *I'm only using it for her, just enough to reach her up there, not for the sake of flying.* And something in the smooth way that presence turned to fly over the street made him certain… even before he caught a proper glimpse, he knew it really was the owl herself.

He leaped after her, a high arch to clear the street and bring him near to where the dark shape soared. He remembered what he'd read about owls' hearing… "Angie!" he whispered as he drew up below her. "Angie, I know it's you."

The bird turned again, circling around, and he strained his neck to watch—no wonder owls' necks could twist all the way around!—as she drew closer to follow above and behind him on his course. He faced forward again, saw a storefront wall looming up ahead, and lifted himself up just in time to stumble across the roof of the building instead. When he turned to look again, breathing hard, the owl was circling above.

"Angie?"

With a stroke of wings, the bird climbed upward. Before she faded into the night Mark leaped after her, trying to push himself up, ahead of her path.

"It's me, it's okay!"

She flapped again, pulling her climb still higher. Mark tightened the magic to lift his path up nearer hers, but she was already peeling off to the side. Avoiding his floating jumps as freely as any bird—and just as ready to stay clear of the human. Like a bird.

Was she just an owl now, was Angie gone? He clamped down an urge to scream.

"That's still you in there, Angie!" he called after her. "You brought the belt back to me, remember? We'll find whoever did this to you, we'll use his magic to… help you, *somehow!"*

She only glided away. Her gray shape was already lost in the dark, and he felt only the flicker of power she carried.

And another energy. Another bird rushing toward her from up ahead.

"No no no—" Mark could only let himself drop, trapped in his leap until he had ground under his feet again. As the air whistled up past him he struggled to track the two pulses in the distance. One closed in, and the other veered away, but the first swept after her. Too fast!

Mark jerked his eyes downward again in time to break his fall for a steep-slanted rooftop. The birds' magic was already fading, at the fringes of his sense—

He flung himself across the roof, just to the edge, before kicking off again to sail over the street. He could feel Angie and the killer's bird closer now—and he could make out the roughness, the wilder quality to her energy that her pursuer lacked—then he hit the far roof and lunged forward. *Cross the roof, clear the wires, keep heading in their general direction. Nothing matters if I'm not fast enough...*

But they were gone. Mark hurdled another roof and found himself arcing through open space high above the streets. He stared down at the asphalt, cursing the dots of light from the few cars that kept him in such long, momentum-bleeding leaps when he needed speed.

No good. He knew it before he reached the far roof and tried a desperate twist across the block in hopes of coming into range of them again. Both birds moved too fast, too freely, for his jumps to keep up. And Angie might be... what, trying to draw their enemy away from him?

That would be like her. He stared around the cold, dim air and the maze of buildings that jutted up just far enough to let a flying creature hide behind them. Angie could have been twisting through that half-world for days now, fighting her own battles, keeping just a wingbeat ahead of the enemy's birds.

And Mark couldn't find her *or* keep up with her. His muscles burned to take the next leap and the next, anything to keep *moving* and somehow run them down… but he knew that impulse. He turned his way toward a private corner on the ground.

Just as he slipped below the skyline he caught a glimpse of the ground to the west, where the city lights thinned out in the distance for some of the wealthier estates. Like Orchard Heights, and Olivia Nolan's home.

And every *minute* Mark waited to beg for her help was one more the killer could be hunting Angie—

He caught himself in mid-lunge before he broke into a wild run. Not this time. Not after breaking into Nolan's home in the middle of just… was it last night when he'd attacked her? If he wanted a dangerous, trigger-happy magician to at least listen to him this time, the least he could do was approach her in daylight.

He banged his fist against the wall. There had to be something he could do *now*…

Instead he turned and trudged back toward his hiding place.

*   *   *

He wouldn't sleep, he was sure. The image of Angie fleeing the killer was pounding through his brain, and he knew that soon he'd be walking straight into Nolan's hands with no weapon; nothing but his need to make her listen… The night should take forever to pass. No matter how much his feet ached and how long the hours were, rolling from side to side on the uneven bed and struggling for another search term to run through his phone…

The sun glared through the gaps in the window's skewed curtains. And a fist was rapping on the door.

Mark twisted on the mattress, eyes going for the corner where the belt lay, all of five feet away. Why would the enemy *knock*—or was it just the owner, demanding another day's cash?

On stiff legs he moved to the corner and settled the belt around his waist again. Catching up the two strips of leather, he called out, "Yeah?"

The knocking stopped. "I know it's you, Mark."

Roger Winton. Again.

Mark's mouth twitched. He wanted to ask how, *why,* Winton was at his door… but no, none of that would be any easier if Winton had to shout his answers through that door.

At least the hall and the block felt clear of the killer's magic. Mark seized the bed and pulled it back from across the door in a scrape of metal on wood, and a final thud when its weight returned as he was still setting it down. Then he swung the door open.

Winton stepped into the doorway at once, but halted there. His eyes flicked around the tiny room, and the bed slanting out of line along the corner.

Mark said "What are you *doing* here?"

"Which one? Daring to come to a pit like this?" He took a step in, as Mark moved back, and he shut the door, then pulled back his coat to show a glimpse of a gun holstered under his arm. "Or tracking you down? That took a night of knowing which cops and surviving gang members to call. With no help from your friend Dennard, by the way," he added. "What I want to know is, what are *you* doing down here?"

Mark edged backward, but with the bed behind him and Winton's pudgy shape in front of the door, the tiny room had barely a step left either way. And with Winton here, after all the warnings—no, because of them—Mark saw no way left to chase him back out.

Trusting him had to be easier than persuading him to go. *Something* had to change.

"So you found me." The bed frame creaked as Mark sank down on it. "Do you have any ideas for finding where Rafe went, or who he's taking orders from these days?"

"I… might. It would probably be harder than finding you. Just what have you gotten yourself into anyway?" Winton's voice lowered to draw their words in to just the room, tucked inside the scattered noises beyond the walls.

"Or, forget Rafe. What do you know about Olivia Nolan? North Star Events, do you know it?"

"What?" This time Winton's face quirked in surprise.

"Well… when Rafe was holding you down, how much of our conversation did you hear?"

"Not much that made sense. And then he put that choke hold on me… no." He stopped, and his eyes closed in thought. "After that there were bits and pieces, when I must have been coming back awake. But then *wham!* I'm just lying on the ground and you two are fighting in the water. But I never felt myself fall over."

Mark heard a quaver in Winton's voice, where he'd be trying to fit the gaps together. Rafe's chokehold was a great cover for the way the puppet master's magic sent people to sleep.

And both of them wanted Winton out, so they could talk freely to me. But how they'd done it also gave Mark more evidence to prove it.

"Rafe and his… boss… have an enemy. Her name is Olivia Nolan. What I need is to understand is if I can trust her."

Winton shifted on the floor; when had he crouched down next to Mark? Up the hall a voice shouted in some strange accent. Mark found he had been holding his breath.

"What if," he began slowly, letting the words come. "What if some of the old forces we call myths were actually real, and someone still knew how to use one of them, but didn't want to be treated like a freak? Besides, how much real good is it to be able to fly when you can just hop on a plane, anyway?" *So strange… after all the searching for clues and begging Kate for explanations about the magic, now I'm laying out all the guesses I've had on my own—and they seem to fit.*

But Winton only frowned. "What are you talking about? Is this some 'would you fly or go invisible' game?"

"More like, would you fly or *not* fly?" Mark leaned forward on the bed. "Do you think someone might hide something like that? For how long?"

Winton's face went still, impassive. Unreadable thoughts twitched at the edges of his eyes. "I... suppose they might."

Mark nodded. "Especially if showing the power made you a target. What if it made you a target for someone who had a stronger power, or one that worked better in hiding. They could steal your secret and add it to their own, and you'd never see them coming. And kill you, probably. Think how careful you'd be then."

Winton pursed his lips. "All right. So you're saying Rafe Martinez has one of these secrets, and he's using it to take another one from this... Nolan. Or someone else."

He paused, and cast a pointed look at Mark—the one he'd heard Rafe make all his demands to.

"And you think it all comes down to how paranoid this Olivia Nolan is. How far... someone... would go in fighting over one of these secrets. You say."

And Winton turned his head in a slow glance around the tiny room, a sneer edging over his lip as he took in the shabby bed, the stained walls, the tattered curtains that barely covered the window in the room Mark had been driven to.

In other words, never mind if Nolan can be trusted, can anyone trust my sanity? Because it was all just delusion unless the magic was real. Unless he proved it to Winton.

Then... Mark's phone rang.

The chime shattered the stillness; he was on his feet and flicking his eyes around for danger, for one awkward instant before his nerves settled and he snatched up the phone lying on his bed.

The name on the screen was *Joe Dennard.*

Mark answered with "Good news!" Words tumbled around in his head, how Winton was already a target, how he'd forced himself into being either a distraction or an ally.

But before he could find a way to start, Dennard said "Nolan's back."

"What?"

"Seems like her. The park Nature Center I'm in has dropped twen-ty degrees in ten minutes. Winds outside don't look too bad yet—but I'll have to pick my time to make a run for it."

"Run? You can barely stand! Let me—"

"Just watch yourself. You could be next." Dennard's voice held only the faintest quaver, as he brushed aside the danger.

Mark stared at the phone, then at Winton trying to follow the con-versation from just one, shocked half. And just when they were talking about how to win Nolan over...

Why am I still standing here? "I'm on my way."

* * *

Winton didn't say a word as he drove. Mark put off trying to explain, saying nothing except directions until the trees of Rosewood were in view... and he saw that they were shaking with wild winds and thick sleet.

"When we get to the corner, stay back and stay safe. Nolan could be anywhere."

"Nolan?" Hard sleet pattered on the windshield, and Winton slowed down to match the hesitant drivers in front of them. "Yester-day you were asking about the Stormday outbreaks..."

"They're all her." Such a simple confirmation, to say someone was controlling the sky itself. *But why? Why's she doing this, when she let us go before?* Hoping to track where the storm came from, Mark reached out for any magic—

Somewhere in the park, near but separate from the source of the belt's power, *another* steady pulse of gravity magic burned, taunting his senses. It was so familiar that even as he felt it resonate through the belt, his elbow brushed his waist to check that his own power was still in place. But how, how could that be—

"Mark? That corner's coming up."

Mark closed the mouth that had fallen open and tried to push that one extra shock down in his mind; focus on Dennard and Nolan. Winter Street looked more like its name every second as cars ground to a crawl in the thickening white air. In the park he saw scattered people stumbling through in the storm.

Then he saw the Nature Center just beyond the Fall/Winter streets' parking lot, where Dennard had called from. Was that window broken?

"Pull in there and stay down. I'll find her—or get him out."

"If he listens to either of us," Winton muttered.

Two cars were trying to edge out of the parking lot while the weather raged, but Winton's BMW was the only one heading *in.* Then he slowed, and Mark stepped out into the teeth of the storm.

I've done this before, I've done this before; the thought did more to shield him than the hand he flung up in front of his face. He braced himself against the buffeting winds and looked around.

A family staggered past him, huddled together under a picnic blanket. Shouts and curses fought for supremacy with the wind's howl. Nolan could be anywhere. Mark squeezed his eyes shut and reached out for magic again... the other gravity presence was *still* lurking near the power source, but his shivering senses couldn't track the void of Nolan's energy in the maddened air.

He pushed forward, past a couple that had slipped on the iced-up asphalt. With the Nature Center in front of him he knew Nolan had to be close to be sure that Dennard didn't escape. But where, where would someone be if watching was all she needed to strike?

The same type of shelter she'd used in the other parking lot? Hoping against hope, Mark stumbled deeper into the lot, trying to make out what cars were parked there. He couldn't see the Porsche Nolan had driven before, and none of the people sitting huddled in their cars looked like her.

But one face in a battered-looking yellow SUV ducked down lower as he looked. No, all he saw was a broad-brimmed *hat* that hid any features. Mark started toward the car.

And the wind slapped out at him, and under its scream the car roared to life and barreled out of the lot with just a glimpse of Nolan's face as the hat fell back.

"Dammit!" Mark staggered after her a step, saw cars honking and twisting as her SUV flung itself into the street, but the wind only swelled and beat him back. *Did she just attack us and then run* away?

But Nolan *could* do that, he realized. Her weather magic let her lash out and barely show herself, and still pull out long before anyone could strike back at her... she'd just come back with another storm later. Compared to that, the belt gave Mark power up close and even more speed to escape, but none of that was safe to use in broad daylight. Was that the battle of opposites he and she were locked in now?

While the killer never has to show his face at all, or leave us any *way to find him.*

Mark heaved out a frustrated breath into the sleet and turned back toward the Center. Somewhere up the street a siren was howling toward him, while behind him park-goers were still stumbling toward the parking lot, looking to take shelter. But... with Nolan gone, he could feel the driving sleet begin to let up.

He sensed no other magic—even the other gravity energy was gone now. Could he have imagined it? No, it *had* been there. And with Nolan back on the warpath it might be connected... somehow...

His head hurt worse than his frozen skin. *Only one thing I can do right now.*

When he looked toward Winton's car, he found it empty, with an ambulance pulling up beside it. But he only had to glance up again to see Dennard hobbling out from the Nature Center with Winton a pace behind him.

Mark stepped around a mother and child that were heading toward the little building. He saw Dennard, still on his crutches, stumble to keep well away from them as they passed. When he slipped, Winton moved to help him, but Dennard lurched away, snarling, "Don't touch me! I can still walk, damn you all."

The way Dennard said *touch,* the way he dodged back from all of them… Mark had a sudden image of Dennard trying to keep everyone he met back beyond arms' length. Sure, since he could never know who might be a puppet, one touch away from possessing him.

As if to prove him right, a paramedic from the ambulance made straight for Dennard, and Mark saw him wave her back with a crutch. "I'm fine! See, no frostbite—" he held up his free hand and spread his fingers—"and I'll recite the Gettysburg Address if you want. Or I can sue you for forcing treatment on me, when that looks like a broken ankle over there." He nodded toward where a family clustered around a boy who was sprawled on the asphalt.

The paramedic glanced over, but Winton moved up behind Dennard again and said, "Will you just let her look—"

Dennard's glare back at him was so fierce, Mark scrambled forward to break in. "They're alright! There's no danger here—"

"Says the man who sees ghosts," Dennard sneered at him.

He took a step toward Mark, or maybe just away from Winton and the paramedic. Those two were talking over each other in a tangle of words, giving Mark a moment to close the distance with Dennard.

"Please, Joe, let's get you out of here! You've been stabbed, frozen--how many more hits like that can you take?"

Dennard's jaw tightened. "One more, I hope." And he reached up to brush his hand against his coat. Or what was under it.

Where he'd keep a gun. *Oh God, he's not just on alert, he's making himself* bait—*but if someone tries to touch him, would he really shoot them?*

"Please! Let me take you away from here!"

"Why? So you can rant about ghosts to your new friend?" He shot a vicious look back at Winton.

"If that's what's bothering you, he's not new—"

Dennard lunged forward one more step. With his face within inches of Mark's, he hissed, "When did you tell him about Angie?"

And a moment later he jerked away from Mark again and turned away.

Mark stared at the man and his wild, darting gaze around the park. And Dennard's words began to work their way in, past the shocking sight of a man he'd known forever, so far gone.

The paramedic rushed in to take Dennard's pulse, and this time he let her. And Mark thought: *He called me here. Now he thinks I'm crazy, for trusting Winton and for thinking Angie's alive.*

Someone shouted "I can see the sun!" and Mark heard cheering. The snow was petering out. *Dennard said, because of Winton and Angie,* Mark thought again.

Winton trudged up beside Mark. "So you're saying all this," and he brushed bits of ice from his suit, "was Nolan?"

"That's right," Mark said automatically, but inside his head the thoughts came together. *Angie. Dennard said Winton knows about her coming back... and I never told him.*

Winton kept talking, right in front of Mark and as calm as ever: "Then Nolan could be back for him, or us. So we head off before she does?"

"Yes. If he won't come with us." Mark even managed to say it calmly, and turn away toward the car.

His heart thundered in his ears. That couldn't be what Dennard meant. Winton couldn't know about Angie and the owl. And if he'd found out, somehow, why would he tell Dennard...

Unless he wanted to fuel Dennard's bitterness about it, to split him away from Mark...

Mark slowed, and Winton wobbled past him, so close. In mid-step, Mark made himself *stop.*

His breath stopped. His sight of the figures around him lost their meaning. In the space between one heartbeat and the next, he went still... still and empty of everything but the tingle of the belt and leather scraps at his waist, and their resonance with the park's energy, and nothing else… except… a tiny flicker, like the scratch of a mouse's toe, somewhere on Winton—

His foot came down at the end of the step, jarring Mark out of the moment. *I have to be wrong, wrong!*

"Are you going after Nolan now?" Winton asked.

"Uh… not yet…"

Winton wasn't possessed, but he *couldn't* have any of the killer's magic on him, he only got involved because the killer sent Rafe to grab him. Didn't he?

Thoughts tumbling, Mark managed to say, "We split up. You go find out more about her; I'll try watching her."

Winton stopped, started to turn back. "But…we haven't—"

"Stay somewhere safe!" Mark spun away and dashed deeper into the park.

He almost crashed into an older woman, limping through the parking lot, but he swerved around her without slowing; he didn't dare slow or he'd have to think *what am I doing, this is Roger Winton, he's been in and out of my life for years, it's insane—and how could he send Rafe to fake his own kidnapping—*

He could almost feel Winton's eyes on his back, so he swerved away from Dennard and the paramedic, but he still heard the woman with the news camera standing next to them, saying, "the man who's been caught *twice* in Stormday—"

The words brought a frown to Mark's lips, to hear someone so close to the truth.

Then the frown stretched into a smile: if the idea worried him, how much more would it bother Nolan, make her hesitate at aiming her "random" weather at Dennard a third time? With a few words to the media the crippled ex-detective had twisted the whole untraceable strength of her attacks into a shield for himself.

And if Dennard was right about how to handle that enemy… could he be right about Winton?

CHAPTER SEVENTEEN

FLY

The car was Mark's first sign of good luck.

Winton was long gone from the park by the time Mark circled back. He could have driven off anywhere—even to hide out from their enemies if he was actually the honest ally he seemed to be. But when Mark peered around a corner to peek at Winton's brownstone, he saw the businessman's blue BMW in the parking lot.

He pulled back out of sight. So Winton had gone home… but why wouldn't he, if he'd rather gamble on walling out his enemies on home turf rather than hiding from them? It didn't mean he *was* the puppetmaster.

When he bought my the last sketch, he had me walk right in that house. Anger clenched his teeth, tangled up with just how maddeningly thin the signs against Winton were, and he pressed his hand on the brick wall to hold himself in place. No more reckless raids, like the one into Nolan's house.

Mark turned back up the street away from Winton, and tried a text to Dennard.

you still ok? more blizzards?

He braced himself for the long, painful wondering about whether Dennard would even answer. Instead, the words came right back.

fine. did you tell Winton about the owl or not??

There it was. Winton really had known more than he'd let on to Mark—and he'd tried to poison Dennard against Mark? But it could still mean anything…

No I didn't. So he was spying on me, just to watch you? I've known him since school. He trusted I wasn't with Rafe's gang. He's bought my sketches for years.

Should've been your first warning. You think your art was that good?

Mark managed a bitter laugh.

The worst of it was, they still didn't *know* about Winton. Or why Nolan had attacked them again, or if Dennard's tale of being a "two-storm survivor" would keep him safe. Or if that fleeting other pulse of the park's magic was tied to it.

Mark tried a call to Kate, to ask if she'd somehow found a new belt, but she never answered.

The one real tool they had was Mark's sense for magic, and the hope that Winton didn't know they suspected him. And Mark could only keep that fragile secret by circling around the blocks out of line of sight, around and around, and trying his best not to look like a ragged burglar strolling in an upscale neighborhood.

Staying within two blocks of Winton was easy. What made him scowl and have to fight to keep every step slow and patient was watching *hours* grind by with nothing happening.

Even when Dennard brought his own car around and left it for him, together with a bag of hamburgers, Mark could only think of how many trails they were ignoring—all because without Nolan they *had no way* to find Angie or any puppetmaster who wasn't Winton. None of Dennard's police tips about enduring a stakeout made it any easier; it was still only parking the car on different corners, pretending to read a map, and watching the sun set.

And yet I'm betting Winton picked me out years ago, as a way to watch the Dennards? He invests a few hours for a visit every year, and flatters a gullible kid about his sketches, just in case other signs start to say the Dennards are the ones with the magic... easy to fit into a calendar full of other schemes...

What kind of person *lived* like that?

Hours later, when the flicker of magic gathered and formed right as he "watched," the sensation that sprang up in his head matched Roger Winton's home like an invisible flag.

Mark found his fingers clenching, crushing the map he was holding. *Steady, steady.* The newly-made spybird moved by above... but it only flew past him, it must have missed him among the dozens of cars. The killer—no, Winton!—hadn't guessed that Mark knew where the birds were first possessed, how he'd been *used*...

Slowly Mark folded the map smooth again, then swung Dennard's car into the street. He'd just take a quick look at the brownstone now. This wouldn't be a reckless raid, like he'd tried with Nolan; he needed to be certain, he needed to find *all* the secrets of Winton's magic to help Angie. This time he'd stay back until he was better prepared.

But it can't be Winton, the killer sent Rafe to grab him, Rafe even choked him... but then Winton fell "asleep" and a bird possessed Rafe... if Winton set it up and Rafe went too far...

The bird swerved in flight. To the side.

Mark felt the magic shift, and not heading back but twisting south, so abruptly that his mental sense dragged his eyes off the road ahead. *What did Winton see?* Mark spun the wheel again and headed after the bird.

The flicker of power was already growing faint with distance. Mark released his sense and pressed the gas pedal, straining to think less about the bird and more like a cabbie, choosing turns that would close the distance in this lighter-traffic hour. The wikis said birds flew, what, twenty, thirty, fifty miles an hour in casual flight? He had to hop onto Garcetti and start weaving between cars to close in on where the bird had been heading.

Three blocks later, when the full lanes ahead forced him to slow, he stretched out his sense again, fearing he'd already followed it blind for too long. Instead, he sensed what must be the reason it had changed course: a second, similar tingling, flying somewhere beyond it.

Angie. And Winton bird's had changed course to follow it.

Stopping at a red light, Mark glared up at the sky, feeling the hidden shapes wing away ahead. If Winton was following her, where was she going—what was she doing that would made him chase her? *How long can one light stay red—even the Garcetti-Fontaine light shouldn't be this slow, she's already fading out of my range!*

Mark glared at the crossing traffic, but it wasn't nearly thin enough to risk running the light.

Along the sidewalk the trees shook in a heavy wind. It was just wind, he told himself. Except… the birds had been heading southeast, and rising wind across town *could* be a ripple from Nolan using magic at her home. *Coincidence. Both birds are gone and I'm desperate.* Still, he gazed out across the rooftops; they really had seemed to fly toward Orchard Heights—

Somebody honked behind him, and he saw the light was green again. *It's all gambles anyway now.* Mark screeched forward and began fighting through traffic with every trick he knew. It left him no time to search for the birds' presence again, only to race forward.

By the time he reached Orchard Heights itself, he found the thicker lines of trees along the avenues and estates were swaying, easing, then struggling again to stand straight as the wind rose and fell. He throttled back his engine to turn through the neighborhood's slow curves, staring through a blur of leaves and twigs spilling through the air ahead of him. *What is Nolan up to?*

As he neared the Nolan estate, he felt it again. Another clear, steady pulse of gravity power, and stronger than his belt.

Of course it's here too.

The roads didn't stretch far enough toward where that power was, so Mark pulled the car over and stumbled out into the storm. Leaves and dirt peppered his skin as he started to lean into the wind, but the gale was already dwindling down to a simple breeze, as if gathering its breath now. Before it could rise again he leaped across to hang from the top of the estate wall and peer over.

For a moment he thought a great snake had stretched down along the side of Olivia Nolan's squat stone house. Then the clouds shifted past the moon and he saw it was simply a long branch tangled in the power lines, one end skittering against the wall as the wind grew fiercer again. But even this storm couldn't have swept something that big all the way across the open yard to the house.

High above, Mark felt a bird winging toward the estate. Just sensing how its course twisted and struggled along made him tighten his own grip on the wall, wondering how any bird could push through that wind. Was Nolan even in control of this gale anymore?

Then the bird started to fall.

Angie! He kicked backward off the wall and broke into a run, shoving forward and gripping magic to stretch his stride and hold him on course as the wind battered him. He'd already swept past the driveway of the next estate when he felt the bird pull up again and start to weave back and forth, trying to fight through the wind, toward the Nolan grounds. Its presence felt like Angie's, and if that bird wasn't her, it was damn well determined enough to be.

The other magic, that felt like his own gravity power, moved upward. Mark whirled around to glimpse a long black shape darting through the moonlight in an arc toward the Nolan grounds—and spin away in the storm, deflected. He didn't see the second attempt, that came in too low behind the estate walls, but he sensed it thrown back as well. Someone out there was using levitation to launch branches as giant javelins at Nolan's home. Wasted effort, in this weather.

"You there! What are you doing? Get inside!" A man's voice pushed through the wind, and Mark turned to see a figure leaning out from the neighboring estate.

He shouted back "I have to find..." and mumbled the rest so that the wind would swallow it, rather than bother making something up.

He pushed back toward the Nolan grounds. *Who's out there? Is all this Nolan trying to fight them off?*

Magic, gravity magic, pulsed somewhere on the estate; Mark felt a single surge and then a fainter push sweeping across at ground level. Like someone clearing Nolan's wall and running for her house. Making their move.

The second Mark left the other property's fence, he sprang up to seize Nolan's wall again, floating only for a moment in the gale before swinging over and dropping to the grass beyond, almost tripping over a long branch that had fetched up inside the wall. He sensed the other gravity energy was just slowing its rush—Mark looked across the bare grayed-out lawn and picked out a shape moving outside a window. Breaking in.

Do I help him, do I stop him? Does his form of magic make him one of us—is there an "us?"

Mark felt the birds close in now, their power moving an instant before he felt the wind against his face ebb. Two points of Winton's magic soared in, high above the estate.

One twisted to veer toward the other. Mark stared up at the sky, hoping to get a glimpse of something among the skidding clouds. He felt the other bird swing away, and the first drop past it—one had dived at the other, but which one had that sense of Angie to it? For long moments he mentally traced their paths, arcing apart and spinning back to lunge at each other.

As they swept over the side of the grounds, he thought of dashing under them and then leaping straight up… but that was just how Angie had been beaten before. Streaks blurred by in the air and started upward again, still too fast and too distant to tell apart.

Glass shattered. The sound barely reached him through the wind, but he sensed the power and looked to see a figure leaping out of an upper-story window, then flaring magic and landing on the grass. Mark caught a glimpse of a heavy male figure, crouching, with a long shape in his hands.

Like one of Nolan's fishing poles? I knew I sensed something odd about them. The thief rose upward, gliding away as the light wind caught him.

Then the air went mad.

With the first blast, Mark crouched down and threw his arms over his eyes, leaving only his inner sense to track pieces of magic. Far above, the birds whirled away into the distance, safe at their altitude. But he felt the thief tumbling down, swatted from the sky at a vicious angle—then a desperate surge of force as he tried to push back—then a drop again, and a slide into a jolting path that Mark knew in his bones was man meeting lawn, and rolling across it.

Snap. The sound didn't reach his ears, but it echoed in his mind; the breaking of something that resonated with magic.

The wind faded in that moment.

Mark peered across again. The thief was a dark shape slumped on the ground, still pulsing with undirected gravity energy. The fishing pole must have broken in his roll, and the worst of the storm had shattered along with it.

The front door of the manor stood open. From the faint light behind it, he saw the outline of a woman that had to be Olivia Nolan, looking out into the night for her enemy. She turned clumsily left and right, blindly—was she the only one here without magical or bird-sharp senses? She took a step to the left, away from the door, to look toward the garage.

Then she jerked once, and slumped back against the wall. The thief's magic pulsed as he leaped up, bounding toward Nolan and raising an elongated gun for what must be another silenced shot at her.

Mark spun away and grabbed at the fallen branch beside him, helplessly knowing he'd be too late to stop anything—

Nolan swung her hand up, and the leaping shooter spun upward in a roar of wind, then soared away, flailing, shrinking in the moonlight.

Bang! This didn't even sound like the same gun; its deeper roar smashed through the wind, and Mark saw the shooter's outline jerk in the air. When it veered to the side, then jetted forward again as more shots erupted, Mark understood—he was using a gun's recoil to push him through the air.

Damn, I never even thought of that one.

And the thief was already swooping down around the house.

The thought crystalized in Mark's head: whatever Nolan was, enemy or something else, he wouldn't let anyone be gunned down before his eyes. He leaped forward, still holding the branch he'd caught up. Two long steps to close some distance, then up, and in midair, he flung the branch at the descending gunman.

For a moment, even as the throw's force tossed him backward in his jump, he thought his missile would hit home. But the thief burst upward, another shot blasting him clear of the branch. Then the gun swung around.

Mark didn't wait for him to aim. He hurled himself to the side with a surge of magic, arcing up to spin away across the lawn. *I've got the whole vast night to lose him in, if I don't give him a clear look at where I am.*

He'd bounced once off the ground before he realized the thief *wasn't* shooting. He hadn't deflected his own course, and Mark could feel him still flying down and then—

This time he saw it as well as sensed it: the thief soaring up into the moonlight, with Nolan in his grasp. He couldn't make out if Nolan was struggling… but he began to feel the wind tear at him again.

While she's right in the thief's hands? Nolan must *be desperate!* Mark was already staring, crouching, trying to match their course above the hills against his own distance to it. He leaped.

It would have been hopeless if he'd tried to aim against the wind. But before the storm could catch him he clutched wildly at the gravity forces around him—and, like he had on the night he'd lost himself in the magic, those forces locked his momentum, not able to shift and change his course but at least they could hold it straight against the wind. He swept upward, senses tracing the others' path, and released himself to ride the wind again when he was just rising above where they'd been.

He spread his arms and legs then, and felt the current catch harder at him. Up ahead he sensed the other magic riding through the air, the gap between them already shrinking. "You call that real flying?" he chuckled softly. "You can't even sense me coming, can you?"

Something in his voice sent a chill through him, a cold that penetrated deeper than the numbed-away bite of the wind. *The magic's influence again. I can't let it get to me.*

Lights swept by below. Block after block passed, Orchard Heights giving way to the brighter streets of downtown, just close enough below that he could make out the widest of the streets in the shadows. Mark watched the two ahead slowly drift off to the left, and he tried tilting his body to catch the wind at an angle and stay with them. But the streets seemed to be slowing, the wind growing weaker.

Then the thief looked up at him.

"You!"

The voice barely reached Mark, but he hardly needed to hear it to know. Of all the people to face in the sky—it *would* have to be Rafe.

And his gun was already swinging up.

Mark clutched at power and yanked himself upward to get clear of the gunsights. *How did he get the power? I only showed him the belt for a moment—now he's got something like it himself?* But the energy was all too clear to deny.

That pulse let Mark pick out the dwindling dot in the air below. Rafe and his prisoner were trembling, thrashing in the dimness. A harsh voice grunted inaudible words.

And Rafe must have lost sight of him at this distance; Mark slipped down again. He had no way to fly across and intercept them, but he held back enough of his weight to sink slowly through the air, trying to shift his balance and angle off the wind to arc just a little nearer.

As he edged closer, he saw Rafe shaking his prisoner, and heard the words across the air:

"Where is it? What's holding your power, what's the word, where do you recharge it? Don't you pass out, *tell* me!"

Did Rafe just forget *me?* And Mark felt his own fists clenching, eager to smash out at Rafe, no matter if that left Nolan to fall. Rafe was losing control of the magic, but Mark knew he himself wasn't much better.

The air twisted. Wind swung around and sucked downward, shrieking in Mark's ears as he locked himself in place. He saw Rafe and Nolan twisting downward, their motion looking slower, weaker.

Magic moved. Not Rafe, not the wind, but a flicker of power swept down past Mark toward them—a tiny bird-shape too small for an owl, its energy surging up to attack.

Somehow Rafe's head turned toward it, saw it. The next instant he plunged down out of the bird's path, but Mark felt it loop around ready to strike again, and knew none of them could outmaneuver something that had real wings. Winton really was through trusting Rafe, and he had him and Nolan just where he wanted them.

Then the wind turned again, weaker now, as Nolan swung an arm around. Whether she'd seen the tiny killer, or only wanted to break their fall, the wave still sent the thing whirling away into the night.

"A bird, another fucking *bird?*" Rafe was shouting at Nolan. "I'm through taking his orders! Tell me how to fight it! Give me the power, or I'll—"

A piece of their confused, floating silhouette shifted, and Mark realized Olivia Nolan's head was lolling back, unconscious. That wind must have taken the last of her strength.

"She can't help you now!" Mark yelled. *"You* can't help you—the magic's frying your brain!"

Why'd I have to yell at him? came the thought as the gun swung around again. Rafe was closer this time—and Mark lifted upward, but saw Rafe's his aim already rising to match him. *He guessed—*

Then Rafe howled in pain. A flicker of pale shadow swept by him, a tiny beacon of ragged magic. When Mark felt it curve around and follow Rafe's clumsy climb away he knew this bird wasn't one of Winton's.

Rafe fired, again and again at the shape below him, each blast filling Mark's ears and slamming his heart as the owl spun through the dimness that was her only protection—

"Stop it!" he yelled.

The gun's thunder stilled. Mark saw Rafe staring over at him—out of his reach, but close enough to shoot at him. But at least he stopped. Angie circled back above them.

Rafe shifted in the air… hanging onto Nolan while he fitted another magazine into his gun. "Beg? You want to beg?" he laughed.

Was that madness what Kate heard in my *voice?*

Before he could shoot again, Mark shouted "You've got what you wanted, right? You're flying! But your old patron won't let you live— that first bird was his, and he'll kill you!"

"Him, kill *me?"* Rafe brought his gun up, staring around the night. For Mark's voice.

We keep giving him targets, I have *to make him listen or we're dead!* "He'll keep sending them, and you've seen what they do! Unless you stop shooting us and we all go after him—you know why you blacked out when you started hurting Roger Winton? *It was him!"*

As the words left his mouth, Mark saw Rafe freeze. Gun aimed high, not moving, he gave no sign of what was passing through his mind. Then—

"Kill me? *This* is what I'll do to him!" Rafe shrieked.

And Rafe erupted with energy. The power surged and poured into his limp prisoner, and he flung Nolan straight up to hurtle away into the dark.

"Damn!"

The rush of air ripped the curse from Mark as he rocketed upward. He risked one glance back to see the streets plunging away below—

Something *smashed* into him—

The impact slapped a moment of clarity through him: chasing Nolan was useless, when he couldn't fly *across* to her. He'd only given Rafe a better target.

Then the rush of air swept that away in wild thoughts of *Faster, push harder, before we drift apart!* He felt the power that dragged at Nolan already tumbling further to the side as they shot up, waves of pain wracking his body from so much force—roaring in his ear, eyes clenched shut as he swept through a layer of something moist enough to be clouds, knew he should be cold but felt only the flare of energy, *just reach that power ahead,* catch *it!*

Something burning fell into his grasp. Hadn't it been out of reach? But somehow here she was, surrounded with blazing force, and with as much upward pull as he had… but this power wasn't quite his own. *It's not mine, not* right—*and you can't stop me.* Fingers tightened, will tightened and wrenched to peel the energy out of her body and fling it away to set them free, his eyes closing in triumph—

Not yet; he felt himself dropping. Mark shook his head and brought up his own magic to steady their fall. "Hold, hold on!" he growled, as icy air stabbed at his lungs.

A blanket of gray wetness pulled back above them, and he saw they'd fallen through the clouds. A lightless stretch sprawled off to their right; was that the lake?

As they dropped he could feel Nolan breathing against him, but she never stirred. What had Rafe shot her with—some kind of tranq gun so he could force her secrets out of her too? Just like his teacher.

Secrets. Rafe's making a grab for Nolan, Winton attacking them after chasing Angie. "A gang-banger, a force of nature, an assassin and an owl… walk into a bar…"

I'm losing it. He shook his head harder and fought to keep his eyes on the ground, not looking away until he stepped down onto the side-street and laid Nolan under a streetlamp.

Then he finally looked down at his other hand, at where it was clamped on his shoulder, against the slowly spreading cold around what had to be a very real wound.

Shot.

The thought made him sway on his feet. He could almost hear the blast again—

And again, again. Distant, but that ragged sound somewhere above could only be Rafe, still firing at Angie.

"No!" He kicked upward... a feeble jump that left him floating slowly past the first window of the wall beside him, until he forced out more magic to drag himself to its angled roof. Why couldn't he sense the two magics out there?

Then he saw the flashes in the sky, like pint-sized, rapid-fire thunderclaps. He stared across the streets; the fight must be too far away to sense, too far for him to hobble across to from below. But still, his legs were already sending him arcing along the roof.

"Let him go, Angie!" he gasped, knowing she'd never hear him. For her to keep after Rafe, owl's claws against bullets—had she lost her mind?

Or she's goading Rafe into losing the rest of his. The thought buoyed him up, and let him catch the edge of the roof and fling himself outward, high above the street. A glance down showed the lights of scattered cars passing as he drifted by. Their glows had an odd haze about them, when he knew they should have been stark against the blackness below.

Magic stirred. Not Rafe's energy, that must be somewhere up nearer the gunshots, not the rough feel of Angie within the owl—no, this was the purer, deadly twitch of Winton's own bird again.

Like a dream, it seemed to move so slowly, slow as his thoughts trying to turn those movements into meaning. Winton swung down along the next street, toward some unknown target. Rafe's gun fired and fired somewhere up ahead. The building across the street edged nearer to him.

Nolan was back there. And Winton was searching around where Mark had left her, helpless.

While Angie was fighting for her life, all alone.

She's doing better than I am. Trust her.

The far building rushed up, and Mark dropped his course enough to meet the wall with his feet and launch himself into a vast arcing leap backward toward Winton's path.

He tumbled in the air, trying to get a clear look at his target. At least in his head he felt Winton still a block from where Nolan had been, somewhere down in the concrete chasm. Another distant shot sounded behind him, but he kept his gaze forward. *Sure, just head Winton off, drop on him from above and crush him, then use his mind magic to* really *save Angie.* Lights, roofs, shapes blurred by below…

Mark blinked. The blurs snapped back into place—with Winton's presence already well ahead of him as Mark's dive cleared the last roof. *What's that wound doing to my head?*

He slammed down on the sidewalk. Far up at the streetlight, he could see he was too late.

Olivia Nolan stood, pulsing with Winton's control; whatever Rafe had used to subdue her, the possession forced through that and dragged her to her feet. Mark saw her wobble as she moved, but her hands were cradling a limp hawk, and never wavered from it. She stared off across the street.

She hadn't seen him. Mark lunged, one long step clearing half the distance. His foot touched down feather-soft, silent, and flung him through the last of the space between them.

She turned. He caught one glimpse of a strange, drunken look before her eyes snapped onto him and her hand slashed across.

The gale caught him in mid-leap. For one heartbeat the world was wind, pitching him over to the side. The wall swept up—

Cold, rough concrete pressed against his cheek. Had he been tumbling along bricks and rolling until his every muscle should be one mass of pain? But he heard the wind raging.

On and off, shifting and swaying like a broken TV screen. Mark forced his head up to stare at the possessed Nolan.

Her features hung slack, but she looked straight at Mark. Winton moved her body with more control than Mark moved his what was left of own. And every second Winton held her magic, the air steadied, his control of it tightened—

If I could just get my hands on him—

It's not only him, that's Nolan too—

But if I can't crush them, she's too strong, all I had was speed—

Speed. Mark dragged himself to his hands and knees, and spat out, "Enjoy the new body. I know where the real Winton is."

The possessed hand swung at him, but Mark dove to the side as air blasted at him. One step, two—he slid around the corner, out of the worst of the wind, and out of Nolan's sight.

The next moment he shot up to settle on the roof and crouch there. *My oldest flying trick,* he realized, *and this time it's just a bluff to pretend I have the strength to reach Winton's house.*

But he could sense the possessed figure stumbling around the corner, stopping there. He'd see Mark was gone.

Then the magic broke free of Nolan and soared upward. Winton must have shifted his control back into the hawk, to hunt him down.

Mark pressed himself flat in the shadows. Just let Winton move away, then he'd drop back and get Nolan out of sight… only his arm didn't seem to work…

Winton's path curved upward, and back, over the roof, over Mark. Of course.

Mark floated to his feet. Some move, some direction, would get him away from the hawk, but what was it?

The trace in his head blurred. The hawk was… circling.

It swung away across the night, closing on the other pulse that swept toward him.

Which bird was which? Mark stared into the sky, straining to hold his sense of which bird had the rougher feel of Angie in it. That shape circled away from the roof, and the other climbed to head her off. Faster.

Can't catch them. I can only watch... or...

He stepped off the roof. He could still get Nolan away.

As he dropped, he felt one bird swing around and dive toward him.

The owl rushed down to head it off. In a steeper, more desperate dive.

The hawk skimmed over, too fast, too strong, sliding into a path above Angie and streaking down at the owl. *His real target,* Mark thought, as Winton cut down at her with magic flaring—

The slower bird flipped over in the air, twisting away at an angle Mark was sure no bird had ever flown. In one instant Angie shot up, spinning off to the side as Winton rushed by. Mark gaped as she weaved once and swept down, all while Winton's bird was still pulling itself from its dive. That bird moved so clumsily Mark could picture the real Winton letting his control slacken as he stared at Angie through its eyes.

She struck, and Winton's presence broke apart with a burst of energy that rang in Mark's head like a scream, as her rush tore the hawk to bloody feathers.

Mark's feet touched the ground.

He swayed to keep his balance, watching Angie twist up again. That scream—had the real Winton been finished along with his hawk? Angie circled in the air, so slowly.

Then she turned and flew away, rising up over the walls and *away.*

Mark moved after her. Each step came lightly, lifting him to a roof and on to the next, teetering in the air but always keeping him going... but if Angie noticed him behind her, she didn't turn back.

Some blurred blocks later, he felt magic ahead. Not hers, not Winton's, but the power like his own. Rafe's.

Right, she couldn't beat him, she could only enrage him to make the magic blind him. So we finish him together?

On the next roof he tipped too far forward, and had to push off with his hands instead of his feet. His one working hand. The roofs seemed more evenly clustered now, along the docks.

The docks. The black expanse of the lake to his left. Hadn't Rafe been drifting over that? Yes, Angie could have trapped him over miles of water with nothing but his madness—but the energy ahead said he'd made it back to shore.

Why's he so still?

Mark's knees trembled, but he only needed one jump... his will swept him up and carried him toward the power.

It lay against the wall of a warehouse, where it might have landed if someone from the lake had thrown it away. No sign of Rafe, *but why would he get rid of it? I knew a reason a moment ago...*

Cold, fumbling, he closed his fingers around the belt. And it *was* a belt, made of stiff new leather with an oversized two-pronged buckle. Nothing familiar about it except how the grain of the leather spoke to his fingertips, just like the battered old shape at his waist did. Just a belt, just a belt, but the magic in it burned.

Burned so hot, until the cold crept through him and sucked him down.

CHAPTER EIGHTEEN

GATEKEEPER

He left the hospital without Joe Dennard. The long days under the doctors' care had given him a new sympathy for Dennard's stiff and bandaged pride, but still Mark had to make this journey alone.

Alone. Even after Dennard's report, of watching a private ambulance agency carry a still but breathing Roger Winton from his house... and disappear in the night. Losing the bird must have hurt him, but he'd had precautions all planned.

Once, it would have mattered more how oddly Henry looked at Mark now. But at least the police had been easy enough to put off; they had known Rafe might make another attempt on his life, and none of them asked what altitude he'd shot at Mark from. *Rafe... they never found him, he's another consequence of all this, if he turned Winton's spying on the magic into stealing his own gravity belt.* That new danger gave Mark a taste of Dennard's regrets as well as his injuries—and an understanding of why the orphaned Kate had tried so hard to push the magic away.

It couldn't go on.

The cool, overcast sky outside the hospital didn't *call* to him anymore, not after so long away from the belts and their influence. Or the lure would have been unbearable. He barely had the strength to shuffle out to the bench and sit; much longer on his feet and he'd have let magic around his waist carry some of his ever-present weight, or lighten his arm in its sling. As it was, he sat straight-backed against the bench waiting for the cab, thoughts running through the same circle they had for days, still looking for another way than what he'd chosen.

"I may have a job out of state soon," a woman on the next bench said to her friend.

"Then you could be out before you see what all this crazy weather does during a Lavine winter."

Mark kept his face still, something he'd gotten too much practice in lately. They hadn't seen a *fraction* of what the magic could do.

I shouldn't even be alive, he thought, for the thousandth time. Too many enemies could have used his hospital time to finish him off; he didn't know why they hadn't. Maybe some thought he could still be useful, with so many players in the game now. Had he ever truly thought it was all about a gang, a choice between arrest or attacking or escaping? Had he really once said, and believed, *There's always a way?*

Angie's motto, that was. Battered and drained, the only thing he trusted now was that any way at all was worth the price, for her.

The cab pulled up, and he stumbled in and gave the driver the address, then lolled his head back to watch the sky, so calm today. *I've looked down from those clouds, I've seen our city from every angle and thought I knew it... but I never cared enough.*

"You got shot!" he heard Henry's words again. "I thought you could fix this, but—what did you do?"

I've never done *anything, the only thing I cared about was always right beside me and I never faced that until I was about to lose her.* But Angie, right from the instant she thought she had a chance to change their lives, she'd never stopped searching for how to make it work. And it cost her everything but her life, and too much of that as well. But if the magic did that, then the magic had to help her, somehow; he only had to make it possible.

When the cabbie let him out at the gate, Mark sent him on his way. Win or lose or stand out here shouting until he got an answer, this bloody stalemate had to change *now.*

This time he did tap into the belt, to buoy him up as he walked and help him stand in place. No other magic pulsed around him, not Rafe's, not even Winton's. Or Angie's.

He buzzed the gate and said, "It's Mark Petrie. I think you want to talk to me." No going back.

He took one more look at the clouds, thicker now. Not like they'd been on the long nights he'd lain in the hospital, staring out the window and trying to see through the haze of painkillers, and thinking he might have seen an owl in the window. There was still a part of Angie free enough to remember him.

That couldn't be all of her that was left. *I won't let it be.*

"You," Olivia Nolan said, standing opposite the gate.

Nolan's voice carried the same tight suspicion it had held when they had faced off atop the parking lot, but this time she said it slowly, eyes watching carefully.

Mark answered simply. "The enemy is Roger Winton."

Nolan's jaw dropped. "The *food cart king?*"

"His magic works on minds, somehow; you've seen him use it through birds," Mark went on. "He tricked me into attacking you, and he's manipulated and killed…" He still didn't want to finish that sentence, but he didn't have to. "My friend Joe Dennard says he hasn't been seen in town since I shouted out that I knew it was him—while I was saving you," he added, for good measure.

"Winton." She gave Mark a searching look, the same look he'd seen when she'd been facing off with Kate, as if sure there had to be a lie in it somewhere. "Then I'll keep an eye out for him."

"That's not enough," and Mark drew his tired body up higher, glad at least he was still tall. "I bet he's hidden somewhere, still working on his next scheme to learn how our magics work. The two of us have to find him."

"Oh, *we* do?" Nolan's eyes narrowed.

"We have to. I've seen how much damage you can do when you want to, but you were only watching me—until Winton and I attacked *you.* I don't know what it is you want, and you don't trust me, but Winton has twisted gangs and who knows what else in this city, and now Rafe Martinez can somehow go beyond leading punks to using some of the secrets too—and yes, I bet he's still out there too. It has to *stop.*

"That's not *all* my cards on the table, but it's more than I had to give you. So, are you ready to trust someone?"

And Mark held out his hand. With the elaborate metal gate between them, he stopped short of reaching between the bars, but that shouldn't matter.

Nolan looked at his hand, then slowly up and down Mark's pale, tired form, as if she could see it was more than muscle keeping him on his feet.

She said, "You really think you're a fit Keeper?"

A what? Mark kept the words off his lips, but he couldn't hide his surprise.

Nolan smiled. "That's what my father called it. Spellkeeper. It was only the word he came up with for himself; he never thought there could be other magic forces like ours..." She shook his head. "And if there were, *I* never thought that they'd turn out to be in such devious—or reckless—hands."

As she said that, she looked down at Mark's hand again, still waiting.

Mark didn't answer. Reckless? Yes, he had been, then and now. But if Nolan listened to her own words...

She added, "Of course, I haven't shown that much restraint under pressure either. And I need *some* kind of ally to fight a war."

Her hand felt harder than the gate's steel.

*****

Mark's adventures continue in:

Freefall

from FREEFALL

Dammit, Angie! Where are you?

Mark Petrie swept a glare around the mist-dimmed sky above the street's rim, but of course his other sense felt none of Angie's magic out there. Why should tonight be any different from the rest?

The thought pushed his feet faster along the pavement, leaving Claremont Road's nighttime murmurs behind and twisting up Smithson, then across Teal until the November-chilled streets thinned down to empty sidewalks. Olivia Nolan's simple white car stood next to a shuttered shop—almost right under their meeting place.

Taking one more turn, he adjusted the bag of tools at his belt… though the real weapons were the two belts themselves that he wore. His shoulder barely ached in the cold mist so far; the bullet wound *was* healing faster than the doctors thought. The back street was as deserted as it looked.

Mark's will tightened around the magic in the belts, and he scampered up the wall.

His fingers barely touched the cold metal of the drainpipe, but that light grip was all he needed. With his weight all but wiped away by the power, he *rode* the pipe up as fast as his hands could move—if someone had come by below he'd be out of their view in moments, and they'd see nothing more than what could have been a person climbing. And nobody came by below anyway.

Not bad, for someone just a year out of high school.

When he swung up to the flat top of the roof, he saw she was waiting there. Just a short, middle-aged woman with a dark coat, looking out a pair of binoculars, standing in the mist and the slow lakeside breeze she'd summoned like she'd been meeting on rooftops all her life.

She hasn't. Nolan's had her magic *for generations instead of months, but I've been chasing our enemies before she even knew she had any. We've fought, I've saved her life—and I need to be sure we do this my way.*

Four easy hops brought him to Nolan's side, and he knelt his rangy height down to put his gaze on a level with her. "So, anything I should know out there?"

If he'd startled her, she didn't show it. "It… just looks like a building, from here. Whatever the commotion was last night, I can't tell anything from here." She handed him the binoculars.

What they showed him was more the two blocks of vaporous air than the East Lavine Youth Center behind it. But he could make out that the windows sat unlit, and he knew the place didn't even have curtains to hide any activity. Just bars, and only on the first floor.

All to promise *The gangs can't reach you here, but we have no secrets.* —None except for how Roger Winton was still backing them from the shadows, to get him influence with the police, while his power played with everyone else's life…

Mark forced his angry fingers to loosen enough to hand the binoculars back. "But it's not just a trap. Winton's got no magic down there. Not working now, anyway." It sounded too pushy in his ears, too quick to remind her that without his sense for different energies they'd be fighting blind.

She still didn't ask about his plan. Instead she said "And you did remember *both* belts, yours and the one you took from Rafe?"

"That's right." Both had drained most of their tingle of power, but he shouldn't need to stop and replenish them yet. Slowly he began pulling on his gloves. "I can do this like at Winton's other holdings: I jump in, look around, and jump out. *Except,* this time I want to grab any computers I see and take them with me; that should give your hacker what he needs."

Nolan's eyes narrowed, for a moment. "That just might do it. Winton can't cover up all the clues to where he's hiding, if he's still sending as many emails to this place as *she* tells me," and she smiled. "Yes, she. I keep my hacking PC."

This time Mark forced an answering smile. Nolan had to know she just couldn't tell a joke right, but she kept trying.

"Their security looks light, too," she went on.

"I know. Joe Dennard said they should have the basic Steel package. Unless they tripled it overnight."

"You told Dennard?" She raised an eyebrow, but Mark met her gaze squarely, and she shrugged. "All right then. But have you thought about this: the real risk is liable to start after you leave the place. We're stealing from an antigang center, and Winton has his friends with the police. That means the authorities will turn over every carpet fiber for any trace of you. This time, you need to use your magic to smash the site up as if one of the gangs had—"

"No."

"What?"

This time she glared at him. Mark thought of snapping back, about all the weather damage she'd thrown around trying to stop Winton herself, but by now he knew that wouldn't convince her. He almost wished she *did* have some magic reading his mind, not her eyes searching his face for one crack in his determination.

Then she said "Is that all your revenge for Angie is worth?"

For a moment Mark heard only his own gasp of breath in his ears, and the breeze over the rooftop. All he could answer was "It's 'worth' still being able to live with myself, when we bring her back. I'm not going to trash a place like that to cover my tracks, or because it *might* hurt Winton—"

He'd motioned out toward the Center as he spoke, but now he froze, and looked down at the new motion closer in on that street. He *knew* that white Ford.

As it pulled up next to Nolan's car, he said "That's Dennard down there."

"What?" Her voice buzzed in irritation. "Is he out here trying to help us, or does he want to scare us off?"

"He's got more reason to do this than we do. But I bet you want to ask him yourself, right?"

Mark glanced at the street below and held out his hand to her, trying to make the motion look casual. Only a breath later Nolan gripped it.

He said a rushed "Three-two-one" to prepare her, and they stepped off the roof. He tried to will just enough antigravity into their bodies to let them settle with something like a smooth elevator's drop, with an extra pull up to slow them well before they reached the pavement. Still, he felt Nolan's fingers clench on his once.

Joe Dennard climbed out of his car, and Mark studied the wounded ex-cop and his cane as they walked to meet him. *All those years growing up, I was so sure Angie's dad had turned vigilante for that one night and never known* how *he'd done it. Magic.*

"Is your ex coming too?" It was Nolan's weakest joke yet.

"Didn't have to. Wherever Kate is, I'd bet she did more to tie Winton to this place than your hacker has." He tapped his cane on the pavement once, and when Nolan only studied his face he went on "So, don't tell me you're about to level the one antigang spot in Lavine that works."

Mark swallowed and fought the urge to step between the two. *Don't make me play peacemaker here.*

"We were just talking about that," Nolan said. "But no, Winton can keep his building. I thought for a moment you might have a problem with going in at all."

"If it *stops* Winton… but right now, no 'freak windstorms.' Not against this place." Dennard's voice roughened, as if he'd felt the irony of a one-time vigilante holding back now—or, learned all too well.

Mark said "Of course not. And like you said, if we find it *would* let us take him down, nothing's saving the place." The words sounded harsher aloud than Mark had meant, but with the stakes what they were…

"That does sound impressive," Nolan said, looking between the two men. "But what would you really do to finish a spellkeeper who's a murderer? Neither of you talk about it, but do you still think this is about making Angie whole? Her body's gone, and what's left of her never comes back to us—"

"Except when she and I saved your life," Mark cut in.

He glanced at Dennard, but Angie's father had gone stone-faced; had he given up hope or not?

It was too much. Mark took a step clear of the two. "Look, I know I'm looking for their computer, that and any hidden clues to his magic. I know what the alarms should be, and I'll watch for anything dangerous. Anything else?"

"Just, stay ready to run," Dennard said. "We don't know what happened there last night or if Winton's up to something you can't sense. If Rafe Martinez is back he might be making his own moves against Winton, or even be back on his side again."

Mark tapped the second belt around his waist, with a bravado he didn't feel. "Rafe can't be everywhere. And I already took his talisman off him once. I *hope* he's standing guard in there; I'd like to know how there could be a second gravity belt at all."

As he mentioned belts he glanced at Nolan, hoping this once she'd take the cue and fill in the gaps with some of how she managed her own weather magic. The more they could see about how their two forces were alike, the closer they were to working out Winton's secrets as well.

Instead she turned away and motioned back to the building they'd watched from. "I lined the breeze up to blow you right in if you start up there. Or I can change it—"

"Don't need it."

This time he didn't pretend to climb; he just took one last glance around the street and leaped upward. *I'm showing off again,* he thought, knowing arguing with his older partners had been wearing him down. One leap brought him rushing up through the damp air along the wall, and a careful look let him aim for the broad notch in the roofs ahead that would be his target, and kick off against the bricks to launch himself toward it.

It was the strangest trick the belt's magic had, one he couldn't describe even to Dennard, who'd had the belt before him. Instead of floating up or pressing down, he could *hold* the forces around him enough to hang in place, or to keep himself on a path he leaped without any of the damp air slowing his momentum. Mark often thought of what it would have meant if he could truly "steer" gravity—to turn and maneuver in the sky like a bird—but following one course should be all the flying he'd need now.

Simpler than the rest of our "war." If Winton stayed in hiding… Nolan called them all "spellkeepers," but even "keeping" the secret of how to use their two magics from Winton's spying wouldn't win the fight if Mark couldn't track down Winton's own power.

He took a deep breath of cold air. Flying over the city should be a moment to savor—looking past the buildings' fronts and the streets that tried to lead people where some old planner had thought was the best route. Far off to the left, the shapes lay larger and more spread out in the mist, like pieces from a whole different set of building blocks. After months of flying he'd begun to see the walls and roofs below like different crowds of people: those would be hulking factory men, each crowded into their own domains with their own offspring of storehouses and labs, smaller shapes at their elbows somewhere in tonight's gray.

Ahead, the squat little two-story space between the taller walls was sliding nearer on his right. He pulled on the ski mask and released the energies enough to let the breeze push him over, drifting downward and in toward the wall.

Even as its rough brick lines emerged from the mist, he still saw no lights inside and no shutters to hide them. He felt none of Winton's magic flickering inside either—*but there'll be traces back to him somewhere, there have to be.*

The roof looked too rough to land on, so he let himself fetch up against the wall like a windblown leaf—with enough momentum left to slam his hands and knees and send him rolling to the side, tumbling once around, before he began sliding down the bricks. Then his elbow caught the frame above a window, and he dangled in place a moment as he tried to take back just enough weight to settle there.

When his breathing steadied, he felt in the bag at his waist. First he drew out a thick block of plastic built more less like his phone than some old walkie-talkie: the bug sweeper he'd learned to carry at all times. This time, instead of searching his home for any non-magic tricks Winton might have tried on him, he played it over the window. The display's tiny lights never moved.

"Okay." He'd read that the sensor was meant to catch radio signals, not all kinds of alarms, but that mainly left simple pressure switches that would trigger if the window swung up. He tucked the detector away and drew out the glass cutter.

It didn't make him a burglar. Not compared to everything Winton had done.

If only the glass would wear away as quickly as it did in the movies. Mark hung on against the wall, looking and listening around the street below, while his gloved fingers worked the tool. At last he'd etched out an opening big enough for his shoulders, to the point where a movie spy would have slid the glass out with a suction cup... except that the "detatched" section would never have budged out of the pane that held it. Instead, Mark simply gave it a slow *push*—and before it could fall and shatter, a twist of magic through his fingertips left it floating in the air inside. Still not a sound, not below or within.

With a sigh of shame that this was becoming so familiar, he slipped his weightless form through the opening.

Sliding out of the night air was stepping down into stillness, and a hint of an odd chemical smell. The dim light from the row of windows caught and glimmered on the floating pane of glass and let him set it in the corner, its weight restored again. He'd landed near one end of a long corridor, with doors along on its unlit side and stairs downward at the far end.

So, he just needed a quick look around for the Center's office computer. It'd probably be right on this floor, not down below where the crowds came through.

He played the bug sweeper over the nearest door frame, more because he had the tool than because he expected more alarms. Inside it he saw nothing but dim shelves; closing the door behind him sealed him in darkness a moment, and let him flick his flashlight on without any light escaping outside. But it picked out only near-empty racks of T-shirts, basketballs, cleaning supplies... All the resources a center might use to lure street kids away from gangs—a merchant "giving back" as if Roger Winton hadn't manipulated the real gangs to flush out the secrets of Dennard's magic.

Had Winton told the young people who came here the same lies he'd strung Mark along with? How some fleeting interest like drawing sketches made them important, made them worth a busy entrepreneur's attention over the years?

Mark's soft footsteps were the only sound. The next room was only more supplies, but he felt a tightening in his gut and asked himself once again: *if I somehow walked in on Winton himself, could I do it?* He'd used to dream of revenge, and now the plan was to catch him or spy on him and use his magic's secrets to help Angie... but if it came down to it?

After Angie, her father's stabbing, the Blades' and the 66s' gang war, and a dead detective? *Yeah, I think I could kill Winton.* The thought felt small, but with deep, cold roots through his mind. As long as he didn't join Nolan in smashing places on a whim—

His light caught the great green chunks of a shattered ping-pong table. The other shelves were as near-empty as the last rooms'… but the picture-frames on one side looked just as broken, and he saw what could have been a TV screen behind the ping-pong pieces. Fragments, all neatly stacked, and how bare the other shelves were—the picture fell into place for him.

The building lay as silent as ever, and as clear of magic, but he still whispered as he pulled out his phone.

"I know what happened last night. Some already attacked here."

"What? Are you alright?" Nolan's gasp in his ear felt all too loud in the tight room.

"It's quiet now. It must have been last night—everything's cleaned up now. Maybe it was Rafe."

The guess felt right. Rafe Martinez had lost his place in the Blades—and somehow gotten his own gravity belt—from being a pawn in Winton's tricks. If he'd survived his clash with Mark and Angie, his first move against his old boss might be to trash Winton's antigang center.

"Hold on," cut in Dennard's voice. "The place was attacked, and all we heard were rumors? They hushed it up, why?"

"Must have. I'll see what's left—"

"Quiet!"

Dennard's word froze Mark in place. He still heard nothing except his heart in his ears. The sharp smell he'd caught when he entered, he should have noticed it was fresh paint.

Then Dennard spoke again, harsher than ever. "Silent alarm! It's on the police band—get out of there!"

Mark swung the door wide. The window to the sky waited just two long strides away…

He turned toward the stairs down. One glance down there first would just add another two of his long steps to his escape—it was what Angie would have done, she'd be already *at* the stairs by now. He crept toward the corridor's end.

"This is all wrong," he heard Dennard say, from the phone he still had at his ear. "It sounds like some special alert, how'd it get on the regular band—Mark? I can't see you getting out—"

Mark lowered the phone and edged around the stairs' corner. A broad, open space stretched below, almost empty. From the windows' light he could just make out several doors scattered along the wall, and a kitchen space. The walls gleamed with fresh paint, but under that smell he caught some whiff of garbage lingering somewhere.

Lights moved by the front door.

Mark ducked back out of sight a moment before the sounds broke through. He caught feet on the floorboards as he backed away, then a man's clipped voice: "Clear." A cop.

A woman answered "Clear. I'll check the office."

And show me where that is? But Mark forced his curiosity down and he padded back up the corridor. He'd pushed his luck too far already.

He almost missed the strange, strangled cry below. Then one cop scrambled across the space, heading away from the stairs—and Mark thought to feel for magic.

Down where the police were, he felt it: the faint, flickering twist he'd learned to sense resonating against his own belts' power. From out of nowhere, Winton's magic had struck at someone's mind.

Mark dove back toward the stairs down, and as he flew he heard the running cop near the other and slow.

Just as Mark turned the corner he saw the uniformed man reaching the woman, where she staggered back through the open doorway, swaying on her feet like some drunk—with Winton's unseen power twisting through her nerves. Mark opened his mouth to shout some useless warning, but the man glanced at her, then started past to her to level his gun at the room beyond.

Just as they brushed together, Mark felt the magic shift. Within a heartbeat, the energy jumped from the woman through the man's shoulder—

His gun whipped around and *crack*ed against her skull. Her body crumpled, against his—

The magic flickered back to her, *so fast!* She slumped for the floor, and the man caught at her with one arm, waving the gun around with the other. Oblivious to the fleeting second that his body had been stolen.

"C'mon, Bennie—" Mark heard him growl to her, all frenzied concern and rage.

And in that moment, Mark felt another pressure against his own magic, a flicker like a more ragged one of Winton's spells out beyond the walls, the presence he had always sworn he'd sense again. *Angie's found me.*

"Freeze, bastard!"

The cop's gun was on him, but Mark flung himself backward around the corner, one move sending him into cover. He slammed back against the wall, then scrambled to get to his feet. Magic pulsing, he skipped up the corridor in a few steps, straight toward the window out.

SHREEE!

The screech blasted through the night outside, and he caught one glimpse of the small gray form darting straight across the dimness beyond. A warning.

Somehow, Mark twisted his step to pivot away and keep his balance, his hand scrabbling for the last doorknob. Somehow, he wrenched it open and darted inside and swung it shut to close himself in darkness.

Heart pounding, he held his breath to listen. No sound of the cop charging up—so far. Mark's elbow brushed something in the black, and he remembered the shelves; it would be all open space in here, nowhere to hide if anyone looked.

The cop's low snarl came from beyond the door: "Anything?" and some softer answer.

It's from his radio, from more cops out in the street. They're watching the windows that Angie warned me not to use!

A door rattled open, down the hall, and he heard the cop take a step inside. He was searching the rooms, one by one. Was that four doors he had left before Mark's, or three?

Mark stared at the crack of light beyond his own door, and struggled to find options. Just dive out the window and hope they'd be slow to shoot? Grab the cop and slam him to the floor with magic—if he could get past the gun?

The second door opened.

Or Mark could press himself to the ceiling to hide; even if the cop looked up, the sight might even make him freeze for that one instant. Hell, he could *stay* on the ceiling and show the cop, show the whole police force, what they were really facing—no, not with this cop furious about his partner's attack—

Through the hush came another sound: another bird cry, right outside again but smoother, less harsh.

That's the best signal I'll get. The third door creaked open next to him—and Mark moved his own door.

For two whole heartbeats he swung it slowly, holding it tight to keep the hinges quieter than the cop's foot taking that one step into the next room. The moment of turning the door inward past himself took longer than the single lunge down the corridor and the dive to freedom.

As he hit the night air he *wrenched* himself straight up with a burst of raw power. The street plummeted away below, giving him one glimpse of a pair of police cars with cops facing the window, but looking away distracted just during the moment she'd signalled. Of course.

In another moment the block shrank away. Just a patchwork of lines…

He felt his thoughts slowing and eased the energy back, and the upward force ebbed to leave him hanging in space while blood thundered back up to his brain again. His glance down showed he could still make out the "notch" of the Center's lower-roofed block, even in the mist, still not so far below.

The last time Angie floated outside a window, it led to our first kiss, when she was still herself. Now…

Mark craned his neck to glance around the streets below and the air around, but of course she'd be like a hay-colored needle in a haystack as big as the sky; that was *why* Winton used weapons like these. But, he could feel her power arcing along below. She was almost close.

One small part of him could still remember the plastic square of the phone clenched in his hand, as he tried to match her course to the breeze blowing against his side. When his moment came, he left himself sink and drift with the current down to meet her.

Out of the shadows below, the little shape emerged… too far right, out of reach. And, she slowly winged on by and let him pass.

Biting down a shout after her, Mark dropped for the roof below, damp air catching at his coat. He thumped down on concrete, then his shoes skidded and he lurched a step to fall against a chimney. He flinched away before the metal cowling over it could burn his hand.

When he looked around, Angie was swooping down toward him.

It was almost his first clear look at the body she was trapped in. Maybe a foot in height and twice that in the spread wings, all in gray-brown feathers nature had meant to dissolve into the night. The barn owl's white disk face bore in closer.

Mark stuffed the phone away and held out his hands for her. He still couldn't catch one sound from her wings against the air, but he sensed the magic she carried gathering itself, like himself holding his breath.

Her weight came down on his gloved hands, so light——

Pure cold fire swept through his senses and blotted out the world. Buffeting, tangling tides of energy—he tried to think of the other time she'd reached for his mind, but he still couldn't make out more than the quicksilver Angie-presence whirling within it. She spun through otherspace, brushed against him, again and again.

She can't get her message through. He reached for his other self that had the body and the belt, for that power's resonance with her own energy—

The world *dimmed,* torrents of power fading to streams and pulling back— He broke off and let the storm rise around him again. Be still, let her come… he felt her twisting somewhere in the mingling forces, tried to be ready and let her in.

She was already on him. Pushing, shaking, struggling to reach into his *self* with whatever she had… eager, wild… useless…

He felt the weight leaving the hands before he felt his hands again. The maelstrom melted away to leave him back in his flesh, but his body moved so slowly now. His eyes couldn't open, his ears couldn't catch if she made a sound as her energy drew away.

"Hold on!"

When he said it, his world snapped back into sync. He could stare around the misty rooftop again, see her climbing into the night sky, and he stumbled over the roof after her. The power she carried, was it weaker now?

Then another energy moved in the dimness.

Mark caught his balance and braced himself. He could only dodge at the moment that other bird attacked, so Winton couldn't know Mark had sensed him. Angie was swinging around toward them, too slow and too far away.

But the bird Winton possessed only floated by above. And some small shape rattled down against the roof.

Back to your old tricks, dropping notes to screw with our heads? Mark moved after the sound, but he kept his attention locked on the trace of power still circling above him. The message was still lost in the roof's darkness, until he remembered his phone and its screen's light.

It was a simple sheet of paper, wrapped around a pebble to give it weight to drop cleanly. The shaky letters could have been penned with the bird's own claws:

"Do you want her mind put back?"

Mark's voice came out as a rough whisper as he read them aloud, knowing Angie's owl ears could catch every word. *Damn you, Winton, after all your tricks you want to make a* deal?

Except… Angie should have been closer by now. Her presence did feel fainter than it had before she'd tried to reach him, and her path through the dark should be smoother. Was she hesitating? The thought was soft and cold as the misty air.

Then Angie dove straight at Winton.

Mark felt the bird twist away from her talons, quicker than the other spybirds had been. Winton arced around in the air and shot upward. Positioning for his own attack.

Mark's leap sent him rocketing up after the killer, before the cold thought caught him in midair: *if he triggers his magic as we touch—*

But the bird was already swinging clear of Mark's clumsy path. Winton turned and closed in on Angie, and she could only veer off along the rooftops. Too slow now.

A wrench of magic let Mark stop from overshooting them further, but now he could only drop helplessly through the empty air, tracking as one tiny pulse of power swept in on the other. Angie had to be in the shadows near that roof—and she dove again, spending what altitude she had left to flit down into the concrete canyons below. Where she'd have even less room to dodge, with her enemy close behind.

She wasn't trying to escape. Was she… keeping Winton down where he couldn't see Mark?

Mark tensed as the surface rushed up, the springboard he could use to leap after them. But he'd only miss them again, he'd *always* miss them trying to outfly actual wings.

Trust her. Take the opening she's fighting to give me.

Winton's building had been somewhere to the left. Mark broke into a long stride as soon as his feet hit the roof, crossing it in four steps and one more to leap to the next. Another leap above the street, faster now… each step off concrete or tile or brick came faster, flinging him through the mist. His sense of the two combatants faded behind him, with Angie's weakened presence dwindling first. She'd always beaten Winton before.

Lights moved below. Between the roofs ahead he caught a glimpse of a police car charging away up one street, then as he crested another roof he saw the other car was already gone. They'd rushed out searching for him, leaving the door open—and he'd only need a minute.

His run flowed into one long leap down toward the street that gave him a few seconds in the air to glance around for anyone to view his landing, before one more flux of power let his shoes barely brush the pavement as he hurled himself through the Center's doorway.

Three smaller steps ahead was the office door the police had tried for. On the first step, as he squinted through the bright building lights again, Mark saw the injured woman cop, still lying slumped by the wall.

His momentum couldn't slow, but he made his second step come down ghost-soft. In the same instant he felt for whatever magic had wakened to defend Winton's office.

ABOUT THE AUTHOR

"Whispered spells for breathless suspense."

Ken Hughes dreams of dark alleys and the twenty-seven ways people with different psychic gifts might maneuver around each corner. He grew up on comics and adventures before discovering Stephen King and Joss Whedon, and he's written for Mars mission proposals and medical devices, making him an honorary rocket scientist and brain surgeon. Ken is a Global Ebook Award-nominated urban fantasy novelist, creator of the Shadowed Steps series, the Spellkeeper Flight, the Mirrorman, and many more series of supernatural thrills.

Don't get him started on puns.

Find more books and join the Overview newsletter at:

KenHughesAuthor.com.